A clamor arose outside the tower as word spread that the keep was under attack. The tattoo-headed man turned to listen for an instant, then calmly returned his gaze to the two guards in front of him. The stranger stepped forward, slapping their halberds aside as if the weapons were no more than sticks.

"Get back!" screamed one of the Cormyrian soldiers, kicking at the bald man.

The guard's boot caught the stranger in the forehead. The blow should have sent him tumbling down the stairwell, but the tattooed head simply rocked back. Then the little man growled and, moving with astounding speed and grace, struck the offending leg and broke it. The guard screamed and fell, his head striking a stone step with a sickening thump.

Adon suddenly knew why the guards had not stopped the attacker. The little man was an avatar.

"Bhaal!" the scarred cleric gasped, unconsciously lifting his mace.

The avatar of the God of Assassins turned toward Adon and drew his thin lips back in an acknowledging smile.

———————————
—————

THE AVATAR TRILOGY

FANTASY SETTING

WATERDEEP

Richard Awlinson

**Cover Art by
CLYDE CALDWELL**

TSR Inc.

For Andria

————————

WATERDEEP

First Printing: August, 1989
Printed in the United States of America.
Library of Congress Catalog Card Number: 88-51725

9 8 7 6 5 4 3

ISBN: 0-88038-759-9

TSR, Inc.
P.O. Box 756
Lake Geneva,
WI 53147 U.S.A.

TSR Ltd.
120 Church End, Cherry Hinton
Cambridge CB1 3LB
United Kingdom

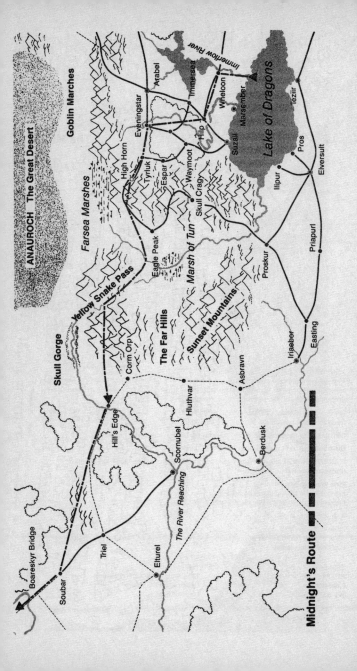

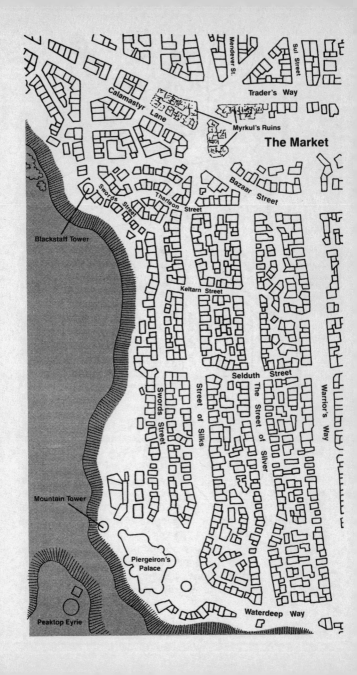

Mendever St.

Sul Street

Trader's Way

Calamastyr Lane

Myrkul's Ruins

The Market

Bazaar Street

Swords Street

Tharleon Street

Blackstaff Tower

Keltarn Street

Selduth Street

The Street of Silver

Street of Silks

Swords Street

Warrior's Way

Mountain Tower

Piergeiron's Palace

Waterdeep Way

Peaktop Eyrie

Prologue

The patrol had been from Marsember, charged with protecting the coastal farms around the tear-shaped grove
called Hermit's Wood. The sergeant, Ogden the Hardrider,
was one of Cormyr's best, well known for keeping his sector
free of brigands.

Twelve riders had served under Ogden. They were typical
soldiers: a half-dozen youthful good-for-nothings, two
drunks, two good men, and two murderers. Ogden gave the
dangerous assignments to the murderers. Predictably, the
pair was insubordinate and had made a pact to add Ogden
to their short list of victims—though neither one had ever
gathered the courage to attack the sergeant.

Now, they would never have the chance. Ogden's patrol
lay a hundred yards north of Hermit's Wood, dead to the last
horse. The Purple Dragon, the crest of King Azoun IV, still
glimmered on their shields, and their armor still gleamed
whenever the moonlight slipped past the stormclouds and
played over their corpses.

Not that spit and polish mattered now. The jackals and
crows had come yesterday, leaving a gruesome mess in
their wake. Ira's ears were gone. Phineas's toes had been
gnawed off. Ogden had lost an eye to the crows. The rest of
the patrol had fared worse. Parts of their bodies were scattered all over the field.

Even without the scavengers, the patrol would have been
a grisly sight. They had been riding through the field when
the ground started belching poisonous black gas. There had
been no reason for the deadly emission. The field wasn't

located close to any volcanoes, near any fens or bogs, or even within a hundred miles of a cavern where fumes might collect. The black vapor was simply one more example of the chaos plaguing the Realms.

That had been two hot days ago, and the patrol had been lying in the heat since. Their limbs were bloated and swollen, sometimes twisted into odd shapes where the riders had broken them. The sides of the bodies closest to the ground were black and puffy with settled blood, while the sides closest to the heavens were doughy gray. The only sign of life that remained in Ogden's patrol was the unsettling red tint that burned in their eyes.

Because their spirits had not yet departed, the soldiers were completely aware of their condition. Being dead was not at all what they had expected. They had been prepared to take positions with the glorious hosts of Tempus, God of War, or to find eternal sorrow beneath the cold lash of the Maiden of Pain, the goddess Loviatar. They hadn't expected their consciousness to linger in their corpses while their flesh slowly decomposed.

So, when Ogden received the command to rise and form a line, he and his soldiers were relieved to find that they could obey. The men and the horses stood, stiffly and without grace, but they stood. The soldiers took the reins of their dead mounts and arranged themselves into a perfect row, just as they would have done had they been alive.

The command to rise had come from the city of Waterdeep, where ninety apostles of wickedness and corruption kneeled in a dimly lit temple. The room was just large enough to hold them all, and looked more like the inside of a moldy crypt than a temple. Its stone walls were black with mildew and slime. The room was lit only by two oily torches set into sconces behind the huge stone altar.

The apostles wore brown ceremonial robes of filthy, coarse material. They stared at the floor, so fearful of disturbing the figure at the bloody altar that they scarcely dared to breathe.

The man at the altar was tall, emaciated, and leprous. His

deformed face was lined by deep wrinkles and covered with lumpy lesions. Where minor injuries had destroyed the diseased skin, patches of stinking gray flesh hung off his face and hands. He had made no attempt to hide his condition. In fact, he cherished his maladies and left his affliction exposed for all to see.

This unusual attitude toward disease wasn't surprising, though, for the figure at the altar was Myrkul, God of Decay and Lord of the Dead. He was deep in concentration, telepathically spanning the continent to give his orders to Ogden's patrol. The effort was taxing on Myrkul's strength, and he had been forced to take the spirits of five faithful worshipers to give him the power he needed. Like the other deities of the Realms, Myrkul was no longer omnipotent, for he had been exiled from the Planes and forced to take a human host—an avatar—in the Realms.

The reason was that someone had stolen the Tablets of Fate, the two stones upon which Lord Ao, overlord of the gods, recorded the privileges and responsibilities of each deity. Unknown to the other gods and Ao, Myrkul and the late God of Strife, were the ones who had stolen the two tablets. They had each taken one and concealed it without revealing its hiding place to each other. The two gods had hoped to use the confusion surrounding the tablets' disappearance to increase their power.

But the pair had not foreseen the extent of their overlord's anger. Upon discovering the theft, Ao had banished the gods to the Realms and stripped them of most of their power. He had forbidden his subjects to return to the Planes without the tablets in hand. The only deity spared this fate was Helm, God of Guardians, whom Ao charged with guarding the Celestial Stairways leading back to the Planes.

Myrkul was now a mere shadow of what he had been before the banishment. But, relying upon the spirits of sacrificial victims for energy, he could still use his magic. At the moment, he was using that magic to inspect the patrol of dead Cormyrians, and he liked what he saw. The soldiers and their horses, which were beginning to decompose nicely, were clearly corpses. But they were not exactly inanimate. Myrkul had been lucky, for he had discovered the patrol before their spirits strayed from their bodies. These zombies would be more intelligent and more graceful than most, since they had died a relatively short time ago. If the soldiers were to accomplish what Myrkul wanted, they would need those extra advantages.

Myrkul had Ogden point toward Hermit's Wood, then gave the patrol its orders telepathically. *There are two men and a woman camped in that grove. In the saddlebags they carry, there is a stone tablet. Kill the men, then bring me the woman and the tablet.*

The tablet was, of course, a Tablet of Fate. It was the one Bane had hidden in Tantras, which was in turn discovered easily by another god and a few humans. The Black Lord had desperately tried to regain the artifact by mobilizing his army. This grand scheme was his downfall. Bane's marauding hosts had alerted his enemies, who gathered their forces and defeated the God of Strife—permanently.

Myrkul was determined to pursue a safer course. Where Bane had used an army to retrieve the tablet, Myrkul would send a patrol to recover it. Nor would Myrkul make the mistake of believing that once the tablet was in his grasp, keeping it would be an easy matter. At this very moment, the trio bearing Bane's tablet was being pursued by a ruthless betrayer. This traitor would stop at nothing to steal the tablet from them or even from Myrkul's zombies. But the Lord of the Dead knew of the cutthroat's plans, and he had already sent an agent to discourage the traitor.

As Myrkul pondered all these things and more, a golden, shimmering disk of force appeared in a part of Waterdeep far removed from Myrkul's moldy temple. The immaculate tower stood nearly fifty feet tall, and was built entirely of granite blocks. Even near the top, it had no visible entrances or windows, and resembled nothing quite so much as a pillar of polished stone.

An ancient man stepped out of the golden disc, then turned and dispersed the portal with a wave of his hand.

Despite his age, the man appeared robust and fit. A heavy maroon traveling cloak hung off his bony shoulders, not quite disguising the leanness of his form. His face was sharp-featured and thin, with alert, dancing eyes and a long straight nose. He had a head of thick white hair, and a beard as heavy as a lion's mane.

"Whom may I say is calling?" The imperious voice came from the tower's base, though no speaker was visible.

The old man regarded the tower with distaste, then said, "If Khelben no longer knows his teacher, then perhaps I've come to the wrong place."

"Elminster! Welcome!" A black-haired man stuck his head and shoulders right through the tower's second story wall. He had a neatly trimmed black beard, steady brown eyes, and handsome features. "Come in! You remember where the entrance is?"

"Of course," Elminster responded, walking to the base of the tower and stepping through the wall as if it was a door. He stopped in a neatly arranged sitting room cluttered with dragon horns, iron crowns, and other trophies from the wizard's adventures. Elminster withdrew his meerschaum pipe from his cloak, lit it from a burning candle, then sat down in the room's most comfortable chair.

A moment later, Khelben "Blackstaff" Arunsun rushed down the stairs, hurriedly pulling a purple cloak over the plain robe of white silk he usually wore while alone in his tower. The dark-haired mage wrinkled his nose at the overly sweet odor from the pipe, then took a seat in the chair usually reserved for guests. "Welcome back to Waterdeep, my friend. What brings you—"

"I need thy help, Blackstaff," Elminster said, pointing his pipe stem at the younger wizard.

Blackstaff grimaced. "My magic's not been—"

"Don't ye think I know that?" the old sage interrupted. "It's the same all over. Not a month ago, my favorite pipe blew up in my face when I used a pyrotechnics spell on it, and the last time I tried a rope trick I had to cut myself loose."

Blackstaff nodded sympathetically. "I contacted Piergeiron the Paladinson telepathically and ended up broadcasting our thoughts to the entire city of Waterdeep."

Elminster stuck his pipe back in his mouth and puffed on it several times. "And that's not the worst of it. Chaos is running rampant through the land. The birds of Shadowdale have started digging burrows, and the River Arkhen is full of boiling blood."

"It's the same here in Waterdeep," the younger wizard said. "The fishermen won't leave the harbor. Schools of mackerel have been sinking their boats."

The old sage absent-mindedly blew a green smoke ring, then said, "Ye know the reason for all of this trouble?"

Blackstaff looked uncomfortable. "I know it started when Ao cast the gods out of the Planes for stealing the Tablets of Fate. I've had trouble learning more than that."

Elminster sucked on his pipe thoughtfully, then said, "Fortunately, I haven't. Shortly after the Arrival, I was sought out by a company of four adventurers—a female mage named Midnight, a cleric called Adon of Sune, a fighter named Kelemvor Lyonsbane, and a thief who went by the name of Cyric. They claimed they had rescued the goddess Mystra from Bane's grasp. Afterward, Mystra had tried to return to the Planes, but had perished when Helm refused to let her pass. With her dying breath, they claimed, Mystra had sent them to warn me that Bane would attack Shadowdale, and to seek my help in finding the Tablets of Fate.

"At first I didn't believe them," Elminster continued, pausing to puff on his pipe twice more. "But the woman presented a pendant that the goddess had given her. And, as they had promised, Bane attacked Shadowdale. The four comported themselves very well in the dale's defense."

The sage purposely left out any mention of the hardship the heroes had suffered as a result of his own disappearance during the Battle of Shadowdale. The townsfolk had accused Midnight and Adon of murdering him. Fortunately, that matter had been cleared up.

"In any case," Elminster noted, "I soon learned that one of the tablets was in Tantras. After briefly being separated as a result of the Battle of Shadowdale, I once again met Midnight, Kelemvor, and Adon in Tantras."

"What of the thief—Cyric, did you say?" Blackstaff asked. He was a keen listener and had not missed the fact that Elminster had left Cyric's name out of his last statement.

"The thief left the party on their journey to Tantras. I'm not sure what happened, but it seems he may have betrayed his fellows. In any case, he's not important to what came next. Bane followed Midnight and her friends to Tantras, then tried to recover the tablet himself. The god Torm, who had taken up residence in the city, met Bane in combat. The resulting battle threatened to destroy Tantras, but Midnight rang the Bell of Aylan Attricus—"

"She what?" Blackstaff interrupted, rising to his feet. "Nobody can ring the bell—not even me!"

"Midnight did," Elminster confirmed. "And she activated the anti-magic shield surrounding the city. The avatars of both gods were destroyed." The old sage sat quietly puffing on his pipe.

After a moment, Blackstaff asked, "And then what?"

Elminster blew a series of smoke rings. "And that is where we begin," he said at last. "Midnight and her friends are bringing the tablet to Waterdeep."

The younger wizard considered this for a long time, looking for some reason for making such a long and hazardous journey. Finally, he could find none and asked, "Why?"

Elminster smiled. "For two reasons," he explained. "First, there is a Celestial Stairway nearby. Second, because the other tablet is here and we need both of them to return the gods to the Planes."

"A tablet is in Waterdeep?" Blackstaff asked. "Where?"

"That's why I need you," the sage said. "All I could learn was that I might find a tablet by going to Waterdeep."

The younger mage rolled his eyes. "Waterdeep's a big city."

Elminster put his pipe away. "Then let's get started. I'd like to find the tablet by the time Midnight arrives."

❦ 1 ❦

Visitors

Midnight's eyes, as dark and deep as the night, followed the shadow as it moved behind the upturned roots of a toppled willow tree. A strong wind whispered through the dark forest, rustling bushes and shaking tree limbs, filling the wood with dancing silhouettes of ambiguous form and size. Overhead, the clouds of a passing storm raced by the moon, dragging heavy shadows through the tangled grove like silent warriors.

Midnight and two companions were camped at the south end of a tear-shaped wood. Her friends were sleeping in a small lean-to shelter erected between two trees. One of the men, Kelemvor, was snoring with deep soft rumbles that sounded like a growling wolf.

While her companions rested, Midnight sat twenty yards away, keeping watch. Not yet thirty and gifted with a lean body, she was a woman of sultry charms. Eyebrows as thin and black as painted lines hung over her eyes, and a long braid of jet-black hair trailed down her back. Her only flaw, if it could be called that, lay in the premature worry lines furrowed over her brow and etched around her mouth.

Those worry lines had grown deeper over the last few days. Adon, Midnight, and Kelemvor had been aboard a small galley bound for the port city of Ilipur, where they intended to find a caravan bound for Waterdeep. As the vessel entered the final leg of its journey, through a sheltered sea called the Dragonmere, an unnatural storm rose out of the calm waters and almost tore the ship to pieces. The storm had lasted for three nerve-wracking days, and the galley had only been saved by the valiant efforts of its crew.

The superstitious captain, already nervous about a Zhentish trireme that had been following them, had blamed his bad luck on his passengers. When the storm finally let up, the captain had immediately turned toward the nearest land and put the three companions ashore.

A rustle sounded from the lean-to and Midnight turned to see Adon creeping toward her. In his right hand, the cleric carried a mace he had bought from a sailor. With his left, he held a set of saddlebags. One bag contained a flat stone about a foot wide and a foot and a half high—the Tablet of Fate their company had recovered in Tantras.

Even now, in the middle of the night, Adon's sandy hair was meticulously brushed. His build was slight, though muscular enough and well proportioned, and his green eyes sparkled with a light of their own. Adon's other features were symmetrical if somewhat plain, save for the red scar that traced a dark path from the left eye to his jawline.

The scar was a grim reminder of the personal crisis that the cleric had suffered over the past few weeks. On the night of the Arrival, when Ao had cast his gods from the Planes, all of the clerics in the Realms had lost their power. Unless they were within a mile of their deity, their prayers for spells simply went unanswered. At first, this had not shaken the optimistic Adon, and he had remained faithful to his deity, Sune, the Goddess of Beauty.

Then, near Tilverton, he had been scarred in an ambush. At first, Adon had feared the blemish was punishment for some unknown offense against his goddess. This feeling had grown steadily stronger. Finally, during the Battle of Shadowdale, Elminster suffered an accident and Adon found himself powerless to help the ancient sage. The cleric then fell into a catatonic depression. When he finally recovered, several weeks later, his faith in Sune had been lost. Instead, the cleric had focused his fervor and dedication on his fellow man.

"Why are you awake?" Midnight asked, whispering loud enough to make herself heard over the wind.

Crouching next to her, Adon answered in a whisper, "Who can sleep with that racket in his ear?" He nodded at Kelemvor's slumbering form, then offered, "I'll take over if you're tired."

"Not yet," Midnight said. She turned back to the toppled willow tree. The shadow she had observed earlier was still crouched behind the tree's upturned roots.

"Is something wrong?" Adon asked, noting Midnight's interest in the willow. He followed her gaze and noted the dark form skulking behind the tangle. "What's that?"

Midnight shrugged and replied, "A shadow I've been watching."

The moon poked its face through the clouds and cast a silvery light into the grove. On the top of the shadow, Midnight could see the silhouette of a head and shoulders.

"It looks like a man," Adon observed, still whispering.

"So it does."

The cleric looked toward the lean-to. "We should wake Kelemvor."

Adon's suggestion made sense. Neither the cleric nor Midnight were at full strength. Like the abilities of all mages, Midnight's powers had become unstable since the fall of the gods. Adon's condition was no better. Even if he had still believed in his deity, Sune was certainly too distant for him to call upon her power.

But Midnight wanted to let Kelemvor snore a while longer. She was not convinced the shadow was dangerous, and if it was, the mage didn't want to alarm it with a sudden flurry of activity. Besides, even without their spells, she and Adon were capable fighters. "We can take care of ourselves if need be," she said. "But I don't think there's any danger."

A cloud covered the moon again, plunging the wood back into darkness. Adon squinted at the root-mass, puzzled by Midnight's assertion. "Why not?"

"If that's a man, he means us no harm. He'd have done something by now if he did," Midnight answered. "He wouldn't be sitting there watching us."

"If he didn't mean us harm, he would have come into camp by now," Adon countered.

"Not necessarily," Midnight said. "He might be afraid to."

"We hardly look like thieves," Adon said, waving his hand at himself and the magic-user. "Who'd have reason to fear us?"

Midnight did not answer immediately and avoided the cleric's gaze. As soon as Adon had asked his question, it had occurred to her that the shadow might belong to Cyric, the trio's missing comrade. It had been only a few weeks since the thief had disappeared on the River Ashaba, but already it seemed that he'd been gone for years. She missed his grim wit, his aloof bearing, even his dark temper.

After Midnight did not respond to his question for several moments, Adon turned toward the lean-to. The magic-user grasped his shoulder to keep him from leaving. "It might be Cyric," she whispered.

Spinning around to face Midnight, Adon hissed, "Cyric! It couldn't be!"

"Why not?" Midnight asked, glancing back at the shadow. "The trireme that worried our ship captain *did* seem to be following us."

"That's still no reason to think Cyric was aboard," Adon countered. "How could he have known we were leaving Tantras, much less which ship we were on?"

"Cyric has his ways," Midnight said grimly.

Adon frowned and squeezed his mace until his knuckles turned white. "Yes, he proved that in Tantras."

Both Midnight and Adon turned to look at Kelemvor. The fighter had seen Cyric last, in Tantras. A Zhentish assassin had attacked Kelemvor, but failed to kill him. When the battle was over, he spotted Cyric in the crowd, watching the attempted murder.

Removing Midnight's hand from his shoulder, Adon declared, "I'm getting Kelemvor."

"But he'll kill Cyric," Midnight said, concern creeping into her voice.

"Good," Adon responded. The cleric again turned toward the lean-to.

"How can you say that?"

"He's joined the Zhentilar," Adon snapped over his shoulder. "Or have you forgotten?"

According to rumor, Cyric had been with one of the Zhentish armies that had come to attack Tantras. Given Cyric's presence at the attempt on Kelemvor's life, Adon believed the rumor.

"What did you expect?" Midnight inquired, still unconvinced of her friend's betrayal. "Cyric's a schemer. Faced with joining Bane's Zhentilar or dying, he'd join. That doesn't mean he's betrayed us."

"That doesn't mean he didn't," Adon said, still speaking over his shoulder. The wind gusted, whipping the grove into a clamor of rattling branches.

"A few weeks ago, Cyric was a trusted friend and a good ally," Midnight said. "Or have you forgotten that he was the one who saved our lives in Shadowdale?"

"No," Adon admitted, finally turning around to face Midnight again. "And I haven't forgotten that Cyric would have left me for the executioner's axe if you hadn't refused to abandon me."

Midnight didn't know what to say, for the cleric was right. After Elminster disappeared during the Battle of Shadowdale, the people of the town had convened a hasty trial and accused Adon and Midnight of the old sage's death. Unfortunately, Elminster's disappearance had also been the event that triggered Adon's catatonic depression, so he was unable to say anything in his own defense. He and Midnight were quickly found guilty and condemned to death.

The night before the scheduled execution, Cyric had come to rescue Midnight. The thief had been disgusted by Adon's collapse during the trial, however, and had taken the cleric along only upon Midnight's insistence. Then, as the trio had fled down the River Ashaba, Cyric had treated Adon like an unwanted dog, speaking to the cleric only to insult him, and occasionally even hitting him. Midnight had been forced to intervene on Adon's behalf many times.

As the magic-user remembered the unpleasant journey, the moon appeared again and pale light bathed the forest.

This time, it looked as though the moon would shine for a while, for the only clouds near it were the ones the wind had just blown past.

Adon took the opportunity to look squarely into Midnight's eyes. "I owe Cyric nothing," he said. "As far as I'm concerned, I'm indebted to you for saving me at Shadowdale."

"Then I want you to pay back that debt," Midnight responded, returning Adon's stare. "Don't assume that Cyric has betrayed us just because he's treated you badly in the past."

"You don't know Cyric like Kel—"

Midnight held her hand up to silence the cleric. "Are you going to honor your debt or not?" she demanded.

Adon frowned angrily. "I'll never trust Cyric."

"I'm not asking you to," Midnight responded, looking back toward the shadow. "All I ask is that you give Cyric the benefit of the doubt. Don't kill him on sight."

Adon's face betrayed his frustration and he looked away. "All right . . . but you'll never convince Kelemvor."

Midnight breathed a sigh of relief. "We'll handle that problem when we come to it. First, I think I'd better find out what Cyric wants."

Without waiting for a reply, Midnight began crawling toward the willow roots. Soggy leaves cushioned her knees and hands, muffling what would otherwise have been a loud rustle.

"Wait!" Adon hissed. "You don't even know if that's him."

"We've got to find out, don't we?" Midnight responded, pausing only an instant. "You can wake Kelemvor if it isn't."

Sighing in frustration, Adon slung the saddlebags over his shoulder and prepared to rush to the mage's aid if the need arose.

As Midnight advanced, the hiss of the wind muffled Kelemvor's snoring, though the soft growl did remain audible. The magic-user gripped her dagger tightly, realizing that the farther away from her friends she crawled, the more she exposed herself to attack. As Adon had pointed out, they could not be sure the man behind the root tangle was Cyric. It could just as easily be a thief or a Zhentish spy who had trailed them from Tantras. But Midnight did not see that she had any choice except to go out and see.

Twenty feet later, the mage put her hand on a stick and snapped it. The shadow didn't stir, but as Midnight glanced back, Kelemvor rolled over, found his swordhilt, then returned to his snoring. She turned back toward the willow roots and advanced another ten feet.

The wind suddenly calmed, leaving the grove eerily quiet. To the north, the pop and crack of snapping sticks rang through the wood. Alarmed, Midnight stopped and looked in the direction of the commotion. Several large silhouettes were moving through the undergrowth.

"Get Kelemvor," Midnight called to Adon. "Something's coming!" She glanced back at the willow's roots and saw that the shadow was gone.

Two hundred feet to the north, thirteen Cormyrian soldiers—once the patrol under Ogden the Hardrider—were slowly riding south, still searching for Midnight and her companions. Most of the men were missing ears, fingers, noses, even whole hands or feet. Jagged wounds laced their torsos where carrion eaters had torn them open in search of an easy meal. The horses were no better off, with great strips of hide ripped away and the tender portions of their bodies gnawed away.

Back at the lean-to, Adon put his hand over Kelemvor's mouth, then shook the fighter's shoulder. The brawny warrior woke with a start, then instinctively thrust Adon aside, knocking the cleric onto his back. A moment later, the fighter realized that it had been Adon's hand on his face and pulled his friend back into a sitting position—not thinking to apologize for knocking him over.

Kelemvor's appearance was as rugged as his manner. Standing just shy of six feet tall, he was heavily muscled and broad-shouldered. Three days' growth of black beard covered the chiseled features of his face, and his green eyes were hidden beneath a frowning brow. The warrior moved with a feline grace that was the only remaining trace of the lycanthropic curse of which he had recently freed himself.

"What is it?" Kelemvor asked, rubbing the sleep from his eyes.

"Something's coming from the north," Adon replied, slinging the saddlebags over his shoulder and hefting his mace. "Midnight didn't say what." The cleric did not mention the shadow that might or might not have been Cyric, for he had promised not to kill the thief on sight. Informing Kelemvor of Cyric's presence would amount to the same thing.

"Where is she?" Kelemvor asked, kneeling.

Adon turned back toward the willow roots. Midnight was nowhere in sight. "She was here a minute ago," he said.

Kelemvor cursed and pulled his sword out of its scabbard. "We'd better find her."

At that moment, Midnight had just crawled to within a hundred and fifty feet of the shadows north of camp. She could see the silhouettes of eight mounted men, though the mage heard the sounds of other riders behind them. The eight riders that she could see were moving slowly toward the lean-to, so the magic-user began looking for a place to hide.

By the time she found it, pressed against the back side of an alder tree, Kelemvor and Adon had begun their search for her. The fighter had crawled behind a fallen tree's tangled roots and was looking for signs of her there. Adon was crouched halfway between the lean-to and the roots.

"Midnight?" the cleric whispered. "Midnight, where are you? Are you safe?"

Though she could barely hear Adon's queries, Midnight did not answer. The horsemen were only a hundred feet away, and she feared they would hear her reply. She gripped her dagger tightly, praying the riders had entered the wood by coincidence and intended no harm. But as they came closer, Midnight saw two dozen red eyes burning out of the darkness and doubted her prayer would be answered.

The magic-user pressed herself closer against the tree, hoping to fade into the shadows against its trunk. She rummaged through her cloak pockets, taking an inventory of spell components. This battle, she feared, would not be won without magic.

While Midnight prepared a spell, the riders continued advancing. In the pale light of the moon, the first sign of life they saw was Adon crouched between the willow roots and the lean-to. The two point riders charged. Behind them, a second wave of six horsemen spread out through the wood and trotted forward, trying to flush Midnight and Kelemvor from their hiding places. The other five riders remained deep in the forest, still hidden from Midnight's sight.

The two point riders made straight for Adon. They did not see the dark figure lurking fifty feet beyond the cleric, hidden beneath a broad-leafed bush. Suddenly, the figure rose to his knees, lifted a short bow, and twanged the bowstring. The arrow took the first horseman in the throat, knocking him out of his saddle. The rider landed on his left arm, rolled four times, and came up holding his sword. With the arrow still protruding from his throat, he rushed into the forest to search for the archer.

Unaware of his companion's fate, the second point rider continued toward Adon. The cleric dove for cover beneath a fallen log that was ten feet to the left of the root mass. The rider hung off his saddle, his shoulder only three feet off the ground, and lifted his sword.

As the horseman rode past, Kelemvor leaped from behind the root tangle. His blade flashed once, and the rider's head bounced along beneath his mount's hooves. The warrior immediately slipped back behind the roots, his thoughts occupied by the arrow that had knocked the first horseman out of the saddle. Kelemvor knew Adon had not fired the arrow, for the cleric had been right in front of him. The warrior also doubted that Midnight had fired it, for he had never seen her use a bow and arrow.

The fighter's deliberations were interrupted when the second wave of riders approached. Five of the horsemen rode past Kelemvor's hiding place without slowing down, but one stopped ten feet in front of the willow roots.

The overwhelming stench of rotten flesh forced the air

from Kelemvor's lungs. The fighter staggered and nearly dropped his guard. Then he saw the rider's red eyes and knew that he couldn't let his attacker's odor put him off guard.

In order to fight through the willow roots, the decaying horseman dismounted, being careful to keep his mount between him and Kelemvor. Then the rider stepped around his horse and quickly thrust his sword through the tangle of roots. Kelemvor sidestepped the blade, then plunged his own sword back through the tangle. The tip bit into the attacker's spongy flesh, but the rider paid the wound no attention. It was then that Kelemvor decided he was fighting a corpse.

As the zombie attacked Kelemvor, Adon rolled out from beneath his tree, leaving the saddlebags—and the Tablet of Fate—hidden there. He scrambled to his feet and rushed toward the fight, hefting his mace. The cleric's first blow caught Kelemvor's undead assailant in the back of the head. Though the attack caused the zombie no pain, it knocked the thing off its feet. Kelemvor rushed around the root tangle, then he and Adon hacked and smashed the body into a dozen different pieces.

While the lone zombie fell to Kelemvor and Adon, the other five riders of the second wave were searching the forest for the elusive archer. So far, they had seen no sign of the woman they were supposed to capture. Incorrectly assuming she had been the one who had fired the arrows, they were determined to capture her before she escaped into the forest.

In actuality, Midnight was still standing next to the tree where she had taken refuge when the battle began. In her hands, she held a pinch of dust and her water flask. If Adon and Kelemvor had not destroyed their attacker, she would have used the components to create a magical ice storm. With luck, the resulting hail would have pounded the riders into bits—provided, of course, the spell had not misfired disastrously. Fortunately, however, Midnight had not been forced to risk using magic.

Like Kelemvor, Midnight was curious about the identity of

the archer who had knocked the first zombie out of its saddle. She suspected the archer was Cyric, but if so, did not understand why the thief had not revealed his presence before the battle had begun. Perhaps he had overheard the discussion between her and Adon, and had decided to wait for a safer opportunity to present himself.

As Midnight contemplated the archer's identity, four more riders thundered past her tree and went to attack Adon and Kelemvor. Adon had retrieved the saddlebags from where he had dropped them, and he and the fighter were again searching for Midnight.

"Midnight?" Kelemvor yelled. "Where in Myrkul's realm are you?"

When Kelemvor and Adon heard the pounding of more hooves, the pair turned toward the reinforcements. The cleric draped the saddlebags holding the tablet over his shoulder, then he and Kelemvor slipped behind the fallen tree's root mass. They intended to force the riders to dismount in order to attack.

Before the riders reached the two men, however, Midnight stepped away from her tree. In her hands, she still held the components for the magical ice storm. "Kelemvor, Adon!" she yelled. "Take cover!"

She poured some water onto the dust, then cast the spell. Immediately, her head began to spin in pain, her limbs went limp with fatigue, and her body started jerking in convulsions. A hundred silver streaks flashed from her fingertips, then, twenty feet behind the horsemen, abruptly gathered into a small cloud and rose into the treetops. An instant later, tiny balls of flame began falling from it. The cloud drifted toward Kelemvor and Adon, setting fire to everything below it. Within seconds, a wall of flame separated Midnight from her friends. The magic-user's spell had misfired.

As the cloud drifted toward them, Adon and Kelemvor slowly rose to their feet. When Midnight had warned them to take cover, both men had realized she was risking a spell and had immediately dropped to the ground in fear.

The four horsemen stopped ten feet in front of the pair,

then dismounted to attack through the root tangle. As the walking corpses came forward, their mounts fled into the forest to avoid the approaching rain of fire.

"Midnight's on the other side of the fire," the fighter said to Adon. "When I say to, get out of here and run into the forest. We'll circle around the flames, then take Midnight and go."

The cleric had no time to acknowledge Kelemvor's plan. The zombies had arrived on the other side of the roots. Two of them immediately began poking their swords through the tangle. The other two tried to circle around to attack unobstructed.

Kelemvor moved to meet the corpses trying to get around the roots. Adon stayed behind the tangle to keep the other two from climbing through. When the second zombie jabbed its sword between the roots, the cleric brought his mace down on the blade and smashed it. The corpse hissed, then threw itself at the roots, pushing its arm through in an angry attempt to grab the cleric.

Meanwhile, Kelemvor met the other two zombies and prevented the pair from flanking his position. The first corpse attacked and the warrior easily parried, then lopped off its sword hand. The second one slashed at Kelemvor's head, but he ducked and backed away.

Behind Kelemvor's attackers, the cloud began dropping tiny fireballs onto the ground. The underbrush immediately caught fire and flames began licking at the zombies' backs.

"Go!" Kelemvor yelled. The warrior kicked the armed zombie in the chest, knocking it into the fire. In the same instant, the other zombie threw itself at Kelemvor, flailing madly. The fighter met its charge with a shoulder, then shoved it back into the fire beside its companion. Both zombies began to burn, but resolutely started back toward Kelemvor. He turned and ran into the forest on his right, confident the corpses would not catch him before being consumed by fire.

Adon simply backed away from the root tangle and climbed over the fallen tree's trunk. He fled in the opposite direction from Kelemvor. The corpses that had been attacking him tried to climb the root tangle, then burst into flame as the cloud passed over their heads.

On the other side of the fire, Midnight tried in vain to see what was happening to her allies. Her limbs trembled and her head still throbbed from the effects of her misfired spell. Finally, she called, "Kelemvor, Adon!"

The magic-user heard no response, but suspected her voice would not carry through the noisy fire that separated them. The raven-haired mage didn't know whether to try circling around the fire to meet her friends, or stay where she was and hope they could reach her.

Then Midnight heard the muffled thunder of more hooves behind her. Without turning around, the magic-user ran back to the shadows of her alder tree. The rider hammered past, the smell of rancid meat riding its wake. Midnight could not help gagging.

The zombie that was once Ogden the Hardrider drew up short and wheeled around to face the magic-user. The mount snorted, expelling an odor so foul it could only have come from the lungs of something dead and rotten.

Midnight presented her dagger in what she hoped was a threatening manner. She thought about reaching for a spell component, but rejected the idea. It would be impossible to use magic before the rider reached her. Besides, the incantation probably wouldn't work.

The rider sheathed its blade, then walked its horse toward Midnight. Even in the pale moonlight, the magic-user could see her attacker in detail. The Purple Dragon of Cormyr decorated its shield. Its helm gleamed with reflections of the moon, and the zombie's leather breastplate shined with oil and polish. But its gray skin hugged its cheekbones like shriveled leather, and a single red eye bulged from a sunken socket.

The horse must have once been magnificent, powerfully muscled, and well groomed. Now, the creature was more frightening than inspiring. Noxious black fumes discharged from its nostrils every time they flared, and the bit drew the beast's lips back to expose a row of huge teeth that seemed fanglike and sharp.

Midnight started to back around the tree, being careful not to turn away from Ogden. The zombie urged its horse forward, quickly catching up to her. The magic-user kept her dagger pointed at the corpse and did not turn to run. Her chance of defeating the thing in combat was narrow, she knew, but her chance of outrunning it was nonexistent.

Finally, the horseman closed the gap entirely and leaned over to grab her. Midnight slashed at its ribs, opening a deep gash. The corpse didn't care. Five icy fingers gripped the mage's wrist and nearly jerked her arm from its socket as the zombie lifted her off the ground and draped her over the horse's back.

A hand, as cold as granite and just as hard, pressed her down onto the saddle. Midnight tried to dislodge herself and slash at her captor, but it kept her pinned firmly in place and completely helpless. The rider started to walk its horse forward.

By now, Kelemvor had circled around the perimeter of the fire, and he saw Midnight being draped over the zombie's saddle. The fighter immediately ran at a full sprint to cut the horseman off.

Before the rancid horse had taken a dozen steps, Kelemvor caught it. The fighter leaped out of the shadows and hit the zombie in the midsection, knocking both it and Midnight out of the saddle. The horse bolted. Midnight landed on the zombie, and Kelemvor landed on her.

The fighter stood up immediately, sword in hand. Using his free hand, he jerked Midnight to her feet. The corpse kicked at Kelemvor's legs, but the warrior hopped out of the way.

"Are you okay?" Kelemvor asked Midnight. At the same time, he used his free arm to push her clear of the battle.

"Fine. Where's Adon and the tablet?" She stepped back from the fight, knowing Kelemvor needed room to maneuver more than he needed the little help she could provide with a dagger.

Before Kelemvor could respond, the zombie drew its sword and slashed at the fighter's stomach. He had to retreat a step, and the corpse leaped to its feet. Kelemvor attacked with a backhand that the zombie blocked easily, then it countered with a series of vicious slashes.

Meanwhile, Adon, still carrying the tablet, had just circled around the other side of the fire. To the east, the cleric saw that most of the remaining zombies were being destroyed by the cloud of fire. A few of the undead were loping into the woods, but the cleric did not think he was in danger, as long as he moved away quietly. Then he heard the clanging of swords and decided to hazard moving faster.

Back with Kelemvor, Midnight hovered on the edge of the battle, dagger in hand. She was ready to strike if the zombie presented her an opening, but Ogden still moved with startling speed and grace. So far, she hadn't even dared to approach within striking range of the undead creature.

Kelemvor slashed and the corpse parried, then thrust at the fighter's head. He ducked inside the jab and smashed his hilt into the zombie's jaw. The blow failed to stun the thing even slightly, so Kelemvor dropped to a knee and rolled away. He stumbled back to his feet just in time to block another of the corpse's blows.

As she lingered on the edge of battle, it became increasingly clear to Midnight that Kelemvor was getting tired and would need help to destroy the zombie. The magic-user's first thought was to try a magic missile, but after her earlier failure, she feared magic would do more harm than good. As risky as it was, she knew the best choice was stabbing the zombie in the back.

Then, as she started to circle around to the thing's rear, Midnight saw Adon coming through the brush. The corpse seemed oblivious to him, so the magic-user decided to make sure the cleric remained unnoticed. She moved directly opposite Adon. Then, as Kelemvor slashed at the zombie's head, Midnight hurled her dagger at its side.

The blade struck point first and sank several inches into Ogden's torso. The zombie parried a thrust, then glanced at

Midnight and snarled. The momentary distraction was all Kelemvor needed to land his first blow, opening a deep gash in the creature's lower back. The corpse whirled on the fighter, slashing at him madly. Kelemvor barely managed to duck the wild swing, then the zombie raised its sword to strike again —and this time Kelemvor was so off balance, he would not be able to avoid the blow.

Adon stepped out of the brush and smashed his mace into the back of the zombie's knees. The corpse dropped to the ground. Kelemvor stepped forward and separated the undead creature's sword hand from its wrist. The cleric smashed his mace into the zombie's nose, the fighter lifted his sword to strike again, and within moments Ogden the Hardrider no longer presented a threat.

For several seconds, Kelemvor stood panting over the foul-smelling body, too exhausted to thank Adon and Midnight for their help.

Regardless of whether he received thanks or not, Adon didn't think it wise to allow the warrior to rest for long. "We'd better get out of here," he said, pulling Midnight's dagger out of the cadaver's ribs and using it to point toward the woods. "There are still one or two zombies out there."

"What about the archer who helped us?" Kelemvor panted. "He may be in trouble."

"If they haven't found him yet, they're not going to," Adon said, sharing a knowing glance with Midnight.

"I'm sure that this particular archer can take care of himself," the magic-user added. If the archer was Cyric, as she and Adon suspected, the last thing he needed at the moment was to have Kelemvor roaming the woods, searching for him.

The warrior frowned. "Do you two know something I don't?"

Midnight started walking to the north. "We'll talk about it later," she said.

❦ 2 ❦

The Warning

"The men will see no rest tonight," Dalzhel said, slipping past the cockeyed door.

A burly man who stood nearly six and half feet tall, Dalzhel resembled a bear both in build and disposition. He had broad, hulking shoulders, a heavy black beard, and a long tail of braided hair that hung down his back. His brown eyes were calm and observant.

Cyric didn't respond to Dalzhel's comment. Instead, he watched warily as his lieutenant entered the room. The thief and his men were five miles north of Eveningstar, in the great hall of a ruined castle. The hall was fifty feet long and twenty feet wide. An imposing fireplace dominated one end of the dusty chamber, the roaring fire within providing the room's only light. In the middle of the floor sat a thirty-foot banquet table, gray and cracked from age and neglect. Around the table and scattered in the hall's corners were a dozen rickety chairs.

Cyric had placed the sturdiest chair before the fireplace and was sitting in it. With a hawkish nose, narrow chin, and dark, stormy eyes, his sharp features were equally suited to sly humor or sinister moods. A recently acquired short sword lay across the thief's lap. The blade's reddish luster left little doubt that it was an extraordinary weapon.

Removing his wet cloak, Dalzhel moved to the fire. Beneath the cloak the Zhentish soldier wore a shirt of black chain mail. Though the armor weighed at least thirty-five pounds, Dalzhel removed it only to sleep—and then only when safely hidden away.

"You could not have picked a darker lair," Dalzhel noted, warming his hands over the hearth. "The men are calling this place the Haunted Halls."

Though he did not say so aloud, Cyric understood the sentiment. Located in the bottom of a deep gorge and overlooking the turbulent currents of the Starwater River, the ruin was as forlorn a place as he knew. The castle had been built before Cormyr had become a kingdom, yet many of its brooding walls and black towers remained intact. It was a hundred yards long and fifty wide, with outer walls still rising to a height of thirty feet in places. The gatehouses showed no signs of the castle's age, though their elaborate portcullises had long since fallen into disrepair.

The great hall, residential apartments, kitchen, and stable had once stood snuggled against the keep's interior wall, their doors and windows opening onto the courtyard. Only the great hall—built from the same black granite as the gatehouses—remained completely intact. The other buildings, constructed of some lesser stone, had fallen into ruins.

Given the castle's combination of crumbled walls and imposing edifices, it did not surprise Cyric that the men found the place unsettling. Still, he had little stomach for their complaints. Dalzhel and the rest of the troops had arrived at the castle that morning, in plenty of time to avoid the storm that had raged all afternoon. Cyric, however, had not come until dusk—cold, tired, and wet after an afternoon in the rain. He had no wish to listen to the men simper.

Heedless of his commander's mood, Dalzhel continued to speak. "There's something beyond the outer curtain," he said, trying to gain Cyric's interest. He removed his scabbard and placed it upon the dusty banquet table. "Or so the watch says."

Cyric had little concern for what lurked outside the walls to frighten his men. He decided to change the subject and asked, "How is my pony? That fellow carried me well, considering how hard I rode."

"With rest it'll recover—provided someone doesn't kill it first," Dalzhel said, returning to the fireplace. "There are those who grumble that it has eaten better than the men."

"It's proven more use!" Cyric snapped. The pony had carried him nearly one hundred and fifty miles over the last three days. A war-horse could not have done better. He considered threatening death to anyone who touched the pony, but rejected the idea. The order would breed resentment, and someone might take up the challenge. "If it survives until morning, take the pony to the plain and free it."

"Aye. That's for the best," Dalzhel responded, surprised at his commander's unexpected hint of compassion. "The men are in a foul mood. Couldn't we have stayed elsewhere?"

"Where would you suggest?" Cyric growled, glaring at Dalzhel's standing form. "Eveningstar?"

"Of course not, sir," the soldier responded, stiffening his posture.

Dalzhel had meant the question to be rhetorical. Given that he and all the men wore Zhentish armor, few things would have been as foolish as seeking lodging in a Cormyrian town.

Cyric looked away and glowered into the fire. "Never question my orders!"

Dalzhel did not respond.

The hawk-nosed thief decided to further chasten his lieutenant by bringing up a sore subject. "Where are your messengers?" he demanded harshly.

"Holed up with two-copper wenches from one end of Cormyr to another," Dalzhel retorted, standing more or less at attention.

Cyric had ordered sentries to watch all roads leading out of Cormyr, and it had fallen on Dalzhel's shoulders to execute the command. So far, not a single messenger had reported.

"And I'd be with 'em," Dalzhel continued, "if my mother had blessed me with the sense of an ox."

Cyric wheeled on Dalzhel, the rose-colored short sword in his hand and the desire to use it in his breast.

In return, the Zhentish lieutenant backed away and snatched his scabbard off the banquet table, then met his commander's angry glare with a puzzled gaze. His reply had been out of line, but Cyric had never before responded to unruliness with such vehemence.

Three tentative raps sounded at the cockeyed door. The intrusion brought Cyric back to his senses and he thrust the short sword into its scabbard. "Enter!" he ordered.

The night sergeant, Fane, slipped into the room. He was a stocky man with a scraggly red beard. Water dripping from his cloak, he turned to Dalzhel and reported, "Alrik is missing from his post."

"You've looked for him?" Dalzhel demanded, laying his scabbard back on the table.

"Aye," Fane replied, hardly daring to meet Dalzhel's gaze. "He's nowhere to be found."

Dalzhel cursed under his breath, then said, "Assign another to his place. We'll deal with Alrik come morning." He turned away, indicating the audience was over.

Fane did not leave. "Alrik isn't one to desert," he insisted.

"Then double the guard," Dalzhel snarled, turning back to the sergeant. "But don't let the men grumble to me about it. Now go."

His eyes betraying irritation, Fane nodded and backed out the door.

As the sergeant left, Cyric realized that he had turned on Dalzhel for a minor infraction. It was not a smart thing to do. Without exception, the men were cutthroats and thieves, and he needed Dalzhel to watch his back. It would not do to have his bodyguard angry at him.

By way of apology, Cyric said, "Everything depends upon those messengers."

Dalzhel understood the explanation for what it was and accepted it with a nod. "It shouldn't be as difficult for the messengers to avoid Cormyrian patrols. The storm must have muddied the roads and slowed their pace. It seems that Talos the Raging One is against us."

"Aye," Cyric replied, dropping back into his chair. "All the deities are against us, not just the God of Storms." He was thinking of five nights ago, when he had been spying upon

Midnight's camp and a group of zombie riders had appeared. It was possible they had been just another aspect of the chaos plaguing the Realms, but Cyric thought it more likely a god had sent them to capture Midnight and the tablet.

"Not that it gives me fright, understand," Dalzhel said, watching Cyric closely. "But this business hardly seems the affair of common soldiers. It makes a man curious."

Cyric kept his silence, for any man privileged to know his intention might try to usurp his place.

"The blood between you and the three we seek must be bad indeed," Dalzhel pressed.

"We were once . . . friends, of a sort," Cyric responded guardedly. He saw no harm in admitting that much.

"And what of this stone?" Dalzhel asked. He tried to sound nonchalant, but his interest was more than casual. Cyric wanted the flat stone the trio carried as much as he wanted them. Dalzhel wished to know why.

"My orders are to recover it." Cyric tried to intimidate Dalzhel with an angry stare. "I don't care to know why."

Cyric was lying. Before the battle of Shadowdale, he and his companions had helped the goddess Mystra attempt to leave the Realms. The god Helm had refused to let her pass unless she presented the Tablets of Fate, which had been stolen from Ao, the mysterious overlord of the gods. Cyric knew little else about the tablets, but he suspected that Ao would pay a handsome reward for their return.

Cyric had spent most of his life putting bread in his mouth by thieving or fighting, always without a sense of destiny or purpose. For more than a decade, this shiftless existence had seemed an empty one, but the thief had been unable to find a higher purpose in life. Every time he tried, the matter ended as in Shadowdale, his efforts unappreciated. Often as not, Cyric found the very people he had tried to help chasing him from town.

After Shadowdale, Cyric finally realized that he could only believe in himself—not in the abstract concept of "Good," not in the sanctity of friendship, not even in the hope of love. If his life was to have a purpose, it had to be his own best interest. After deciding this, Cyric began to formulate a plan that not only gave meaning to his life, but one that would literally allow him to choose his own destiny. He would recover the Tablets of Fate and return them to Ao in return for a reward that would doubtlessly make him as wealthy as any king.

Without knocking, someone brushed past the heavy wooden door and stepped into the room. Cyric stood and brandished his short sword. Dalzhel grabbed his own weapon. Both men turned to face the intruder.

"I beg your pardon, my commanders!" It was Fane again, still dripping wet. His eyes were locked on the naked blades in the hands of Dalzhel and Cyric, and his eyebrows were arched in fright. "I've merely come to report," he gasped.

"Then do it!" Dalzhel ordered.

"Edan's post is also empty." Fane winced as he said the words, half-expecting Dalzhel to strike him.

The Zhentish lieutenant merely frowned. "He could be hiding with Alrik."

"Edan *is* unreliable," the sergeant admitted.

"If two men have abandoned their posts," Cyric interrupted, addressing Dalzhel, "your discipline is not half as strict as you claim."

"I'll fix that come morning," Dalzhel growled. "Still . . . have you doubled the guard?"

"No," Fane replied, blanching. "I didn't think you meant that as an order."

"Do it now," Dalzhel snapped. "Then find Alrik and Edan. Your punishment for disobeying my order will depend on how quickly you find them."

Fane gulped, but did not reply.

"Dismissed," Dalzhel said.

The sergeant turned and scrambled out the door.

Dalzhel turned to Cyric. "This is bad. The men are unruly, and unruly men fight poorly. Perhaps their spirits would be lifted if they saw a reward in sight—that halfling village we raided provided little enough loot."

"I can't help how the men feel. We have our orders," Cyric

lied. If he could keep the men in line a week or two longer, the tablets would be his.

Dalzhel didn't put his sword back in its scabbard. "Sir, the men know better. We followed you from Tantras because you had brains enough not to get us killed there. But we've never believed your orders come from Zhentil Keep. You're no more a Zhentilar officer than you are the High Lady of Silverymoon, and we've known it for a long time. Our loyalty is to you and you alone."

Dalzhel paused, looking squarely into Cyric's eyes. "A few answers would go a long way toward holding that loyalty."

Cyric glared at Dalzhel, angered by his lieutenant's half-spoken threat. Still, he recognized the truth in the words. The men had grown resentful and rebellious. Without the promise of reward, they would soon desert or mutiny.

"I suppose I should be flattered that the men chose me over their homeland," Cyric said, then paused and pondered what he should reveal to Dalzhel.

He might tell him about the Tablets of Fate or the fall of the gods. Cyric could even tell his bodyguard that he suspected that one of the trio they were chasing held the power of the dead goddess Mystra. The hawk-nosed thief shook his head. If he was hearing that story for the first time, he might not believe it.

"What are you after?" Dalzhel asked, his curiosity aroused by Cyric's long pause.

"I'll tell you this much," the thief said, looking at Dalzhel. "The stone I want is half of a key to great power. The other half lies in Waterdeep, where the woman and her friends are going. The woman, Midnight, has the power needed to turn that key. We'll capture her and the stone, then go to Waterdeep and find the stone's twin. When that's done, Midnight will put the key in the lock—and I'll turn it! I'll be more powerful than any man in the Realms, and I'll reward you and the men with gold or whatever you desire."

Cyric turned back to the fire. "That's all I'll say. I don't want anyone to make the mistake of believing he can take my place."

Dalzhel stared at Cyric for a full minute, considering the story. The promises were grand, but they were also vague. Cyric sounded as though he expected to make himself an emperor without a battle. Dalzhel had once fought for a petty Sembian noble, Duke Luthvar Garig, whose delusions of grandeur had resulted in the destruction of an entire army. It was not an experience Dalzhel was anxious to repeat.

However, Cyric spoke with a purpose and lucidity Luthvar lacked, and Dalzhel had never thought of his commander as a man given to wild imaginings. Besides, the Realms were in chaos, and Dalzhel knew his legends well enough to know that kings were just mercenaries who had enough courage to carve a realm out of anarchy. It seemed he had found himself in the service of a king in the making.

"If any other man made such promises," Dalzhel noted, "I'd count him a fool and leave. But I swear my allegiance to you, and so shall the others."

Cyric smiled as warmly as he could. "Be careful of what you swear," he warned.

"I know what I'm doing," Dalzhel replied. He pulled his cloak over his shoulders and put his sword back into its scabbard. "If you'll excuse me, I'll attend to our men."

Cyric nodded and watched Dalzhel go, wondering if his lieutenant knew that he might be standing against the gods themselves. The thief had no doubt that one or two of the gods, at least, would be chasing Midnight as soon as they learned she had the tablet.

In following Midnight from Tantras, Cyric's original intention had been to seize her and the tablet when her ship docked in Ilipur. But, as they entered the Dragonmere, a squall had risen from a calm sea. It had been impossible to say whether the storm was a deity's work or just another of the chaotic phenomenon plaguing the Realms.

Regardless of its source, the storm had driven Midnight's ship north. Cyric had followed as best he could, but maintaining contact had proven impossible. Finally, on the afternoon of the third day, the storm had died. Cyric had sailed north, correctly guessing the galley would limp toward the

Port of Marsember. He quickly intercepted the small ship, but discovered that the superstitious captain had set his passengers ashore somewhere near the mouth of the Immerflow. Cyric had reversed his course and, over a span of sixty miles, set scouts ashore to search for his old friends.

It had been Cyric himself who located Midnight's camp, in a small wood near the mouth of the Immerflow. He had sent his companion to summon Dalzhel and the twenty-five men held in reserve with their ship. Then he had crept up to the camp, hoping for an opportunity to kidnap Midnight or steal the tablet.

But the storm had muddied the fields and delayed his reinforcements. Before Dalzhel could arrive, the mysterious zombie riders had attacked Midnight's camp. Without showing himself, Cyric had used his bow to aid his former allies enough to keep the tablet from falling into the zombies' hands.

During the combat, one of Midnight's spells had misfired and set the wood ablaze. Unfortunately, Cyric had been trapped on one side of the fire, Midnight and the tablet on the other. She, Adon, and Kelemvor had escaped before he could follow.

By the time Dalzhel had arrived with reinforcements, Cyric had been forced to adopt a desperate plan. Because he had little hope of finding Midnight and his old friends in Cormyr, where soldiers wearing Zhentish armor would be killed on sight, Cyric had to force Midnight to find him. He decided to herd her north, making sure she and her company had little opportunity for rest. His intention was to attack after they reached Eveningstar.

He posted patrols of six men along all the major roads leading south. The patrols were to remain inconspicuous until they saw Midnight's company. Then they were to attack and drive her north.

Cyric and the rest of his Zhentilar marched northwest on foot, moving at night to avoid Cormyrian patrols. Along the way, Cyric visited the towns of Wheloon and Hilp, arranging unpleasant receptions in case Midnight and company stopped there. North of Hilp, Cyric's Zhentilar had stumbled across an isolated halfling village. Of course, they had plundered it, which was where Cyric had acquired his new sword and the pony.

Afterward, Dalzhel and the men had continued north on foot, dispatching sentries to watch key crossroads. Cyric had taken the pony and arranged more trouble for Midnight's company in the other cities they might visit.

The hawk-nosed thief felt that his plan was both a sound and subtle one. But with no word from his messengers, he didn't know whether or not it was working.

Fane rapped on the door, interrupting Cyric's reflections, then entered without awaiting permission. His face was as pale as bone. "We've found Alrik and Edan," he said. "Dalzhel requests your presence."

Cyric frowned, then rose and grabbed his cloak. "Lead the way." He kept his short sword in his hand, just in case Fane was leading him into a mutinous ambush.

They slipped past the hall's crooked door into the dark courtyard. Cyric's boots sank to the ankle in mud. A driving rain, so cold it should have been sleet, stung his face. The eerie wail of the wind echoed from the keep's stone walls.

In the opposite corner of the courtyard, torchlight flickered between what had once been the guards' barracks and the blacksmith's shop. That was where the well was located. Fane led the way across the yard, each step creating a slurp that punctuated the hard patter of the raindrops. Three men stood beneath the inner curtain's eaves, trying to shelter their torches and themselves from the rain. Two of the men were pointedly looking away from the well. Since it still provided water, it was the one item the castle's periodic inhabitants kept in good repair.

A moan, low-pitched and feral, issued from the well's depths. Tied to the blood-smeared crossbar was a gray cord that descended into the dark pit. Dalzhel stepped forward and grabbed the cord. Without speaking, he began to pull. An anguished scream rang out deep down the well. Dalzhel allowed the cry to continue for several seconds before dropping the cord.

"What was that?" Cyric asked, peering into the black depths.

"Edan, we think," Dalzhel reported.

"He's still alive," Fane added informatively. "Every time we try to pull him up, he screams."

Though he had seen many slow deaths, and had caused one or two himself, Cyric's stomach turned as he tried to imagine what had happened at the other end of the rope.

Fane drew his sword to cut the rope.

Cyric grabbed Fane's arm and said, "No, we need the well." He turned to the two men holding torches. "Pull him up and end his misery."

They paled, but did not dare object.

Next, Dalzhel and Fane led the way to a latrine on the outer curtain. The castle had been abandoned too long for the thing to stink from use, but it exuded a coppery odor that was equal parts blood and bile. From inside came a plaintive groan.

"Alrik," Fane reported.

Cyric peered inside. Alrik faced the corner, kneeling in a pool of his own blood. He held his hands cupped in front of his stomach. A barbed, wooden tip protruded from his lower back, suggesting that a stake had been driven through his body. Because of the barbs, the stake could not be removed without dragging Alrik's intestines out with it.

When Cyric pulled his head out of the cramped room, Dalzhel said, "I've never seen such cruelty. I'll lay my blade into whoever—"

"Don't promise what you might not dare to deliver," Cyric said coldly. "Put an end to Alrik's misery. Fane, wake every man and send them out on patrol in threes."

"They're awake already," Fane reported. "I could not have—" He was interrupted by a terrified yell from the inner gatehouse.

"No!" A high screech followed. It did not fade, even after the man's throat should have gone hoarse.

Cyric turned toward the gatehouse, unsure of what he

would find. Few humans were capable of the efficient brutality with which Alrik and Edan had been tortured. Still, the thief moved at his best pace. If he appeared frightened of the murderer, his men would no longer be afraid of him—and that was an invitation for mutiny.

Dalzhel and Fane followed close behind. By the time they reached the gatehouse, the scream was no longer audible. A dozen men had gathered in the stairwell, standing in a line running up to the second floor. Their torches cast a flickering yellow light on the walls.

The men did not even notice Cyric when he arrived, so Fane bellowed, "Out of the way! Stand aside!"

When the onlookers made no move to obey, Fane muscled a path up the stairway. Cyric and Dalzhel followed, eventually reaching a doorway. Five men stood inside, staring at a crumpled form in the center of the room. A dark pool was spreading about their feet, and the barest whisper of a croak came from the shape on the floor.

"Let your betters have a look!" Fane ordered, pushing his way into the crowded chamber.

Cyric and Dalzhel shadowed Fane into the room. "Put a stop to that moan," Cyric ordered. "And nobody walks alone tonight."

Fane obeyed immediately, delivering the stroke of mercy with an unnerving lack of emotion.

A man standing in the doorway growled, "And come morning, I walk out of here!" The speaker was Lang, a lanky fighter skilled with both sword and bow. "I didn't sign on to fight ghouls."

Dalzhel immediately pulled his sword on the mutineer. "You'll do as you're told, and nothing else!" he said. Cyric moved to Dalzhel's left and stood shoulder-to-shoulder with him. If this came to blows, they would stand or fall together.

"I've had too much danger and not enough loot, myself!" cried Mardug, who stood in the room behind their backs. "I'm with Lang!"

A muted chorus of agreement rustled down the stairs.

"Then you'll go with Lang to the Realm of the Dead,"

Dalzhel said evenly, turning and swinging his sword. He slapped Mardug in the head with the flat of his blade. The mutineer dropped to his knees.

Lang drew his blade and lunged at Dalzhel's back. Cyric intercepted the attack and easily parried it with his short sword, then kicked Lang in the stomach and sent him crashing into the doorjamb.

Before Lang could recover, Cyric touched the tip of his sword to the mutineer's throat. "On any other night, I would finish you," he hissed, trembling with exhilaration. A bloodlust such as he had never known was coursing through Cyric's veins, and it was all he could do to keep from pushing the sword forward.

"But we're all upset by the deaths of our friends," Cyric continued, "so I'll make this allowance."

The hawk-nosed thief let a heavy silence hang in the room for several moments, then turned to Dalzhel. "Lang and Mardug can leave now," he said, speaking loudly so the men on the stairs would hear him. "Anybody else who wants to leave can join them. Everybody that's still here at dawn is with me until the end."

"Aye." Dalzhel turned to the two mutineers. "Be gone before the commander changes his mind."

The two men took their leave and pushed their way down the stairs. Nobody else moved to join them.

Cyric remained quiet. When he had lifted his sword, a powerful bloodlust had invaded his body, but it still hadn't died away. If anything, it had grown stronger. Although he had never felt any compunction about killing, this was something new to him. Not only did he want to draw blood, he wondered how he would sleep if he did not.

After several moments of silence, Fane asked, "What are we going to do?"

"About what?" Cyric asked absently.

"The murderer," Fane replied. He used his toe to turn the body over, strangely fascinated by its grotesque wounds. "We've got to find him."

"That might be foolish," Dalzhel said, grimacing at the way

Fane played with the body. "If we send men to look for the murderer, we're exposing them to attack."

Cyric and his lieutenant were thinking along the same lines. During his life, Cyric had known many evil men. Not one was capable of what he had seen tonight. "Have the men gather in groups of six," the thief ordered. "One group in the great hall—" A terrified whinny sounded from outside, interrupting the instructions.

"The stable," Dalzhel observed.

The men mumbled, but stood still and waited for their orders.

Again, the pony whinnied, this time sending chills down Cyric's spine. "We'd better have a look," he said, cringing at the thought of what they would find.

The men on the stairs reluctantly started toward the stable, Cyric and Dalzhel close behind.

By the time the hawk-nosed man reached the ground floor, the pony was quiet. As Cyric stepped into the courtyard, a ghostly wail whistled through the castle. Outside the stable, ten men stood with their swords drawn, peering inside and clearly reluctant to enter. Cyric slopped his way across the ward and pushed them aside. Grabbing a torch, he entered the stable, his sword arm aching with the desire to lash out at something.

The pony lay dead in its stall, a withered and puckered hole over its heart. The lips of its muzzle were twisted back in horror, and one eye stared directly at Cyric.

Dalzhel approached and stood next to his commander. For a moment, he observed in silence, wondering whether or not Cyric was mourning the beast's death. Then he noticed something on the beam over the stall. "Look!"

A circle of drops had been drawn in blood. Cyric had little trouble recognizing the Circle of Tears. It was the symbol of Bhaal, Lord of Murder, God of Assassins.

❧ 3 ❧

Black Oaks

Kelemvor reined his horse to a stop and lifted his waterskin to his lips. He thought he smelled smoke, but that was no wonder. Despite the absence of the sun, which had simply failed to appear that morning, the day was blistering. A flickering, swirling orange fog clung to the ground, bathing everything it touched in dry heat.

The fog had leached all moisture from the soil, turning the road into a ribbon of powdery dust that choked man and beast alike. The horses moved slowly and resentfully, stopping every few steps to sniff for the cool odor of a river or pond. Kelemvor knew they would find no water. The company had already crossed several brooks, and the only thing in the streambeds had been billows of orange mist.

After washing the dust from his mouth, Kelemvor turned his rugged face to the left. Through the fog, the forest that ran along the road's left flank was barely visible. He sniffed the air and definitely smelled smoke. It carried a greasy odor resembling burned meat. Visions of battles involving razed towns and villages came unbidden to his mind.

"I smell smoke," Kelemvor said, twisting around to face his companions.

The second rider, Adon, stopped and sniffed the air. "So do I," he said. He kept his head slightly turned to hide the scar beneath his left eye. "I would guess there's a fire, wouldn't you?"

"We should have a look," Kelemvor said.

"What for?" Adon demanded, waving his hand at the fog. "It wouldn't surprise me if the air itself were burning."

Kelemvor sniffed again. It was difficult to be sure, but he still thought he smelled scorched meat. "Can't you smell it?" he asked. "Burned flesh?"

The third rider stopped behind Kelemvor and Adon, her black cape now gray with road-silt, her hair braided into a pony tail. "I smell it, too," Midnight said, inhaling. "Like charred mutton?"

Sighing, Adon turned to face Midnight. "It's probably a campfire," he said. "Let's go."

Absent-mindedly, the cleric rested a hand on the reason for his concern, the saddlebags containing the Tablet of Fate. Nothing was more important than getting it to Waterdeep as quickly as possible. Adon did not want to waste a single moment with detours, especially after the troubles of the last few days.

Kelemvor knew the source of Adon's concern. After escaping the zombie riders, they had gone to Wheloon to rest. However, the trio had scarcely arrived when Lord Sarp Redbeard accused Kelemvor of murdering a local merchant. When the town watch attempted to seize the fighter, the trio had been forced to escape on stolen horses.

If Adon wasn't worried about the Wheloon Watch, then he was concerned about the Zhentilar. After Wheloon, the three companions had ridden to Hilp and turned south toward Suzail. From there, they intended to take passage across the Dragonmere to Ilipur, where they could join a caravan bound for Waterdeep.

They had made it only as far as the Starwater Bridge when six Zhentilar had ambushed them. Kelemvor had wanted to stay and fight, but Adon had wisely insisted upon fleeing. Though the green-eyed warrior had been strong enough to fight, Adon and Midnight had been too weary to face two-to-one odds.

Kelemvor doubted that the Zhentilar or the Wheloon Watch was pursuing them. The watch consisted of merchants and tradesmen. They had surely turned back after a day's ride. It was even more certain that the Zhentilar were not following. Inside Cormyr, they might survive hiding by day and skulking about at night. But if the Zhentish soldiers dared to move openly, it would be only a day or two before a Cormyrian patrol tracked them down and finished them.

"Don't worry, Adon," Kelemvor said. "We have time to do a little exploring. I'm sure of that much."

"What are you unsure about?" Midnight asked. She had long ago learned what Kelemvor left unstated could be more important than what he said.

Knowing it would be futile to hide his concern, Kelemvor said, "I don't understand why we met Zhentilar in Cormyrian territory. It makes no sense."

Midnight relaxed. "It makes plenty of sense. They serve Cyric. He's trying to keep us from using the southern route."

Kelemvor and Adon exchanged knowing glances. "If I believed Cyric wished us to go north," Kelemvor snapped, "that would be reason enough to go south."

"At any cost," Adon added, nodding.

"Why do you say that?" Midnight asked sharply.

"Because Cyric wants me dead," Kelemvor replied.

It was an old subject. For nearly a week, Midnight had been laboring to convince her friends that Cyric had not betrayed them by joining the Zhentilar.

"Whose arrows saved us five nights ago?" Midnight demanded, referring to the mysterious archer who had aided them against the zombie riders. She looked away and stared into the forest, confident they could not provide a satisfactory answer.

"I don't know," Kelemvor responded, determined not to let Midnight have the last word. "But they weren't Cyric's. He wouldn't have missed me and hit the riders instead."

Midnight started to protest, but thought better of it and dropped the subject. Kelemvor would not change his opinion easily. "Let's get on with it," she said sternly.

"Yes," Adon agreed, urging his horse onward. "Every hour forward is an hour closer to Waterdeep."

Kelemvor grabbed Adon's reins. "Into the forest," he said.

"But . . ." Frustrated by Kelemvor's refusal to accept his leadership in even this simple thing, Adon jerked his reins out of Kelemvor's hand. "I won't go," he pouted. "It's just someone roasting a sheep."

Annoyed by Adon's obstinacy, Kelemvor set his jaw and narrowed his eyes. But he stopped himself from being as stubborn as Adon. Instead, he said, "If you're right, this will only take a minute. But if you're wrong, somebody might need our help."

Despite his reasonable tone, Kelemvor was determined not to leave without investigating the smoke. It carried the smell of death by fire, and to him that meant someone was in trouble.

And now that he could, Kelemvor Lyonsbane was anxious to offer his help to anyone who truly needed it.

For five generations, the men in Kelemvor's family had been forced to sell their fighting skills because of their ancestor's greed. Kyle Lyonsbane, a ruthless mercenary, had once deserted a powerful sorceress in the midst of battle so he could loot an enemy camp. In retaliation, she had cursed him so that he changed into a panther whenever he indulged his greed or lust. In Kyle's descendants, the curse had reversed and manifested itself whenever they attempted to perform selfless acts.

The curse had been more of a prison than any man could imagine. Forced into a career as a mercenary, Kelemvor had appeared to be as ruthless as his ancestor had been. Consequently, his life had been one of isolation and loneliness.

As strange as it seemed, Lord Bane, the God of Strife, had changed all that. Through a complicated series of events, Kelemvor had tricked Bane into removing his family curse. He was now free to help others, and he was determined to never again turn away from someone in need.

When Adon showed no sign of agreeing to Kelemvor's request, it was Midnight who settled the matter. Sniffing the air again, she said, "I do smell burned flesh." Despite the fact that she was still angry at the fighter for his condemnation of Cyric, Midnight agreed with Kelemvor. "Come on, Adon. Kel's right."

Adon sighed, resigned to the detour. "Then let's make this

as fast as we can."

Kelemvor led the way into the forest. There, the fog did not seem as thick, nor the temperature as hot. As far back into its depths as they could see, the forest was ablaze with blood-colored sumac leaves. The three companions continued forward, pausing every few minutes to sniff the air and make sure that they were continuing in the right direction.

Presently, they found a path leading farther into the wood. As they progressed, the odor of smoke and charred flesh became stronger. Eventually, they had to dismount and lead their horses, for the trail was narrow and ran beneath low-hanging branches. After five minutes of walking, the path started up a small hillock. Every now and then, gummy black smoke rolled down the trail, mixing with the orange fog. Presently, the sumacs thinned out, giving way to a ring of black oaks that towered eighty feet over the tops of the smaller trees nearby.

In the center of the ring of oaks was a scorched and trampled circle fifty yards in diameter. A fire had cleared the entire area. Here and there, rubble lay heaped in knee-high mounds. Though the village had obviously burned some time ago, several wrecked houses still emitted thin columns of greasy smoke.

Pointing at a pile of stones around a pit, Midnight was the first to speak, "That must have been a well."

"What happened?" Adon gasped.

"Let's see if we can find out," Kelemvor said, tying his horse to a sumac tree. He went up the hillock to the first pile of rubble, then began tossing aside sooty stones.

The small structure, no more than fifteen feet on a side, had been constructed with great care. A fine mortar and rock foundation extended four feet into the ground, and someone had used mud to chink the walls and keep out the wind.

Eventually, Kelemvor came upon a tiny hand. Had it not been wrinkled and weathered, he would have assumed it belonged to a girl. He quickly pulled the rest of the body from beneath the stones. The hand belonged to a woman. Though no taller than a child and lighter than Kelemvor's sword, she had been old. The oils and pigment had long ago drained from her skin, leaving it ashen and cracked. Her face had been a kind one, with eyes that were friendly and soft even in death.

Kelemvor gently laid her on the ground beside her collapsed home.

"Halflings!" Midnight exclaimed. "Why would anybody raze a halfling village?"

Kelemvor simply shook his head. Halflings did not hoard gold or treasure. In fact, they usually had little of value to creatures other than halflings. The fighter went back to his horse and began taking the saddle off.

"What are you doing?" Adon demanded, calculating they had at least two hours of light left.

"Making camp," Kelemvor replied. "This may take some time."

"No, absolutely not!" Adon objected. "We came up here, and now we've got to go! I'm very firm about that."

"A man—even a small man—deserves a burial," Kelemvor said, pausing to glare at Adon. "There was a time when I would not have needed to remind you of that."

Adon could not hide the hurt Kelemvor had caused him. "I haven't forgotten, Kel. But Waterdeep is weeks away, and each hour we delay brings the world closer to ruin."

Kelemvor dropped his saddle, then removed the bit from his horse's mouth. "There may be survivors who need help."

"Survivors?" Adon screeched. "Are you mad? The place has been sacked to the last rat." When Kelemvor did not respond, Adon turned to Midnight. "He'll listen to you. Tell him we don't have time. This may take days."

Midnight didn't respond immediately. Though he was as stubborn as ever, this was not the Kelemvor she remembered. That man had been selfish and untouchable. This one was consumed by the misfortune of a people he didn't even know. Perhaps his curse had been responsible for more of his callousness and vanity than she realized. Perhaps he had truly changed.

Unfortunately, Midnight knew that Adon was right.

Kelemvor had picked a poor time to exhibit his new personality. They had a long journey ahead of them and could not afford to waste a single day.

The mage dismounted and moved to Kelemvor's side. "You've changed more than I would have believed possible," she said, "and this gentle Kelemvor is one I like. But now is not the time. We need the old Kelemvor these days, the man whom a titan could not sway."

He looked at Midnight. "If I turn away from these halflings, what good has it done to remove my curse?"

It was Adon who answered. "If you let the Realms perish, what will it matter that your curse has been lifted? Stop thinking of yourself and let's be on our way!"

Kelemvor simply turned toward the halfling village and, over his shoulder, said, "You do as you must and I'll do the same."

Midnight sighed. There would be no reasoning with Kelemvor now. "I'll make camp," she said. "We need a rest anyway, and this place looks well hidden." She tied her horse to a tree and began clearing brush away from an area at the hillock's base.

Frowning, Adon resigned himself to Kelemvor's stubbornness and also tied his horse. Then he gave the saddlebags with the tablet to Midnight and moved to help Kelemvor.

"I suppose you'll finish sooner with an extra pair of hands," the cleric said gruffly. The statement sounded more harsh and vindictive than he'd meant it to. Adon had no wish to see the halflings remain unburied, but he couldn't help being angry at Kelemvor.

The fighter eyed Adon coldly. "I suppose the halflings are beyond caring who lays them to rest," he said.

They worked for an hour and a half, uncovering two dozen bodies, many of them burned horribly. Adon's mood turned from angry to downcast. Although three halfling males had perished defending the outskirts of the village, the victims were mostly women and children. They had been beaten, slashed, and trampled. When they had run into their homes for refuge, the structures had been put to the torch and pulled down on top of them.

There were no survivors, at least in the village, and no indication of why the settlement had been destroyed.

"Tomorrow, we'll dig their graves," Kelemvor said, noting that the daylight was fading and it was almost dusk. "We should be finished and on our way by noon." He hoped the delay would be acceptable; he had no wish to antagonize Adon further.

"I saw no sign of a burial ground," Adon said. "It might be better to cremate them tonight."

Kelemvor frowned. He suspected Adon was trying to rush him, but he was no expert on halfling funerals. If anybody knew the form of the ceremony, it would be Adon. "I'll think it over while we rest," the fighter replied.

They returned to the edge of the hillock, where Midnight had created a small clearing and made beds from cut brush. As Kelemvor and Adon approached, Midnight said, "I'm starving! Where are the corn biscuits?"

"In my saddlebags," Kelemvor responded, pointing at his gear.

Midnight grabbed his saddlebags and looked inside, then turned them upside down. A few crumbs fell out, but nothing else.

Kelemvor frowned. "Are you sure those are mine?" he asked. "There should be a dagger, a heavy cloak and gloves, a bag of meal, and several dozen cakes of cornbread in there."

"I think they're yours," Midnight replied. She grabbed another set of saddlebags and turned them over. The tablet and Adon's mirror spilled out, but nothing else.

"We've been robbed!" Adon yelled. His cloak, food, and eating utensils were gone.

Alarmed, Midnight grabbed her own saddlebags and began rummaging through them. "Here's my dagger, my spellbook, my cloak. . ." She pulled each item out as she named it. "Nothing's missing."

The three companions stared dumbly at their camp for a minute, hardly able to believe that someone had robbed them. Finally, Adon picked up the tablet and hugged it.

"At least they didn't take this," he said, putting it back in his saddlebags. Though he would miss the rest of his gear, he was so relieved not to have lost the tablet that he felt happy.

Kelemvor wasn't so optimistic. "We'll have a hungry night unless I catch us something to eat," he said. "Perhaps you should start a cooking fire, Adon." He removed the flint and steel from the pouch that hung at his neck and handed them to the cleric.

Midnight nodded, then gathered her things and placed them near Adon. "I saw a butternut tree as we came in. Its fruits are nourishing, if bitter." The mage stood up and brushed herself off. "Take care of what the thieves left us, Adon," Midnight said, turning toward the forest.

"Don't worry," Adon assured her. "It's one thing to rifle unwatched packs and quite another to steal from beneath an attentive guard's nose."

"Let's hope so," Kelemvor grumbled, heading into the forest in the direction opposite Midnight. Though he did not say so, the fighter hoped that he would run across some sign of the thief.

An hour later, Kelemvor returned with nothing save a healthy dread of the nuts he would have to call dinner. Night had fallen quickly, and he had been unable to see any tracks or droppings. Even when he'd sat quietly alongside the trail, the fighter had heard nothing but the hooting of an owl.

Midnight sat beside a small fire, opening gummy husks with her dagger. In her lap was a pile of shriveled nuts that looked about as appetizing as gravel. Adon had gathered a sizable stack of wood and was using his mace to smash it into fire-sized sticks.

"No meat?" the cleric asked, obviously disappointed. He had already tasted some of the butternuts and was hoping that Kelemvor would bring back something else for eveningfeast.

"Plenty of meat," Kelemvor answered. "All on the hoof and far away." He grabbed his saddlebags and poked around inside, hoping the thief had missed a broken corner of corn cake. Save for a few crumbs, the sack was completely empty. Kelemvor sighed, then decided to put away his remaining belongings before they also disappeared. "Let me have my flint and steel," he told Adon.

"In your sack," the cleric replied, throwing a stick onto the fire.

"They're not there," Kelemvor said, turning the saddlebags over.

"Look again," Adon snapped, irritated by the fighter's failure to return with a decent meal. "I put it there a half-hour ago."

Kelemvor's heart sunk. "The thief has returned," he announced.

Midnight grabbed her own saddlebags and turned them over. They were empty. She turned on Adon. "You stupid oaf, my spellbook's gone!"

"You were supposed to be guarding—" Kelemvor stopped in midsentence and fought back his rage. Anger would not recover their belongings. "Forget it. Anybody who can rifle packs beneath your nose is no ordinary thief."

Midnight studied the fighter in open astonishment. "You can't be Kelemvor Lyonsbane!" It was not like him to be so forgiving. The fighter's calm demeanor made Midnight feel embarrassed by her own anger. Still, she couldn't contain it. Without her spellbook, she was powerless.

Adon was paying no attention to either of them. He snatched up the saddlebags containing the tablet and slung them over his shoulder. He felt like a fool for letting the thief return, but he could live with embarrassment as long as they had the tablet.

Though he had conquered his anger, Kelemvor wasn't ready to give their possessions up for lost. He went to the edge of the campsite and carefully inspected the shrubbery. After several minutes of searching, he found a few crumbs of corn biscuit. The warrior quietly called his companions over and pointed out the crumbs.

Midnight started into the forest at a sprint, heedless of the noise she was making. Kelemvor and Adon quickly caught her.

"Slowly," the fighter suggested, placing a hand on her shoulder.

"We don't have time!" she retorted. "The thief has my spellbook!"

"He won't get far tonight," Kelemvor replied. "But if he hears us coming, we'll never find him."

"What makes you think he's afraid of the dark?" Midnight snapped, twisting free of Kelemvor's grip.

"Fan out and be quiet," Adon ordered, taking charge of the situation. He knew Kelemvor was right about moving quietly, but he also thought it unlikely they would find the thief on the basis of a few crumbs. "We need another clue before we know which way our thief went."

Midnight sighed and did as the cleric suggested. Ten minutes later, she found a ball of sulfur wax on the ground. It was one of the extra spell components she had kept in one of her saddlebags.

"It's not much," Adon noted, turning the ball over in his hand, "but it's all we have to go on." He traced a line from where Kelemvor found the crumbs to where Midnight found the wax. It led away from camp at an angle ninety degrees to the direction Midnight and Kelemvor had originally intended to go. "I'd say he's out there somewhere. We'd better approach quietly."

The trio began picking their way through the dark forest. Several times, a foot fell on a dry stick and snapped it, and once Adon tripped and could not contain a groan as he landed. Nevertheless, the heroes' eyes quickly grew accustomed to the dark and they became more adept at moving quietly.

Soon, the telltale glimmer of a campfire danced off the tree trunks ahead. The companions slowed their pace and crept up to the edge of a clearing.

Two dozen halflings, mostly women and children, sat in a circle. They wore the same simple cotton clothes as the dead halflings from the village. A matronly woman was using Kelemvor's dagger to slice corn cakes into bite-sized portions. Three juicy rabbits, each large enough to feed the entire camp, roasted over the fire.

Several halfling children huddled together beneath a tent made from Kelemvor's heavy cloak, while an old man poured wine down his throat from the thumb of Kelemvor's glove. Although the camp did not appear cheerful, neither was it melancholy. The halflings were resolutely continuing their lives under adverse conditions, and Kelemvor could not help but admire their determination.

Adon signaled the fighter to circle around to the left side of the camp, then instructed Midnight to circle around to the right. The cleric silently indicated that he would stay where he was.

Kelemvor moved to obey and, seven steps later, put his foot on a stick. It cracked with an alarming pop. The halflings turned toward the sound, and the adults grabbed nearby large sticks to serve as weapons.

The warrior shrugged and stepped into the clearing. "Don't be afraid," he said softly, holding his empty hands in plain sight.

The matronly halfling stared at Kelemvor in astonishment and fright. The others stepped away, brandishing their weapons and chattering between themselves in their own language. The children began to cry and ran behind the adults.

Kelemvor kneeled, hoping to appear less intimidating. "Don't be afraid," he repeated.

A moment later, Midnight stepped into the light on the opposite side of the campfire. She said, "We're not going to hurt you." Her voice was comforting and melodious. The halflings looked startled, but they did not flee.

A shrewd look of comprehension crossed the matron's brow, then she turned to Kelemvor. "What you want? Come back to finish job?" She held the stolen dagger toward the fighter.

Adon stepped into the light, taking advantage of the opportunity to say, "No. We're not the ones who—"

"Phaw!" the woman spat, turning Kelemvor's dagger in Adon's direction. "Tall Ones all the same. Come to loot rich halfling cities." She waved the weapon menacingly. "Not take Berengaria without fight. Cut off—"

"Please!" Adon cried, pointing at the dagger. "That's our knife you're using to threaten me!"

"Mine now," Berengaria replied. "Spoils of war, like tent—" She waved at Kelemvor's cloak. "—and wineskin." She pointed at his glove.

"We're not at war!" Kelemvor interrupted, his patience strained. Considering how close they lived to Hilp, these halflings seemed remarkably wild and uncivilized. Perhaps they weren't welcome in the city, for halflings were commonly considered to be a race of thieves. Apparently, it was a well-earned reputation.

"We at war," Berengaria snarled. She nodded at two old men and they stepped forward, bearing spears folded into two pieces. Despite the old men's trembling arms, Kelemvor was nervous. Their spears were woomeras, a special weapon he had seen used to good effect. The woomera was simply a three-foot stick with a groove along the length and a cup at the end. The halfling warrior placed his spear in the groove, then used the stick like an extension of his arm, launching the spear with incredible speed and accuracy. In the proper hands, the weapon was as accurate and powerful as a longbow.

Adon stepped forward, careful to keep his empty hands in sight. "We didn't destroy your village. We're your friends."

"To prove it," Kelemvor added, "we'll make a gift of the dagger, the tent, and the wineskin." He pointed at the items as he mentioned them.

Adon frowned but said nothing. The "gifts" Kelemvor had named belonged to him, and it was his business if he wanted to give them away.

The matron studied the heroes for a long time, shrewdly appraising their words. "Gifts?"

Kelemvor nodded. "To help your village recover."

"What you want in return?" Berengaria demanded,

squinting at the warrior.

"The book," Adon said. "And Kelemvor's flint and steel. We need those to survive."

Berengaria frowned in concentration, but the children began giggling and she said, "Done. We all—"

Midnight, silent until now, let out a cry of anguish and rushed to the fire. Pulling his sword, Kelemvor leaped past Berengaria and her two old men. "What's wrong?" he demanded.

"My spellbook!" the raven-haired mage yelled. "They burned it!" She snatched Kelemvor's sword, then started poking at a wide strip of shriveled leather in the fire. Kelemvor knew the book was where Midnight stored her spells when they were not committed to memory, so he could understand why she was so upset. Still, he grabbed his sword away from her and put it back into its sheath; fire was no better for a sword's temper than it was for a spellbook.

Midnight stared into the fire, a single tear running down her cheek. "Gone," she whispered.

"It's not so serious," Kelemvor said, trying to comfort her.

Midnight whirled on him, her hands clenched into fists. "Serious!" she screamed. "You oaf! Those were my spells— without them, I'm nothing!"

A pall of silence fell over the camp. For several minutes, Midnight stared at Kelemvor as if the fighter had burned the spellbook himself. Finally, she hissed, "Was burying those halflings worth this?" She turned away and stared into the fire.

A moment later, Berengaria approached Adon. "We still have deal?" she asked timidly. "We still friends?"

Adon nodded. They had nothing to gain by punishing the halflings. "We're still friends. You didn't understand."

"She might not have realized what the spellbook was," said a clear, masculine voice. "But that'd be all she didn't understand." A gaunt halfling male stepped into the clearing. His skin was the color of ash, his eyes were rimmed with red, and a sloppy bandage circled his forehead.

The other halflings backed away from the newcomer,

whispering amongst themselves. He knelt beside the fire and picked up two roasted rabbits. "Have these," he said, giving one to Adon and one to Kelemvor. "There are plenty more where they came from, and it's only a fair trade for all you've lost."

Kelemvor accepted the rabbit, but made no move to eat it. The warrior had an uneasy feeling about this halfling, and it was not just because the others feared him. "Who are you?" he demanded.

"Atherton Cooper," the halfling replied, his gaze never faltering from the fighter's. "But most call me Sneakabout. Now eat up. Berengaria has not been a good hostess this night."

"Yes, please do," Berengaria added. "We can always catch more coneys." The matronly halfling put the dagger away and smiled.

It did not escape Adon's notice that Berengaria's Common had suddenly improved. It was clear to the cleric that the halfling had been playing them for fools.

"You've known all along we didn't attack your village, haven't you?" Adon demanded. "You were stealing our gear while we collected your dead!"

"That's correct," Berengaria replied, wincing. Then she turned to Kelemvor and added, "But that doesn't negate our deal. What's done is done. Besides, our need is great."

The green-eyed fighter grunted and took a bite from the rabbit. He had no intention of demanding back what he had offered to the halflings, for Berengaria spoke the truth about their need. Nevertheless, he didn't enjoy losing his possessions through guile and trickery.

The warrior chewed slowly, considering Atherton Cooper. Sneakabout was taller and thinner than most of his race, and there was a certain menace to his manner. The tall halfling was the only able-bodied male in the camp, and that in itself was suspicious. Still, Sneakabout was the only halfling who had not stolen from or lied to the heroes, and Kelemvor was determined to treat honesty and respect in kind.

"Where are the other men?" the fighter asked between mouthfuls of rabbit. "There weren't many in the village, and there are fewer here."

"Gone to massage their vanity while their womenfolk starve in the forest," Sneakabout replied.

Berengaria turned from Midnight, whom she was trying to comfort, and added, "The menfolk were hunting when the Zhentilar—"

"Zhentilar?" Adon interrupted. "Are you sure?"

"Aye, I'm sure," Berengaria replied. "They wore the armor of Zhentil Keep, didn't they? Anyway, the men were gone, or there would have been a different story to tell in Black Oaks. Now our warriors have gone to track down those sons-of-sows!"

"And to get themselves killed," Sneakabout added bitterly.

Berengaria glared menacingly at Sneakabout. "They'll be fine without your company," she snapped.

Sneakabout snorted in reply. "They'll be outnumbered, outsized, and outwitted."

Kelemvor agreed with Sneakabout, though he didn't say so. Even if the halflings caught the raiders, the Zhentilar would cut the inexperienced warriors to shreds. The soldiers of Zhentil Keep were vicious sneaks and backstabbers who would never fight unless assured of an easy victory.

After a thoughtful pause, Sneakabout glumly noted, "I wish I were with the fellows."

"Why aren't you?" Adon asked, watching the halfling suspiciously, still not comfortable with the demihuman's sinister bearing.

"They wouldn't have me," the halfling answered, shrugging.

"It was his fault they came in the first place!" grumbled Berengaria, pointing a gnarled finger at Sneakabout's face. "He had his own pony and a magic sword. That's what they wanted!"

Adon turned to Sneakabout. "Is that right?"

The halfling shook his head and looked at the ground. "Maybe," he mumbled. Then he lifted his gaze. "But I doubt it. They wouldn't have needed to raze the whole town to get what they wanted—they caught me on their way in."

The halfling's red-rimmed eyes grew hard and distant. "Say, you wouldn't be going north, would you? I'd sure like to catch those Zhentish pigs!"

Kelemvor swallowed a bite of rabbit and said, "As luck would have it—"

"Kelemvor!" Adon hissed sharply. "We've got our own trouble."

Sneakabout drew himself up before Adon. "Without your spellcaster's book, you'll need all the help you can get. I'm as fine a scout as you'll meet outside of Elventree."

Adon shook his head firmly. "I'm afraid—"

"He can ride with me," Kelemvor noted flatly, his voice a throaty growl. "Where's your sense of courtesy, Adon?"

The young cleric glared at the warrior for a long moment, once again irritated by Kelemvor's refusal to listen to him. At last, he decided not to argue the point, as long as the fighter was willing to yield something to him. "Then we leave at dawn!" Adon said, summoning his most command-ing voice.

Kelemvor would not be bullied. "No. The halfling dead—"

"Will be buried by halflings!" Adon finished, pointing at Kelemvor with a grease-covered finger. "You don't care about these people! You only want to prove your curse is gone. Don't you think we know that?" He glanced at Mid-night, who was still staring at the remains of her spellbook. "Your test has cost us too much, Kel."

The cleric put his hand on the raven-haired mage's shoul-der. He looked at the fire and added, "I just hope we can make it to Waterdeep without Midnight's spells to aid us."

* * * * *

The four companions left Black Oaks at dawn—hungry, cold, and wet. During the night, the orange fog had changed to a chill drizzle that continued to fall through the morning. Breakfast had been nonexistent. The halflings had eaten the last of the corn biscuits the night before, and in the gray morning light, the greasy hare looked appetizing only to Kelemvor.

Adon took the lead, suggesting they travel north to Eveningstar, then rethink their route to Waterdeep. Sneaka-bout made the mistake of saying he knew a shortcut, so Adon insisted that the halfling ride with him to act as a guide. Neither enjoyed the experience. Despite his loss of faith, Adon's conversation was no less pedantic, and Sneaka-bout was not a tolerant listener.

Kelemvor, his brow gloomy and troubled, followed next. Twice, he tried to apologize to Midnight for losing her spellbook. Each time his voice failed him and he barely managed a croak.

Midnight came last, still too upset to speak. There was a hollow knot of panic and sorrow in her stomach. Since her sixteenth birthday, she had carefully recorded every spell she could learn in the book, and it had become almost an extension of her soul. Without it she felt barren and worthless, like a mother without children.

Still, all was not lost. Midnight still had several spells firmly committed to memory, and she could copy these down in a new book. Some were so common that, given time and the help of a friendly mage, she could easily relearn them. With a week or two of research, the raven-haired mage might be able to rebuild others. But a few, such as the phantasmal force and plant growth spells, were so alien to her way of thinking that she could never reconstruct them. Those spells were gone, and there was nothing she could do about it.

All in all, the situation was not as terrible as it had at first seemed. Unfortunately, that realization had not yet diminished Midnight's anger. She desperately wanted to blame somebody for the book's destruction, and since Kelemvor had been the one who had led them to Black Oaks, he was the easiest target.

But in her heart, Midnight knew that the warrior was no more responsible for the crisis than she was. He hadn't thrown the spellbook in the fire, and even the halflings had not burned it in malice. It had been an accident, pure and simple, and nothing would be accomplished by venting her anger on friends.

However, Adon wasn't helping to cool anyone's temper. Several times, he had chastised Kelemvor for leading the company to Black Oaks, reminding the gloomy fighter that the spellbook would be intact if not for that detour. Amazingly, the warrior had accepted the assertion. Adon's angry insight the night before had subdued the brawny warrior as no sword ever would, and Midnight resented the cleric for it. Despite her own pain, she did not enjoy seeing Kelemvor's spirit broken.

Consumed by her melancholy reflections, the magic-user barely noticed as morning passed. By midday, the company was deep in the forest, and she still hadn't set things right with Kelemvor. In part, this was because the path was too narrow for their horses to walk side by side. So, when Adon unexpectedly called a halt, she guided her mount forward and stopped at Kelemvor's right.

"Kelemvor—," she began.

Adon twisted around and held up a silencing hand. "Listen!"

Midnight started to object, then heard a loud rustle ahead. It came from far up the trail, and sounded as though an army were marching over a plain of dried leaves. Creaks and rasps, and then dull, distant thuds began echoing toward the company.

"What is it?" Midnight asked.

"I can't imagine," Adon replied.

Sneakabout slipped off Adon's horse. "This is where I earn my ride," he said, hustling up the path.

The halfling disappeared around a bend. For ten minutes, Midnight, Kelemvor, and Adon sat on their horses. The rustle grew louder, until it could more properly be called an uproar, and the creaks and rasps became squeals and groans. The thuds assumed a rhythmic cadence and grew into thunderous booms.

Finally, Sneakabout quickly came running back, his short

legs carrying him at his best sprint. "Off the trail!" he screamed. "Now!"

The halfling's face was so terror-stricken that no one even thought of asking for an explanation. They simply spurred theirs mounts and crashed into the forest, regrouping thirty yards off the trail.

When Sneakabout joined them, Adon started to question him. "What—"

The cleric didn't have an opportunity to finish. A hundred-foot-tall sycamore tree stepped into sight, swinging dozens of branches like arms. As its roots twisted forward, an ear-splitting creak echoed through the forest. The ground trembled as the roots flopped onto the trail. Another sycamore marched behind the first, and behind it, a hundred more.

For an hour, the company watched in flabbergasted silence as grim sycamores marched down the trail. By the time the thousandth tree passed, the company's ears were ringing and their heads were spinning. Kelemvor's horse grew skittish, and he managed to keep it under control only with the greatest effort.

Finally, however, the last tree passed out of sight and the company returned to the trail. Their ears rang for the rest of the afternoon, precluding discussion of the peculiar sight. But as they rode northward, they saw thousands of huge holes where every sycamore tree in the forest had torn its roots free and marched off.

Just before dusk, they reached the northern edge of the forest. Eveningstar lay a mile ahead, oil lamps already lighting its windows. The town was unfortified, with about fifty buildings of significant size. The companions rode to the outskirts of town, then paused before entering. Memories of the murder accusations in Wheloon were fresh in their minds.

As a crossroads village, Eveningstar had a few stables, inns, and provision markets at the edge of town. Toward the center stood shops of skilled craftsmen who produced wine, wool, farm tools, and, Midnight noted, parchment.

The streets were clean and peaceful enough. Although the shops had already closed, men and women moved freely about, paying no attention to the four strangers.

After pronouncing it safe to proceed, Adon nudged his mount forward. Midnight asked the party to wait while she knocked at a parchment shop, hoping the proprietor was still there. Unfortunately, except for businesses serving travelers, it appeared Eveningstar closed at nightfall. She would have to wait until morning to buy the materials for a new spellbook.

On Sneakabout's suggestion, the heroes went to the Lonesome Tankard, the only inn in Eveningstar. The inn was clean and warm—a welcome relief after the chill ride. An expansive dining room, crowded with travelers and locals, occupied most of the ground floor. Midnight noted with approval that its wooden floors were free from dirt and grime. A stairway along the left wall led to the lodgings on the upper stories.

Sneakabout bribed the guard who was stationed at the desk to watch for unregistered companies. After accepting the halfling's money, the guard studied Midnight warily. "You wouldn't be a thaumaturgist?" he inquired.

"No, no," Sneakabout answered for her, "she's nothing of the sort. A lady of the arts, that's all."

The guard looked doubtful. "His Majesty King Azoun IV has decreed that enchanters of any type must register with the local herald when traveling in Cormyr."

Sneakabout held out another gold piece. The guard snatched the coin away and said, "Of course, with all the folks on the roads these days, nobody can keep track of 'em anyway." With that, he left the desk and allowed the company to conduct their business with the inn's steward. After the company rented two rooms, the steward showed the four to a table near the back of the taproom.

A young serving girl immediately brought ale and wine, then asked if the company wished to eat. A few minutes later, she returned with steaming plates of sliced turnips, boiled potatoes, and roast pork. In spite of her mood, the aroma was enough to make Midnight hungry. She helped herself to generous portions of turnips and potatoes, but had only one slice of the pork.

Even with the fine food, the group had a dreary meal. Midnight wanted to apologize to Kelemvor, but not in front of her other companions. Adon and Sneakabout were the only ones who felt like making conversation, but not to each other. Adon tried to liven things up with a discussion of their route, but everybody else insisted upon postponing that chore until morning. Kelemvor was lost in his own thoughts, and Midnight's patience was chafing under the relish with which Adon pursued his temporary position as group leader.

When the meal finally ended, the four climbed the stairs to the second floor. The hour was early for sleep, but they had ridden hard that day and would ride as hard tomorrow. Their rooms each contained two cots and a small window overlooking the dark currents of the Starwater.

"The men will take this room," Adon said, indicating the one on the right. "You take that one, Midnight. I don't think anyone will mind if we move a bed into the other room."

"It'll never fit," Sneakabout said. "I'll stay with Midnight."

Kelemvor frowned jealously, but it was Adon who objected. "You can't be serious!"

Midnight ignored Adon and smiled at the halfling. "Thanks, but I prefer Kelemvor's company."

Adon's jaw dropped slack. "But you're—"

"I don't think it's necessary to dictate sleeping arrangements, Adon," Midnight said, her voice calm and even.

Adon shrugged. "You haven't spoken to Kelemvor all day," he said. "But it's none of my business if you want to spend the night with him. I was only being considerate."

Sneakabout sighed. After sharing the saddle with Adon all day, he had hoped to avoid spending the night with the pedantic ex-cleric.

Midnight stepped into her room without saying anything else. When Kelemvor didn't follow her, she stuck her head back into the hall. "Are you coming or not?"

Kelemvor shook his head as if to clear it, then stepped inside. Midnight closed the door behind him, leaving Adon and Sneakabout in the hall.

Kelemvor glanced around the room nervously and fumbled at the clasp of his swordbelt. He finally released it and laid the scabbard on the nearest cot.

"What's wrong?" Midnight asked, slipping her damp cape from her shoulders. "This is hardly our first night together."

Kelemvor studied her, wondering whether she had forgiven him or lured him in here to take vengeance. "Your spellbook," he said. "I thought you were angry."

"Angry, yes, and more. But you aren't the one who threw it in the fire." She managed a weak smile. "Besides, I can rebuild it, given time and parchment."

The fighter's face showed no sign of relief.

"Don't you understand?" Midnight asked. "The book's loss wasn't your fault. The halflings threw it in the fire. You couldn't have prevented that."

Kelemvor nodded. "Thanks for forgiving me. But Adon was right. I went to the village for selfish reasons."

"Your reasons weren't selfish," she said, taking his hand. "There's nothing wrong with helping strangers."

For a moment, Kelemvor's fingers remained limp and passive, his emerald eyes searching Midnight's. Then he returned her grasp and pulled her close. A long-smoldering ember flared to life in both their bodies. Midnight's apology had gone further than she intended, but she did not care.

Later that night, Midnight sat awake, Kelemvor snoring in the cot next to hers. Making love with him had been different than it had been before Tantras. The warrior had been gentler, more considerate. She had no doubt that he had truly changed with the lifting of his curse.

But her lover's curse, or lack of it, was not the source of the magic-user's wakefulness. This new Kelemvor was more appealing and attractive than the man he had been before Tantras, and Midnight was thinking about what that difference meant to her. He was more dangerous, for he gave more and therefore demanded more in return. But the mage didn't know how much she could give, for her art had always been, and always would be, her first love.

Also, there was the mission to consider. She was growing more attached to Kelemvor, and the mage feared that an emotional attachment would influence her if she were forced to choose between his safety and the safety of the tablet.

In the hall, a foot scraped on the floor. Midnight slid out of bed and put on her cloak, fully alert. An hour ago, she had heard Sneakabout's soft steps as he slipped out of Adon's room. Where he had gone, she did not know. The little man had his own secrets, as she had hers, and it was not her place to intrude.

But this step had been too heavy to be Sneakabout's, for halflings could walk as quietly as snowfall. Midnight slipped her dagger from its sheath and went to the door.

Visions of thieves and cutthroats dancing in her head, Midnight cracked the door open and peered out. A single oil lamp that hung over the stairs lit the hall. Its feeble light revealed a man standing at the top of the stairs, waving the steward away. The dark man's other hand was tucked beneath his dripping cloak. He turned slightly to study the hallway, and his hawkish nose was silhouetted against the lamplight.

Cyric! Her heart pounding with joy and fear simultaneously, Midnight stepped into the hall. The thief turned to meet her, his eyes wide with alarm.

"Cyric!" she whispered, advancing toward him. "It's so good to see you!"

"You—er, I'm happy to see you as well," he said, removing his hand from beneath his cloak.

"What are you doing here?" she asked, taking his arm and guiding him farther down the hall. It was less likely they'd be heard there, and Midnight didn't want to awaken Kelemvor or Adon. "Were your arrows the ones that saved us from the zombie riders?"

Cyric nodded, his eyes narrow slits. "I trust the tablet is safe?"

"Of course," Midnight replied, nodding. "And the Zhentilar who've been forcing us north? They're yours as well?"

"Right again," he replied. "I wanted you in Eveningstar." His hand slipped beneath his cloak.

Midnight grew serious. "Why? What hazards lie to the south?"

Cyric frowned for a moment, then smiled. "The forces of Bane's allies, of course," he said flatly. "The Black Lord may have perished, but he had many allies—and the zombie riders are the least of them." The thief withdrew his hand from the cloak again and laid it across Midnight's shoulder. "That's why I'm here."

A sense of dread overcame Midnight. "If you've come to rejoin us, we must be careful. Kel and Adon have not forgotten Tantras."

Cyric pulled his arm back hastily. "That's not what I mean. I've come for you," he said, "and the tablet."

"You want me to abandon—"

"They cannot protect you," Cyric snapped. "I can."

Midnight shook her head, thinking of Kelemvor. "I can't," she said. "I won't."

Cyric studied her angrily for several seconds. "Think! Don't you realize the power that you possess?"

Midnight shook her head. "I lost my—"

"With the tablets, we can be gods!" the thief snapped.

Midnight had the uncomfortable feeling that Cyric was talking to himself. "Are you mad?" she asked. "That's blasphemy!"

"Blasphemy?" Cyric laughed. "Against who? The gods are here, tearing the Realms apart in search of the Tablets of Fate. Our only gods should be ourselves. We can forge our own destinies!"

"No." Midnight backed a step away.

Cyric grabbed her elbow. "The gods are on your trail. Two nights past, Lord Bhaal butchered three of my best men. I'll not burden you with the details of their deaths." The thief's eyes seemed to glow red for an instant. "Had Bhaal wished to stay for a day or two, he could have killed me and all my men," the thief continued. "But he didn't. Do you know why?"

Midnight did not respond.

"Do you know why?" Cyric repeated, gripping her elbow harder. "Because Bhaal wants you and the tablet! You'll never make it to Waterdeep. He'll catch and kill Adon and Kelemvor, kill them in ways more painful than you can imagine."

"No." Midnight pulled her arm away. "I won't permit it."

"Then come with me," Cyric insisted. "It's your only chance . . . It's *their* only chance."

Down the hall a little ways, the door to the mage's room opened. "Midnight?" It was Kelemvor's sleepy voice.

The thief's hand slipped beneath his cloak and closed around the hilt of his sword.

"Go!" Midnight said, shoving Cyric toward the stairs. "Kel will kill you."

"Or I'll kill him," Cyric said, drawing his weapon. The short sword's blade had a reddish sheen.

The drowsy fighter stepped into the hall, pants hastily fastened and sword in hand. Upon seeing Cyric, he rubbed his eyes as if unable to believe what he was seeing. "You? Here?" The warrior brought his guard up and advanced.

Midnight stepped away from Cyric. "Don't force me to choose between friends," she warned.

The thief looked at her coldly. "You're going to have to make that choice soon." With that, Cyric slipped down the stairs and disappeared into the dark.

Kelemvor did not follow, knowing that in the dark, the advantage would belong to Cyric. Instead, he turned to Midnight. "So, you were right. He followed us. Why didn't you call me?"

"He came to talk," Midnight replied, unsure whether Kelemvor's tone showed hurt or anger. "You'd have killed him."

Just then, Sneakabout came bounding up the stairs with a rope slung over his shoulder and a book of parchment in his hands. When he saw Midnight and Kelemvor, he nearly fell over himself. "You're awake!"

"Yes," Kelemvor grumbled. "We had a visitor."

"You're about to have more. A Zhentilar band is riding this way." The halfling gave the book to Midnight without explaining where he'd gotten it.

Kelemvor opened the door to Adon's room. "Get up! Gather your things!" Then he turned to Midnight. "Do you still believe Cyric wanted to talk?"

"You drew your weapon first," she replied, pointing at Kelemvor's sword.

"Uh—can you finish this later?" Sneakabout interrupted. He took the rope off his shoulder.

"We may not have a chance," Kelemvor answered. "We'll never reach the stables—"

"No need to," the halfling chimed, grinning widely. "When the Zhentilar started nosing around, I saddled our horses. They're beneath my window."

Kelemvor slapped Sneakabout on the back, nearly knocking him down. "Good man!" Then the fighter turned to Midnight and said, "Collect our gear. We'll discuss this later."

Though resentful of his tone, Midnight immediately did as Kelemvor asked. While the magic-user hastily packed, the fighter took the rope and looped it over a beam. Adon and Sneakabout climbed out the window and slipped into the saddle of the first horse. The warrior dropped the tablet and their gear to them. A moment later, Midnight returned with the remaining bags, then climbed out the window and slid down the rope to her waiting horse. Kelemvor dropped their packs to her and followed an instant later. The halfling guided them out of town by way of a back street, and they didn't see even one of Cyric's men.

❧ 4 ❧

Hígh Horn

"Let down your guard, friend Adon," said Lord Commander Kae Deverell. A robust man with red hair and a deep, jolly voice, Lord Deverell sat at the head of a long oaken table. Behind him, a fire roared in a magnificent hearth, illuminating the room with flickering yellow light.

To Deverell's right sat Kelemvor, and to Kelemvor's right, stretched down the table like horses at a trough, sat fifteen Cormyrian officers. A mug of ale and a plate of roasted goat rested before each man. Iron candelabras stood on the table every few feet, supplementing the light from the fireplace.

Sneakabout occupied the first seat to Lord Deverell's left, followed by Adon. The saddlebags containing the tablet rested on the floor next to the cleric's chair. To Adon's left sat Midnight, who was drinking wine instead of ale, and on her left sat six Cormyrian war wizards.

Three serving wenches bustled in and out of the shadows at the room's edge, keeping everyone's mug filled and making sure no plate was ever empty.

"You and your friends are safe enough here," Deverell continued, still addressing Adon.

The cleric smiled and nodded, but did not relax.

Midnight grimaced inwardly, embarrassed by Adon's rudeness. After losing her spellbook, she could sympathize with his caution. But he was acting as though the company were camped along the road. There was no reason for his insulting behavior in a Cormyrian stronghold.

Inside High Horn, the tablet was safe—if any safe place existed in the Realms. Protecting the only road across the

Dragonjaw Mountains, the fortress had been built for defense. It stood upon the summit of a cragged peak, and its curving walls overlooked thousand-foot cliffs. Only three paths, each heavily fortified and guarded, led to the mighty castle. Even then, each road ended in a drawbridge and a triple-doored gatehouse as secure as any in Cormyr.

Due to the chaos in the Realms, seventy-five men-at-arms and twenty-five archers manned the outer curtain's frowning towers at all times. A similar force guarded the inner curtain, and eight more soldiers stood constant watch at the entrance to the keep tower. The guest enclave had been converted into barracks for the fortress's expanded complement. Travelers now had the choice of camping in the mountains or staying outside the walls at a cold, hastily erected guesthouse.

The four companions had been spared this discomfort because Kae Deverell was a Harper, and he wished to atone for the poor treatment Midnight and Adon had suffered at Harper hands during their trial in Shadowdale. Unknown to the four companions, the Cormyrian commander had also received a message from Elminster requesting that he aid Midnight and her company if they passed his way.

Deverell grabbed a mug of ale from a serving wench's hand, then sat it in front of Adon. "Don't ridicule my hospitality by drinking less than your fill," he said. "Not a rat enters High Horn without my permission."

"It is not rats that concern me," Adon replied, thinking of Cyric's visit to the inn. The thief had said that Bhaal was pursuing them. Adon doubted that even High Horn's defenses could keep the Lord of Murder at bay.

A surprised murmur rippled down the long banquet table and a dark cloud settled on Deverell's face.

Before the lord commander voiced his indignation, Midnight spoke, "Please forgive Adon, Lord Deverell. I fear his weariness has crushed his sense of courtesy."

"But not mine!" Kelemvor said, grabbing the cleric's mug. The warrior had spent many evenings with men like Deverell and knew what they expected of guests. "To please

Your Lordship," he said, draining the mug in one long swallow.

Deverell smiled and turned his attention to the fighter. "My thanks, Kelemvor Mugbane!" The lord commander grabbed a full mug and gulped it down as fast as Kelemvor had. "Of course, host duty dictates we match you cup for cup!" He called the serving wench and motioned to the officers seated to Kelemvor's right. "Until he can lift it no longer, see that no man's mug goes empty!"

The Cormyrians gave a perfunctory cheer, though more than one man grimaced at the command. Adon also groaned inwardly; when Kelemvor drank too much, he could be difficult. The cleric thought they might have been safer camping in the guesthouse.

As the officers finished their cheer, a page rushed into the room and approached Deverell. The lord commander nodded for the page to approach. Though the young man whispered into Deverell's ear, his words were not lost to Sneakabout's keen hearing.

"Milord, Captain Beresford bids me inform you that two guards are absent from the outer curtain."

Deverell frowned, then asked, "Is it still raining?"

The page nodded. "Aye. The drops are as red as blood and as cold as ice." The boy could not keep his fear from showing itself in his voice.

Deverell stopped whispering. "Then tell Beresford to worry no more, and we'll discipline the derelicts come morning. I've no doubt the guards are hiding from the strange weather."

The page bowed and left. Deverell returned his attention to the banquet table. "What a night we shall have!" he cried, addressing Sneakabout. "Shall we not, short friend?"

Sneakabout smiled and lifted his mug to his lips. "I will long remember it."

Adon made a mental note to be sure all the pewterware remained on the table at the evening's end. He had seen for himself that the halfling's fellows were incorrigible thieves, and Sneakabout had already provided reason to doubt that he had the sense to leave their host's property alone.

After escaping The Lonesome Tankard in Eveningstar, Sneakabout had tried to convince the company to ambush the Zhentilar. He was convinced that Cyric's band was the one that had destroyed his home. The halfling had been so determined to take vengeance that Kelemvor had been forced to restrain him. Afterward, Sneakabout had been furious. The halfling had claimed then that the only reason he didn't leave the companions immediately was because Cyric would soon catch them again.

It was a reasonable assumption. The company's head start from the Lonesome Tankard had earned them only a fifteen-minute advantage. Twenty-five riders had appeared on their trail as soon as they'd left town. Six exhausting hours later, when the company rode into Tyrluk, Cyric and his fastest riders were barely two hundred yards behind. Adon had led the way straight through the village, hoping the local militia would assail Cyric's company of Zhentilar. But the hour had been early, and if any watchmen had seen Cyric's band, they had elected not to sound the alarm.

From Tyrluk, the companions had fled in the only possible direction: into the mountains. An hour later, they had caught a troop of Cormyrian mountain soldiers on the way to High Horn. It had taken little effort to persuade the captain that Cyric's company was Zhentilar, especially after the band fled at the first sign of the Cormyrians. The captain had pursued, but Cyric's men had escaped easily. On the open road, the Cormyrians' mountain ponies were no match for horses—even when the horses were exhausted from hours of hard riding.

The Cormyrian captain had assigned a few scouts to trail the Zhentilar band, then resumed his journey, saying that High Horn would dispatch a charger-mounted patrol to deal with the intruders. This plan had not thrilled Midnight, who still had no wish to see Cyric hurt, but she could hardly have objected.

After chasing Cyric away, the captain had invited the company to ride with him to High Horn. The rest of the journey had been uneventful. When they had reached the fortress and the captain had made his report, Kae Deverell had offered the companions the safety and comfort of the keep. After thirty-six hours in the saddle, there had been no thought of refusing. Kelemvor and Midnight were glad to let down their guards and relax—though certainly not around each other. In fact, they had barely spoken since Eveningstar.

Thinking about his friends' relationship, Adon could only shake his head. He did not understand what attracted Midnight and Kelemvor to each other; the closer they grew, the more they fought. This time, Kelemvor was angry because Midnight had not sounded the alarm upon discovering Cyric outside their rooms. Midnight was angry because Kelemvor had pulled his sword on their old friend.

The cleric had to take the warrior's side in this particular dispute. Cyric wouldn't have crept into the inn if he had not intended them harm. Adon rubbed the ugly scar beneath his eye thoughtfully, for finding himself in agreement with Kelemvor always gave him pause.

"Does it hurt, milord?"

Snapping out of his reverie, Adon looked at the serving girl who had asked the question. "Does what hurt?"

"The scar, milord. You were rubbing it awfully hard."

"Was I?" Adon asked, dropping the offending hand to his lap. He also turned his head so the red mark would be less visible.

"I have a small jar of soothing ointment. Could I bring it to your chamber this night?" she asked hopefully.

Adon could not help but smile. It had been a long time since a woman had presented herself so boldly. And the serving girl was pretty enough and had a generous figure that had been toned by plenty of hard work. Her yellow hair spilled onto her shoulders like a silk shawl, and her blue eyes sparkled with an innocence that in no way implied lack of experience. She seemed much too beautiful to spend her life serving ale in the halls of this bleak outpost.

"I fear the ointment wouldn't do any good," Adon noted

softly. "But I'd welcome your company."

The chatter at the head of the table died, and Kelemvor glanced at the cleric with a raised eyebrow.

Realizing he had made a social gaff, Adon quickly added, "Perhaps we could discuss your—er, your—"

"Milord?" the girl asked, impatient with his floundering.

"Are you happy as a serving wench? Surely, you have other ambitions. We could talk—"

"I like what I do," she answered in a huff. "And it wasn't talking I had in mind."

Lord Deverell roared in laughter. "Your charms are wasted on him, Treen," he said to the wench, breaking into a new fit of laughter.

The officers slapped the table and guffawed. Kelemvor frowned, uncertain as to whether he had missed the joke or the situation simply wasn't funny. Finally, Deverell brought his mirth under control and continued, "Perhaps, Treen, you'd have better luck with Kelemvor—a tower of virility if ever I saw one!"

Treen obliged her liege by rounding the table to Kelemvor. She ran her hand over his arms. "What do you say, Sir Tower?"

Midnight and Adon were the only ones who did not burst into laughter.

Kelemvor took a long swig of ale, then sat his mug on the table. "Why not?" he asked, glancing at Midnight. "Someone must make amends for Adon's rudeness!" The warrior was intentionally trying to provoke Midnight. He was confused and hurt by the bitterness of their disagreement concerning Cyric, and could not help but believe there was more to it than he understood. If his flirtation angered Midnight, then at least he would know she cared enough to become jealous.

When Treen slipped her fingers beneath Kelemvor's shirt, Midnight could hold her temper no longer. She sat her wine goblet down hard. "This is one thing Adon should do for himself," she said coldly.

A surprised mutter ran around the table. Kelemvor smiled at Midnight, who simply glowered back. Treen withdrew her fingers from beneath the warrior's shirt. "If this man belongs to you, milady—," Treen began.

"He belongs to no one!" Midnight snapped, standing. She did not doubt Kelemvor had meant to hurt her, and he had succeeded. The raven-haired magic-user frowned and turned to Deverell. "I am weary, Lord, and wish to retire." With that, she spun on her heel and disappeared into the gloom.

The table remained silent for several moments, then Treen turned to Lord Deverell. "I'm sorry, Lord. I meant—"

Deverell held up a hand. "A jest gone awry, girl. Think no more of it."

Treen bowed, then retreated into the kitchen. Kelemvor drained his mug, then lifted it to be filled again.

Adon was glad to see the girl go. In the days ahead, it would be difficult enough for Midnight and Kelemvor to get along. The cleric knew the pair loved each other, though at the moment petty anger prevented them from realizing that fact themselves. But if they didn't come to grips with their feelings soon, the journey ahead would be a long one. It would have been much simpler, it seemed to Adon, if Midnight had been a man, or, better yet, Kelemvor a woman.

The page entered again and approached Lord Deverell. In the room's silence, it was impossible not to hear his whisper. "Milord, Captain Beresford orders me report the absence of three sentries from the inner curtain."

"The inner curtain?" Deverell exclaimed. "There, too?" He considered this for a moment, mumbling to himself. Like most of the men in the hall, he was rather drunk—too drunk to be making command decisions. "Beresford's discipline must be sorely lacking," he said at last. "Tell the captain I will personally correct this problem—in the morning!"

Sneakabout frowned at Adon. That five guards would abandon their posts in one night seemed strange. "Perhaps we should sleep lightly tonight," the halfling whispered, glancing at Kelemvor. The warrior had just downed his third mug of ale since Midnight's departure.

Adon nodded, a sudden sense of doom and foreboding

overcoming him. "I'll see if I can slow him down." Like Sneaka-bout, the cleric did not feel comfortable sleeping in a castle where the guard abandoned its post. He would feel even more uncomfortable if Kelemvor went to bed inebriated.

Before Adon could speak to Kelemvor, though, Lord Deverell lifted his mug. "Let us drink a health to Sir Kelemvor and the Lady Midnight. May they both rest well—" He winked at Kelemvor. "—though it be in separate beds!"

A wave of laughter ran around the table and the officers chorused, "Here, here!"

"I don't know about Lady Midnight," Kelemvor said, raising his mug to his lips. "But Sir Tower will not sleep this night!"

"If you have another mug of ale," Adon noted as he stood up, "the choice will be out of your hands. Come along— we've had a hard ride and need some rest."

"Nonsense, nonsense!" Lord Deverell cried, glad to see his party resuming a festive air. "There will be time enough to rest tomorrow. Midnight said she wanted a day to replenish her spellbook, did she not?"

"True enough, milord," Adon replied. "But we've been on the trail a long time and aren't accustomed to such rich fare. Kelemvor may feel this night for days to come."

The green-eyed fighter frowned at Adon, resentful of the unexpected supervision. "Come morning, I'll be as strong as my horse," he bragged, standing and swaying slightly. "Besides, who named you captain?"

"You did," Adon answered quietly, speaking the truth as he knew it. Kelemvor had lost his sense of purpose. The detour to Black Oaks had been only one example of the warrior's inability to focus on recovering the tablets. Someone needed to fill the void, and Midnight, intelligent as she was, seemed unwilling to take charge of the company. That had left only Adon to be the leader, and he was determined to fill the role as best he could.

"I did not," Kelemvor responded slowly, dropping back into his chair. "I wouldn't follow a faithless cleric."

Adon winced, but made no retort. He knew the warrior

had to be very upset—and very drunk—to lash out at a friend so fiercely.

Sighing, the cleric said, "Have it as you will." He picked up the saddlebags with the tablet.

Kelemvor frowned, realizing that he had treated Adon cruelly. "I'm sorry. That wasn't called for."

"I understand," Adon replied. "Even if you don't go to sleep, try not to drink too much." He turned to Lord Deverell. "If you'll excuse me, I'm very tired."

Kae Deverell nodded and smiled, glad to be rid of the kill-joy.

After Adon had gone, Kelemvor's mood grew even darker. He spoke little, and drank even less. It fell on Sneakabout's shoulders to keep Lord Deverell's party jolly and exuberant, which he did by reciting halfling stories and poems. Finally, two hours later, Lord Deverell drank one ale too many and slumped into his chair, unconscious.

The six Cormyrian officers who had outlasted their commander breathed sighs of relief and stood. Grumbling about the lateness of the hour, they picked up the lord commander and went to put him to bed. From their impatient attitude, the halfling guessed that similar duties fell on their shoulders with too great a frequency for their liking.

After seeing Kelemvor to his room on the tower's third floor, Sneakabout went down to the second floor and peeked in on Midnight and Adon. Both were sleeping soundly, so he began an investigation of the keep tower.

While the halfling explored, Adon drifted through the night in the mists of a sleep as deep and peaceful as he could remember. Though the cleric had not realized it until leaving Lord Deverell's table, the previous two days of riding had truly exhausted him. He had collapsed into bed without undressing.

But Adon had not forgotten the five missing guards or the danger that pursued their company, and part of his mind remained alert. So when he suddenly found himself completely awake with the dim memory of hearing a scream, he did not doubt for an instant that something was wrong. His first thought was that Bhaal had come for the tablet. The cleric slipped his hand beneath the straw mattress and felt the reassuring texture of the leather saddlebag.

Adon lay motionless, listening for another scream. The only sounds were his own panicked breath and the patter of rain on the shutters. For another thirty seconds, nothing stirred in the black room. Adon began to suspect he had dreamed the scream and silently chuckled to himself. It had been a long time since he'd been afraid of the dark.

But Adon knew better than to feel silly for being frightened. Bhaal was on their trail, and from the Lord of Murder, there was only one protection: the blessing of another god. Adon could no longer provide that protection, and he worried for an instant that it had been wrong to turn away from Sune Firehair. The cleric caressed the ugly scar beneath his eye. Certainly, it had been wrong to turn away because she hadn't removed the blemish. In a time of so much strife, it had been selfish to expect her to repair his marred visage. Adon could accept that fact now, just as he accepted the imperfection.

What he could not accept, however, was the gods' indifference to their worshipers. Since his youth, he had venerated Sune, believing the goddess would watch over him in return for his dedication. When she had allowed him to be scarred, Adon had fallen into a deep despair, realizing Sune cared little about her worshipers. Recovering from that disappointment had been a slow and tedious process. His confidence and will to live had returned only when he'd turned his devotion to his fellow man.

But this newfound devotion had not renewed the cleric's faith in Sune. In fact, the more dedicated to other men he became, the more Adon resented Sune—and all the gods—for abusing the faith of their mortal worshipers.

Unfortunately, it had been faith in Sune that supplied Adon with clerical abilities. No matter how deeply felt or sincere, devotion to fellow man would never restore those powers. Gods were magical, supernatural, and, for reasons of their own, they rewarded fervent belief in their existence with the barest fraction of their power.

The door to the stairwell creaked open, abruptly ending Adon's reflections. A sliver of yellow light slipped into the room. Watching the partially opened door, Adon reached for his mace and put his feet on the floor.

As the cleric stood, a black shadow flew out of the doorway, striking his face with a cold weight. Shrieking in surprise, Adon fell back onto the bed.

"Quiet!" Sneakabout hissed. "Put that on."

Adon angrily peeled the mail shirt from his head, then slipped into it. "What's happening?" he asked.

But Sneakabout, who had spent the last three hours examining every trap in the keep tower, had already disappeared. As the halfling reached the bottom of the stairs, the doors to the banquet hall opened. Six Cormyrian guards rushed into the room carrying torches and weapons.

"Jalur, help me bar the doors!" ordered the sergeant, waving his drawn sword at the entrance. "Kiel, Makare, and you others—to the stairwell!"

Surprised at how quickly the Cormyrians had retreated into the keep, the halfling crept toward the kitchen. His destination was the room directly below Adon's, the steward's office. Unfortunately, the office was locked and Sneakabout would have to pick the lock or find a key. Then he would have to rearrange the furniture so he could reach the crank. It would take time—time he might not have. The halfling had no idea what it was that the guards were fighting, but he knew that it had torn through them with frightening speed.

The guards knew little more about their opponent than Sneakabout. Orrel had seen something crawl down a dark corner of the inner wall. A moment later, a timid-looking man had stepped out of the shadows and walked nonchalantly to the keep's entrance. Orrel and another guard had stepped out of the foyer to challenge him. He had knocked their halberds aside, then slipped a dagger out of his sleeve and killed them both with a single, long slash.

A third guard had yelled an alarm, which had also proven

fatal. The stranger had thrown a dagger through the guard's throat, silencing him in midscream. Fitch, the sergeant, had ordered the survivors to retreat inside. He felt foolish for running from a lone attacker, but the smooth efficiency with which the man killed left no doubt that he was no ordinary assassin. Because their assignment was to protect the keep tower, Fitch thought it wisest to retreat and bar the door, then send a man to call for help.

His strategy didn't work. The doors were thick and heavy, designed for strength instead of maneuverability. As the sergeant and a guard pushed them into place, the stranger stepped out of the foyer. The guard died an instant later, the attacker's fingers wrapped around his larynx.

Brandishing his sword, Sergeant Fitch yelled his last order to the men on the stairs. "In Azoun's name, keep him downstairs!"

On the second floor, Adon heard the sounds of a brief scuffle, which was followed by a few words he could not understand. A flickering torch lit the landing that separated his room from Midnight's. Her door was also ajar, but the chamber was too dark for him to see inside. The magic-user might be there, or she might have already fled.

To Adon's left, the stairs descended in a gentle, clockwise spiral. Five feet down, another torch hung in a sconce, casting its dingy light upon the cold stone steps. Where the stairwell curved out of sight, the shadows of four Cormyrians were retreating up the stairs. Each silhouette held a polearm.

Judging from the shadows, it appeared a single man was pursuing them. One of the Cormyrian silhouettes lunged. A flurry of activity followed, then a weak chuckle rolled up the stairs. An instant later, a man screamed in agony.

The other three guards retreated another step. Their chain-mailed backs were visible to Adon now, but the attacker remained unseen. Adon could not believe a single man pressed so fiercely, but the shadow appeared to be nothing more.

The cleric had no doubt that the mysterious attacker had

come for the tablet. He went to the window inside his room and opened the shutters. An icy, driving rain struck him full in the face. Dismissing any thought of the storm, Adon propped the tablet in the window. If necessary, he would shove the tablet out the window rather than let it fall into an enemy's hands. With any luck, one of Deverell's men would pick it up at the tower's base and flee.

When Adon returned to the door, clutching his mace, only two guards remained. They stood on the second floor landing, facing their attacker despite the terror in their faces. Two steps below them stood the mysterious assassin. When Adon saw the little man, he could not help but be puzzled by the Cormyrians' fear.

The man stood no taller than five and a half feet, and had a slight build. His bald head was tattooed with swirls of green and red, but that was the only thing about him that was even remotely frightening. From the stranger's apprehensive brow hung a timid nose, with nervous, bulging eyes on either side. The only prominent features on the entire face were two flaplike ears and a set of buckteeth. The face was the kind that made Adon thankful for his own good looks, scar and all. The man's body had been allowed to wither into a gaunt bag of bones held together by sinew and willpower alone. Small gouges and cuts covered him from head to toe.

"What's wrong?" Adon demanded. "Stop him!"

One of the Cormyrians glanced in the cleric's direction. "You try it—or get out of the way!"

A clamor arose outside the tower as word spread that the keep was under attack. The tattoo-headed man turned to listen for an instant, then calmly returned his gaze to the two guards in front of him. The stranger stepped forward, slapping their halberds aside as if the weapons were no more than sticks.

"Get back!" screamed the second Cormyrian, kicking at the bald man.

The guard's boot caught the stranger square in the forehead. The blow should have sent him tumbling down the stairwell, but the tattooed head simply rocked back. Then the little man growled and, moving with astounding speed and grace, struck the offending leg and broke it. The guard screamed and fell, his head striking a stone step with a sickening thump.

Adon suddenly knew why the guards had not stopped the attacker. The little man was an avatar.

"Bhaal!" Adon gasped, unconsciously lifting his mace.

The avatar turned toward the cleric and drew his thin lips back in an acknowledging smile.

A wave of fear washed over Adon, and he could not force it away. When he had faced the god Bane in similar circumstances, Adon had had his faith to strengthen him. Death had not been frightening then, for he had believed that dying in Sune's service was a high honor that would bring a great reward in the afterlife.

There were no such guarantees now. Adon had abandoned the goddess, and if he died, only endless despair and nothingness would follow. Worse, there would be nobody to set the matter straight. Bhaal would take the tablet and plunge mankind into darkness and misery.

The last guard dropped his halberd and drew his sword. He crouched into a fighting stance and slowly traced a defensive pattern in the air.

Still two steps below the landing, Bhaal turned his attention back to the guard.

The Cormyrian hazarded a glance at Adon. "Are you with me?"

Adon swallowed. "Aye," he said. The cleric stepped out of his room and stood over the guard who had fallen a moment earlier.

The remaining live soldier shifted to the other side of the landing, then raised his sword. The guard was deliberately giving the god an opening so Adon could attack.

Heedless of the trap, Bhaal stepped forward, and Adon swung his mace at the avatar's head. The god easily ducked the blow. Before the Cormyrian could slash, however, the Lord of Murder punched him in the abdomen. The man barely retained his balance and stumbled back on the landing. Bhaal now stood next to Adon.

Staring the avatar in the eyes, Adon brought his mace into a guarding position. The Cormyrian staggered a step forward and lifted his sword, too.

"What now?" the guard asked, gasping for breath.

"Attack!" Adon yelled.

The Cormyrian obliged with a vicious overhead slash. Bhaal sidestepped it easily, moving backward toward Midnight's chamber.

The magic-user's door flew open. Midnight stood in the entrance to her room, dagger in hand. She had been watching the battle in silence, cursing the loss of her spellbook and waiting for an opportunity to strike. Finally, it had come. She thrust the blade into the avatar's back.

Bhaal's eyes widened in surprise. He started to turn, and Adon seized the chance for an easy attack, smashing his mace into the avatar's ribs. The god's knees buckled and he tumbled down the stairs, roaring in a rage.

The avatar came to rest six steps down, Midnight's dagger still planted in his back.

"Is he dead?" Midnight asked.

Bhaal rose and glared at the magic-user, cursing in a language no human could duplicate. Without paying any attention to his wounds, the Lord of Murder jumped for the landing.

The Cormyrian yelled and leaped to meet the avatar, blade flashing. Bhaal met the guard in midair, blocking the soldier's sword arm with a bone-crunching blow and simultaneously driving his fingers into the man's throat. The avatar reached the landing with the guard's gasping body in his hands, then dropped the corpse down the stairs without a second thought.

It was then that Adon understood. Nothing they could do would stop the avatar. Bhaal was animating the body with his own life force.

The tramp of boots and a chorus of yells announced that reinforcements had entered the keep tower.

"Run, Midnight!" Adon yelled. "We can't kill him!"

The cleric turned toward his own room, intending to shove the tablet out the window. Bhaal grinned, then turned toward Midnight.

"Adon!" the magic-user screamed. "What are you doing?" She could not believe her friend would desert her.

Midnight's cry brought Adon back to his senses. In his concern to protect the tablet, he had forgotten she was defenseless. He turned and hefted his mace, finding Bhaal's back to him. It was as good a chance as he'd ever have.

Adon brought the mace down hard on the back of Bhaal's head. Bone splintered beneath the weapon. The surprised avatar teetered and stumbled, and Adon thought for a moment the god might actually fall.

Bhaal lifted a hand and felt the wound. His fingers came away bloody. Without so much as turning around, he kicked backward, catching the cleric in the ribs. Adon flew into his chamber, crashed into his bed, then crumpled to the floor gasping for breath and wondering how he would ever pick himself up.

Adon felt the floor tremble faintly, then metal screeched against metal. He had no idea what could be causing the strange noise and vibration.

"What's happening down there?" Kelemvor yelled from up the stairway. His voice was hoarse with grogginess.

Bhaal looked up the stairs, his head little more than a bloody pulp.

"By Torm's mailed fist!" Kelemvor cursed, descending the keep's stairs with heavy, unsteady steps. "What are you, I wonder?"

Bhaal turned back to the magic-user, apparently unconcerned with the warrior. Heart pounding with fear, Midnight held on to her door for support while searching her mind for a way to defend herself without a weapon.

A mighty roar echoed from the walls. Kelemvor flew into view, swinging his sword in a mighty arc. Bhaal dropped his shoulder, letting the fighter land on his back, then stood up and catapulted the warrior down the stairwell. Kelemvor flashed out of Adon's sight as quickly as he had entered it.

A series of thumps and curses announced that the Cormyrian reinforcements had broken the fighter's fall—and
that they would be delayed even further. Adon forced himself to stand, his breath coming in short, painful gasps. His
doorway was aligned directly opposite Midnight's, and he
could see Bhaal slowly advancing on the magic-user.

Midnight remained motionless as the Lord of Murder
moved toward her. She had thought of a way to delay Bhaal,
but it depended upon surprise. When the god reached the
threshold to her room, she slammed the door, using its bulk
as a weapon.

The move did catch Bhaal by surprise, and the heavy door
hit him squarely in the face. The avatar stumbled back two
steps, then Midnight pushed the door shut, slid the bolt into
place, and braced her body against it. The tactic would not
hold the Lord of Murder for long, but it might allow her
time to think of something better.

Bhaal stood in the middle of the landing and stared at the
closed door, venting his anger in a stream of guttural curses.

Adon could easily understand how Midnight's move had
stunned the evil god, for it had certainly astonished him.
What he could not understand, however, was why Bhaal
was concentrating so intently on her. Perhaps the god assumed that she carried the tablet, or, not realizing that her
spellbook was lost, feared her magic more than Adon's
mace. Whatever the reason, the cleric decided to take
advantage of the situation.

Adon stepped into his own doorway. Six feet down the
stairs, Kelemvor and eight Cormyrians lay in a heap, dazed
and groaning.

As the cleric raised his mace, the floor vibrated beneath
his feet again, and faint metallic clinks echoed around the
landing. Though he could not imagine what caused them,
Adon shrugged off the strange vibrations and prepared to
attack.

In the same instant, Bhaal rushed forward and kicked
Midnight's door. The bolt snapped off and the door flew

open, sending the magic-user sprawling.

Adon missed Bhaal's head and his mace struck the floor with a hollow clang. Two stones fell out of the landing. The cleric stepped back into the doorway to his room and frowned at the hole in astonishment.

Bhaal turned to face Adon, the avatar's face betraying irritation. Then the entire landing collapsed, carrying the Lord of Murder and the body of one fallen guard with it. The landing crashed onto the first floor with a deafening clatter. Clouds of dust billowed up out the newly opened pit.

Midnight crawled back to her doorway, and, for a moment, both she and Adon stared down into the hole. When the air finally cleared, they both saw that Bhaal's crumpled form lay in the rubble, its neck cocked at a severe angle and obviously broken. The small body, sprawled and twisted, had been crushed in a dozen places.

But the avatar's eyes remained opened, and they were staring at Adon with deliberate wrath. The god curled first his left hand into a fist, then his right.

Midnight gasped, unable to believe the avatar still lived.

"What does it take to kill you?" Adon cried.

As if in answer, Sneakabout stuck his head out of a hole below the cleric's doorway. It was where the beam supporting the landing should have been.

"That didn't do it?" the halfling asked. "What have you dragged me into?"

"What happened?" Midnight asked, still staring in wonder at the collapsed landing.

"It was a trap," Sneakabout noted casually. "A last line of defense. The landings in this tower are designed to collapse, in case the keep is breached and the residents need to slow down pursuit while they retreat to the roof."

As the halfling spoke, Bhaal drew a knee up to his chest, then propped himself into a sitting position.

"Never mind," Adon said, pointing at the avatar.

Sneakabout gestured at the top of Adon's doorway. "There's a crank behind the door!" he cried, waving his hand for emphasis. "Turn it!"

The cleric stepped behind the door. The crank was where Sneakabout said it would be. The cleric began turning it. A terrible, rusty screech filled the room. The beam overhead—the one that supported the landing on the third floor—began moving.

"Hurry!" Sneakabout screamed.

Midnight backed away from her door, sensing it might be wiser to be completely inside her room when the landing fell.

Adon cranked harder. The supportive beams slowly withdrew, and a stone dropped out of the landing. Then two more dropped. Then a dozen. Finally, the whole thing crashed down, falling through the hole where the second floor landing should have been.

Sneakabout poked his head out of his hole again, and Midnight crawled to look out her doorway. The Cormyrian reinforcements finally reached the second floor, Kelemvor stumbling along behind them. Everybody peered through the hole and stared at the rubble on the first floor.

"Is he dead?" Sneakabout asked.

Adon shook his head. "No. When a god's avatar dies, the destruction is immense."

"A god!" Sneakabout gasped, nearly tumbling out of his hole.

Adon nodded. "Cyric wasn't lying. Bhaal is chasing us." The cleric paused and pointed at the rubble. "That's him."

As if in response to Adon's revelation, the dust clouds cleared. Bhaal lay buried under a small pile of rock, a hand and foot protruding from beneath the stones.

"He looks dead to me," Sneakabout declared.

The hand twitched, then it pushed a stone away.

Midnight gasped. "If we can't kill him," she said, looking to Adon, "isn't there some way to imprison him?"

Adon frowned and closed his eyes, searching his memory for some trap that might hold a god. Finally, he shook his head, "Not that I know of."

The hand pushed another stone away.

"To the first floor, men," ordered the Cormyrian sergeant.

"Quick, before he frees himself!" Kelemvor added, turning and leading the way down the stairs—to die in a hopeless fight, Adon thought.

"Perhaps we should leave now," Sneakabout offered weakly.

Midnight was not listening. As soon as she had suggested imprisoning Bhaal, a spell unlike anything she had ever studied had formed in her mind.

The mage went back into her room and rummaged through her cloak, then emerged with two balls of clay and some water. After soaking the first ball in water, Midnight crumbled it between her fingers and sprinkled it over the pile of rubble below.

"What are you doing?" Sneakabout asked, watching the bits of mud fall.

"Encasing him in stone," Midnight explained calmly. She continued crumbling the clay.

"Magically?" Adon asked.

"Of course—do I look like a stonesmith to you?"

"What if you miscast it?" Adon objected. "You might bring the tower down around our ears!"

Midnight frowned. The spell's appearance had excited her so much that she hadn't considered the possibility of it going awry.

Bhaal shoved away several more stones.

"What do we have to lose?" Midnight asked. The magic-user closed her eyes and focused on her magic. She quickly uttered the chant, crushing the last of the first clay ball.

When she opened her eyes, the rubble had turned to a syrupy, translucent fluid the color of ale. She had expected mud, not pine sap, but at least Bhaal's mangled form remained encased. His hateful eyes were focused on Midnight, and he was struggling to free himself.

Kelemvor and the Cormyrians charged into view on the first floor, then stopped at the edge of the golden glob. One tried to stick his sword through the goo and stab Bhaal, but the syrup gripped his blade and would not release it.

"What's the meaning of this?" the sergeant demanded.

"How are we supposed to attack through that mess?"

"I wouldn't advise attacking at all," Adon replied, "unless you have no other choice."

Midnight soaked the other clay ball, then began sprinkling it over the yellow glob.

"Just what do you think you're doing?" the sergeant demanded, pointing at Midnight's hand with his sword.

Sneakabout replied for the magic-user. "Never mind. By the way, I'd stand back if I were you."

Midnight closed her eyes and recited another spell, this one designed to turn the sticky mess solid. When she finished, the golden fluid began hardening. The avatar's struggles slowed and completely stopped within seconds.

The Cormyrian sergeant tapped the yellow glob with his sword. The blade chimed as if he had tapped granite.

"Where did you learn that?" Adon asked.

"It just came to me," Midnight replied, her voice weak and tired. "I don't understand myself." She suddenly felt very dizzy, and realized that the spell had taken more out of her than she'd expected.

Adon stared at Midnight for a moment. Each day, it seemed the mage learned something new about her magic. Thinking of his lost clerical powers, he could not help but feel a tinge of jealousy.

"Will this hold?" Kelemvor asked, tapping the glob.

Adon looked at Bhaal's prison. The liquid had dried into eighteen inches of clear, crystalline rock. Inside, the avatar continued to stare at Midnight.

"I hope so," Adon replied, resting his own gaze upon Midnight's weary face.

❦ 5 ❦

A Green Sun

Despite a fitful night of sleep, Midnight woke just an hour after dawn. Slivers of light slipped through the seams in the window shutters, illuminating her room in eerie green tones. She pulled her cloak on and opened the window. Where the sun should have hung was an immense, multi-faceted eye similar to a fly's or spider's. It burned with a radiant green light that turned the entire sky to emerald and cast a lush glow over the gray mountains around High Horn.

Midnight blinked and looked away. Atop the keep's inner wall, the sentries marched their routes without paying the eye any attention. The magic-user wondered if she were imagining the thing, but when she looked back, the eye still hung in the sky.

Fascinated by the magnitude of its hideousness, Midnight studied the green orb for several minutes. Finally, she decided her captivation was pointless and dressed.

The mage proceeded with the task of dressing slowly, stopping to yawn often. After imprisoning Bhaal, Midnight had fallen into a restless sleep that did little to replenish her energy. Though the god's attack had terrified her, the ride from Eveningstar had fatigued the mage to the point where staying awake had been out of the question.

Her slumber had been short-lived, however. Two guards had come to lay planks over the collapsed landing, interrupting her rest. Midnight had spent the next two hours flinching at High Horn's unfamiliar sounds, then finally drifted into an unsettled sleep that had lasted until she woke to the green dawn.

Though still drowsy and exhausted, Midnight knew it would be pointless to return to bed. Sleeping during the day was difficult for her, especially with the clamor of castle life outside the window. Besides, the magic-user was anxious to turn her thoughts to the spell she had used last night.

The spell had simply appeared in Midnight's mind, which both puzzled and delighted her. Magic was a rigorous discipline, demanding careful and tedious study. The mystical symbols that a mage impressed upon her brain when studying a spell carried power. Casting the spell discharged the power, draining all memory of the symbols until the spell was studied again. That was why Midnight's spellbook had been her most valued possession.

But the stone-to-mud spell had appeared in her mind without study. In fact, she had never studied it, and had considered it beyond her ability to cast.

Flushed with excitement, Midnight decided to summon another spell. If she could call mystical symbols at will, the loss of her spellbook would be a trivial—perhaps even lucky—thing.

She closed her eyes and cleared her mind. Then, remembering how Kelemvor had spurned her last night, she tried to trace the symbols for a charm spell into her brain.

Midnight did not need to try for long, however. Nothing happened, and the magic-user immediately knew that nothing would. She sat down and analyzed every detail of the previous night's events. After the collapsed landings had failed to kill Bhaal, she had realized their only hope was to imprison the god—and a method for doing so had come to her.

But Midnight couldn't remember any of the spell's mystical symbols, and realized that the incantation had come to her in pure, unadulterated form. She puzzled over this for several minutes. In effect, mystical symbols were spells, for symbols put the spellcaster in touch with the magic that powered her art. It was impossible to cast a spell without using a mystical symbol.

With sudden clarity, Midnight understood what had hap-

pened. She had not cast a spell at all, at least not as most
magic-users thought of one. Instead, she had tapped the
magic weave directly, shaping its power without symbols or
runes.

Her stomach fluttering, Midnight decided to try summoning the charm spell again. This time, she concentrated upon
the desired effect instead of the symbols associated with it.
The power swelled within her and she intuitively knew
how to say the words and make the gestures that would
shape the magic into her charm spell.

Midnight's hand went to her chest and she ran her fingers
over a flat, smooth line crossing her collarbone. That was
where, just weeks before, the chain of Mystra's pendant
had grafted itself to her chest.

"What have you done to me?" she asked, looking toward
the heavens. Of course, no one answered.

As Midnight contemplated the magic weave in her room
on the second floor, a dozen hungry Cormyrian officers
stood in the banquet room on the first floor. They had been
awaiting the arrival of Lord Deverell, and dawn repast, for
over an hour.

Finally, the lord commander stumbled into the room. His
eyes were sunken and bloodshot and his skin pallid yellow.
His condition had nothing to do with Bhaal's attack of the
night before. Lord Deverell had slept through the entire
battle and knew about it only because his valet had recounted it for him.

Although he had drunk less ale than Lord Deverell,
Kelemvor was less accustomed to the potent drink and was
in a condition similar to the lord commander's. However, he
was still in bed, having earlier informed a maid that he
would not be rising before midday. Adon, too, remained in
bed, finally resting quietly after a series of dreams involving
Bhaal and various forms of slow death.

Sneakabout was the only one of the four companions
present when Lord Commander Deverell took his seat.
Though any other host might have found the absence of
Sneakabout's friends strange, perhaps even rude, it did not

trouble Deverell. In fact, it made him feel less guilty about rising so late, and these days he could do with less guilt. The night officers were sure to grumble about his valet's inability to rouse him last night, and Deverell couldn't blame them. Lately, there had been too many occasions for similar remarks. But he felt he could not be blamed for keeping himself entertained in the forlorn halls of High Horn.

Deverell waved the officers and Sneakabout to the table. "Sit," he said wearily. "Eat."

The officers sat without comment. From conversations he'd had earlier, the halfling knew that the Cormyrians were in a foul mood. Most had spent the night on cold ramparts and were anxious to go to bed, though ceremony dictated they break bread with their lord first.

Serving wenches brought out steaming bowls of hot cereal. Deverell looked at the gruel and pushed it away in disgust, but Sneakabout dug in with a hearty appetite. He liked boiled grains more than roasted meat or sweet cake.

A moment later, Deverell turned to the halfling. "My steward tells me you broke into his office last night."

Sneakabout gulped down a mouthful of oats. "The need was great, milord."

"So I hear," Deverell replied, shaking his head sadly. "My thanks for your quick thought."

"Think nothing of it, milord. It was but gratitude for your hospitality." Though raised in Black Oaks, Sneakabout had seen the inside of enough palaces to know the mandates of courtesy.

A murmur of approval rippled through the room. The lord commander tried to smile and inclined his head. "Your words are kind, but I must apologize. I promised safe refuge, and my failure to provide it is a grievous violation of host duty."

"It wasn't your fault, Lord Deverell," Midnight said, stepping into the room.

Lord Deverell and the others stood to acknowledge her presence. "Lady Midnight," Deverell observed. "You look well this morning."

Midnight smiled, appreciating the flattery—though she knew her fatigue showed. The magic-user approached the table, continuing to speak. "You mustn't feel bad on our account. Our attacker was Bhaal, Lord of Murder."

Whispers rustled round the table. She had just confirmed the rumor that had circulated through the ranks all night. A few men cast nervous glances toward the courtyard, where Bhaal still lay in his amber prison, but no one made any comments.

Sneakabout added, "There was nothing you could do. Nobody could have stopped him."

"But you slowed him down, friend halfling," Deverell responded, motioning Midnight to a seat. "Perhaps *you* should be my watch captain."

One of the officers, a lanky man named Pell Beresford, frowned. So did Midnight. In the few days she had known him, she had developed a fondness for the halfling—and the cleverness he had shown in twice saving their company. The prospect of parting with him did not make her happy.

"I know you haven't traveled long with Midnight and her friends," Lord Deverell continued, resuming his seat. "If you wish to stay here, my offer is serious. I can always use men with keen wits."

"You flatter me," Sneakabout said, astonished. Humans rarely offered positions of authority to halflings.

Midnight bit her lip. If Sneakabout took the offer, she would have to congratulate him and appear happy.

"I'd like to accept," the halfling replied, looking into Deverell's blurry eyes. "But my path runs with Midnight's for a while yet."

Midnight breathed a sigh of relief.

Then, thinking Lord Deverell deserved further explanation, Sneakabout added, "I've certain unfinished business with a Zhentilar band pursuing them."

"Black Oaks," said Pell Beresford, pushing aside his empty bowl.

Sneakabout nodded. "How did you know?"

"Before dawn, forty of your people passed this way. They

were trailing a troop of Zhentilar that one of our patrols chased off during the night."

"No doubt the same Zhentilar that chased you into our company," Lord Deverell observed.

"I must leave at once!" Sneakabout exclaimed, hopping out of his chair. "Where did they go?"

"Patience," said Lord Deverell. "They undoubtedly fled to the west, and those lands belong to the Zhentilar—if they belong to anybody. You'll never find the ones you seek, though plenty of evil will find you. It would be wiser to forego your vengeance and accept my offer."

"If it were only a matter of vengeance, I would," Sneakabout sighed. He meant what he said. As much as he ached to repay the men who destroyed Black Oaks, he knew that no good would come of trailing them into the Tun Plain.

But Sneakabout had no choice. When the Zhentilar had attacked his village, they had stolen his sword. Now, as evil as it was, he had to steal it back. The thing had a will of its own—a will that had long dominated Sneakabout, forcing him to murder indiscriminately and often. If the red blade's absence had not been driving him insane, Sneakabout would have been happy to be rid of the thing.

But an irrational desire to recover the sword dominated all of his thoughts and he had not slept an hour since losing it. Sneakabout knew his symptoms would get worse. The sword's previous owner had turned into a raving lunatic—before dying in a poorly planned attempt to recover the weapon.

The lord commander, misinterpreting the desperation in Sneakabout's eyes as resolve, said, "Do as your honor dictates. No matter how great my need, I can't command you to stay."

Sneakabout bowed to Deverell. "My thanks for your hospitality." He turned to Midnight. "Please say good-bye to Kelemvor and Adon for me."

"Where are you going?" Midnight demanded, rising to her feet.

"To track down the Zhentilar who destroyed my village,"

the halfling answered, glancing at the door anxiously. "As I remember, you wanted to avoid them."

Midnight ignored his barbed comment. "You're going to catch your people and join the war party?" she probed.

"You know they won't have me," Sneakabout replied testily.

"If you go alone, the odds are twenty-to-one," Deverell said. He shook his head in disbelief.

"Are you mad?" Midnight added, grabbing the halfling's shoulder.

Noticing that the Cormyrian officers were listening to the exchange, Sneakabout hesitated before replying. Midnight did not know about the sword's curse. Nobody did, and he thought it wise to keep it that way. Finally, the halfling pulled away from the magic-user and snapped, "I've slipped into better guarded camps."

"And then what?" Midnight demanded. "Will you slit twenty throats as the Zhentilar sleep?"

Just one, the halfling thought. He'd done that often enough. But all he said was, "I must go."

"You'll be killed!" Midnight cried. She clenched her fists, angry at the little man's stubbornness.

"Perhaps not," Lord Deverell noted, turning to halfling. "We often send heavy patrols into the Tun Plain. It's time for another. If you rode with it, you'd be safe until you caught the Zhentilar who raided your village."

Before Sneakabout could reply, Deverell turned to Midnight. "The patrol could also escort your company as far as Yellow Snake Pass, if you're going that way."

Several officers arched their brows, thankful they had been permanently assigned to garrison duty.

"We'd certainly welcome that," Midnight said. She and her companions had not yet discussed their new route to Waterdeep, but she knew both Adon and Kelemvor would agree. They'd been driven so far north that risking the Tun Plain and Yellow Snake Pass would be much easier than going south to join a caravan.

"Good," Deverell said wearily. "I'll have the quartermaster

assemble a few supplies. You'll need mountain ponies, cold weather gear, spare weapons, rope, a map. . . ."

* * * * *

Cyric sat huddled behind a boulder, a wet cloak drawn over his shoulders. To all sides, white-streaked peaks eclipsed the horizon, scraping their jagged snouts against the sky's gray belly. Cyric's men were camped on the only flat space visible for miles, a field of man-sized rocks at the base of a towering cliff. The field ended atop another cliff that overlooked the road from High Horn.

A gentle, cold breeze washed down the valley, carrying with it the sour odor of skunkweed. Though a few scrappy bushes grew in sheltered pockets, there wasn't a tree or plant taller than a dwarf in sight.

Dalzhel stood next to Cyric, having just relayed what he thought was a reasonable request from the men.

"They can't build fires," Cyric replied, not that he could see where anybody would find the wood to start one. After a night of icy drizzle, an insect eye had risen in the sun's place. Though the eye had cast a green light over the mountains, its rays had lacked warmth, causing more grumbling among Cyric's already disheartened men. Mercifully, clouds had finally moved in at midday and concealed the eye. At least the day now looked like it should be cold.

The chill did not trouble Cyric. Though the water in his canteen was frozen solid, he could not have been warmer if he had been sitting before a roaring fire. Although the thief did not fully understand the reason for his warmth, he suspected the red sword had something to do with it.

"We're ill prepared for mountain travel," Dalzhel grumbled, his nose and ears white from the cold. He looked toward the west, where eighteen of Cyric's company sat huddled in the rock field. "The men are frozen and hungry."

One of the Zhentish soldiers let out an agonized wail, as he had every few minutes since dawn. The howls unsettled the horses and put Cyric's nerves on edge.

"No fires," the hawk-nosed thief repeated. Though his

men were freezing, there could be no fires, for fires created smoke, and smoke was visible for miles. "When our spies sight Midnight and we start moving, the men will warm up."

"That's little comfort," Dalzhel replied, rubbing his hands together. "Half the men will be frozen corpses by then."

"Think!" Cyric snapped. He touched the tip of his sword to a nearby rock. "This is us." The thief moved the tip of his sword a few inches to the east. "And here is High Horn. The Cormyrians are over five hundred strong, with patrols crawling all over."

Dalzhel winced at the mention of High Horn. Last night, they had camped a mile from the fortress. A patrol of fifty Cormyrians had surprised them. After losing quite a few of his men, Cyric had been forced to flee into the mountains.

The Cormyrians, mounted on sure-footed mountain ponies, had dogged their trail through most of the night. The enemy patrol had only turned back when Cyric's band of cutthroats ambushed them in a narrow gorge. The Zhentish outlaws had taken the rest of the night to find the road and their present resting place. Along the way, the Zhentish sergeant, Fane, had broken both his legs in a bad fall, two horses had stepped off cliffs, and half the mounts had gone lame stumbling through the rocky terrain. Though he had originally snickered when he saw the Cormyrians' riding ponies, Dalzhel would now gladly trade three men for a dozen of the sure-footed beasts.

Cyric placed his swordtip north of the spot representing his company. "The Farsea Marshes. Home to the Lizard People." He touched the sword to the west. "Darkhold, Zhentilar stronghold."

"We have nothing to fear from that direction, at least," Dalzhel said. "Darkhold's forces were decimated in the battles at Shadowdale and Tantras."

Fane wailed again, causing the horses to whinny. Both men glanced in his direction, then returned to their conversation.

"We have plenty to fear from Darkhold," Cyric snapped. "With his numbers decimated, the garrison commander is surely sending raiders into the Tun Plain to look for recruits. Don't you think they'd come after us?"

Dalzhel reluctantly nodded. "Aye." A puff of steam came out of his mouth with his voice and obscured his face. "We'd be stuck on garrison duty for the rest of our lives."

"If they didn't recognize us as deserters," Cyric added.

Dalzhel shivered. "This had better be worth the trouble. Fighting Cormyrians I can take—but being tortured as a deserter is another matter."

"You don't have a choice, do you?" Cyric snarled, irritated. A staggering urge to kill his lieutenant washed over him. He lifted his sword, then realized what he was doing and stopped. The thief closed his eyes and calmed himself.

"Is something wrong?" Dalzhel asked.

Cyric opened his eyes. The anger had faded, but bloodlust had replaced it—a bloodlust more powerful and more sinister than anything the thief had ever felt. The emotion was not his own, and that made Cyric truly angry.

"You'd better check on the watch," the hawk-nosed man grumbled, thinking of an excuse to get Dalzhel out of his sight. "And let me know the minute our spies report from High Horn."

Dalzhel obeyed immediately and without question. He had no wish to add to the tension that was playing over his commander's face.

Cyric sighed in relief, then laid his sword across his knees. The blade had paled and was now beige instead of a healthy red. Pity for the weapon washed over him.

Cyric laughed aloud. Feeling sorry for a sword was no more his emotion than the thirst he had felt for Dalzhel's blood.

Fane howled again, sending a shiver of irritation down the thief's spine.

Kill him.

Cyric hurled the sword off his knees and watched it clatter to the rocky ground. The words had come unbidden to his mind in a wispy, feminine voice.

"You're alive!" Cyric hissed, the cold biting his ears and

nose for the first time.

The sword remained silent.

"Speak to me!"

His only answer was Fane's pitiful groan.

Cyric retrieved the sword and immediately grew warm. The desire to kill Fane washed over him, but he made no move to act on the urge. Instead, the thief sat back down and laid the sword across his knees again.

"I have not decided to kill him," Cyric said, glaring angrily at the weapon.

Before his eyes, the blade began to pale. Hunger and disappointment crept into his heart, and the thief found himself completely absorbed with pangs of hunger. As the blade grew more pale, Cyric became increasingly oblivious to his environment. By the time the weapon had turned completely white, he was aware of nothing else.

At Cyric's back, a girl's voice said, "I'm hungry."

He stood and spun around. An adolescent girl, perhaps fourteen or fifteen years old, stood before him. She wore a diaphanous red frock that hinted at ripening womanhood, but which also betrayed a half-dozen protruding ribs and a stomach distended with starvation. Black satiny hair framed a gaunt face, and her eyes were sunken with fatigue and desperation.

Behind her stretched an endless white plain. Cyric was standing in a wasteland as flat as a table and as featureless as the air itself. The boulders on which he had been sitting were gone, as were the mountains that had surrounded him, and even the sword that had been lying across his knees.

"Where am I?" Cyric asked.

Ignoring his question, the girl dropped to her knees. "Cyric, please help me," she pleaded. "I haven't eaten in days."

The thief didn't need to ask how she knew his name. The girl and his sword were the same. She had moved him into a sphere where she could disguise her true form and assume a more sympathetic one.

"Send me back!" Cyric demanded.

"Then feed me."

"Feed you what?" he asked.

"Feed me Fane," the girl begged.

Though the plea might have shocked Midnight or Kelemvor, Cyric did not recoil from its hideousness. Instead, he frowned, considering her request. Finally, he shook his head. "No."

"Why not?" she asked. "Fane means nothing to you. None of your men do."

"True," Cyric admitted. "But *I* decide when they die."

"I'm weak. If I don't eat, we can't return."

"Don't lie to me," Cyric warned. An idea occurred to him. Without taking his eye off the girl, he turned his attention inward. Perhaps she was manipulating his imagination and he could break free by force of will.

"I'm dying!" The girl staggered a few steps and collapsed at the thief's feet.

The girl's scream broke Cyric's concentration. They remained in the wasteland. The young girl's skin had turned gray and doughy, and it truly looked as though she would perish. "Then, good-bye," Cyric said.

The girl's eyes glazed over. "Please. Have mercy on me."

"No," the thief growled, returning her gaze with a cold stare. "Absolutely not."

Whatever the sword's true nature, there was no doubt it was evil and manipulative. Cyric knew that to give in to its plea was to become its servant.

The girl buried her head in her arms and began to sob. Cyric ignored her and looked at his feet, trying to visualize the jumbled, gray rocks upon which he had been sitting. When that didn't work, he turned his gaze to the sky, trying to see the soft, curved lines of clouds in the barren bowl above.

The sky remained a white void.

Cyric stared at the horizon, searching for the towering peaks that had encircled him just minutes ago. They were gone.

As if reading his mind, the girl said, "Disbelief won't save you." Her voice had grown deeper, more sultry and mature.

Cyric looked at her. She had become a woman, her red frock now clinging to a full, round figure. As he watched, the void upon which she lay formed itself into a white bed and lifted her off the ground.

"You're in my world now," the woman purred. "And it's as real as your own."

Cyric didn't know whether to believe her or not, but he realized that it made no difference. Whether she had truly transported him or was only playing games with his mind, he could not leave this place on his own. He had to force her to return him.

"I'm yours," the woman cooed.

Despite the dark circles beneath her eyes, she was voluptuous, and Cyric might have been tempted had he not known that she was trying to lure him into servitude.

"Every gift has a cost," the thief said. "What is the price of yours?"

The woman tried to redirect the conversation. "I'll keep you warm when others are cold. When you're wounded, I'll make you well. In battle, I'll give you the strength to prevail."

Her promises interested Cyric, for he would need magic in the days to come. Still, he resisted his desire to go to the bed. "What do you want in return?"

"No more than any woman wants from her man," she replied.

Cyric did not respond. The meaning of such a statement could easily be twisted. He was determined to master the sword, not be indentured to it through some vague covenant.

"Let's be more specific," he said coldly. "I'll feed you only when and where it pleases me. In return, you'll serve me as your master."

"What?" the woman screamed. She twisted her face into a grotesque mask of rage. "You dare to suggest that I become *your* slave?"

"That's your only choice," Cyric replied. "Serve me or

starve."

"You're the one who'll starve!" she snarled, baring two long fangs.

A crash sounded behind Cyric and he spun around. A dirty gray wall stood where moments before there had been nothing. Then another wall slammed into place on his right, and a third to his left. The thief turned around again, just as the fourth wall and a ceiling appeared. The floor turned hard and dirty, and the thief suddenly found himself standing in a prison.

Beneath her blood-colored robe, the woman's body had withered into a grotesque and frightening parody of womanhood. Her sunken eyes had grown cold with hatred and malice. A pair of silvery manacles appeared in her hand. She stepped toward Cyric. "Give me Fane."

With her sinewy muscles and clawlike fingers, the woman looked as though she could disembowel Cyric in seconds. But he didn't retreat or show fear. To back away was to surrender, to become her slave—and he was determined to rot in the foulest dungeon before serving someone besides himself.

"I want Fane!" the woman hissed, opening a shackle.

As the hag reached for his arm, Cyric punched her with all his strength. The blow connected squarely with her jaw. She staggered two steps back, her mouth agape in astonishment. He struck again. This time, the woman caught his fist in her open hand, stopping it in midair.

"Fool!" With her free hand, she closed one shackle over the thief's wrist. "You'll pay for that!"

Cyric slammed his other fist into the woman's head, surprising her once again. She released the manacles and stumbled away, puzzlement showing on her face. "I can kill you," she gasped, as if surprised that she had to mention that fact.

"If you want to starve!" Cyric replied. He began twirling the chain hanging from his wrist. With nearly two feet of steel links between shackles, the manacles made a serviceable weapon. "Return us to Faerun," he ordered.

The woman sneered at him. "Not until you feed me."

"Then we'll both die," Cyric told her flatly.

He swung the chain. The hag barely managed to duck the attack.

"Stop!" she hissed. Her expression was a mixture of disbelief and fear. It had never occurred to her that, despite being marooned, the thief would attack.

Cyric did not stop. He swung the chain again, but it suddenly disappeared from his hand. Without an instant's pause, he stepped forward and punched the woman's chin. She took the blow with a painful grunt and fell on her back.

"You're mine!" Cyric yelled. "Do as I say!"

Instead of replying, she swept her feet at his ankles, knocking his legs from beneath him. He dropped to the floor, landing on his shoulders with jarring abruptness.

The woman sprang to her feet and leaped at Cyric. He rolled to his left, and her claws raked his back. He came up on his knees, facing the gruesome woman eye-to-eye. She brought her elbow across his chin, snapping his head back.

But Cyric didn't allow himself to fall unconscious, and he did not retreat. If he wanted to be the sword's master, he could not shrink from facing the weapon's spirit in its most hideous form. He grinned and smashed his fist into her temple, then immediately stood and slipped his other arm across her neck.

The woman rammed her fist into Cyric's ribs, driving his breath away. Nevertheless, the thief slipped around behind her, locking his hands together. With all his strength, he pulled his forearm across her throat.

The hag's face turned white and she snarled, then clutched at the thief's arm with her spindly fingers. Cyric pulled harder. Her claws ripped deep grooves into his arms.

When Cyric still did not release her, the woman stopped clawing at his arms. Instead, she tried to slash at his eyes, but he pulled his head away. Then, stiffening her fingers like fork tines, she tried to reach behind her back and drive her fingers into his rib cage. By then, however, she was too weak and the attack did little damage.

"Take us back!" Cyric ordered. "Take us back or I swear I'll kill you now!"

The hag's arms fell limp, but Cyric maintained his choke-hold. After a time, the woman's body went slack and her head drooped onto her shoulder. Her eyes had rolled up into their sockets. After a few more moments, the outlines of the woman's face began to soften, and it became a white smear.

"Take us back!" Cyric said again, this time subdued. All he could see before him was a white blur.

"Sir, are you feeling well?"

Cyric looked toward the voice and saw that the speaker was Shepard, one of his Zhentilar. Behind Shepard stood another five men, their faces wrinkled in concern.

"I'm back!" Cyric gasped. It was true. He stood at the side of a boulder, holding his short sword in his hand. The blade was pale as ivory.

"Begging your pardon, sir, but did you go somewhere?" Shepard asked. For the last minute, he and the others had been watching Cyric talk to himself and wrestle with his short sword. Some of the men—Shepard included—were beginning to suspect their commander had lost his mind.

Cyric shook his head to clear it. The fight could not have been an illusion. Everything had felt so real.

When Cyric didn't reply, Shepard suggested, "Perhaps the cold—"

"I'm warm enough!" Cyric responded testily. "Do you know the penalty for approaching me without leave?" He did not know how to explain what had happened, and thought it better not to try.

"Aye, Lord," Shepard replied. "But—"

"Leave me, before I decide to enforce it!" Cyric ordered.

The men behind Shepard breathed a sigh of relief and began drifting away. Their commander's petulance had convinced them he had returned to normal.

After glaring resentfully at Cyric for a moment, Shepard bowed his head. "As you wish, sir. But I'd have Dalzhel look at those scratches if I were you." He turned and left.

Cyric looked at his forearms and saw that they were

striped with cuts. He smiled. "I won!" he whispered. "The sword is mine."

The thief sheathed his weapon, then sat down. He pressed his cloak over his wounds and passed the time by listening to Fane's screams. They no longer seemed as irritating as they once had.

An hour later, Dalzhel scrambled through the boulder field and approached. He looked alarmed. "The spies have returned from High Horn," he reported. Though he noticed the scratches on Cyric's arms, he wasted no time by asking about them.

Cyric stood. "And?"

"The woman and her companions are riding this way."

"Set up an ambush," Cyric said sharply.

Dalzhel held up his hand. "There's more. They ride with fifty Cormyrians."

Cyric cursed. His twenty men were no match for a patrol of that size. "The Cormyrians will break off eventually. We'll have to trail the patrol."

Dalzhel shook his head. "They're watching their back trail. They don't want to be followed."

"Then we'll ride ahead and use scouts to watch them from an advanced position."

Dalzhel smiled. "Aye. They won't be expecting that."

"Then prepare the men," Cyric said, pulling his blood-soaked cloak over his shoulders.

Dalzhel did not turn to obey. "One more thing."

"What?" Cyric demanded angrily, picking up his saddle-bags.

"The lookout on the road saw forty halflings ride past this morning. They missed us, but he thought they were looking for our trail."

"Halflings?" Cyric asked incredulously.

"Aye. They're about half a day ahead of us. There's no telling when they'll realize they missed us and circle back."

Cyric cursed. He did not like being trapped between the halflings and the Cormyrians. The halflings he could handle, but an engagement with them would attract too much attention.

Fane let out a bloodcurdling scream. It echoed off the mountains and caused both men to wince. Given the Cormyrians and the halflings, it was obvious they would have to do something to keep the wounded man silent.

"Tonight," Cyric said slyly, ignoring Fane for the moment, "send a few men ahead to lay a false trail. Steer the halflings toward our friends in Darkhold."

Dalzhel grinned. "That's why you're the general. But what about—"

"Fane?" Cyric interrupted. A crooked smile on his lips, the thief went over to the wounded sergeant and chased away the attendants.

Dalzhel followed, then asked, "What are you doing?"

"He can't ride," Cyric responded, drawing his sword. "Even if he could, he'd give away our position. Cover his mouth."

Dalzhel frowned. He did not like the idea of killing one of his own men.

"Do it!" Cyric ordered.

The lieutenant obeyed automatically and Cyric plunged his pale sword into the injured man's breast. Fane struggled only briefly, biting Dalzhel's hand as he tried to cry out. A moment later, when Cyric pulled the blade from the wound and cleaned it, the weapon's rosy luster had returned.

❧ 6 ❧

The Tun Plain

Sneakabout stopped his pony and scanned the plain. Nothing lay ahead but an undulating sea of pale green grass. The day was a clear one, so the halfling could see their destination, the Sunset Mountains, to the northwest. The range was so distant it looked like a reddish cloud on the horizon.

As the halfling studied the mountains, the tall prairie grass at his mount's feet began hissing and writhing like snakes. The pony whinnied and stomped its hooves, displeased with the pause. Since morning, the grass had clutched at the horses' knees whenever their legs weren't moving.

Ignoring the discomfort this latest chaos caused his mount, Sneakabout dropped his gaze and searched the nearby ground for signs of other riders. The squirming grass made it difficult to see, but the halfling didn't consider dismounting for a closer look. The grass stood three feet high, and he had no desire to test his strength against its tangles. Despite this difficulty, Sneakabout spotted a dozen clumps of earth that passing horses had kicked up.

Radnor, a Cormyrian ranger with deep blue eyes, rode up and joined Sneakabout. Though initially hesitant to accept the halfling's help in scouting ahead of the patrol, Radnor was now glad that he had. The small man was experienced in trail lore, with senses as sharp as any Radnor had ever seen. Given the task he'd been assigned, the ranger could use some help.

Radnor's job was to keep the patrol undetected as it passed through the Tun Plain, the prairie between the Sunset and Dragonjaw Mountains. Located in the gap of control between Darkhold and High Horn, the plain was a no man's land both fortresses tried to dominate. High Horn did this by regularly sending heavy patrols into the plain.

Darkhold exerted its influence through puppet lords, roving bandits, and other nefarious agents. So, whenever a Cormyrian patrol encountered someone on the plain, the captain never knew if he was meeting a Zhentarim agent or not. Normally, a patrol's mission was to search out and interrogate suspicious characters. But Captain Lunt, the leader of this company, was adopting a different strategy. Because his orders were to penetrate clear to Yellow Snake Pass, which was near Darkhold, Lunt had charged Radnor with avoiding the plain's residents altogether.

So far, Radnor had done his job admirably. The patrol had left High Horn five days ago, crossing the River Tun two days ago, and still it remained undetected.

"What signs, friend halfling?" Radnor asked. Like Sneakabout's pony, the ranger's mount snorted and stomped at the grass.

Sneakabout pointed at the overturned earth. "Another group riding toward Darkhold. I'd guess no more than twenty, mounted on chargers."

This was the tenth set of tracks they had crossed going toward Darkhold, but neither man commented on it. Instead, Radnor asked, "Why chargers?"

Sneakabout smiled. He always enjoyed showing off his scouting skills. "The gait is too long for ponies, the line is disorderly. The horses are spirited, so the riders give them plenty of head. Draft horses plod, chargers dart."

Radnor leaned forward in his saddle and studied the earthen clumps. "Yes, so I see."

The halfling's pony nickered angrily. It sidestepped away from Radnor, uprooting several tufts of grass wrapped about its legs. The two scouts took the hint and let their ponies walk while they spoke.

"Anything to the north?" Sneakabout asked.

"A caravan passed two or three days ago."

Sneakabout frowned. "Any tracks from those lame horses?"

Radnor shook his head. "Just oxen pulling wagons."

The halfling's interest in the lame horses aroused the ranger's curiosity, but he did not bother seeking an explanation. Sneakabout had already dismissed two inquiries with superficial answers.

What Sneakabout would not reveal was that the lame horses belonged to Cyric's raiders. The halfling knew this because, while scouting alone shortly after leaving High Horn, he had found their hastily abandoned camp. There were a lot of scuffed rocks where horses had banged their hooves, and lame tracks had led away from the camp. Cyric's men had left little else behind: a few crumbs of un-eaten food and the bloodless body of an injured companion. To Sneakabout, the body confirmed that someone in Cyric's company had taken his sword—he knew of no other weapon that drank blood.

The halfling had not reported his find, for the captain's order to avoid contact had angered him. Lord Deverell had suggested Sneakabout ride with the patrol in the hope of engaging the men who had raided his village. But upon leaving High Horn, the patrol captain, concerned only with reaching Yellow Snake Pass, had issued the command contradicting Deverell's promise. The halfling was determined to force Lunt to keep the lord commander's word, even if it meant leading the patrol into the middle of Cyric's camp.

Two days after leaving High Horn, the halfling had found a broken woomera cord. This he did report to Radnor. The cord meant that his fellows were also looking for Cyric. For their sake and his, Sneakabout wanted to find the Zhentish thief first. The halfling couldn't kill all of Cyric's men, but at least he could kill the one with his sword—and prevent a fellow villager from taking it. Fortunately, the halfling war party had no idea where to find the Zhentilar and was traveling straight toward Darkhold.

For two days after finding the woomera cord, Sneakabout had periodically run across a lame hoofprint or glimpsed a straggler's limping horse on the horizon—always in advance of the patrol. At first, this had puzzled him, for Kelemvor had told him that Cyric wanted Midnight and the stone tablet that Adon carried. Given that fact, he could not understand why the raiders were ahead of the patrol, as if fleeing from it.

But Sneakabout had finally realized that the stragglers were keeping tabs on the Cormyrians. From that point on, the halfling had made a point of scouting the southern flank, where the spies always lurked, and where he would be the only one who noticed them.

After Sneakabout had been brooding for a few moments, Radnor said, "I'd better return to my position. Keep a sharp eye out for trouble." He turned his pony toward the northern flank.

The halfling withdrew from his thoughts long enough to acknowledge the scout's departure. "I will," Sneakabout called. "You do the same."

Radnor, along with Kelemvor and Midnight, was one of the few humans the halfling liked. Though an accomplished ranger with an important position in the Cormyrian army, Radnor was not threatened by Sneakabout's scouting abilities. To the contrary, the ranger had often complimented the halfling on his keen observations.

In fact, the more time Sneakabout spent with humans, the more he liked them. Unlike the villagers in Black Oaks, they did not find his serious nature insulting or arrogant. In fact, they respected him for it and treated him as an equal, a rarity in relationships between halflings and humans.

But Sneakabout knew that this growing affection could be his downfall. As he became more fond of his companions, he was beginning to feel guilty about betraying them. The halfling had even considered reporting Cyric's spies to Radnor and Kelemvor, although he had resisted the urge so far.

Unfortunately, the decision might be taken out of his hands. There had been no signs of the spies for two days. Sneakabout feared Cyric's raiders had lost the patrol, or had finally been forced to stop by their lame horses.

The halfling felt helpless. He could leave the patrol and look for Cyric alone, but the Tun Plain was too large to search without help. Frustrating as it was, the only thing to do was wait for the spies to return. Cyric had not trailed Midnight and the tablet this far simply to let them go.

But, even if the Zhentish spies did not return, the halfling suspected he had a chance of survival without the sword. Sneakabout still had not slept a wink since Black Oaks, and constantly longed after his stolen weapon, but there were no other signs of insanity. It seemed vaguely possible his condition would grow no worse. Perhaps he had the will-power to endure the sword's absence. Perhaps not.

Twenty miles south of Sneakabout and the Cormyrian patrol, there was an immense bog known as the Marsh of Tun. Located in the middle of the plain, the marsh was a dismal, foul-smelling place. Most men went to great lengths to avoid it, for vicious, evil beasts lurked in the shelter of its watery confines.

Such beasts did not concern Cyric, who knew the marsh could contain nothing more sinister than his own heart. Taking advantage of its seclusion, the thief and his men had made camp on the marsh's northern edge. He and Dalzhel were discussing the failure of their spies to track the Cormyrians.

"Where are they?" Cyric roared. It had been two days since they'd lost sight of the patrol.

"If we knew that, I'd be after them!" Dalzhel snapped back.

Cyric turned and stared over the Tun River. Its slowly churning currents had turned the coppery color of boiling blood. Despite his frustration, the unusual scene calmed the thief. Without turning back to his burly lieutenant, he said, "My plan is worthless if we cannot find Midnight!"

"And perhaps if we do," Dalzhel replied.

The hawk-nosed man turned and stared at him with such cold malice that Dalzhel dropped a hand to his swordhilt.

"I know Midnight," Cyric said. "She won't betray her friends, but she won't betray me either."

"I'd never trust my life to a woman's whim," the burly lieutenant grumbled.

"I don't ask you to," Cyric replied evenly. "All I ask is that you find her. If I had not listened to you and stopped to raid that stable—"

"All our mounts would be lame and we would have lost the Cormyrians anyway." Dalzhel realized he was still holding his swordhilt and released it. "At least now we have fresh horses."

The thief sighed. His lieutenant was right. Horses were not men. One could not force them to walk upon crippled legs. "If Darkhold captures her—"

"Darkhold won't get her," Dalzhel stated calmly. "Most of their raiding parties are farther south than we are. I've positioned sentries near the three groups that might intercept the patrol."

Cyric's eyes widened in alarm. "How do you know one of your sentries won't betray us?"

Dalzhel shrugged. "We must run that risk. When Midnight and her company leave the Cormyrians and turn south, there's no other way to be sure we'll be the first to sight her."

A thought occurred to Cyric and he laid a hand on Dalzhel's shoulder. "Darkhold's gangs are working in the southern towns?" he asked.

"All ten that we know of, milord."

"We can assume Bane took most of the patrols out of Yellow Snake Pass to attack Shadowdale and Tantras, can't we?" the thief asked, staring into space.

"Aye," Dalzhel replied, frowning. He did not see the point his commander was working toward. "That would make sense."

Cyric grinned. He had originally assumed Midnight and her company would stick close to Cormyrian protection and follow Dragonjaw Road south to Proskur. It had been a reasonable assumption, for Darkhold's grip on the western Tun Plain was secure. Once in Proskur, Midnight's company could easily join a caravan traveling to Waterdeep.

But the Cormyrian patrol had ridden due west, and the thief had been forced to change his thinking. Cyric had decided the soldiers were escorting Midnight across the desolate sections of the northern Tun Plain. Once they had crossed the plain, the patrol would turn back and Midnight would drop south. The thief had assumed Midnight and her companions would cross the Far Hills south of Darkhold, trying to reach the walled town of Hluthvar.

But Cyric suspected he had been wrong. "What if Midnight isn't riding for Hluthvar?"

"Where else could she go?" Dalzhel demanded, rubbing his chin.

"Yellow Snake Pass lies due west of High Horn," Cyric said, looking northwest.

"Not a beggar passes through there without Darkhold's permission," Dalzhel objected. "Your friends would never try it!"

"They would," the thief replied. "We're not the only ones who might suspect the pass is empty."

Dalzhel's eyes widened in shock. "I'll tell the men to break camp. We can leave in an hour!"

* * * * *

Seven mornings after leaving High Horn, the Cormyrian patrol awoke at the base of Yellow Snake Pass. Named for a fearsome, yellow dragon that had inhabited it several hundred years ago, the forested pass now seemed calm and safe.

In the sharp morning light, Yellow Snake Pass looked no less impressive than it did at dusk. A wide, deep canyon snaked its way to the Tun Plain from the heart of the Sunset Mountains. Bushy conifers and white-barked poplars covered the valley floor, except where tremendous red bluffs poked smooth-edged rips through the green carpet. These cliffs rose one after the other like a titan's staircase leading toward the range's summit.

Sheer, spike-shaped peaks flanked the valley like rows of sharp teeth, forming canyon walls as steep and as slick as slate tiles. The peaks were stained deep red, giving the whole valley an eerie feeling of twilight. Every now and again, the silvery ribbon of a mountain stream rushed off a canyon wall, dissipating into a misty spray. The trail twisted its way along the valley floor, climbing slowly toward the distant summit.

Midnight studied the scene with equal parts of awe and fear. Beside the magnificence of Yellow Snake Pass, she felt at once peaceful and insignificant, as if she could lose herself in its reaches. The magic-user knew the beauty of the pass was misleading. Like any mountain trail, it was fraught with potential disasters ranging from mysterious fevers to avalanches.

Had the dangers been only of the natural variety, she would not have been frightened. But Zhentilar dominated Yellow Snake Pass, and Midnight had no doubt that they wanted her and the tablet as badly as anyone did. Fortunately, as she and her friends had hoped, it appeared the Zhentilar had abandoned the pass.

Captain Lunt and Adon approached. Lunt said, "My men and I will be taking our leave now."

Midnight turned to face the captain. He was a man of forty, his curly black hair lined with gray streaks. "Our thanks for your escort, Captain. You saved us a great deal of time."

Lunt looked up into the mountains. "Even if the Zhentilar have left, there are other hazards in the pass." He paused, then set his jaw as though he had resolved a troublesome conflict. "We'll go with you—orders be damned."

Midnight looked at Captain Lunt and smiled. "How much do you know of our journey?" she asked.

"Not much. Lord Deverell said Faerun's safety depends upon your success." The Cormyrian officer paused again, then noted, "But I mean what I say about coming along."

"We'd be glad for your company, Captain," Adon said. "But Lord Deverell wanted you to stop here for a reason. A small party will fare better in the mountains."

Lunt's face sank. "Aye, you're right." He turned toward

Midnight. "Until swords part, then."

"Until swords part," Midnight responded.

Captain Lunt returned to his men. The Cormyrians left without further ceremony, save that Sneakabout and Radnor exchanged daggers as tokens of friendship. The halfling threw his saddlebags over his pony's back, then mounted. "Shall we be on our way?" he asked. "This path looks like a long one."

"You lead, Sneakabout," Adon ordered, loading his own pony's saddle. "I'll follow, then Midnight and Kelemvor."

Kelemvor groaned. Though the others looked at him expectantly, he said nothing.

Finally, Adon asked, "What's the problem, Kel?"

The warrior looked away, picking up his saddlebags. "It's nothing. I was thinking of the trail dust, that's all."

"I'm sorry," Adon responded, puzzled. It wasn't like Kelemvor to object to a little thing like riding order. "But we need a rear—"

"Adon, why don't you and I switch places?" Midnight interrupted. "I suspect Kelemvor's groaning has less to do with trail dust than trail company."

Adon frowned. "This is ridiculous," he snapped. "You two haven't stopped fighting since Eveningstar."

Midnight ignored him and mounted her pony. "Lead the way, Sneakabout."

The halfling obligingly started up the trail, but Adon was determined to make his point. He mounted his own pony and quickly caught the magic-user. "From Kelemvor, I can understand this. But you, Midnight?"

From the rear of the line, Kelemvor called, "It's Cyric. He's got her so confused—"

Midnight twisted in her saddle. "Me! You're the one who's confused—but that's nothing new," she spat. The statement felt hollow and fiery to her, the way angry words often did.

"Midnight," Adon said, "Kel's right about Cyric. Why can't you see that?" Without waiting for an answer, he twisted around to face the warrior. "But you're just as much to blame—"

"Who asked you?" Kelemvor roared, dismissing Adon with a wave of his hand.

Sneakabout interrupted the argument to say, "I think I'll scout ahead." When nobody paid any attention to him, the halfling shrugged and urged his pony into a trot.

After a short pause, Adon added, "You're both being stubborn." He was growing more exasperated by the second. "Don't let your spat interfere with our mission."

"Adon, be quiet," Midnight snapped. She spurred her pony ahead.

The cleric ignored her order. "Like it or not, we're in this together—"

"Adon," Kelemvor interjected, "one of your sermons won't solve the problem."

The warrior's statement quieted the cleric for a little while, but the rest of the day was filled with bitter arguments and long periods of silence as sharp and as distressing as the peaks overhead. The mountain ponies Lord Deverell had given them climbed the conifer-lined trail slowly, kicking up puffs of powdery dust each time they set a hoof down. Time passed slowly. Each minute of choking on the dust seemed an hour, and each hour an endless, wearing day. Twice, Sneakabout led them into the forest to avoid approaching Zhentish caravans. Otherwise, despite their growing fatigue, the companions did not stop. So great was their animosity that they even ate the midday meal in their saddles.

In his heart, Kelemvor knew that Adon was right—as he had been so often lately. The warrior and the mage could not allow their anger to interfere with the task at hand. Too much depended on the completion of their mission.

As she rode, Midnight was having similar thoughts. However, she was determined not to apologize first. Kelemvor was the one who had deliberately prolonged the argument back at High Horn. In addition, the magic-user thought she was right about Cyric. It was true that their old friend was self-serving and mercenary, but Kelemvor had been more so, and he had found redemption. It was unfair to deny that same redemption to Cyric, and Midnight would not give up on her friend so quickly.

Finally, dusk came. Sneakabout led the group off the path, stopping in a forested area near a cliff. The cliff overlooked the portion of the valley they had already climbed, so the heroes could watch their trail until night fell completely.

When Midnight crept up to the cliff's edge, her heart sank with disappointment. The grove of trees where they had camped last night was still visible.

As soon as he had unpacked and tethered the ponies, Adon took the tablet and disappeared into the forest. The cleric was disgusted with the petty argument between Midnight and Kelemvor and just wanted to be alone tonight. Sneakabout also went into woods, but only to see if he could forage something for dinner.

Night was already falling when Midnight spread out her sleeping roll. Left alone with Kelemvor and nothing to do, she decided to make tomorrow a more pleasant day. After digging through the cloaks, spare weapons, and miscellaneous supplies Deverell's quartermaster had given them, she finally found a sack of corn tash. The magic-user removed a handful of biscuits and offered one to Kelemvor.

The warrior accepted it with a grunt.

"Adon's right," Midnight said. "We can't let our emotions interfere with our quest."

"Have no fear," Kelemvor grumbled. "I won't make that mistake again."

Midnight threw her tash to the ground. "Why are—"

"Cyric," he interrupted.

She puffed in exasperation. "Cyric won't harm us. We might even persuade him to our cause, if you wouldn't allow your mistrust to color your judgment"

"Cyric has earned my mistrust," Kelemvor said evenly. "And it's your judgment that's colored." Realizing further discussion would lead to another argument, the warrior abruptly left and went to his bedroll. Angered by the rude manner in which Kelemvor had ended the conversation, Midnight walked over to the cliff and sat down to brood.

Twenty minutes later, Sneakabout startled her when he suddenly appeared at her side. She had not heard the halfling approach.

"Everyone went to bed early tonight, I see," he said, opening a sack and offering a handful of berries to Midnight. "I guess I picked too many of these."

Deep in the forest, Sneakabout heard a faint snap. Midnight showed no sign of hearing it, so he decided to investigate later. "I'll stand watch tonight," the halfling offered. "I can't sleep anyway."

Midnight nodded, taking a handful of raspberries from the sack. She had long been aware of the halfling's insomnia. She suspected it was related to the magic sword that had been stolen from him in Black Oaks. Whenever the magic-user questioned him about the sword, however, the halfling always changed the subject, and she had given up trying to learn more about it. Instead, she asked, "Did you see Adon?"

Sneakabout nodded. "I don't understand why you and Kelemvor take orders from him."

"At the moment, he's wiser than Kelemvor or I."

"He's a fool."

Another faint snap came from the forest, and this time Midnight also heard it. "I'll go and see what that is," the halfling whispered, rising. "It's probably nothing. I'll be back in a few minutes."

As Sneakabout faded into the woods north of camp, Midnight remained seated. She continued to watch the spot where the halfling had entered the forest.

A minute later, the magic-user heard a familiar voice at her back. "Your companions are getting shorter, Midnight."

The mage spun around to face the speaker. He wore a hooded, dark cloak, but his hawkish nose was still visible.

"Cyric!" Midnight hissed.

The thief smiled. His band of Zhentilar was sneaking through the woods on foot, encircling the camp. While he waited for his lieutenant to position the men, Cyric had been watching Midnight and the halfling. Hoping to convince the magic-user to come with him willingly, the thief wanted one last chance to speak with Midnight alone.

"Aye," Cyric replied. "You didn't think I'd be easy to lose, did you?"

"What are you doing here?" Midnight demanded, standing.

The smile dropped from the thief's face and he crossed his arms. "I've come to talk some sense into you."

Several sticks snapped in the trees north of camp. Midnight frowned, glancing toward the forest. "If Kelemvor sees you, he'll cut—"

"Let him. It's time we had this out."

As if on cue, Kelemvor roared, "Cyric! You won't escape this time." The fighter rushed out of the night, sword firmly in hand.

Midnight stepped in front of Cyric. "Hold your sword, Kel! He came to talk."

Kelemvor slowed his charge and tried to circle around the raven-haired mage. The thief stood perfectly still, a hand on the hilt of his sword.

Outside camp, a surprised yell arose. A moment later, Adon screamed, "Wake up! We're surrounded!" He ran out of the forest, waving his mace. The saddlebags with the tablet were slung over his shoulder.

Cyric drew his sword.

Ignoring Adon's tardy warning, Midnight said, "Kelemvor, Cyric, lay down your weapons!" She looked from one to the other.

Both men scorned her plea. Hefting his mace, Adon came to Kelemvor's side.

"You were foolish to come here," the cleric said, glaring at Cyric. "But you won't live long enough to make the same mistake again."

"No!" Midnight objected. "He came to talk!"

"If that's what he said, he's lying," Adon snarled. "His men are sneaking toward us right now."

Cyric waved his rose-colored short sword. "If that's how you want it, old friends," he hissed, "that's how it will be." His voice cracked with a sharp command: "Dalzhel!"

The sound of snapping sticks echoed from the edge of the forest. Kelemvor and Adon looked over their shoulders. A hundred yards away, a dozen shadows were emerging from the woods.

Kelemvor looked from the shadows to Cyric. "You'll die with us, you know."

"No one's going to die tonight," Midnight said, stepping toward the fighter.

The warrior snorted and roughly pushed her out of his way. "Somebody will."

"Stop!" Midnight ordered sharply, but her command went unheeded.

Kelemvor lifted his sword and charged. Hefting his mace, Adon followed.

Cyric met Kelemvor's charge first, ducking under the swing. He came up standing behind the warrior, but Adon arrived in the same moment. The cleric leveled his mace in a blow vicious enough to smash a giant's skull.

Cyric's short sword flashed and blocked Adon's stroke, stopping the mace in midair. The cleric's whole body trembled, then he stumbled back a step, shaking his head in disbelief. The thief swept his feet at Adon's ankles, taking him by surprise and dropping him to the ground.

Cyric swung at Adon. Kelemvor deflected the red blade, though, then slashed at the thief's head. Cyric ducked, and the warrior stepped forward again, slicing down toward his opponent's throat.

Midnight cried out. The fight had broken out so quickly that she'd been unable to prevent it. Now she felt helpless to stop it. To the north, the mage saw one of the shadows point his sword at the fight. His followers began to run toward camp. Sneakabout still had not returned, and the magic-user hoped he had not perished at the hands of the men coming from the forest.

Midnight knew those men had to be stopped. She decided to risk creating a magical wall of fire ahead of them. Given the current instability of magic and the recent changes in her relationship to the weave, she didn't know if the spell would work properly. Still, if Cyric's men reached the fight, all was lost. The magic-user reached into her robe and withdrew a few pinches of phosphorus to serve as a material component.

The proper gestures and words for creating a wall of fire came to Midnight's mind. To her surprise, there was no indication as to what she should do with the phosphorus.

While Midnight prepared to cast her spell, Cyric blocked Kelemvor's slash. Their blades clanged loudly, but the block held. As Kelemvor's eyes widened in surprise, Cyric brought his sword down and lunged for the warrior's unprotected chest.

Kelemvor barely managed to save himself by kicking the thief squarely in the stomach and knocking him toward the cliff. Cyric landed flat on his back six feet away.

Meanwhile, Cyric's men had closed to seventy yards. Midnight sprinkled the phosphorous in a semicircle around her body, then called upon her magic to create a wall of fire.

The white granules simply fell to the ground.

An instant later, a loud pop sounded in front of the charging Zhentilar. Tendrils of glowing yellow smoke sprang out of the ground between them and Midnight. The tendrils began to wave in the breeze, as if they were corn stalks. Dalzhel and the others slowed their advance, uncertain of what to make of Midnight's strange magic.

Oblivious to the misfired spell, Kelemvor, Adon, and Cyric continued to fight. The thief scrambled to his feet. Adon did likewise.

The cleric and Kelemvor advanced cautiously. Cyric backed away, buying time to plot a strategy. The cliff dropped away a mere ten feet beyond his back.

Then Kelemvor noticed a shadow creeping up behind the hawk-nosed thief. It stood about as high as a man's waist, and could only belong to a halfling.

"Your swordsmanship has improved," Kelemvor observed, trying to keep Cyric's attention focused on him. "Or is it that blade you now carry?"

"You'll know soon enough," Cyric responded.

Kelemvor nodded to Adon. They charged from opposite directions. Cyric stepped away, then heard a soft patter at his back.

Sneakabout sprang just as the thief turned. Back on the Tun Plain, the halfling had dared to hope he could forget the sword. But one sight of the weapon had rekindled his desire to recover it.

Cyric stepped aside, catching Sneakabout's arm in his free hand and hurling the halfling at Adon. An instant later, the thief had to defend himself against Kelemvor, and barely managed to stop a powerful slash.

But Kelemvor was not finished. He kicked Cyric in the ribs, knocking him three steps backward. The thief now stood at the edge of the cliff, bent over and gasping.

Kelemvor kicked again, this time knocking Cyric off his feet. The thief landed with his sword arm twisted awkwardly beneath his body, balanced precariously on the cliff. A scream of pain and rage escaped his lips.

Upon hearing his commander's scream, Dalzhel swore he would allow the smoke to delay him no longer. He ran into the writhing mass of yellow tendrils. When the wisps did not hurt him, the burly lieutenant waved his men forward.

As the Zhentilar approached, Kelemvor stepped forward to finish Cyric.

In a forceful voice, Midnight yelled, "Stop, Kelemvor!"

Kelemvor responded without looking away from Cyric. "No." He pointed the tip of his sword at the thief's throat.

Adon and Sneakabout picked themselves up, then noticed the approaching Zhentilar. The cleric quickly retrieved the saddlebags with the tablet, while Sneakabout disappeared into the shadows.

"If you kill him," Midnight cried, "we die too."

Without looking away from Cyric, Kelemvor said, "We're not going to die alone."

"We don't have to die at all," Adon yelled, turning to face the approaching company, who were now only thirty yards away. To them, he yelled, "Stop, or Cyric's dead!" The cleric pointed at Cyric, who still lay beneath Kelemvor's blade.

Dalzhel's first instinct was to charge the scarred man. But upon seeing his commander's predicament, he halted and motioned for his subordinates to do likewise. "Milord?" asked the burly lieutenant.

For the first time, Cyric dared to move. He slowly pulled his sword arm from beneath his body. "Wait there."

Kelemvor frowned. "Now what are we going to do?" the warrior asked Adon. "Zhentil Keep sent Cyric for the tablet. He's not going to give up."

Cyric laughed bitterly. "You're mistaken. They're no longer my masters. I want the tablet for my own reasons."

"To satisfy your lust for power," Kelemvor snapped.

Cyric ignored him. "I have twenty men. Let us join forces. We all want to return the tablets to the Planes."

Adon snorted. "You'd slit our throats while we slept."

"Can you look into men's hearts, Adon?" Midnight demanded. "Are you a paladin that you can tell when a man is being untrue?"

The cleric didn't reply.

"Then how do you know what he intends?" Midnight was relieved that her friends had to hear Cyric out.

After a long pause, Kelemvor answered Midnight's question with his own. "How do *you* know what he intends?"

"I don't," Midnight admitted. "But he was our friend. He deserves our trust until he abuses it."

Kelemvor snorted. "He's done that already."

A maniacal gleam sparkling in his eye, Sneakabout returned to the group with a long rope. He began anchoring one end to a boulder at the cliff's edge.

Dalzhel watched the halfling carefully, ready to charge.

"What are you doing?" Midnight asked.

"I'll hold him hostage while you three climb down the rope," Sneakabout replied. "You'll be long gone before his men ride back around the cliff."

"What about you?" Adon asked.

The halfling shrugged. "I'll think of something."

In reality, Sneakabout already had a plan in mind. He intended to kill Cyric, then recover his stolen property. With luck, he could slide down the rope a short distance, then climb onto the cliff before the rope was cut. The plan was risky, but it was the only way to both save his friends and get the sword back.

Cyric frowned at the halfling's resourcefulness. "I know when I'm defeated," the thief lied, hoping to stall and looking at Midnight. "If you let me go, I'll take my men and never bother you again."

"He's lying!" Sneakabout yelped, finishing his knot.

"No doubt," Adon said, "but at least we'll live through the night."

"I still want to kill him," Kelemvor said, pressing the tip of his sword against Cyric's throat. "Can't you stop his men with a spell, Midnight?"

"No!" the raven-haired mage exclaimed. "I won't even try."

Kelemvor sighed in frustration. Still holding his sword to the thief's throat, he said, "Then you live, Cyric . . . for now. Stand up."

Cyric carefully stood, acutely aware that Kelemvor could kill him with a mere twitch.

"Your command, milord?" Dalzhel asked.

"Tell him to go down the trail to the bottom of the cliff," Kelemvor ordered, never taking his eyes off the thief.

Cyric hesitated before obeying. "How do I know you'll release me?"

"My promise is better than yours," Kelemvor spat. "You know that. After they're gone, you can climb down the rope. Now tell them."

Cyric hesitated for a long moment. He had no doubt the warrior would do as promised. But, after coming so close to capturing Midnight and the tablet, the thief could not bear to let them escape.

Kelemvor pushed gently against his sword and the tip drew blood. "I don't know how much longer I can resist the temptation," the fighter warned. "Send them away!"

Cyric had no choice and he knew it. Kelemvor could kill him in an instant. "Do as he says, Dalzhel," the thief ordered.

Dalzhel nodded and sheathed his sword. But before leaving, he addressed Kelemvor. "If you do not release him unharmed, we will be back."

The burly lieutenant turned and led the others away.

A few minutes later, Adon walked to the edge of the forest and peered into the darkness. "I think they're gone."

"Good," Sneakabout said. "Kill him now."

Kelemvor shook his head. "I won't betray my word," he rumbled. Then, never taking his sword from Cyric's throat, the warrior steered his prisoner to the rope. "If I ever see—"

"You won't have the chance," Cyric yelled.

Without sheathing his short sword, the thief ran the rope around his thigh and over his shoulder. Then he began picking his way down the face of the cliff, using his free hand to feed the rope through the makeshift rappelling harness. Cyric's sword arm remained free to hold his weapon.

"Don't make me regret saving you," Midnight called.

The thief simply grunted and continued down the cliff.

As he watched Cyric go, a groan of disappointment escaped Sneakabout's lips. Overwhelming despair overcame him, and the halfling knew that he could not let his sword go. Drawing his dagger, Sneakabout grabbed the rope and wrapped his legs around it, then disappeared down the cliff after Cyric.

The halfling's action surprised everyone and it was a moment before they reacted. By the time they peered over the cliff's edge, Sneakabout was no more than a dark form moving down the rope.

When Cyric felt the rope jerk, his first thought was that Kelemvor had cut it. But when the thief didn't fall, he knew that something else was happening. Cyric looked up and saw the halfling sliding down the rope.

"I want my sword!" Sneakabout screamed.

"Come and get it," Cyric called. He stopped descending and braced himself.

A moment later, the halfling reached him and lunged. Cyric easily blocked the attack and sent the halfling's dagger flying into the night.

The lack of a weapon did not deter Sneakabout. He slid farther down, landing atop Cyric's shoulders. Holding the rope with one hand, the halfling clawed at Cyric's sword arm with the other.

Cyric wrenched his arm free, then laid the edge of his blade against the halfling's neck. "You're mad!" he hissed.

Sneakabout resisted a powerful urge to grab the weapon. At the moment, the halfling was completely at Cyric's mercy and knew it. "Give me my sword," he begged.

As the thief began to comprehend the reason for Sneakabout's mad attack, a cruel smile creased his lips. "As long as I have this, you'll never stop hounding me, will you?"

The halfling started to lie, but realized there was no point in it. Even if Cyric was foolish enough to believe him, Sneakabout would only have to hunt the thief down again. "You shouldn't have taken it," the halfling said, making a feeble grab for his sword.

"Oh, yes, I should have," Cyric answered. He pulled the blade across Sneakabout's throat.

On top of the cliff, the three companions did not hear Sneakabout's gurgle. They simply saw a small form plummet soundlessly into the darkness at the bottom of the cliff.

For several moments, Midnight, Adon, and Kelemvor remained in motionless shock, unable to believe the halfling was gone. Then, as Cyric resumed his descent, Midnight tried to call Sneakabout's name. A strangled gasp was all that escaped her lips.

Not so for Kelemvor. "Cyric!" he roared.

The thief looked up and saw the fighter raising his sword to cut the rope. Fortunately, he had been prepared for something like this. As Kelemvor brought his blade down, Cyric grabbed hold of the cliff's face.

Adon saw the rope fall, but Cyric's silhouette simply disappeared against the cliff's face. "We'd better leave immediately," the scarred cleric murmured. "Cyric's still alive . . . and I don't think he intends to keep his word."

❧ 7 ❧

Over the Summit

The afternoon had come and gone and still the task remained uncompleted. Outside High Horn's inner gatehouse, a dozen Cormyrian soldiers were struggling with pulleys and ropes to raise Bhaal and his amber prison off the ground. Earlier that day, the masons had mortared support posts into the wall, high over the gate. The soldiers were attempting to hoist Bhaal onto those support posts and fasten him there as a trophy.

In the fading light of dusk, Lord Commander Kae Deverell paced back and forth outside the gatehouse, a parchment scroll crushed in his fist. The crest of the Purple Dragon, King Azoun's royal seal, still clung to the scroll's edge where the lord commander had broken the wax. Deverell slapped the parchment against his leg, as if venting his frustration would speed the work.

The message from Suzail had come at noon: *Lord High Marshal Duke Bhereu riding to High Horn to investigate drunkenness and sagging morale. Especially in this time of crisis, such behavior must be avoided. Take his recommendations as my wishes. Hope this message finds the weather fair. His Majesty, King Azoun IV.*

"Drunkenness and sagging morale!" Deverell hissed to himself. "We'll see about that."

The lord commander had a plan to convince Duke Bhereu the king was misinformed. That was why his soldiers were hanging the Lord of Murder over the gatehouse. When Bhereu entered High Horn, the high marshal would have to look Bhaal right in the eye. The duke would have no choice except to inquire about the trophy. When Deverell explained what it was, Bhereu would be forced to report that matters were well in hand at High Horn. After all, drunks and cowards did not capture gods.

The breeze came up, bringing with it a chill rain. Deverell looked into the wind and saw a bank of swarthy clouds coming toward the fortress. The watch would have a cold night.

The lord commander turned to Pell Beresford, captain of the night watch. "I'm expected at dinner. See that the amber is raised and secured."

Pulling his hood over his head, Pell looked toward the storm. "If I may, sir, it might be wiser to leave the thing down until morning. The wind could give it a battering."

Deverell also looked toward the storm, but he shook his head. "I want it in place when the sun rises. You'll just have to be sure it's well secured."

The lord commander left without further comment. He did not notice his subordinate's eyes burning with resentment, nor Bhaal's hand, the only part of the avatar that protruded from the amber, closing into a fist.

"As you wish, sir," the watch captain hissed.

Pell had to admit his anxiety was not for the amber alone. As far as he was concerned, the blob was no prize to be displayed. The creature inside, along with Deverell's drunkenness, had cost the lives of many good men.

If the incident had been isolated, Beresford would not have found it so disturbing. But, often as not, the captain stayed on duty long past dawn because the lord commander had kept the day officers carousing into the morning hours. Pell had yet to see Deverell lucid, or even sober, at morning repast. Having his post offered to a halfling—of all things—had been the last straw.

So the captain had dispatched a rider to Suzail and lodged a formal complaint. He had not expected the king to send the lord high marshal to investigate, but Pell knew his grievance had not been the first against Deverell. Whatever the reason, though, Duke Bhereu was due tomorrow—and if that grotesque amber was not hanging above the inner gate as "proof" of Kae Deverell's competence, Pell would be just as happy.

Nevertheless, Deverell had issued a direct order, and Beresford was too good an officer to disobey. As though it had been his own idea, Pell set about hanging the amber. Without Deverell's presence to make the men nervous, the captain completed the task within the hour.

Beresford spent the rest of the night huddled deep within his cloak, methodically making the rounds, keeping the men alert and at their posts. The captain passed beneath Bhaal a dozen times, pausing each time to inspect the trophy's moorings and make sure it remained secure in the heavy wind. Pell even posted two men beneath the amber blob, just in case the wind tore it loose.

In the dark, however, Beresford and his guards failed to notice that the Lord of Murder was using his free hand to fray the rope that held him in place. By the time the night wind blew itself out and false dawn's gray light appeared behind the eastern peaks, only a strand held Bhaal's prison in place.

Pell stood along the western wall, enjoying his favorite hour of the watch. The night air would grow no more biting, and the castle was as still and as quiet as a snow bank, only the crisp coughs and whispers of the men echoing from the cold stones. It was a peaceful time, a time when a man could turn his thoughts to breakfast and a warm bed.

But a loud crash told the watch captain that he would not enjoy that luxury this morning. Beresford turned to his page and said, "Rouse Lord Deverell and tell him his trophy has fallen." Pell started toward Bhaal's prison immediately. He needed no report to know what had happened.

What the captain found at the gate was far worse than he had expected. In the middle of the entrance, the amber lay broken and empty. The two sentries posted beneath it were dead, the cobblestones red and slick. Two more men kneeled in the blood, picking up pieces of the amber like children who had overturned their mother's favorite vase.

"Where's Bhaal?" Pell demanded, kicking at the amber fragments.

The sentries stood. "Not here, sir," said one.

"I see that," the captain answered, waving his hand at Bhaal's shattered prison.

"He was gone when we arrived," explained the second sentry, still holding a handful of fragments.

Pell's heart sank. He could not understand how the avatar had survived his imprisonment, but now was not the time to ponder the question. "Sound the alarm. Wake and arm every man—"

Beresford's page came running out of the gate. "Bhaal, sir! He's in Lord Deverell's chamber!"

Without another word, Pell and the sentries ran for the keep, charging up the central staircase in less than a minute. When they reached the top floor, the captain shoved open the lord commander's door and rushed into the apartment, his sword drawn.

A dozen guards stood in a circle, their halberds lowered and pointed at a motionless form. Beresford pushed into the circle. A gaunt, lifeless body lay on the floor. The tattoos on the corpse's head left no doubt that this had been the man trapped in the amber. But the fire had left his eyes, and he no longer looked even remotely menacing. Pell had no doubt his soul had long since departed.

"Who killed him?" the captain demanded.

"Nobody," answered the page. "That's how I found him."

Pell looked up. "Where's Lord Deverell?"

The page's eyes roamed the chamber as if searching it. Finally, he answered. "Gone, milord."

* * * * *

Kelemvor took another step, stumbled, and sent a rock bounding down the mountainside. The warrior took a deep breath, jerked his pony along by its reins, then stepped forward again. His skull throbbed with a terrible headache.

Hoping to keep his thoughts focused on something besides the pain in his head, Kelemvor thought back over the last few days. After Sneakabout's death, he, Midnight, and Adon had continued up Yellow Snake Pass. Two days later, the companions had encountered a huge curtain of black nothingness. The curtain was not physical. Rather, it was simply a boundary beyond which they could not see.

Unfortunately, the barrier had stretched clear across the canyon, precluding any hope of slipping around it. The trio had debated the curtain's nature for several minutes, finally concluding it was either the residue of a misfired spell or one of the chaotic phenomena plaguing the Realms. Whatever the curtain's origin, no one had been anxious to step inside it. Adon had picked up a stick and pushed it into the blackness. When he withdrew it, the part that had been inside the curtain had vanished.

The company had decided not to risk entering. Instead, Kelemvor had pointed out a small, recently blazed trail leading up the south wall of the canyon. The companions had followed the trail, hoping that whoever had laid it knew his way through the Sunset Mountains. That had been one and half days ago, three and half days since Sneakabout's death.

The trail had quickly started up a steep scarp of jumbled stones and rosy dirt, becoming the chain of zigzags upon which Kelemvor now struggled. Every step ended with his foot sinking into sand or shifting unsteadily on a loose stone. A dozen yards above, the slope ended in a saddle slung between two jagged peaks. Only blue sky showed beyond, but Kelemvor took no comfort from that fact. Too many times, he had crested a similar saddle only to find another looming in the distance.

An icy wind gusted over the ridge and stung his face. The warrior paused for a rest. Just breathing took effort, and the effort made his head hurt even more. Two hundred steps behind Kelemvor, Adon was slowly working his way up the trail. A thousand steps beyond him, Midnight rested where the trail switched back on itself. To avoid kicking rocks down on one another, Kelemvor had recommended the climbers keep some distance between them. Midnight was taking the suggestion to an extreme.

Below Midnight and to the left, Kelemvor could still see the black curtain that had forced them off the pass. To the right, the main canyon snaked its way back to the Tun Plain. The distance was less than thirty miles in a straight line, but more than twice that far following the trails that wormed along the valley floor. A carpet of pine trees stretched from the plain to the base of the slope, but ended there and came no higher.

Kelemvor had no doubt that Cyric and his Zhentilar were somewhere down there, following at their best pace. What would have surprised the warrior, had he been able to see them, were the forty halflings near the entrance of the canyon. Sixty miles outside of Darkhold, one of their scouts had stumbled across Cyric's trail, and the men from Black Oaks had turned north in pursuit. They had just found Sneakabout's body, and, puzzled as they were by what had befallen him, were now certain they were on the right trail.

Oblivious to the halflings, Kelemvor turned his gaze to the terrain upon which he stood. Nearby, tiny white flowers grew out of lumps of fine grass resembling bread mold. Here and there, pale green lichens clung to the largest of the rust-red rocks. No other plants could endure the rigorous climate, and the barren environment made the fighter feel disheartened and isolated.

"Come on, Adon," Kelemvor called, hoping that offering encouragement would make him feel better, too. "We're bound to reach the top sooner or later."

"Later," came Adon's strained reply.

Kelemvor shivered and resumed climbing. He had broken into a sweat during the hard climb, and the wind chilled him. The warrior thought of putting on the winter clothes Deverell's quartermaster had provided, but decided against it. More clothes would only make him sweat more.

The mountainside was a cold and solitary place, and the warrior could not help but regret that he was risking his life there. When the trio had begun their journey to Waterdeep, the mission had seemed compelling enough. Now, with Sneakabout gone and the trouble between him and Midnight, Kelemvor felt like a mercenary again.

His anger with Midnight colored his mood, and he knew

it. Twice, Cyric had been in his grasp, and twice the mage had freed the thief. The fighter couldn't understand why she was so blind to Cyric's treachery.

Kelemvor's love for Midnight only made matters worse. When she had saved the thief, the warrior had felt she was betraying him. He knew that there was nothing between Cyric and Midnight to cause his jealousy, but that knowledge provided little comfort.

The fighter had tried to explain away his fury a hundred times. Midnight had not seen Cyric slipping from one camp to another as a spy during Arabel's Knightsbridge Affair, and did not know how treacherous he could be. The naive magic-user truly believed the thief was possessed of a noble character and would help them.

"This had better be the top," Adon called. "I've lost my stomach for climbing."

"Perhaps you'd rather try the curtain," Kelemvor returned, waving his hand at the black screen that still blocked the valley.

Adon paused and looked down, as if contemplating the warrior's suggestion. Finally, he said, "Don't tempt me."

Kelemvor chuckled, then took one more step. His foot found solid purchase. A steady, stiff wind pushed at his chest with force enough to make standing difficult. The warrior looked up and found himself on top of the little ridge. Ahead, the mountain range dropped steadily away. He had reached the top.

The trail followed the other side of the saddle down to a sharp ridge. This ridge ran straight ahead for about fifteen miles, like the spine of some huge book, until it joined a small chain of needle-tipped peaks. At the top of the ridge, the trail split. The best-used trail ran to the left, leading down into a basin of lush green grass. It eventually disappeared into a heavily forested canyon that twisted in a westerly direction into a distant grassland.

The other trail descended the right wall of the spiny ridge, eventually touching the shore of a small mountain lake. From there, the path ran along the edge of the violet-blue water to an outlet, then followed a river into a steep-walled gorge to the northwest.

After taking in the view, Kelemvor turned and waved to Adon. The warrior's load no longer seemed heavy, and his dreary mood faded as though he were drinking Lord Deverell's fine ale again.

"This is the top!" he yelled.

Adon looked up and shrugged, then held his hand to his ear. Kelemvor couldn't raise his voice above the wind, so he made an arcing motion, pointed down the other side of the pass, then raised his arms in a sign of triumph.

Adon immediately perked up, then began tugging his pony's reins in an effort to speed up his ascent. Kelemvor would have signaled to Midnight too, but she had fallen so far behind he feared he would discourage her.

A few minutes later, Adon reached the summit, scrambling on his hands and knees.

"Are we finally at the top?" the cleric gasped. He was so winded he could not lift his head to look.

"See for yourself," Kelemvor replied.

After catching his breath, Adon stood and peered down on the lake. The view lifted his spirits, as it had Kelemvor's. "We're there! The journey's downhill from here!"

Looking back to Midnight, Kelemvor asked, "How's she doing?"

Adon turned, suddenly feeling morose. "Sneakabout's death still grieves her."

Kelemvor gave his pony's reins to Adon, then started back down the trail. The cleric quickly placed a restraining hand on his shoulder. "No."

"But she's tired!" Kelemvor objected, turning to face the cleric. "And I'm strong enough to carry her."

"She doesn't want help," Adon replied. Two hours ago, he had offered to take her pony's reins. The magic-user had threatened to change him into a crow.

Kelemvor glanced back at Midnight's slow-moving form. "It's time we spoke."

"I agree!" Adon exclaimed, relieved that the warrior had

finally overcome his stubbornness. "But let her finish the climb alone. Now isn't the time to imply she can't carry her weight."

Kelemvor was not inclined to agree. "Five minutes ago, I'd have given my sword to somebody who'd carry me up the pass. I don't think she'd take it wrong."

The cleric shook his head. "Trust me. Climbing gives you time to think. Despite the cramps in your legs, the pounding in your ears, and the fog in your head, climbing promotes thought."

The fighter frowned. In him, it promoted nothing but a pounding headache. "It does?"

"Yes," Adon insisted. He released the warrior's shoulder. "While I was struggling up the trail, a few things occurred to me. Midnight saved Cyric, then Cyric killed Sneakabout. If you were her, wouldn't you feel responsible?"

"Of course I would," Kelemvor responded quickly. "And I told her—" He stopped in midsentence, recalling the bitter argument that had followed Sneakabout's death.

"Exactly!" Adon said, nodding. "What did she say?"

"It didn't make any sense," Kelemvor replied defensively. "She said it was our fault that Sneakabout had died. She said Cyric came to talk and we attacked him." The warrior frowned. "You're not saying she was right?"

Adon grew serious. "We did strike first."

"No," Kelemvor objected, holding up a hand as if to ward off an attack. "I don't kill lightly, not even before . . ." He let the sentence trail off.

"Before Bane lifted your curse?" Adon finished for him. "You're worried that being free of the curse might not mean you're less of an animal."

Kelemvor looked away.

"We all have self-doubts," Adon replied, sensing that now was a good time to open up to the fighter. "With me, it's wondering if I was right to turn away from Sune."

"A man has to follow his heart," the warrior said, grasping the cleric's shoulder warmly. "You could have done nothing else." Kelemvor's mind returned to what Midnight had said about attacking their former ally. "Could we be wrong about Cyric?"

Adon shrugged. "Midnight certainly thought so."

Kelemvor groaned.

The cleric quickly added, "But I'm convinced we're right. Cyric's men were surrounding our camp, so I doubt he came to talk. It isn't wrong to strike first if your target means you harm."

Adon paused, letting his reassurances take their effect. Finally, he proceeded to the main point. "But that doesn't matter. What matters is how you and I reacted to Midnight."

"What do you mean?" Kelemvor asked, glancing at the mage again. She was still plodding up the trail, making slow but steady progress.

"When I suggested we were wrong to attack, you felt defensive, didn't you?"

Kelemvor nodded.

"How do you think Midnight feels? Since Sneakabout died, you've hardly spoken to her. I've done nothing but lecture her about Cyric. Don't you think she feels worse than we do?"

"Probably," Kelemvor muttered, looking at the ground. Midnight always seemed so composed that it had never occurred to him she might be suffering the same sort of inner turmoil he was.

Studying the warrior's bowed head, Adon continued. "With us blaming Sneakabout's death on her, it seems likely that—no matter how she protests otherwise—Midnight blames herself, too."

"All right," Kelemvor said, turning toward the west side of the ridge, away from both Adon and Midnight. "I see your point. She feels bad enough without us rubbing it in."

Kelemvor was ashamed of his behavior since Eveningstar. Without facing Adon, he said, "Life was much simpler when the curse prevented me from thinking about anybody else. At least I had an excuse for being selfish." The warrior shook his head angrily. "I haven't changed at all! I'm still cursed."

"Sure," Adon replied. "But no more or less than any other man."

Kelemvor turned back toward Midnight. "All the more reason to carry her. I can apologize for my harsh words."

Adon shook his head, wondering if the fighter had understood anything that had been said. "Not yet. Midnight already feels like a burden, and offering to carry her will only convince her she is. Sit down and wait until she gets here herself."

Though clouds were gathering in all directions, Kelemvor did as the cleric asked. The saddle was no place to be during a storm, but Adon's words seemed wise. Besides, even if a storm broke, descending the west side of the ridge would take only a fraction of the time it had taken the heroes to ascend the east side.

Adon went to his pony and rummaged through the supplies from High Horn. A minute later, the cleric pulled out a parchment map and, retaining a secure grip on it because of the wind, carefully studied it.

Kelemvor, on the other hand, contemplated the changes in Adon. The cleric's self-confidence had returned, but was tempered with a compassion that had been lacking before Tantras. Where the transformation had come from, the fighter could not imagine. But he was glad for the newfound wisdom—even if Adon still required a thousand words to convey what could be said in ten.

"You surprise me, Adon," Kelemvor said at last, watching his friend study the map with diligence. "I didn't think you so cunning in the ways of the heart."

Adon looked up. "I'm as surprised as you."

"Perhaps Sune is closer than you think," the green-eyed fighter suggested, remembering what the cleric had said regarding misgivings about turning away from her.

Adon smiled sadly, thinking of how distant he felt from his old deity. "I doubt it." He grew reflective for a moment, then pulled himself out of his reverie. "But thanks anyway."

Embarrassed by the unaccustomed sentimentality of the moment, Kelemvor looked away and watched Midnight struggling up the trail. She moved slowly, resting with each step, keeping her eyes focused on the ground ahead of her. The warrior found himself admiring her grace and how it mirrored her inner strength.

A wave of concern for her washed over him. "Will Midnight survive all this?" Kelemvor asked.

"She will," Adon replied. He didn't even look away from the map. "She's as fit as you or I."

Kelemvor continued studying the magic-user. "That's not what I mean. We're just two soldiers who happened to be in the wrong place at the wrong time. But there's more to it for her." The warrior was remembering the amulet she had carried for Mystra. "This involves her. Could her magic—I don't know how to put it—but could it remake her somehow?"

Adon grew reflective and lowered the map. "I don't know magic," he said at last. "And it wouldn't help if I did. There isn't any question that Midnight's power is increasing. What that means is anybody's guess, but I suspect it will change her."

As if sensing she was the subject of conversation, Midnight looked up. Her eyes met Kelemvor's and the warrior felt a jolt of euphoria. "I couldn't bear to lose her. I've just found her again," he said.

"Be careful, my friend," Adon replied. "Midnight alone will determine whether she is found."

Abruptly, the wind died. Gray clouds hung over the mountains in all directions. Midnight was only five hundred steps from the top now, and still Kelemvor resisted the temptation to go to her. If it rained, it rained. He was determined not to make her unhappy by helping her.

Adon passed the map to Kelemvor, oblivious to the change in weather. "Look at this," he said. "The shortest way to Hill's Edge is through the western canyon." The cleric pointed at the canyon on the map. "But if we build a small boat, it might be faster to float down the River Reaching." He indicated the river leaving the small lake. "What do you think?"

Kelemvor didn't bother with the map. Looking at the river, he said, "After the Ashaba, I thought you'd have had your fill of boats."

Adon grimaced at the memory of the difficult journey from Shadowdale to Blackfeather Bridge, but he continued undaunted. "This might save us a week."

Kelemvor simply shook his head. Adon might have learned something about people, but when it came to route-finding, the cleric still lacked the sense of a mule. "No raft we can build will stand up to the rough water in that canyon," the warrior said, pointing at the rugged valley below the lake. "Even if it didn't fall apart and drown us, we'd be killed going over some waterfall."

Adon studied the canyon. "Of course. I see what you mean."

Five minutes later, the sky had grown ominously dark. Midnight was only a dozen steps from the summit, and Kelemvor could barely wait until she reached it. Remembering how his own spirits had lifted when he stepped onto the saddle, the warrior was determined to take the opportunity to apologize. After that, the rest of the trip would go smoothly.

Midnight slowly plodded up those last feet and stepped onto the ridge. She breathed a sigh of relief when she saw that they had, at last, reached the top.

Kelemvor could not contain himself. "You're here," he said enthusiastically.

Midnight looked around. "I see that." Though she could not miss Kelemvor's cheery tone, she didn't share his delight.

The magic-user was still too angry, though she could no longer say why. Initially, Midnight had blamed Sneakabout's death on Kelemvor and Adon. After all, they had attacked Cyric without provocation, and everything else had followed. But she was beginning to fear their old friend might be playing her for a fool. She wished she had seen what had passed on the rope between Cyric and the halfling, whether Cyric had acted in self-defense or had killed Sneakabout in cold blood.

A driving rain of black drops began to fall. The water was so cold it should have been ice, and where it touched the companion's skin, it left itching red circles.

From the surrounding peaks echoed a quiet wail that would not have been out of place had there been a breeze. But the wind was calm and the air still. In another time or place, they would have puzzled over the black rain and the unnatural howl, but at the moment it merely seemed another irritation.

Shrugging off the rain, Kelemvor exclaimed, "From here, it's all downhill!"

"Then I suggest we continue downhill before this rain burns us to death." Midnight yanked her pony's reins and started down the trail.

The magic-user's curtness deflated the spirits of both Kelemvor and Adon. As they scrambled to follow, Kelemvor whispered, "How much longer must we wait before she'll let us forgive her?"

"I wouldn't hold my breath," Adon responded.

It had taken them nearly two days to climb the east side of the saddle, but it took only a quarter that long to descend the west side. Cold and itching from the black rain, the three companions reached the ridge separating the lake and the forested canyon just before dusk. Kelemvor noticed a small cliff in the western basin. In a niche at its bottom, they found beds of mossy grass and a shelter from the unnatural weather. After assigning watches and gulping down a drab meal, the company settled in for a dreary night of sleep.

The first two watches passed without incident, save that it stopped raining during the second. Still, Midnight, who had the third watch, slept little and knew it was useless to try. She attempted to occupy her mind by puzzling out the reason her magic had failed against Cyric's men. The magic-user could not understand why smoke tendrils instead of a wall of fire had appeared. She had executed the gestures and words exactly as they had come to her.

Any number of things could account for the unexpected results. Perhaps the wrong words and gestures had appeared in her mind. Or dropping the phosphorous beforehand could have altered the magic's form. But it was just as likely the magic had simply gone awry, as magic had done so often since the night of the Arrival.

Midnight could conclude only one thing from the whole incident: her relationship to the weave was definitely different than that of a normal magic-user. Otherwise, the incantation, whether correct or incorrect, would never have come to her in the first place.

But through most of the night, Midnight could not keep her thoughts from returning to the battle on top of the cliff. Over and over, she heard Kelemvor asking her to keep Cyric's men at bay so he could kill the thief, and heard herself flatly refusing. Then the image returned of Sneakabout sliding down the rope after Cyric, and time after time she saw his silhouette plunging to the ground. Then she would hear Kelemvor blaming her for the halfling's death.

By the time her watch came, Midnight had decided to leave the company. Back in Eveningstar, Cyric had said she was endangering her friends' lives. The thief had been trying to persuade her to join him instead of staying with Kelemvor and Adon. But Sneakabout's death had convinced her that Cyric was right. As long as she remained with the fighter and the cleric, they were in danger—from Cyric, the Zhentilar, and Bhaal.

An hour before dawn, Midnight judged it would be safe to leave her companions unguarded. The night had passed without incident, and the two of them were hidden beneath the cliff. The mage saddled all the ponies, then slipped the tablet from its resting place next to Adon and tied it on to her own mount's saddle.

Finally, she bade a silent farewell to her friends and led all three ponies away. She would leave Kelemvor's and Adon's mounts somewhere down the trail, after she had ridden far enough to insure they would find it difficult to catch her.

❧ 8 ❧

Dangerous Crossing

Midnight kneeled behind the twisted trunk of a shagbark tree. A small expanse of grassland lay at her back. Beyond the prairie stood the rosy crags of the Sunset Mountains, where she had abandoned Kelemvor and Adon just four days ago. The morning was a dreary and gray one, but behind the peaks, the sun had bleached the clouds to bright white.

The scrawny shagbark stood atop a bluff overlooking the River Reaching. A narrow flood plain separated the river's eastern shore from the embankment. Both the plain and the slope were covered with tall scraggly brush. A well-used trail led down the bluff to an inn and livery stable that sat in a small clearing at the river's edge.

Built from river rock and mortar, the inn was a one-story structure. The stable had been constructed with twisted planks hewn from gnarled shagbark trees. Currently, over thirty ponies and horses stood crowded within its confines. One end of the corral protruded a short distance into the River Reaching so that the animals had a constant supply of water.

Outside the inn, two Zhentilar sentries lay dead with short spears protruding from their chests. Another sentry had fallen in the doorway. Thirty halflings lay scattered throughout the clearing, black arrows in their breasts. A handful of the small warriors had reached the inn and hacked eight window shutters off their hinges. Beneath three sills, bloodstains darkened the stone walls, and half-ling bodies lay beneath two more windows.

With a sad heart, Midnight realized that she had stumbled across the men from Black Oaks, Sneakabout's village.

Sleeping only four hours a day, the halflings had marched straight through Yellow Snake Pass. Two nights ago, they had slipped past Adon and Kelemvor, finally catching up to their prey the previous evening. The war party had attacked just before dawn, surprising the sentries with a vicious volley of woomera-launched spears.

If they had stopped there, the halflings might have returned to Black Oaks with their pride and their bodies intact. But they had foolishly rushed the stone building. The Zhentilar inside, well trained and disciplined, had awakened the instant the sentries screamed. The soldiers had fired several volleys of arrows out the windows. Most of the short fighters had fallen before reaching the inn.

Midnight found herself curiously angry at the halflings. Over thirty of them had died, and they had gained nothing. The foolhardy attack against the inn had wiped out their company, and the survivors would have been no match for the strength of full-sized men in hand-to-hand combat.

Though it was clear the halflings had lost the battle, Midnight realized that there might be survivors. If so, the mage had to aid them. Part of her conviction was due to guilty feelings about Sneakabout's death, but the magic- user was also a compassionate woman who despised needless suffering. She simply couldn't bear the thought of leaving any halflings in merciless Zhentish hands.

Midnight also wanted to sneak down to the inn for another reason. She had long suspected Cyric's Zhentilar were the ones who had raided Sneakabout's village, and the halfling's crazed attack on the thief had gone a long way toward confirming that suspicion. If so, then Cyric would be at the inn, and his presence would mean that he had violated his promise not to follow her. The magic-user had to see if her suspicions were true.

Midnight crawled away from the shagbark tree and retreated to the gully where her pony was tied. As the raven-haired magic-user approached, the pony stomped its hooves and snorted.

"What do you want?" Midnight asked. "We left Hill's Edge

an hour ago. You can't be hungry again."

Of course, the pony said nothing. Midnight shook her head and sighed heavily, feeling silly for addressing a dumb animal as if it could respond. The magic-user had grown so lonely she thought of the beast in human terms. Midnight missed Adon and, especially, Kelemvor. Sneaking out of camp, she had felt no special need to make amends with her friends. Now, she ached to take back the anger between them.

But it was too late. The magic-user had a mission to accomplish, and she knew that it would be better to forget Kelemvor and Adon for now. Perhaps that was why she had begun thinking of the pony as a companion.

At least this newfound empathy had served Midnight well. Twice, the pony had smelled something that frightened it. If the magic-user had not been attuned to her mount's moods, she would have missed the pony's skittishness and pressed forward into disaster. The first time, Midnight would have stumbled into a goblin patrol. Though it might have been easy to escape using her magic, Midnight was just as glad she had not needed to try.

The second time, the pony had smelled something that frightened it badly. When the mage had investigated, she found one of the few patrols Darkhold had kept in Yellow Snake Pass. Midnight's magic might have handled the Zhentilar, too, but the patrol had been escorting a humanoid stone statue standing ten feet tall. As soon as she had looked into its vacant eyes and had seen it walking under its own power, Midnight had recognized the statue as a stone golem and hurried away. By their very natures, stone golems were almost immune to magic.

Other than that, her journey down Yellow Snake Pass had been uneventful. Last night, she had stayed in a small hostel in Hill's Edge. Though most residents of the town had been cold and distant, the innkeeper was a warm man not averse to offering good advice to his customers. When Midnight had asked where she could discreetly buy a fast horse, he had suggested the livery before which the mage now stood. Fortunately, Midnight had approached it cautiously, for

Hill's Edge had been crawling with Zhentilar, and she had correctly suspected there might be more at the stable.

The pony nuzzled Midnight under the arm, looking for something to eat. The mage ignored it and took the saddlebags off its back. Without Adon and Kelemvor to help guard the tablet, she didn't want to leave the saddlebag containing the artifact unattended.

She started to pick her way down the slope, being careful to stay well hidden in the heavy brush and not to kick loose rocks or snap twigs. When the mage reached the bottom of the bluff, a cold drizzle began. The rain smelled foul and rotten, as though something in the clouds had died. The inn remained dark and still.

Midnight paused to search for signs of a sentry. Then she heard a faint chorus of deep laughter behind the inn. A high-pitched voice cried, "Not again, I beg—aaaaghh!"

Taking care to remain concealed in the brush, the magic-user circled around to the southern side of the building. The high-pitched voice screamed again, then fell silent. A few seconds later, the foul drizzle changed to a shower, and Midnight reached the edge of the clearing. She stopped a hundred feet away from the building, where she had a clear view of the area between the inn and the river.

Standing up to their chests in water, four Zhentilar held a ten-foot long log in place against the current. They had carved a deep groove in the center of the wood, and in this groove rested the joint of two long poles lashed together at right angles. The Zhentilar had tied a halfling to the far end of each pole, leaving his arms free so that he could swim and hold himself above water.

The diabolic result of this construction was that a prisoner could not hold himself above the surface without forcing his comrade at the other end beneath the water. Two wet halflings already lay on shore, one dead, the other coughing weakly.

Four more Zhentish soldiers stood at the river's edge, chuckling quietly and betting on which prisoner would survive. Another man stood apart from them, evidently uninterested in the cruel sport. He was a large man with black braided hair, a bushy beard, and gleaming blue-black chain mail.

A cloak-shrouded figure left the four wagering Zhentilar and walked toward the lone black-haired man, pulling his cape tight over his shoulders. Midnight immediately recognized Cyric.

"Come on, Dalzhel, join the fun!" the hawk-nosed thief cried.

"You're wasting time, sir."

Cyric looked back to the water torture. "Nonsense. The men are enjoying themselves." He did not add that he found the diversion entertaining, too.

"What of the woman? We should ride after her."

"There's no need," Cyric said confidently. "The spies in Hill's Edge spotted her and tell me that she's alone." He paused and smiled. "She'll come to us."

A roar went up from the Zhentilar, and Midnight saw that one prisoner had broken the surface of the river, plunging his companion beneath the waves.

"Another plan, milord?" Dalzhel asked, ignoring the cheering spectators.

Cyric nodded, then looked back at the struggling halflings and chuckled. "She's going to ride right into our arms," he said absently.

Midnight licked her lips and tasted an angry sweat. She had nearly done just that. In fact, she might yet be captured.

Dalzhel raised an eyebrow doubtfully. "Even if she knows where to find us, I doubt she'll trust you after you killed the halfling."

"Trust me?" Cyric guffawed, grabbing Dalzhel's massive shoulder for support. "I don't expect her to trust me any longer. I'll no longer play those games with her."

Dalzhel frowned in puzzlement. "Then why would she join us?"

Cyric laughed even harder and pointed to the river. "The ford," he said. "It's the only one within sixty miles. She has to come this way."

Embarrassment crept over Dalzhel's face and he smiled

sheepishly. "Of course, milord. We'll ambush her."

"Without Kelemvor to buy her time, we'll have her bound and gagged before she casts her first spell!"

Midnight's heart felt as though it had turned to ice. Kelemvor had been right—Cyric was a traitor. She needed no more proof. The magic-user exhaled quietly and choked back her anger. The icy feeling in her heart remained, and she vowed Cyric would pay for his betrayal.

The shower increased to a downpour. An eerie wail came down the river and the fetid rain fell as though driven by a hardy wind. Even though the air remained deathly calm, Midnight ignored the bizarre rain. Since the night of Arrival, she had seen many things a thousand times stranger.

But Cyric and Dalzhel did not share her lack of concern. The last time they had heard that wail, in the Haunted Halls, they'd lost several good men. Both men frowned and looked skyward.

"I'll check the sentries," Dalzhel said.

Midnight's scalp bristled with alarm. She had seen no sentries, and the fact that she remained undiscovered proved they had not seen her. Something was wrong.

"I'll finish with the halflings," Cyric grumbled, turning back to his men and prisoners.

Midnight saw that the soldiers had forgotten about the halflings. They, too, remembered what had happened the last time they heard a wail like the one that echoed around them now. Several of the Zhentilar held their hands on their hilts, nervously glancing in every direction, expecting Bhaal to appear at any moment.

As Dalzhel turned away, Cyric called out a last instruction. "If Midnight doesn't show within the hour, we'll go to Hill's Edge."

"Aye," Dalzhel replied, "assuming we're not fighting for our lives."

"You will be," Midnight whispered. "I promise." Though she did not understand the source of Cyric's distress, she intended to use it to maximum effect.

Her first order of business, however, was to free the halflings. Though fearing her magic might misfire, she had no choice except to rely upon it. She summoned the words and gestures for telekinesis magic to mind. A normal telekinesis spell simply moved objects horizontally or vertically. The magic-user was gambling she could manipulate the ends of the ropes with enough dexterity to loosen them.

Midnight immediately performed the incantation. To her astonishment, all the ropes in the area, not just the ones binding the halflings, immediately loosened and began to unravel of their own accord. The two halflings on the torture device came free and floated down the river. Then their ropes began swimming for shore, as though they were snakes. The cord lashing the poles came undone, too, and crawled onto the log, coiled itself, and struck at one of the Zhentilar.

Cyric's men voiced astonished shouts and angry curses. The thief started toward the river. "Kill the prisoners! Kill them this instant!" He pulled his short sword. In the gray light, its pink blade seemed especially threatening.

His men immediately moved to obey, drawing their blades. The halflings swam as fast as they could, and the men lunged after them clumsily, hacking and swinging— sometimes at the escapees, and sometimes at the ropes squirming past them. The halflings were exhausted and it was all they could do to keep their heads above the water. Still, the current was a fast one, and it seemed possible the river would carry them out of danger's reach. Cyric growled angrily and waded into the river to intercept one of the escapees.

When Midnight noticed that the living ropes were crawling toward her, she backed into the brush, moving closer to the river. The ropes adjusted their course and kept crawling toward her.

One of the Zhentilar noticed what the animated ropes were doing and pointed at them. "Look!" he yelled. "They're after something!"

Cyric glanced at the ropes. "See what it is!" he ordered. At the same time, he adjusted his position to intercept his prey.

Midnight backed away again, through the bushes. If the Zhentilar's attention had not been focused in her direction already, the resulting rustle would have gone unnoticed. But the squirming ropes were crawling straight toward Midnight's hiding place, and it was impossible for the soldier to miss the noise. An instant later, he saw Midnight's form huddled in the brush.

"There's someone in there!" He yelled, stopping. "A woman!"

Midnight stood, ready to flee.

In the same instant, Cyric turned toward the brush and saw the mage's familiar black cloak. "Midnight!" he called. "You're here at last!" Without looking away from the thicket, he reached out and snagged the halfling who was drifting by.

"I am," she growled. In that instant, the raven-haired magic-user decided not to run. As of yet, Cyric and his men had made no move toward her, but they would obviously give chase the instant she fled. The longer Cyric talked, the longer Midnight had to develop a plan of escape. "And I know you for what you are."

Cyric shrugged. "What's that?" Moving smoothly and casually, he pulled the half-drowned halfling to him and slit his throat.

"Monster!" Midnight yelled, taken by surprise. "You'll pay for that!"

An instant of doubt flashed across Cyric's brow. He let the halfling's body slip into the water, then waded toward shore. His men started after Midnight, but he waved them back. "No," the thief said. "You won't make me pay. We were friends once, remember?"

"That's over!" The magic-user thought of killing Cyric and the appropriate incantation came to her, but she did not cast it. Before he died, Midnight wanted Cyric to know what she was punishing him for. "You betrayed me, Cyric. You betrayed all of us, and by Auril's blue skin, I'm going to—"

"Be careful by whom you swear," Cyric cautioned, stepping onto the riverbank. "The Goddess of Cold is more of my persuasion than—"

The thief's eyes suddenly bulged in terror and his lips pursed to form a single word. "No!"

Cyric's unexplained fright caused Midnight to hesitate. She sensed movement behind her—then the ambusher was upon her. A vicelike hand clamped over the mage's mouth, burning her lips where it touched them, and a steely arm snaked around her waist, causing her intestines to churn in revolt.

Midnight tried to cast her death spell, but found that she could not. The thing held her immobile; she could not voice the words or make the gestures to execute the incantation. The iron-gripped attacker lifted the mage off her feet and retreated into the brush.

* * * * *

When that day became night, it did not grow dark. The sky twinkled with a thousand different colors, as though the heavens were filled with glittering gemstones. Kelemvor could not deny that the flickering light cast a certain macabre beauty over the land. But he would have been happier with the customary stars and moon overhead, and he envied Adon for having found a retreat from the eerie night.

Adon sat cross-legged before the small fire, his attention focused on the yellow flames. Though he knew Kelemvor sat beside him, that it was night and they were camped on the bank of the River Reaching, he was not "aware" of these things. His mind had retreated into itself, following the convoluted pathways of prayerful meditation.

"Anything yet, Adon?" the green-eyed fighter asked. Though he was not well versed in these matters, it seemed to him that something should have happened by now.

The interruption shattered the trance and Adon came spinning back to the world with dizzying speed. The cleric closed his eyes and shook his head from side to side, digging his fingers into the cold mud.

He had been sitting before the fire since dusk, without eating, drinking, or so much as shifting his weight. His back ached, his legs were numb, and his eyes burned. Irritated with Kelemvor's intrusion, Adon asked, "How long has it been?"

"Half the night, maybe more," the warrior muttered, doubting the wisdom of interrupting the cleric's meditation. "I've been to gather wood a dozen times."

He didn't add that someone was watching them. If he told Adon now, the cleric would react with surprise and the mysterious figure would know that she'd been discovered.

Adon rolled his neck, letting his aggravation drain away with his stiffness. He could not blame Kelemvor for being impatient, and the interruption had not changed the trance's result. "I found nothing," the scarred cleric reported. "Sune cannot hear me . . . or will not answer."

Adon wasn't surprised by this fact or even disappointed. Attempting to contact Sune had been Kelemvor's idea. Even though it was a desperate plan with little chance of success, the cleric had agreed because they stood to lose nothing by trying.

The fighter, however, was disappointed. He snapped a stick and threw it into the fire. "Midnight's lost, then," he said sadly.

Adon laid a gentle hand on his friend's shoulder. "We'll find her."

Kelemvor shook his head. "She's been gone four nights. We'll never catch her."

The cleric could say nothing. When she had abandoned them, Midnight had ridden north, well into the gorge of the River Reaching. Mounted on her sturdy mountain pony, Midnight could have taken no more than three or four hours for the first leg of her escape. But on foot, it had taken Adon and Kelemvor a full day to reach the clearing where she had left their mounts. By the time they had returned to the main route, Midnight had a head start of a day and a half.

Her desertion would have been disturbing in itself. But when they found Midnight's trail again, Kelemvor had also discovered the hoofprints of a dozen horses following her.

He and Adon had both agreed the horses could only belong to Cyric and his men.

"Well, what should we do now?" Kelemvor asked.

Adon didn't have a single idea to offer, and he wished Kelemvor would stop looking to him for answers. Still, he knew someone had to make a decision, and, with Midnight missing, Kelemvor would not be the one. So Adon stood and unfolded the map Deverell had given them. After a moment of thought, he placed a finger on a dot a few miles down the river. "We'll go to Hill's Edge," he said. "Midnight will need a strong horse to cross the plains, and so will we."

Adon started to kick dirt on the fire, but Kelemvor stopped him. Placing a hand on the hilt of his sword, the fighter turned toward the river. Fifty feet away, the woman who had been watching them was approaching.

The cleric followed Kelemvor's gaze. "Is that you, Midnight?" he called.

The woman continued to approach. "No, it's not," she replied, her voice soft and melodious. "May I approach your camp anyway?"

Having spent the night staring into the fire, Adon's eyes were unaccustomed to the dark. Even in the eerie light of the sparkling sky, he couldn't see the mysterious woman clearly. Nevertheless, he was the one who replied. "You're welcome here."

A few seconds later, she stepped into the firelight and Adon gasped. The woman stood as tall as Kelemvor, with silky brown hair and deep brown eyes. Her complexion was fair, though the glittering sky cast over it a multihued tint that lent an ethereal quality to her beauty. Her face was oval-shaped, with a leanness that contrasted the fullness of her striking figure. In contrast to the eloquence of her beauty, she wore the rugged clothes of one who lived in the wilderness.

A wave of hope washed over Adon. Perhaps his prayers had been answered. "Sune?" he asked meekly.

The woman blushed. "You flatter me."

Adon could not help frowning as his momentary excitement faded.

Noticing the cleric's disappointment, the woman feigned disappointment herself and said, "If only the Goddess of Beauty is welcome in your camp—"

Kelemvor raised a hand and said, "Don't be offended. We didn't expect anybody to wander into our camp, especially you—er, I mean a beautiful woman."

"A beautiful woman," she repeated distantly. "Do you think so?"

"Certainly," Adon said, bowing. "Adon of—well, just Adon, and Kelemvor Lyonsbane at your service."

The woman bowed in return. "Well met. Javia of Chauntea at yours."

"Well met," Adon replied. If she served Chauntea, the Great Mother, that meant the woman was a druid. That explained her presence in the wilderness.

"I've been watching your prayer fire," Javia explained. "Was it Sune you were praying to?"

"Yes," Adon responded glumly.

Javia stared at the scar on the cleric's cheek. Her compassionate eyes showed that she understood the remorse the blemish would bring to a follower of the Goddess of Beauty.

Adon turned his head to hide the scar.

Javia blushed and smiled shyly. "Forgive me. I don't often meet travelers here and I forget how to act."

"What are you doing out here?" Kelemvor asked.

Sensing the fighter's suspicion, the woman said, "Perhaps I'm interrupting your service—"

"Not at all, Javia," Adon protested, taking her by the hand and guiding her to a log beside the fire. "Sit. Please."

"Yes," Kelemvor said moodily. "Praying wasn't solving our problems anyway."

Javia arched her eyebrows in alarm. "Don't say that!"

"I didn't mean—," Kelemvor began, recoiling from Javia's vehement response. Then he decided it was better to be honest and explain what he meant. "In our case, it's true." He pointed at Adon's cheek. "All the praying in the world didn't get rid of that scar, and Adon got it in Sune's service."

"Surely not in Sune's service!" Javia exclaimed, her voice

sharp with reproach. "She is no goddess of filthy war."

"Do you think that's why she let me suffer?" Adon asked, his grief working its way to the surface again. "Because I fought in the wrong cause?"

Javia's face softened and she turned to Adon. "Your cause may have been right enough," she said. "But expecting a goddess to serve a worshiper . . ." She let the sentence trail off as though Adon ought to know better than to expect something like that.

Adon felt his anger rising. "If not a worshiper, then who?" he demanded.

Javia looked puzzled for a moment, as if she had never considered the question. Finally, she answered, "Herself— who else?"

"Herself," Adon echoed indignantly.

"Yes," Javia replied. "Sune, for example, cannot concern herself with the welfare of her followers. The Goddess of Beauty must think only of beauty. If she contemplates ugliness, no matter how briefly or for what purpose, then she brings ugliness into her soul. If that happened, we would no longer have a pure ideal—all beauty would contain some ugliness."

"Tell me," the cleric demanded angrily, "what do you think worshipers matter to the gods?"

Kelemvor sighed. To the warrior, many things were worth arguing about—but religion was not one of them.

Javia regarded Adon for a long time. Finally, her voice warm but condescending, she replied, "We're like gold."

"Like gold," Adon repeated, sensing that Javia's meaning was not to be found on the surface of her words. "So we're the coins in some godly purse?"

Javia nodded. "Something like that. We are the wealth by which the gods measure their—"

"By which they measure their status," Adon interrupted. "Tell me, what contest are they playing at now? Is it worth the destruction of the world?"

Javia looked up at the sparkling sky, then, oblivious—or indifferent—to Adon's anger, she said, "I fear this is no game. The gods are fighting for control of the Realms and the Planes."

"Then I wish they'd take their battle someplace else," Kelemvor said hotly, waving his hand at the sky. "We want no part of it."

"That is not our choice," Javia said sternly, wagging her finger at Kelemvor as though he were a child.

"How can you be so dedicated to them?" Adon demanded, shaking his head in amazement. "We don't matter to them!"

Though he disagreed with Javia, the scarred cleric was glad that she had wandered into camp. Despite the intensity of the argument, he felt more at peace with himself than he had in ages. Javia's succinct opposition helped him see that he had been right to abandon Sune. Serving a goddess who did not care about her worshipers was not only foolish, it was wrong. Mankind had too many problems to waste its energy in the unproductive worship of vain deities.

The debate continued for twenty minutes without any resolution. Javia was too vehemently faithful and Adon too determinedly heretical for them to reconcile their differences.

When the conversation deteriorated into a pointless and repetitive argument, Kelemvor excused himself and went to his bedroll. "If the two clerics are going to stay up all night arguing," he muttered to himself as he closed his eyes, "they can keep the watch."

❧ 9 ❧

Bad Company

The trail bent south and ran along the base of some rolling hills. The sun kindled a golden hue in the tufts of drab grass that speckled the dusty soil. Here and there, a few reddish cliffs dotted the barren hillsides, the crisp morning light igniting blazing tones in the sandy rock.

Without warning or reason, one cliff burst into fire, burned for a few minutes, then collapsed. Flaming boulders bounced down the hill, touching off small fires wherever they touched the greenery.

Ignoring the mysterious eruption, Bhaal—who now used Kae Deverell's haggard body as an avatar—guided his and Midnight's mounts into the hills. Though the cliff's spontaneous combustion frightened the magic-user, she did not have the energy or strength to object to the change in route. Midnight felt more asleep than awake, and was almost delirious with pain. Where Bhaal had closed his hand over her mouth, her lips and chin still burned. The mage's stomach was worse. Her entrails still churned from the Lord of Murder's polluted touch.

As the horses picked their way up the hillside, Midnight flopped helplessly to and fro. Too exhausted and disheartened to hold herself in the saddle, she remained mounted only because it was impossible for her to fall off. Bhaal had bound her hands to the saddle's horn and her feet to the stirrups.

Had she not suffered through the last thirty hours, Midnight would never have believed a human being could endure so much. After snatching the magic-user from the confrontation with Cyric, Bhaal had bound and gagged her, making magical incantations impossible. Then the god had lashed Midnight to a waiting horse, mounted his own, and, leading her mount, ridden away at a trot.

The pace had not slackened since. The Lord of Murder had ridden through an entire day and night without slowing for rest or explanation. If the horses did not collapse first, Midnight feared her bones would crumble from constant jarring. Confirming its own exhaustion, the magic-user's horse struck its hoof against a rock and stumbled. The mage lurched left to keep her balance. The saddlebag with the tablet, still slung over her shoulder, shifted. A streak of pain ran up her spine.

Midnight groaned. When he had abducted her, Bhaal had left the saddlebag slung over her shoulder and simply secured it into place with a leather thong. The saddlebag had already rubbed the skin on the mage's shoulder raw. A warm, wet stain spread from the abrasion and ran down her back in ticklish streams.

Bhaal paused. He turned to face her. "What do you want?"

Unable to speak through the gag, Midnight shook her head to indicate the groan meant nothing.

The foul god frowned, then resumed riding.

Midnight exhaled in relief. Despite the pain in her shoulder, she did not want Bhaal to take the saddlebag away. The magic-user still clung to the hope of escape, and she wanted the Tablet of Fate with her when the opportunity came.

Unfortunately, Midnight did not know what to do if she did escape. Unless she disabled Bhaal, which seemed unlikely, he would simply track her down again. The magic-user wondered what Kelemvor would do. As a warrior, he had certainly faced capture and knew methods of escape. Even Adon might have a solution. He had studied the gods and would know if Bhaal had any weaknesses.

Midnight could not help longing for the presence of her two friends. She had never been more frightened, nor more lonely, in her life. Despite the need for their company and counsel, however, she did not regret abandoning her allies.

Had they been at the ford, Bhaal would have murdered them both. If Kelemvor had died, the magic-user might have lost the strength to continue her struggle. Midnight could not allow that to happen.

The magic-user chastised herself for trying to rescue the halflings. She had placed the tablet in peril, and doubted that she had saved even one life. But Midnight quickly realized that abandoning the survivors of the war party would have changed nothing. Bhaal would have tracked her down anyway. In the end, it was making the task easy for him that upset her.

The Lord of Murder suddenly stopped the horses. They had reached the top of a hill, and Midnight could see dozens of miles in all directions. Fifteen miles back, an expanse of orange and red stretched toward the south. It was the forest that had hugged their left flank through the night.

Bhaal dismounted, then removed his horse's bridle and tethered the beast.

"The horses need rest," he grumbled, untying Midnight. Whenever the avatar touched the mage's skin, her skin grew red and irritated. "Dismount."

Midnight gladly obeyed. The instant her feet touched the ground, Bhaal grabbed her wrist. Scorching pain shot through her arm up to her shoulder. She screamed in agony.

"Don't try to escape," Bhaal snarled. "I'm strong. You're still weak." Confident that he had made his point, the fallen god released her.

The fresh agony jolted the magic-user into full alertness. She pulled the gag off her mouth and considered summoning her magic. Midnight quickly rejected the idea, however. The Lord of Murder would not have untied her—or allowed her to remove her gag—unless he was prepared to counter any attack.

Instead, the mage cleared her throat and asked, "What do you want?"

Bhaal stared at Midnight, but did not respond. The face of the avatar—Lord Deverell's face—was pale and sickly yellow. The eyes were sunken, the skin stretched over the bones like leather over a drumhead.

"Hold your hands together like this," Bhaal said, pressing his palms together.

Midnight briefly considered being uncooperative, but decided to obey. At the moment, she was too exhausted to argue, and there was more to gain by letting Bhaal believe she had lost hope.

As Midnight pressed her palms together, she asked again, "What do you want?"

Bhaal produced a leather thong. "You," he answered.

This answer did not surprise Midnight. When the Lord of Murder had first abducted her, she had assumed he wanted the tablet. After he had not killed her, however, the mage had begun to suspect he wanted something else. "Me? Why?"

Bhaal tied the mage's thumbs together, pausing to consider his response. Finally, he answered, "You're going to kill Helm."

He spoke the words so rapidly and quietly that Midnight thought she had misunderstood him. "Kill Helm?" she asked. "Is that what you said?"

The Lord of Murder tied her little fingers together, then repeated the process with each of her other digits. It was obvious to Midnight that the god was binding her hands so she could not trace the gestures necessary to call on her magic. "Yes, kill Helm," he finally confirmed.

"I can't kill a god!" Midnight yelped, astounded.

"You killed Torm," Bhaal growled. "And Bane." He pulled the thongs painfully tight.

"All I did was ring the Bell of Aylan Attricus! I saved Tantras. Bane and Torm killed each other."

"There's no need for modesty," Bhaal said. He finished binding Midnight's hands and stepped away. "Lord Myrkul is the one who's angry about the Black Lord's death. After Bane destroyed my assassins, I was happy to see him die."

"But I didn't kill him . . . or Torm. And I can't kill Helm!" Midnight insisted, gesturing with her bound hands. Bhaal's misconception both angered and frightened her. If he had abducted her in order to destroy Helm, the fallen god had made a terrible mistake. "It was the bell!" she insisted.

Bhaal shrugged and removed her horse's saddle. "It's all the same. You rang the bell when nobody else could. Now you will kill Helm."

"Even if I could," Midnight replied, finding a place to sit, "I wouldn't. You must know that."

"No," Bhaal told her sharply. He tossed the saddle on the ground near his. "We know you'll do as you're told."

"What gives you that idea?" Midnight asked. She found it interesting that Bhaal had referred to Myrkul as an ally. The mage decided to make the most of her captivity by learning as much as she could from the Lord of Murder.

Bhaal stared at the mage with a steady gaze. "Though you left your friends, we know how much you care for them."

"What do you mean?"

Bhaal walked around to the other side of her horse and removed its bit. "It's rather obvious, don't you think?"

"Kelemvor and Adon are no longer part of this," the magic-user snapped, fear growing inside of her.

"We understand that," Bhaal sighed, squatting to tether the horses. "And it will stay that way—providing you do as we wish."

"I can't do what you want!" she yelled, rising to her feet. "I don't have the power. You're supposed to be a god—why can't you understand a simple thing like that?"

Bhaal studied her with his dead, coal-black eyes. "You don't lack the power," he said. "You just don't know how to use it yet. That's why you need Myrkul and me."

"Need you?" Midnight cried. The idea of "needing" the Lord of Murder and the Lord of the Dead sent shivers of revulsion up the mage's spine.

"You think it will be easy to wield the might of a god?" Bhaal asked, walking over to her. "Without us, you'll burn up. The Goddess of Magic was very powerful when she transferred her power to you."

"The might of a god?" Midnight repeated. Her mind wandered back to the night she had collapsed praying to

Mystra—the night of the Arrival. That had been when her life changed, when the Realms themselves had fallen into supernatural disarray.

For several weeks now, the suspicion that she carried Mystra's power had been growing in the mage's mind. Midnight had tried to blame the changing nature of her magic on the chaos infecting the Realms, but it had grown increasingly difficult to ignore the evidence: her power over magic was expanding; she no longer needed her spellbook; and finally, she could now use incantations she had never studied.

But having suspected the truth did not lessen the impact of its confirmation. The Lord of Murder's revelation left Midnight stunned and frightened, and she could not help retreating from all that it implied.

Bhaal took advantage of Midnight's dazed state to pressure her. "When he exiled us, our master stripped us of our power. Now, you alone are Helm's match." The God of Assassins turned away from Midnight and looked toward the sky. "If we are to return to the Planes, you must destroy the God of Guardians."

"Wouldn't it be easier to give Helm the Tablets of Fate?" Midnight asked, speaking to Bhaal's back. "Won't Lord Ao open the Planes to the gods when the tablets are returned?"

Bhaal whirled around, his eyes flashing with rage. "Do you think we enjoy being trapped in this puny world? This facade has cost me all of my worshipers!" he snapped. "We'd return the tablets in an instant if it were possible."

Midnight was not sure she believed the Lord of Murder. From what she had learned, the gods were fighting over who would get credit for returning the tablets. But Bhaal's words gave her cause for doubt.

"Are you saying it's impossible to return the tablets?" the mage pressed.

The god pointed at the saddlebags on Midnight's shoulder. "Why do you think we've permitted you to keep that one? It's useless."

"Useless!" Midnight gasped, her heart sinking.

"We can't get the second one. Nobody can," Bhaal

explained, waving his hand angrily. "Without both tablets, Helm won't let us back into the Planes. That's why you must kill him."

"Where's the other tablet? Has it been destroyed?"

Bhaal sneered. "In a manner of speaking, yes. It's hidden in Bone Castle, in Myrkul's Realm of the Dead." He pointed at the ground. "And there it will stay until we are freed from the Realms."

"If you know where it is, why don't you—" Midnight stopped in midsentence, realizing her question was silly. The gods had been banished from the Planes. The Realm of the Dead, being Myrkul's home, was undoubtedly closed to them since it was in Hades.

Bhaal allowed Midnight a moment to consider what she had learned so far. Finally, he said, "You see? We're on the same side: we want to return to the Planes, and you want to get us out of Faerun. But you'll need to kill Helm before that happens. Do you see that now?"

Midnight did not answer immediately. It had occurred to her that if she could destroy Helm, she could also recover the other tablet from Bone Castle. But the mage did not want to reveal her idea to Bhaal, although he claimed that he also wanted to return the tablets. Even after thirty hours in the saddle, she was not muddled enough to believe she could trust the word of the Lord of Murder.

Still, if her plan was to work, Midnight needed more information. "If I must kill Helm in order to save the Realms, then I will," Midnight lied. If she was going to learn what she wanted from Bhaal, he had to think she was convinced. "But before I agree, you've got to answer some questions. I want to know that you've tried every other possibility."

"Oh, we have," Bhaal replied, using his saddle as a chair.

Midnight did not believe the fallen deity's words were sincere, but she pretended otherwise. "The gods are barred from the Planes, not anybody else. Why haven't you sent a mortal into the Realm of the Dead to retrieve the second tablet?"

Bhaal's jaw dropped just for an instant, but long enough to

betray his surprise. "That's not as easy as you make it sound," he said.

Midnight did not miss the shock on Bhaal's face, but was unsure what to make of it. She could not believe that the Lord of Murder and the Lord of the Dead would not have thought of something so simple.

"Answer the question," Midnight demanded. "Why haven't you sent some mortal after the tablet? There must be ways for humans to reach the Realm of the Dead."

"There are ways," Bhaal conceded.

"How?" Midnight asked. She sat down facing Bhaal, now, using her own saddle for a stool.

The God of Assassins twisted Deverell's emaciated face into a sour grin. "They can die," he said.

Midnight frowned. That was hardly the answer she wanted. "You can *try* to force me to cooperate by threatening Kelemvor and Adon, but you won't be able to trust me unless you answer these questions. Why haven't you sent a mortal after the second Tablet of Fate?"

Bhaal studied her for a long time, malice in his eyes. Finally, he dropped his gaze and said, "We have tried. Lord Myrkul has sent dozens of his most loyal priests to Dragonspear Castle and—"

"Dragonspear Castle?" Midnight interrupted. From what she had heard, Dragonspear Castle was little more than an abandoned ruin on the road to Waterdeep.

"Dragonspear Castle," Bhaal confirmed, nodding. "Beneath it, there is a—" He paused, as if searching for the proper word. "—there is a bridge between this world and the Realm of the Dead."

"Then why don't you have the other tablet already?" Midnight asked. By mentioning Dragonspear Castle, Bhaal had already told her what she wanted to know: where to find the entrance to the Realm of the Dead. It was better not to dwell on the subject, or he would quickly discover his mistake.

Bhaal shrugged and looked away. "The mortals go in, but they don't come out. The Realm of the Dead is a dangerous place for the living."

"In what ways?" Midnight asked and she shifted her weight uncomfortably in the saddle. "Surely, Lord Myrkul's priests—"

"We've talked enough about the Realm of the Dead," Bhaal snapped, suddenly rising and snarling in anger. "You *will* help us, Midnight . . . or your friends will suffer for your stupidity and your obstinacy."

Midnight stared at Bhaal, feigning surprise and indignation, but said nothing. From the foul god's sudden anger, she knew that she had asked one question too many.

Bhaal pointed at the ground next to her saddle. "Sleep while you can," he grumbled. "We leave as soon as the horses are rested." With that, he turned away—then allowed himself a satisfied grin. So far, everything with the mage had gone as Lord Myrkul had predicted.

*   *   *   *   *

Kelemvor kept a wary eye turned toward the forest on the south side of the road. A hundred inky shadows hung in rust-colored boughs, ferociously chittering at a dark thing skulking in the underbrush. As the warrior watched, a lone squirrel dropped out of a tree and bounced out to the middle of the dusty road. It had tufted ears, a bushy tail, and eyes darker than its fur. Where the morning sun's yellow rays touched it, the creature's dark fur absorbed the light. The rodent looked more like a tiny demon than a squirrel.

Kelemvor continued to ride toward the little animal. It stood its ground, studying the warrior and his horse with ravenous eyes.

"Strange creatures," Adon commented.

"They certainly don't seem natural," Kelemvor agreed.

Inside the wood, a stick snapped with a loud pop. The mass of squirrels gathered in the trees shrieked in anger and dropped to the ground. Within seconds, a man rose, cursing and screaming as the rodents swarmed him. Kelemvor and Adon could not see the man well enough to tell whether he was a huntsman or someone else with a less honorable reason to lurk in the wood.

"Too mean," Kelemvor added, referring to the squirrels.

The fighter hoped Adon would not insist upon chasing the beleaguered man down. The cleric was making a habit of interrogating strangers, and it was beginning to annoy Kelemvor. Twenty-four hours ago, they had discovered Midnight's pony near the ford at Hill's Edge. They had also found close to forty dead halflings, and signs of the torture that had occurred behind the inn. Though unsure of how to interpret these signs, Kelemvor and Adon had decided to assume Cyric had captured Midnight.

They had been in the saddle ever since, looking for their enemy at every campfire they passed. Kelemvor had grown tired of this methodical search. He knew that Cyric was increasing his lead while Adon wasted their time harassing honest merchants.

But the cleric was convinced that, at last, they had caught up to the thief. "After that man!" he ordered.

Kelemvor made no move to obey. "I'll waste no more time. Cyric's ahead of us, and we won't catch him by chasing woodcutters."

"Woodcutters!" Adon exclaimed. "Why would a woodcutter be so far from town?"

"A hunter then," Kelemvor responded.

"So you're certain that isn't Cyric's sentry?"

"No," Kelemvor said. "But—"

"Then we've got to go after him."

"No," Kelemvor insisted. "We can't look behind every rock for Cyric. We'll lose him for good if we keep this up!"

Adon saw the wisdom of Kelemvor's argument, but believed the fleeing man was more than a hunter. "All right. But hunters don't lurk at roadsides. Trust me."

Kelemvor sighed. Lately, he'd found it increasingly difficult to disagree with Adon for long. Warily eyeing the black squirrels, the warrior spurred his mount into a gallop. The sturdy caravan horse easily broke through the thicket at the forest's edge. A dozen rodents leaped from the trees, attacking Kelemvor and his mount with tiny claws and teeth.

The horse ignored them and continued forward while Kelemvor swore and ripped the creatures off his body. By the time they were free of squirrels, the warrior and his horse were deep within a multihued world of shadows and autumn light.

Adon followed close behind, cursing and ripping black rodents off his body.

The man they were chasing was nowhere in sight.

"What now?" Kelemvor asked.

Adon flung the last squirrel into the forest, then said, "We argued too long. He's gone."

To their left, Kelemvor heard the muffled patter of hoofbeats. He turned his horse to pursue, motioning Adon to follow. The sooner they caught the fellow, the sooner the cleric would let them get back to chasing Midnight.

As he rode, Kelemvor kept an eye turned toward the forest floor. Several minutes later, he stopped. He hadn't seen a single hoofprint, scuffed rock, or freshly broken stick upon which he could base a trail.

"Where is he?" Adon asked.

Kelemvor hushed his friend, then listened carefully. The hoofbeats were gone. But deep in the forest, he heard something else—the nicker of a tired horse.

He turned his mount toward the sound and rode slowly ahead. "Follow me . . . quietly."

A minute later, the warrior heard the soft murmur of a voice. Kelemvor dismounted and gave his reins to Adon, then crawled through the thick underbrush with his sword drawn. He had to go slowly, for the ground was littered with dried twigs and leaves that made it nearly impossible to move silently.

Eventually, he came to the edge of a small clearing, where a rider in Zhentish armor held the reins of a winded horse. Beside the rider stood a large, black-bearded man. Behind the horse, hidden from view, stood a third man. A hundred feet to the trio's right, seven Zhentilar were sleeping on the ground, their armor stacked neatly beside them.

Adon was right, Kelemvor realized. The man at the roadside had been a sentry.

"You're sure they couldn't follow you?" asked the bearded man.

"I'm certain," replied the sentry.

The unseen man spoke. "We can't take chances, Dalzhel. Stupid as he is, Kelemvor has a certain cunning."

The voice was Cyric's.

Kelemvor's heart pounded with anger and excitement. "*Stupid!*" he muttered under his breath. "We'll see who's stupid when my sword creases your neck!" The only thing that kept the warrior from attacking immediately was that he did not see Midnight. He would not risk her life to vent his wrath.

Cyric continued speaking to Dalzhel. "Wake the men."

"But they've slept less than three hours!" Dalzhel objected.

"Wake them," Cyric snapped. Turning to the sentry, he added, "And you ride back over your trail. Be sure the two men didn't follow you."

As Dalzhel and the sentry turned to obey, Kelemvor started to back out of his hiding place. He intended to reach Adon before the sentry did. The stocky warrior, however, was not accustomed to skulking in the bushes. In his rush to beat the Zhentish soldier, his scabbard caught on a bush and rustled it loudly. Kelemvor cursed under his breath and froze, hoping Cyric and his men would not notice the sound.

But Cyric, Dalzhel, and the sentry all stopped and turned to look in the fighter's direction.

Kelemvor realized he had two choices—attack or retreat. He made the same choice he always did: he leaped from his hiding place and charged. The sudden assault took his opponents by surprise.

Dalzhel was first in Kelemvor's path. The huge Zhentilar's weapon had not even cleared its scabbard when Kelemvor leveled a vicious slash at his undefended side. The Zhentilar stepped forward and blocked the slash by smashing his fist into Kelemvor's elbow.

The blow nearly knocked the sword out of the stocky

warrior's hand. Dalzhel grabbed for Kelemvor's wrist, but the green-eyed fighter pulled free and stepped back. This allowed the huge Zhentilar to draw his weapon, but it also freed Kelemvor to attack again.

The exchange occurred so rapidly that Cyric and the sentry didn't have time to react. If Dalzhel's reflexes had not been so quick, Kelemvor would have killed all three men with their weapons still sheathed. The initial melee was over, however; Cyric and the sentry drew their swords.

Kelemvor studied his opponents. Though it wasn't his battle style, he knew he would have to fight carefully and cautiously. Dalzhel lifted his sword into a high guard, inviting a lunge. The warrior refused the bait. He had no intention of closing within arm's length of the black-haired Zhentilar.

While Kelemvor and Dalzhel stared at each other, Cyric slipped around the sentry's horse and stopped out of sword reach. The sentry advanced and stood to Kelemvor's right, much too close for the fighter's comfort.

"Kel, my friend!" Cyric said. "Meet Dalzhel. Alone, he might be your match. But at three-to-one—"

While Cyric bragged, Kelemvor evened the odds. His blade flashed once, opening a deep gash in the sentry's abdomen. Screaming in agony, the man stumbled away and collapsed.

"Two-to-one," Kelemvor corrected, bringing his sword back to guarding position.

Back with the horses, Adon heard the scream of the wounded sentry. He wrapped Kelemvor's horse's reins around a limb, then lifted his mace and urged his horse through the underbrush.

Dalzhel allowed his annoyance to flicker across his face. Kelemvor was truly dangerous, he realized. Cyric would be wiser to let him handle this fight alone. But the burly Zhentilar did not dare say that. Cyric was far too vain to accept such a suggestion.

Out of the corner of his eye, Kelemvor noticed that the seven sleeping Zhentilar had awakened. They were pulling on their helmets and gathering their weapons.

Being careful not to ignore Dalzhel, Kelemvor addressed Cyric, "Before I kill you, tell me where Midnight is."

A sneer crossed Cyric's lips. "If you've come for her, you die in vain. You, Dalzhel, and I together couldn't save her."

At that moment, Adon reached the clearing. To his right, Kelemvor faced Cyric and one other man. In the middle of field, seven Zhentilar were preparing to go to Cyric's aid. Adon decided to make sure they never arrived. The cleric knew his friend had survived two-to-one odds many times, but eight or nine-to-one would have been a challenge for even Kelemvor. The cleric kicked his mount into motion and charged.

As soon as Kelemvor heard Adon arrive, he attacked, beating Dalzhel back with a series of overhand slashes. Cyric jabbed at the warrior's side, but Kelemvor easily blocked, then sent Cyric reeling with a kick to the stomach.

Meanwhile, Adon smashed two skulls as his horse thundered through the Zhentilar camp, then turned around and charged again. This time, however, the Zhentilar were ready for him and stood in a loose group. At the last instant, Adon veered to the left. The cleric's target lifted his sword to block, but the momentum of the charging horse overpowered the defense. The sword went flying, and the mace smashed the victim's ribs. A second Zhentilar fell when Adon's horse trampled him. An instant later, the horse and rider galloped away.

On the other side of the clearing, as soon as Kelemvor kicked Cyric out of the way, Dalzhel fell upon the warrior and thrust for his abdomen. Kelemvor blocked with a low sweep, then Dalzhel's foot came from nowhere and smashed him in the head. Kelemvor's vision darkened and he felt his knees buckle. The warrior fell to his right, trying to put distance between himself and Dalzhel.

As Kelemvor dropped, Adon turned his horse around for another pass at the remaining Zhentilar. The three men stood huddled together, fear showing on their faces. "Get out of here!" Adon called, spurring his horse into a third charge.

The three Zhentilar glanced at each other uncertainly, then at the bodies of their dead and wounded fellows. An instant later, they turned and ran. Adon followed long enough to make sure they would not return. It did not occur to the cleric that Kelemvor might be in trouble.

In fact, Kelemvor was about to die. He rolled away from Dalzhel but quickly bumped into Cyric's legs. The thief immediately pressed the tip of his sword against the warrior's throat and held it there. Kelemvor did not move, expecting Cyric to say something.

Instead, the thief remained quiet, searching his old friend's eyes for signs of fear. To his disappointment, the warrior's face betrayed anger and hatred, but no fear. Though Cyric begrudgingly admired his old ally's bravery, he did not find it admirable enough to spare him.

Kelemvor saw the thief's eyes harden and knew Cyric had decided to kill him. The warrior swung his left hand and smashed his forearm into Cyric's wrist, knocking the sword away from his throat. The red blade grazed the side of the Kelemvor's neck, but didn't draw blood. At the same time, the warrior spun and swung his feet at Cyric's ankles, sweeping the thief's feet from beneath him.

As Kelemvor struggled to save his life, Adon decided the three Zhentilar would not be coming back. He swung his horse toward the other end of the clearing, turning just in time to see Cyric fall, then Kelemvor roll away. Dalzhel rushed forward to defend his fallen commander, but the green-eyed fighter rolled right into the Zhentilar's feet. Kelemvor wrapped his arms around the burly man's ankles. Dalzhel fell, cursing and beating the hilt of his sword against Kelemvor's back.

Adon spurred his horse toward the fight just as Cyric rose to his feet again.

Though he had knocked Dalzhel to the ground, Kelemvor was no match for the bearded man in unarmed combat. Not only was Dalzhel's strength greater, but he was a more experienced wrestler. Dalzhel worked his way onto Kelemvor's back and clamped his arms around the warrior's throat. Kelemvor rolled and pulled at his opponent's arm, but could not shake off the chokehold.

Cyric reached the fight before Adon. The thief hovered over the struggling pair, looking for an opportunity to plunge his blade into Kelemvor's back. A moment later, the scarred cleric rode up and Cyric turned to face him. Adon stopped twenty feet away and did not attack. Although being mounted gave him a combat advantage, it also prevented him from picking his target carefully. If he struck from horseback, he was as likely to trample Kelemvor as kill Cyric or the Zhentish soldier.

"Let him go!" Adon yelled, hefting his mace.

Dalzhel glanced at Cyric for instructions, but the thief shook his head. The burly Zhentilar continued choking Kelemvor.

"It's come down to the four of us," Cyric observed, noting that Adon had killed or chased off his men.

"I guarantee that you won't survive this, Cyric. Release Kelemvor and tell me where Midnight is," Adon threatened.

Cyric broke into a fit of maniacal laughter, thoroughly enjoying the irony of the situation. While he, Adon, and Kelemvor fought, Midnight was facing a danger far greater than death.

"What is it?" Adon demanded. "What have you done with her?"

Cyric managed to control his hysterics. "Me? I've done nothing with her," he said. "Bhaal has her—and now that we're about to kill each other, he'll keep her."

"Bhaal!" Adon yelled. "You're lying!"

Cyric waved his hand around the clearing. "Where is she?" he asked. "I'm not lying. We've all lost her."

Upon hearing this, Dalzhel relaxed his chokehold, but did not release it. Cyric's words had made him realize that this battle was senseless. Neither side had Midnight or the tablet, and he saw no profit in dying or killing over a pointless vendetta.

"I know I'm an outsider here," the burly lieutenant said, eyeing Adon and his mace. "But I'm in no hurry to die, which is what's going to happen to at least three of us."

Nobody bothered to argue. Dalzhel and Cyric clearly had Kelemvor at a disadvantage. But as soon as they killed the fighter, there would be nothing to prevent Adon from charging. From there, nobody could predict what would happen, but Dalzhel suspected that either he or Cyric would fall to the horseman.

Dalzhel continued. "And if three of us die, nobody's going to get what he wants. The survivor, if there is one, will hardly be in any condition to take the woman back from Bhaal."

"What's your point?" Kelemvor gasped.

"You and your friend are good fighters," Dalzhel said flatly. "So are Cyric and I. Together, we stand a chance of defeating Bhaal, but—"

"I'd sooner die here," Kelemvor gasped, struggling to free himself from Dalzhel's grasp.

"That's fine and good," Cyric responded. "But how does it help Midnight? If Dalzhel kills you, then Adon kills Dalzhel—"

"I'd kill you first," Adon interrupted.

"I'm sure you'd try," Cyric responded, glaring at the cleric. "But what happens to Midnight? No matter who kills who, Bhaal keeps Midnight and the tablet. Is that what you want?"

The thief's words had an effect on Kelemvor. He did not trust Cyric, but at the moment that did not matter. He was about to die, which meant he could not save Midnight. What Dalzhel proposed would give him the opportunity to help her. Kelemvor would simply have to be ready for the thief's inevitable betrayal.

"What do you think, Adon?" Kelemvor asked.

Cyric's face betrayed his surprise. The thief had little respect for the cleric's opinion, and when the three of them had traveled together, neither had Kelemvor. "Don't tell me this fool does your thinking now?" the hawk-nosed man exclaimed.

Kelemvor ignored the thief and waited for Adon's reply.

"Oh, yes. Come, friend Adon. Let's have a truce until we recover Midnight," Cyric said sarcastically. "Then we'll let her choose her own company."

There had been a time when Adon would have accepted the proposal at face value. But he was not the same naive person the thief had once known. Still, what Cyric and Dalzhel proposed was the only hope he could see for Midnight.

"We'll accept," Adon said at last. "But I know you won't keep to your word." The cleric paused for a moment, then looked into the thief's eyes. "As I said once on the Ashaba, Cyric, I know you for what you are. Don't think for a moment that we'll let our guard down."

"Then it's agreed," Cyric replied quickly, ignoring the cleric's comments. He turned to Dalzhel. "Let Kelemvor up, then let's prepare to ride with our friends—"

"We are not friends," Kelemvor warned, rubbing his throat.

Cyric smiled weakly. "As you wish."

Dalzhel retrieved his sword and sheathed it, then turned to Kelemvor. "Well met. May our blades fail before they cross again."

To Kelemvor, the archaic mercenary greeting seemed sadly appropriate. The fighter had once again found himself pursuing an uncertain goal with companions he could not trust, just like the time he had helped Lord Galroy "recover" several herds of "stolen" horses from the honest ranchers of Kulta. Just like the hundreds of other quests he had gone on for profit before his curse had been lifted.

Kelemvor sheathed his own sword and replied, "But only after we have broken our backs with bounty."

Completing the ritual with the traditional sign of respect, the two men grasped wrists and gave each other's arms a healthy tug. Kelemvor noted that Dalzhel's grip was sure and strong.

❧ 10 ❧

Boareskyr Bridge

The four riders, Cyric, Dalzhel, Adon, and Kelemvor, stopped their horses at the crest of a bluff. After three rigorous days of riding, their uneasy alliance was still intact.

The night was a moonless one. But the clouds, which were drifting into and out of different patterns of geometric precision, quivered with milky incandescence. The result was a shifting, silvery light that illuminated the land with a dusklike gleam.

The bluff overlooked the shimmering currents of the Winding Water. Ahead and to the company's left, five stone arches spanned the river: Boareskyr Bridge. In front of the bridge, the remains of a perpetual tent city hugged both sides of the road. All that remained of it now were fire scars, a few charred horses' carcasses, and the fire-blackened foundations of the city's only two permanent buildings. On both sides of the deserted settlement, brush as high as a man's head covered the river's flood plain.

Kelemvor didn't even wonder what had happened to the nomadic city. In these times of chaos, it could have been anything.

"The winged horses are over there," Adon said, pointing a hundred feet east of the bridge. Two pegasi were cavorting low in the sky.

"Then let's go," Dalzhel ordered gruffly, urging his horse forward.

Ten minutes ago, when they had first seen the pegasi, the four had debated the wisdom of chasing the winged horses. Adon had won the argument, claiming that the pegasi were as intelligent as men and might have seen some sign of Midnight and Bhaal.

Unseen to the four riders, the objects of their search were lying hidden in the closest fire-blackened foundation. Midnight was asleep, bound and gagged, her head resting on the saddlebag with the tablet. Bhaal was watching the frolicking pegasi, his eyes burning with an appetite for their lives.

Finally, the Lord of Murder could resist the temptation no longer. He decided to go after the winged horses. If Midnight tried to flee while he was gone, it was just as well. Myrkul's plan called for her to escape near Dragonspear Castle, but Bhaal could see no harm in letting her go earlier. The fallen god thought about taking the tablet with him, but decided against it. If the mage woke and found it gone, she would realize he had lied to her about it being worthless. Besides, it would only be in his way while he hunted.

Bhaal's contemplation came to an abrupt end when he heard a horse nicker in the brush ahead. The pegasi were still sailing through the air, but he was sure that the sound had come from the ground. That meant someone was out there. Without making a sound, the Lord of Murder climbed out of the foundation and disappeared into the heavy brush.

A minute later, when she was confident Bhaal had truly left her unattended, Midnight opened her eyes. She sat up and began pushing her hands back and forth in her bindings. The magic-user had been working her hands against the leather thongs all day, and had finally stretched them far enough that she now might be able to free herself.

Meanwhile, several hundred feet away, Dalzhel's horse reared at the edge of a dry gully. On the opposite bank, something rustled the spindly bushes. The Zhentish lieutenant reached for his sword, then a man's form leaped from the hedge. The horse reared again, lashing out with its forehooves. Two sharp cracks sounded as it struck the attacker.

The dark form growled, then grabbed one of the horse's forelegs. There was a hollow pop, then tendons and cartilage began cracking. When the horse dropped back to the ground, whinnying in terror and pain, it was missing a leg. Dalzhel leaped free as his mount collapsed.

On the other side of the fallen horse stood Kae Deverell's form. He hardly looked human. His body had bloated and taken on a doughy texture made more sickening by the silvery light of the luminescent clouds. Because it had been used without regard to preserving it, the body was covered with wounds and bruises from head to toe. The fecund odor of infection hung in the air around the avatar.

The four riders immediately knew they had found Bhaal—or rather, Bhaal had found them. Choking his gorge back, Kelemvor spurred his mount forward and lifted his sword. Bhaal raised his fist and rushed forward. Kelemvor transferred his free hand from the reins to the saddlehorn so he could lean down to Bhaal's level.

They met with a crash and Kelemvor's sword sliced into soft flesh. However, Bhaal's fist also found its mark. The warrior slipped from his stirrups and landed on his back. The impact knocked the breath from his lungs.

Cyric came next, leaping over Kelemvor the instant the fighter hit the ground. The thief's sword flashed. A sharp hiss sounded as its red blade bit into the avatar. Bhaal roared in anger and turned. The Lord of Murder grabbed a handful of hide, then tore a long strip of flesh off the flank of the thief's horse. Cyric's mount screeched in alarm and kicked, throwing its rider.

As Cyric fell, Bhaal retreated into the hedge on the far bank.

Adon spurred his mount forward, barely clearing Kelemvor as the warrior tried to rise. The horse's hooves landed in front of Kelemvor's nose, then Adon galloped on in pursuit of Bhaal. The cleric's horse crashed into the hedge and slowed to a dead stop, unable to penetrate the thick brush into which Bhaal had disappeared. The horse then slipped down a steep bank and stumbled, spilling Adon onto the creek's bed.

By the time the young cleric and his three companions

recovered, Bhaal was gone. Cyric's horse had run off. Kelemvor's and Adon's mounts were nervously pacing up and down the dry wash. Dalzhel's horse lay on the ground whimpering. Its left leg had been snapped off at the knee, leaving a white, rounded knob exposed.

Approaching the wounded beast from behind, Dalzhel quickly ended his mount's suffering. Afterward, he said, "No animal should have to face the likes of that."

"Nor any man," Adon replied. "But here we are."

Cyric quickly joined them. His eyes sparkled with excitement and the blade of his sword was deep red. "Dalzhel, take the point," he ordered. "Kel, Adon, take the flanks. We'll flush him out."

"And do what?" Dalzhel demanded.

The burly Zhentilar seemed a prudent and not altogether evil man, and Kelemvor had trouble understanding why Dalzhel followed the likes of Cyric. In the three days they had ridden together, Kelemvor had come to regard the man not altogether unkindly.

"We'll kill Bhaal, of course!" Cyric said.

"You're mad," Kelemvor replied, shaking his head.

Cyric turned. "Mad?" he exclaimed. The thief lifted his sword, being careful not to appear threatening. He merely wanted Kelemvor to look at the blade. "Mad? . . . perhaps. But with *this*, I wounded Bhaal. Imagine, I injured a god!"

"We chased him away," Adon said, "that's all." He picked something out of the sand, then held it up for the others to see. It was a dirty, bloated thing: a hand severed at the wrist. "We can hack the avatar to pieces, but we'll never kill Bhaal."

"No," Cyric insisted. "I can destroy him—I can feel it!"

"Maybe we'll kill Bhaal and maybe we won't," Kelemvor grumbled. "But that's not why we're here. We came to find Midnight."

"Look!" Adon pointed skyward. The clouds had arranged themselves into a mass of perfect rhombuses. But that was not what had excited the cleric. The pegasi were flying away.

"They're fleeing!" Adon said. "They must have seen Bhaal."

Kelemvor nodded. "We've got to hurry!"

"Why?" Dalzhel asked. "Adon just said we couldn't—"

"Bhaal has Midnight and the tablet. He could be leaving," the green-eyed fighter replied.

By the time Kelemvor finished the sentence, Cyric was halfway up the bank. Kelemvor was soon close behind the thief. Adon and Dalzhel had no choice except to follow.

At the top of the gully, they split into two groups. Dalzhel and Cyric took the left flank, Adon and Kelemvor the right. In the heavy brush, the two pairs soon lost sight of each other. Kelemvor and Adon moved as quietly as possible, as much to hide their position from Cyric as from Bhaal. Midnight was here somewhere. If they found her, the thief would turn on them the instant she was safe. They preferred to make that eventuality as difficult as possible.

Dalzhel's surprised yell announced that he and Cyric had found the Lord of Murder. Kelemvor and Adon went toward the scream, moving as rapidly as possible without making much noise. When they finally reached the battle, it nearly took Kelemvor by surprise. Dalzhel's burly form rushed past him a few yards ahead, his black armor gleaming in the glowing clouds' silvery light. Bhaal was only four steps behind the Zhentish lieutenant. Then came Cyric, slipping noiselessly behind the foul god, maneuvering for a surprise attack.

Kelemvor started forward, but Adon quickly pulled him back. "Let them deal with Bhaal," the cleric whispered. "We should find Midnight."

Without warning, Bhaal stopped and spun on his pursuer, jabbing at Cyric with the sharp bone protruding from his severed wrist. The fallen god followed the jab with an open-handed strike from his other hand. Cyric barely dodged the blows, then returned the attack with a wild slash and backed away.

Dalzhel finally noticed his pursuer had turned on his commander, then stopped and turned around. Moving cautiously but quickly, he advanced on Bhaal's back.

The Lord of Murder ignored the other Zhentilar and

moved toward Cyric. The god's attention was focused intently on the red blade, as if it was his only concern. The thief stopped, then made a foolhardy lunge. Bhaal dodged easily, but Cyric followed the blow with a ferocious kick and caught the avatar in the ribs.

Bhaal did not fall. Instead, he grabbed Cyric's leg and grinned. Remembering what Bhaal had done to Dalzhel's horse, the thief turned and tried to dive away. Luckily, Cyric pulled his leg free and landed in a somersault. Bhaal sneered and advanced, moving out of Dalzhel's striking range just as the Zhentilar lifted his sword.

Afraid to take the time necessary to stand, Cyric continued forward with a series of rolls. Bhaal followed three feet behind, prepared to strike the instant the thief stopped moving.

"They need help!" Kelemvor whispered.

"Do you think they'd help us?" Adon objected.

"No, but—"

"Save your strength," the cleric insisted. "Whether it's Bhaal or Cyric, there's no doubt we'll have to kill the winner."

If Cyric had been fighting the God of Assassins alone, Kelemvor would have honored Adon's wish without hesitation. The thief deserved to die. But so far, Dalzhel had treated them fairly. Kelemvor did not like standing by while the Zhentish lieutenant risked his life.

Sensing his friend's thoughts, Adon suggested a more compelling reason to stay out of the action, "Now's our best chance to free Midnight . . . while Cyric keeps Bhaal busy."

Kelemvor sighed and nodded. "Then let's go find her."

Adon started crawling around the melee.

Only two hundred feet away, Midnight had finally pulled a hand free of her bindings. A few moments earlier, she had heard a scream in the brush and knew that Bhaal was attacking someone. Though Midnight had no idea who the victim was, the magic-user wanted to help him. She freed herself from the leather thongs and her gag, gingerly laid the saddlebags over her raw shoulder, then peered over the edge of the foundation.

As Kelemvor and Adon circled around the battle, the warrior could not help pausing to watch. Dalzhel finally caught Bhaal and swung with his mightiest stroke. His blade whistled straight for the avatar's neck.

The Lord of Murder ducked the attack with casual ease. He turned and met Dalzhel with his stump, plunging the sharp bone deep into the soldier's shoulder. Dalzhel screamed and dropped his sword, but did not fall or retreat. Instead, the Zhentilar stepped forward to wrestle the god, tearing at the avatar's eyes with his left hand.

Cyric used this respite to good effect, standing and moving toward Bhaal. Once again, the avatar had turned his back to the thief. Cyric lifted his sword and charged, hoping to take advantage of the distraction Dalzhel provided by wrestling with the fallen god.

Adon grabbed Kelemvor's shoulder, tearing his attention away from the battle. "Who's that?"

The cleric pointed at a dark silhouette creeping toward the battle on its hands and knees. Through the heavy brush and in the dim light, Kelemvor could not see the shadow well enough to see who it was, or even if it was a man or a woman.

"I can't tell," Kelemvor said softly. "But whoever it is, he's interested in this fight." He glanced back to the battle.

Cyric was at Bhaal's back. The thief attacked with a vicious slash he hoped would cleave the avatar down to the breast bone. But Bhaal heard him coming and, easily breaking free of Dalzhel's hold, pivoted out of the way. The God of Assassins caught Cyric's arm, then used the thief's own momentum to throw him ten feet into the brush.

As Cyric sailed past, Dalzhel snatched his sword off the ground, then plunged the blade into the avatar's rib cage. Bhaal snarled and kicked the Zhentish soldier in the stomach. Dalzhel fell backward and landed with a crash.

The Lord of Murder casually plucked Dalzhel's sword from between his ribs and tossed it aside. Then he leaped onto his opponent's prone form, thrusting the splintered stump of his wrist into Dalzhel's throat. Dalzhel screamed once, then fell quiet.

Cyric scrambled to his feet, shaking his head. He had heard Dalzhel's scream and knew that Bhaal had killed his lieutenant. Though the thief did not feel anything resembling grief, there was a hollow sensation in the pit of his stomach. Dalzhel had been a valuable aid, and Cyric would miss his service.

Upon hearing the terrible scream, Midnight knew Bhaal had killed again. Then, through the brush, she saw the avatar rise and turn toward another victim. The magic-user could not see who Bhaal was attacking, for the evening's silvery light was too dim to reveal his face at this distance. But whoever it was, Midnight did not want to abandon him to the fallen god.

The magic-user summoned the incantation for a lightning bolt. Since imprisoning Bhaal at High Horn, she had not used her magic successfully. There was no reason to believe it would work now, but that did not matter. She could not help Bhaal's victims any other way, and if she did nothing, the Lord of Murder would kill them anyway. As soon as the proper gestures and words came to mind, the magic-user stood and pointed at the avatar.

Adon and Kelemvor both saw the silhouette rise, then they heard a feminine voice reciting an incantation.

"Magic!" The men hissed the words in the same instant. They pressed their bodies flat to the ground. Neither knew what to expect, but both were sure it would be hazardous.

Midnight finished her incantation and a lightning bolt shot from her finger. Then, it abruptly gathered into a brilliant ball of sputtering light. The bright sphere rose over the thicket, hanging behind Kelemvor and Adon like a tiny star. The shining globe illuminated the ground within a hundred yards as clearly as if it were the midday sun.

In the bright light, Kelemvor and Adon immediately recognized the dark-haired spellcaster. "Midnight!" they cried, rising simultaneously.

Bhaal and Cyric also noticed the tiny sun's appearance,

but could not see what had caused it. The globe hung between them and Midnight. All they could see was a circle of brilliant light.

Cyric swore, then focused all of his attention on the avatar. He did not know what had caused the light. What he did know was that, without Dalzhel's aid, he was no longer a match for the Lord of Murder. The thief wasted no time cursing Kelemvor and Adon for abandoning him. He knew he'd been a fool for expecting them to come to his aid.

After squinting at the miniature sun for a moment, the Lord of Murder nonchalantly turned back to the thief and advanced. Cyric slashed. Bhaal easily dodged, slapping the thief's sword hand aside. Cyric kicked, hoping to keep his attacker away. The avatar blocked the foot, then stepped in close and clipped his opponent's jaw with a fist as hard as stone.

Cyric's ears rang and his head swam. He tried to swing his sword, but Bhaal hit him once more. The thief felt his body going limp. The Lord of Murder struck his jaw again, then his stomach, then continued pummeling Cyric until he dropped his weapon and flopped to the ground in a half-conscious heap.

While Bhaal battered Cyric, Adon and Kelemvor rushed toward Midnight. The magic-user's miscast lightning bolt hung at their backs, its overpowering glow casting their faces into deep shadows. It did not matter. Midnight recognized their voices and rushed to meet them.

"How did you find me?" the raven-haired mage cried, hugging Kelemvor. She spun him around so the miniature sun was at her back and she could see his face. "Never mind. It's just good to see both of you. I'm so glad you're still—"

The magic-user broke off in midsentence. She was going to say "alive," which returned her thoughts to whoever was currently fighting the God of Assassins. She still had not seen his face.

"Who's fighting Bhaal?" she asked, hooking a thumb over her shoulder. She still could not take her eyes off Kelemvor's face.

Kelemvor and Adon looked toward the fight, squinting against the glare of the miniature sun. "Cyric," Kelemvor answered. "We're working together—"

Midnight raised an eyebrow. "Together?"

"It's a long story," Adon said. "We don't have time to explain—"

The miniature sun flared brilliant white, sending daggers of pain through the eyes of both Kelemvor and Adon. Then a thunderclap sounded and a shock wave knocked them to the ground.

After the blinding flash, the thicket grew relatively dim. Only the silvery incandescence of the geometric clouds lit the brush. Bhaal dropped Cyric, battered and bloody, and looked to where the globe of light had been.

Fifty feet away, Midnight was picking herself up off the ground, but her two companions still lay holding their hands over their eyes.

"You escaped," Bhaal called to the mage. "I'll have to punish you for that."

Without responding, Midnight looked from Bhaal to Cyric's bruised and bloodied body, then back to the avatar's face. Without taking her eyes off the vile god, she retrieved the saddlebags from where they had fallen, then laid them over her shoulder. To her friends, she hissed, "Get up!"

But Kelemvor and Adon had been looking toward the ball of light when it had burst. When they opened their eyes, they saw nothing but white.

"I'm blind!" Kelemvor cried.

To his left, Adon groaned. "I—I can't see anything either!"

"Then be quiet!" Midnight said. "Don't draw attention to yourselves."

The magic-user did not need to worry. Bhaal was thinking about other things. It had never occurred to him that, upon slipping her bonds, Midnight would not flee immediately. Now he had to recapture her or the woman would know that he had let her escape. If that happened, she might figure out what he and Myrkul really wanted from her. The fallen god walked toward Midnight.

"Stay where you are," Midnight warned.

Bhaal snickered. "Why? You don't have the power to kill me—yet."

Before Kelemvor's eyes, the white faded to gray. Perhaps his blindness was temporary.

"We've got to do something," Adon whispered. His vision had returned enough so that he could vaguely see a shape advancing toward Midnight.

"What?" Kelemvor responded.

"Attack. Perhaps Midnight—"

"We can't. I'm still blind!"

Adon fell silent, knowing Kelemvor was right. Unable to see clearly, they would only get in the way.

As the Lord of Murder walked toward the mage, Cyric began to stir. The thief was surprised he was still alive, for Bhaal's blows had felt like hammer strikes. He ached from head to toe, and the simple act of breathing sent waves of agony through his torso. Still, Cyric knew that if he did not act, he would lose his chance to capture Midnight and the Tablet of Fate.

He retrieved his sword. "You've tasted Bhaal's blood," he whispered. "If you want more, help me."

Yes, more, the sword responded. *I'll help you.* The words came to mind in a sultry female voice.

The sword's hilt warmed in his hand and Cyric felt vigor and strength flow back into his body. He rose to his knees, then stood and stumbled after the Lord of Murder.

Bhaal stopped moving forward. "Surrender, Midnight." As an afterthought, he added, "And give me the tablet."

"No," Midnight replied, stepping away.

"You have no choice," Bhaal said, gesturing at Kelemvor's prone form.

Midnight summoned the incantation for another lightning bolt, then pointed at Bhaal. "I have plenty of choices. Most of them involve killing you."

The Lord of Murder studied the woman, uncomfortably, knowing she might be able to carry out her threat. "Destroying my avatar will kill your friends—and possibly you, too," the god said. "You know that."

Midnight frowned, remembering the immense power that Torm and Bane's destruction had unleashed outside Tantras. And Mystra's death had leveled a castle in Cormyr. This time, at least, Bhaal was telling the truth. She could not kill him without destroying her friends.

Then she saw Cyric creeping up behind Bhaal, his sword poised to strike. The thief's body looked battered beyond recognition. Midnight found it incredible that Cyric could still move, much less move as silently as he did.

"You have no choice," the Lord of Murder repeated.

Before Bhaal could notice she was looking elsewhere, Midnight returned her attention to the god's face.

"I'll destroy you anyway," she said. "What do I have to lose?"

Cyric was only two steps away from Bhaal. Midnight let the lightning bolt drop from her mind, then called the incantation for a teleportation spell. The mage knew that her plan was born of desperation, for she could not remember the last time her magic had worked properly. But if it worked at all, the results would be better than surrendering to Bhaal—or dying in the explosion if Cyric's attack was successful.

Bhaal twisted Deverell's torn lips into a smile. "If you do as I ask, your friends will live."

Cyric's boot scraped a rock. The avatar's face betrayed alarm and he whirled. The thief brought his red blade down and plunged it deep into Bhaal's breast.

"You fool!" the Lord of Murder screamed.

The blade's color deepened to vibrant burgundy, and the fallen god howled in rage. His roar was as loud as thunder and as eerie as the wail of a ghost.

"At least I killed a god before I died," Cyric said triumphantly through clenched teeth. At the same time, the raven-haired mage uttered the words to her incantation.

Bhaal's scream ended and his body exploded. Then the earth dropped away beneath Midnight and her allies.

* * * * *

A flickering ocher flame. A candle stuck in a bottle in the center of a wooden table, its wood, gray and cracked and as dry as tinder. A flimsy, unpadded chair in a dark, wet room hidden in the sewers of Waterdeep.

This was what his glory had come to.

Ao would pay, Myrkul swore. The Lord of the Dead did not enjoy modesty in accommodation, he did not enjoy hiding from mortals, and he most certainly did not enjoy being confined to the Realms. For all these indignities, Ao—and Helm—would pay.

But he had to be careful. The Lord of the Dead had seen what came of carelessness. Tantras had been a disaster, and it had only been through his foresight that Myrkul had not suffered the same fate as Bane. He was in the realm of mortals now. In a certain sense he was mortal, for now he could perish—as Bane and Mystra and Torm had perished.

Imagine, the Ruler of the Dead dying. The thought would have made Myrkul laugh, had it not been so unnerving.

No, it would not do to go meeting rivals head-to-head. He had to remain hidden, where enemies could not find him, where they had no reason to suspect his presence. He had to work through agents, to plot out intricate plans and alternate contingencies, as he had concerning Midnight and the Tablets of Fate.

It would have been a simple matter to kill the dark-haired magic-user and take the tablet she held. The Lord of the Dead had agents and priests all over the land, and no one could survive the unrelenting series of attacks he could bring to bear. But then his followers would have had to deliver the tablet to him in Waterdeep, and none were as capable a deliveryperson as Midnight.

Of course, Myrkul had no intention of letting the woman keep the tablet. He would not feel secure until both Tablets of Fate were in his hands. Indirectly, that was why he had not ordered the magic-user's death. He needed her to go to Bone Castle and recover the second tablet, too.

The Lord of the Dead had plans within plans, and they all depended on the woman. Bhaal had simply wanted to capture Midnight's entire company, then use her friends as hostages to force her to recover the second tablet. But so far, Midnight had displayed an alarming fortitude, and Myrkul believed she would easily thwart such crude methods of persuasion. It was wiser to trick her into doing his will, to make her think that retrieving the second tablet was her idea. To accomplish this, Bhaal had captured her, then let her "trick" him into revealing the second tablet's hiding place.

Even this plan had a weakness, and the Lord of the Dead was not blind to it. Once the woman had both tablets, she could easily return them to Helm. To prevent that, Myrkul had instructed Bhaal to let her escape near Dragonspear Castle once sne knew about the castle's hidden entrance to the Realm of the Dead.

At Dragonspear, Myrkul had prepared a trap to recover the first tablet. This trap would also force Midnight to go to the Realm of the Dead to recover the tablet in Bone Castle. Of course, no strategy could foresee every eventuality. That was why Myrkul made a habit of contacting Bhaal to confirm that everything was proceeding according to plan.

The Lord of the Dead concentrated on the candlelight. The flame wavered and flared. Myrkul waited, expecting it to coalesce itself into the ugly, bloated head of Bhaal's avatar.

But the flame remained a flame.

Myrkul tried once more to work his variation of a commune spell, and again the flame remained a flame. The Lord of the Dead considered the possibility that magical chaos had caused his spell to fail, but rejected the idea. If the failure had been due to chaos, the magic would likely have misfired somehow. His spell had simply failed to go off.

That could only mean Bhaal had perished. The avatar had been destroyed and the Lord of Murder's essence had been dispersed through the Realms and the Planes. The thought distressed Myrkul, and not only because it reminded him of his own mortality. Of all the gods, perhaps he and Bhaal had been the closest. Bhaal presided over the process of death and killing, while Myrkul had dominion over those already dead. Theirs was a symbiotic relationship. One could hardly exist without the other.

Myrkul allowed himself a moment of distress for his fellow god's passing, then turned his thoughts back to his plans. The last time they had communed, Bhaal had reported that the woman knew about the entrance to the Realm of the Dead. Therefore, she would be going toward Dragonspear Castle. His plan remained unchanged, save that the woman would arrive at the castle unescorted. He could still spring his surprise and separate her from the first tablet.

But Myrkul was far from happy. If she had defeated Bhaal, Midnight possessed the power to counter his trap and take the first tablet with her into the Realm of the Dead. Then, if she succeeded at Bone Castle, she would have both tablets. After returning to the Realms, it would be a simple matter to find a Celestial Stairway and present them to Helm.

If that happened, Myrkul would be defeated.

He and Bane were the ones who had stolen the Tablets of Fate. By now, Ao had surely discovered that, and Myrkul doubted there would be a reward if he returned what he had stolen in the first place. Though the Lord of the Dead had not revealed this to Bhaal, he had no use for either of the tablets. His sole purpose for recovering them was to be sure that no one ever returned them to the Planes, for Myrkul suspected the overlord of the gods would destroy him as soon as the tablets were recovered.

But the Lord of the Dead knew that preventing the return of the tablets was a temporary solution. Sooner or later, Ao would grow tired of waiting and deal out his punishment anyway. If Myrkul wanted to survive, he had to strike first. And that was why, through another complicated series of plots, the Lord of the Dead had arranged for Midnight to recover the second tablet.

After stealing the Tablets of Fate, Myrkul and Bane had each taken one and hidden it away. Bane had placed his in

Tantras. Myrkul had hidden his tablet in Bone Castle, in the heart of the Realm of the Dead. To prevent anybody from stealing the artifact, the Lord Myrkul had placed a trap on it.

The minute Midnight took the second tablet out of the Realm of the Dead, she would release the realm's denizens and all the spirits of the dead. When that happened, Myrkul intended to be waiting. He would kill Midnight and take the second tablet from her. Then, utilizing the same methods he used to power Bane's avatar in Tantras, he would harness the souls of the dead—this time for his own avatar.

After that, he would be prepared to meet Ao. Myrkul was far from certain that even given the energy of millions of souls, he would prevail. Above all, the Lord of the Dead hated to reveal himself to his enemies. Still, this desperate plan was his only chance to turn defeat into victory.

But, if Midnight took her tablet to the Realm of the Dead, Myrkul's plan would grow even more dangerous. When she returned to the Realms with both tablets, it would prove difficult to find her in the confusion accompanying the emergence of his denizens. The mage would be able to slip away and take the tablets to Helm.

The safest plan, Myrkul knew, was to make sure she did not take the first tablet into the Realm of the Dead with her. He would have to take extra precautions at Dragonspear Castle to insure the mage lost the tablet she had recovered in Tantras.

* * * * *

The sword remained in his hand. Cyric knew that and no more. His thoughts drifted aimlessly through the fog that had become his mind.

He felt as though he had been beaten to death.

Fists. Fists as hard as stone. Bhaal, beating him senseless, smashing his jaw and ribs and nose, finally stopping and leaving the job undone. Then Cyric remembered rising to his feet, despite his serious injuries, and stabbing the Lord of Murder.

That had been his undoing. The avatar had turned white

and flashed into oblivion. Cyric wondered where he himself was now. Probably the Realm of the Dead, he thought for an instant.

No, he was alive. His head hurt too much, and the agony in his ribs came only when he breathed. He felt as though he had been trampled.

The hawk-nosed man opened his eyes and found it was dark. He lay face down in snow, apparently in the middle of a road. Around him, three figures were rising to their feet.

"Where are we?" Adon asked, studying the snow-covered fields on both sides of the road. His vision had completely recovered.

"Farther up the road to Waterdeep, I hope," Midnight answered wearily. "That's where I was trying to take us, anyway." Her limbs felt heavy with fatigue. Her last incantation had been taxing on her body.

"How'd we get here?" Kelemvor muttered, rubbing his eyes. His vision had partially returned, but the fighter still saw spots of light dancing across the snowy landscape.

"I teleported us," the mage replied. "Don't ask me to explain how."

Cyric decided to remain motionless. He was outnumbered three-to-one and doubted that he could have moved even if he tried. With the return of full consciousness, his pain had grown worse.

Kelemvor chuckled, a bit nervously. "It's good to see you again!" he said, hugging Midnight. Back at Boareskyr Bridge, their initial greeting had been too hurried for his liking. "I can hardly believe you're alive!"

"Why should that surprise you?" Midnight asked, returning his hug warmly.

Assuming a stern tone, Adon grumbled, "After the way you ran off—"

"It's a good thing I did," Midnight interrupted, freeing herself from Kelemvor. She could not believe how quickly the cleric's condescending manner had set her nerves on edge. "Or you'd both be dead!"

"We'd be dead?" Adon exclaimed, stepping backward in

frustration. "Bhaal didn't—"

Before the cleric finished, he tripped over Cyric and crashed to the ground. Only Adon's scream of astonishment kept the wounded thief's muffled groan from being heard. Cyric kept his eyes closed and did not move. His only hope was to convince his rivals that he was harmless.

Kelemvor came over and casually kicked Cyric's body. "Look what's lying here in the road like a dungheap!" the warrior growled. He felt the pulse in Cyric's neck. "And he's alive!"

The thief made sure he had a solid grip on his sword.

"Cyric!" Adon hissed, standing and turning to Midnight. "Why'd you bring him?"

"Believe me, it wasn't intentional," Midnight snapped, frowning at the thief's immobile body. "Besides, I thought you were working with him."

"We were," Kelemvor said. His sword scraped free of its scabbard. "But we're finished with that now."

Cyric peeked out of a half-opened eye, trying to find the strength to lift his sword.

Adon stepped between Kelemvor's blade and Cyric's body. "We can't kill him in cold blood."

"What?" the warrior demanded. "Ten minutes ago, you wouldn't let me fight Bhaal with him." He tried to step around the cleric.

"At that time, he was dangerous to us," Adon said, shuffling to keep himself between the warrior's sword and the motionless thief. "That's not true any longer."

"I saw him slay a drowning halfling and torture another," Midnight objected, pointing an accusing finger at Cyric's head.

"We can't kill him while he's helpless," Adon insisted. He looked past Kelemvor and addressed the magic-user.

Midnight, however, was not easily convinced. "Cyric deserves to die."

"It's not our right to judge our fellows," Adon said softly, still holding off the fighter. "Any more than it was the right of the Harpers to condemn you and I to death."

Kelemvor frowned at that memory, then sheathed his weapon. During the Battle of Shadowdale, Elminster had disappeared. The locals had leaped to the conclusion that someone had murdered the sage, then falsely accused Adon and Midnight of the crime. Had Cyric not broken them out of jail, the pair would have been executed.

"This is different," Midnight insisted. "He betrayed us, and he played me for a fool." She reached for Kelemvor's sword.

The warrior placed a restraining hand on his hilt. "No," he said. "Adon's right."

"If we kill him," Adon said, waving a hand at Cyric's help-less form. "We're murderers—just like he is. Do you want that?"

Midnight pondered that for a moment, then jerked her hand away from the sword. "Leave him, then. He'll die any-way." She turned and started up the road.

Kelemvor looked to Adon for instruction.

"We shouldn't kill a helpless man," the cleric said. "But we don't have to help him, either. He can't do us any more harm. He's lost his men and if we hurry, we'll put some miles between us before he wakes up." He started after Midnight. "Let's hurry, before she disappears again."

They caught Midnight quickly, then Kelemvor asked, "Where are we going?"

Midnight paused.

Though just barely, she was still within Cyric's earshot. Had she looked at the thief, she might have noticed him turning his head to hear her answer.

"*I'm* going to Dragonspear Castle," the raven-haired mage said, her hands on her hips.

"Then we're all going to Dragonspear Castle," Adon noted calmly. "Are Kelemvor and I going to have to split the watch to keep you from sneaking off, Midnight?"

"The gods themselves are against me," the magic-user warned, looking from the cleric to Kelemvor, then back again. "You'll be risking your lives."

"We'd be risking more by leaving you alone," Adon retorted, a smile growing on his face.

Kelemvor caught Midnight's elbow and turned her so he could look straight into her eyes. "Gods or no gods," he said firmly, "I'm with you, Midnight."

Midnight was warmed by the devotion of her friends, but still was not ready to accept their offer. Though she was talking to both Adon and Kelemvor, she looked only into the warrior's eyes as she spoke. "The choice is yours, but you'd better hear me out before you decide. Somewhere below Dragonspear Castle, there's a bridge to the Realm of the Dead."

"In Waterdeep?" Kelemvor cried incredulously. He was thinking of the city's famous cemetery, which was properly known as "The City of the Dead."

"No, the *Realm* of the Dead," the mage corrected. Then Midnight looked at Adon. "The other tablet is in Myrkul's castle."

Kelemvor and Adon stared at each other in dumfounded silence, hardly believing that she meant the resting place of souls.

"Don't feel bad if you choose to go home," Midnight replied, interpreting their astonishment as hesitancy. She gently removed her elbow from Kelemvor's grasp. "I really don't think you should come anyway."

"I thought the choice was ours," Adon said, snapping out of his shock.

"Aye! You're not going to lose us that easy," Kelemvor added, taking Midnight by the arm again.

It was Midnight's turn to be astonished. She had not allowed herself to hope that Kelemvor and Adon would *want* to accompany her. But now that they had declared their intention to do just that, she felt less lonely and immeasurably more confident. Midnight threw herself into Kelemvor's arms and kissed him long and hard.

❧ 11 ❧

Dragonspear Castle

The rise was so gentle Adon hardly knew he was walking uphill. Halfway up, the cleric stopped and shifted the saddlebags with the tablet to his other shoulder. It was the most exciting thing he had done in almost four hours.

Along with Kelemvor and Midnight, Adon had been traveling along the desolate road for five days. To the west, coarse stems of tall golden grass rose from a prairie of wet, slushy snow. A mile to the east stood the dark cliffs of the High Moor. Ahead, running mile after mile, was the straight and endlessly boring road to Waterdeep. Adon had never thought he would long to feel a steep mountainside beneath his feet, but right now he would have gladly traded a mile of easy road for twenty miles of precarious mountain trail.

Despite a hard morning's march, Adon's toes were shriveled and numb. Three inches of slushy snow covered the road, soaking through even the well-oiled boots High Horn's quartermaster had provided. Judging from the pearly complexion of the sky, more snow would soon fall.

Even accounting for their northward progress, the season had changed early this year. A white shroud already blanketed the High Moor, and sheets of ice crowned the streams that poured from the wild country's heart.

Adon felt as if the nature gods were conspiring to make his journey difficult and cold. It was far more likely, he realized, that the unseasonable cold was a reflection of the absence of those gods. Without their supervision, nature was running rampant, randomly changing as one mindless force gained supremacy over another.

The unpredictable weather was just one more reason he and his companions had to succeed in their quest. Without an orderly progression of the seasons, it would not be long before the farmers lost their crops and whole populations starved.

As Adon pondered the importance of his mission and the dreariness of completing it, a sharp bark sounded from the other side of the rise. He immediately turned and waved Kelemvor and Midnight off the road, then began searching for a hiding place himself. The land was so barren he finally had to settle for kneeling behind a scraggly bush.

A band of gray appeared at the top of the rise. The cleric squinted and looked closer. Twelve wolves were walking abreast in a straight line. Another rank followed the first, and then another and another, until a whole column of wolves was marching down the road in perfect step.

As the column advanced, Adon wondered whether he should run or continue hiding behind his pathetic bush. One of the wolves barked a sharp command. The first line drew abreast of the cleric's hiding place, then each wolf snapped its head to face him in a perfect dress left maneuver. Each succeeding line repeated the drill as it passed.

Adon gave up hiding and returned to the roadside, shaking his head in disbelief. Kelemvor and Midnight joined him.

"Nice parade work," the fighter noted, observing the wolves with a critical eye. His voice was as casual as if the trio had been watching an army of men instead of animals.

With studied disinterest, Midnight asked, "I wonder where they're off to?"

"Baldur's Gate or Elturel," Kelemvor observed, turning and looking to the south.

"How would you know that?" Adon demanded, frowning at the warrior.

"You haven't heard?" Midnight asked. She lifted her brows to indicate incredulity at Adon's ignorance.

"The sheep are revolting in the south," Kelemvor finished.

The cleric put his hands on his hips. "What are—"

Both Kelemvor and Midnight burst into fits of laughter.

Adon flushed angrily, and turned toward the road.

"There's nothing funny about the breakdown of Order," he snapped.

Midnight and Kelemvor only laughed harder.

Adon turned away, but after five minutes of watching the column pass, he chuckled. "Sheep revolt," he muttered. "Where did you come up with that?"

"Why else would you need an army of wolves?" Kelemvor asked, grinning.

Finally, the last rank of wolves passed, leaving the trail black and muddy. Kelemvor stepped back onto the road and sank past the ankles in cold muck.

He cursed, then said, "We need horses."

"True, but what can we do?" Adon asked, stepping into the road. "We'll never find horses out here, and if we stray off the road, we're likely to get very lost."

In five days of marching, they had met only one small band of six hardy warriors. Although the small company had been kind enough to confirm that Dragonspear Castle lay ahead, they had refused to part with even a single horse.

"At this rate, the Realms will be dead a year before we make Dragonspear Castle," Kelemvor complained, his humor now completely drained.

"Don't be so sure," Adon responded. "We should be close. It might be over the top of that rise." The cleric was determined not to let the fighter's sudden bad mood infect him.

Kelemvor snorted and kicked at the mud, sending a black spray toward the roadside. "Close? We're not within a hundred miles of the castle."

Adon stifled an acid reply. Despite Midnight's return, the cleric still found himself serving as company leader. It was not a position he enjoyed, but Kelemvor had shown more interest in keeping Midnight company than in assuming command. As for the mage, she seemed content to let someone else guide them, though it should be her, by all rights, who was the group's leader. Adon didn't understand why the magic-user shirked the responsibility, though he suspected the reason might concern Kelemvor. Perhaps she feared the fighter could not love a taskmaster. Whatever the cause, Adon was left to play the captain. He felt distinctly uncomfortable in the role, but he was determined to do his best.

"I'm sure Dragonspear Castle is close by," Adon said, hoping to buoy Kelemvor's spirits. "All we've got to do is keep putting one foot in front of the other."

"*You* put one foot in front of the other," Kelemvor snapped. He turned to Midnight. "You got us away from Boareskyr with a wave of your hand. Why don't you try again?"

Midnight shook her head. "I've thought of that. But it's risky to teleport—especially with magic so fouled up. I only did it because we would have died anyway. We're lucky we didn't appear in the middle of the Great Desert."

"How do we know we didn't?" Kelemvor muttered.

Midnight stepped onto the edge of the muddy road and started up the rise. "I'm sure," she said.

Midnight was relieved that the teleport incantation had worked, and not only because it had saved their lives. It was the first time that her magic had worked correctly since High Horn. In Yellow Snake Pass, her wall of fire had resulted in harmless stalks of smoke, and at the ford she had animated the ropes by accident. Even at Boareskyr Bridge, her first incantation had failed pathetically, producing a ball of light in place of a lightning bolt.

The mage had feared that she misunderstood the change in her relationship to magic. When she summoned an incantation, only words and gestures appeared in her mind—never any indication of the proper material component or what to do with it. At first, this had disturbed Midnight and she had feared that she was misinterpreting something. But each time she tried to cast a spell, there was never a need for material components. The magic-user had finally decided that, because she tapped the magic weave directly, no intermediary agent—like a spell component—was required to transmit the mystical energy.

The horizon suddenly seemed distant and Midnight realized that she had reached the crest of the gentle rise. She paused to look around. Even though it was barely noticeable, the rise was the highest ground nearby and afforded a view of the terrain ahead.

Twenty yards behind the magic-user, Adon was still trying to encourage Kelemvor. "For all we know, we're only ten miles away from Dragonspear Castle."

"Actually," Midnight interrupted, studying a sprawling ruin to the right of the road, "I'd say we're closer than that."

Adon and Kelemvor looked up, then rushed to her side. Nestled against the base of the High Moor, atop three small hillocks, stood the deteriorating walls and toppled spires of an abandoned citadel. From this distance, it was difficult to say how large the castle was, but it might have rivaled the fortress at High Horn.

"What have we here?" Kelemvor asked. He was looking down the road, but neither Midnight nor Adon noticed.

"Dragonspear Castle, what else?" Adon replied. He had no way of confirming his guess, but he suspected there were no other ruins of such size on the way to Waterdeep.

"Not the castle," Kelemvor snapped. He pointed down the road, where, over a mile away, ten caravan drivers had just left the trail. They were slowly fleeing toward the ruined castle, pursued by a dozen sluggish attackers.

"Someone's attacking a caravan!" Midnight exclaimed.

"The battle's not moving very fast," Adon said, watching the two groups. "Maybe the attackers are undead."

"You're probably right," Kelemvor said, turning to look at the cleric. "And the drivers are moving slowly because they're probably tired after a long chase." The warrior's eyes betrayed his desire to intercede.

Adon silently cursed his companion. While the trio could easily destroy one or two undead, there were a dozen attacking the caravan. Even with Midnight's magic, they could not defeat so many creatures. He wished Kelemvor would consider the value of their own lives, as most men would. But the fighter was no longer a common man—if he ever had been. A common man would not be looking for the entrance to the Realm of the Dead, nor would he have undertaken a mission that made such a journey necessary.

"We can't get involved," Adon said thoughtfully, pretending to think aloud. "If we get killed, the Realms will perish."

Adon suspected that Midnight would not involve herself with the caravan if he said not to. But Kelemvor would resent an order to abandon the drivers. Therefore, the cleric wanted the fighter to make the decision for himself. Besides, Adon had no wish to let the burden of abandoning the caravan rest upon his shoulders alone.

Midnight studied the scene for a full minute, weighing Adon's words against her desire to help. If they abandoned the drivers, she would feel guilty for the rest of her life. But the mage also knew that helping could endanger the tablet.

"We can't interfere," she said, turning away. "There's too much at risk."

Adon breathed a sigh of relief.

"I don't know about you two," Kelemvor grumbled, eyeing his companions with disapproval, "but I can't abandon innocents to their deaths. I've done that too often—"

"Think with your head, not your heart, Kel." Midnight's words were surprisingly gentle. She laid a hand upon his arm. "With the gods themselves against us, we cannot—"

"But they'll die!" Kelemvor objected, pulling his arm free. "And if you allow that, you're no better than Cyric."

Nothing could anger the mage more than being compared to Cyric. "Do what you want," she snapped. "But do it without me!"

Midnight's outburst upset Kelemvor, but he didn't let that prevent him from starting toward the battle. Before Kelemvor had taken a dozen steps, Adon called, "Wait!"

The cleric could not allow the company to separate again. No matter what danger lay ahead, they stood a better chance of survival if they faced it together. "We can't let the undead into the castle, or we'll be cut off from the Realm of the Dead."

"True," Midnight muttered grudgingly. She didn't know whether to be angry that Kelemvor had forced Adon to change his mind, or to be happy that the cleric had found a way to justify saving the caravan.

"As slow as the battle's moving, we can reach the castle before the undead." Adon sighed. "Perhaps we'll find the inner ward in defensible condition."

"If we do," Kelemvor said, "we'll let the drivers in and keep the undead outside. That's the caravan's best chance—"

"And ours," Midnight agreed. She had misgivings about intervening in the fight, but at least Kelemvor was willing to do it safely. "If we're going to do this, we'd better hurry." The three companions started toward the castle at a trot.

Ten minutes later, a lone rider approached the top of the rise. After his one-time friends had abandoned him, Cyric had crawled off the road. There, sustained by the vigor of the sword, he had fallen into a slumber more deep and profound than he believed possible. It had not been a peaceful sleep, filled as it was by the stench of death and the screeches of the damned, but it had been a restorative one.

Then, after two days of walking, he had met the same six riders that Midnight's company had passed. The thief recited a cleverly fabricated story of how the trio had robbed him and left him for dead. The riders sympathetically reported that the scoundrels were on the road ahead. Despite Cyric's clever story, however, they refused to give him one of their horses. Instead, they offered to allow him to ride with them until they reached the nearest stable. That same night, the thief had killed all six—five of them in their sleep. Then, taking a horse, a bow, and a quiver of arrows, he had turned north after Midnight's company and the tablet.

When Cyric reached the top of the rise, he realized that he had caught his enemies just in time. Dragonspear Castle stood to the right of the road, and Midnight's company was just slipping into the outer ward. Then the thief saw the caravan moving toward the gate, their awkward attackers following. Noting that there was about to be a battle, Cyric strung his stolen bow and spurred his stolen mount. He did not want to miss the chance to put a few arrows in his old friends' backs.

In the outer ward of Dragonspear Castle, Midnight had

almost given up any hope of defending the crumbled fortress. The outer wall was so pocked with holes and breaches that nothing short of an army could man it. Fortunately, the inner ward was in better condition. All four of its towers still stood, and the walls remained more or less intact. The inner gate hung askew on its hinges, but looked as though it could still be closed.

After a quick inspection, Kelemvor declared, "We can hold the inner ward. Midnight, go to the southwest tower and let us know when the caravan reaches the outer wall." The warrior stepped behind the inner gate and inspected the hinges. "Adon and I will close this when the time comes."

Midnight quickly climbed to the top of the wall, then went to the southwest tower. It was the tallest and most secure of Dragonspear's remaining towers. A spiral stairway ran along the wall facing the courtyard, and the only entrances to its rooms were from the staircase. The stairway itself had only two entrances, one from the top of the wall and one from the courtyard. At one time, each entrance could be sealed in case the courtyard or walls were overrun, but the doors had been battered off their hinges long ago.

Midnight entered the tower's staircase and climbed to the top room. It had once served as the office of someone important, perhaps the steward or bailiff. A heavy, age-worn desk sat near the door, and the remnants of tapestries, now moth-eaten and faded, hung on two walls. In the center of the room hung a rusting iron chandelier, three of its sockets still containing the stubs of ancient and yellowed candles. So that the chandelier could be lit easily, it was suspended by a grimy rope running through a pulley system and tied off to an eyehook in the wall.

The room had two small windows. One overlooked the outer ward, and through it, Midnight could see the path from the outer gate to the inner. Through the other window, she could see the inner ward and the inner gate.

Kelemvor and Adon had found a long beam and were using it to lever the gate closed. Midnight could see that there would always be a gap between the gate and the wall, but she still felt more secure. The gate would certainly make the inner ward defensible.

Despite her increased sense of safety, though, Midnight was upset with Kelemvor for dragging the company into this conflict. To satisfy the warrior's sense of virtue, he was risking all of their lives and letting the fate of the world hang in the balance. Still, Midnight wasn't surprised. The fighter had always been a shortsighted, stubborn man, and that had not changed when Bane lifted his curse. The only difference was that, instead of seeking payment for even the slightest favor, he now insisted upon correcting each and every iniquity he encountered.

Even if it was frustrating and inconvenient, Midnight thought she could live with Kelemvor's stubbornness, but only after the tablets were returned to the Planes. Until then, even if it meant distancing herself from her lover, she could not let her feelings interfere with her duty any longer.

But at the moment, Midnight's duty was to make sure her friends were not surprised when the caravan arrived. As long as she continued watching Kelemvor and Adon, she was neglecting that duty. The magic-user turned to the other window.

Fifteen minutes later, the first caravan driver reached the outer gate, leading a string of four frightened packhorses. Midnight saw no sign of his undead pursuers, though she had not expected to. Zombies were slow and easy to outrun—at least in the short term. The trouble was that they kept coming, eventually exhausting their prey.

Midnight went to the rear window of the tower. "They're at the outer wall!" she called.

Adon and Kelemvor, who had just pried the heavy gates into place, drew their weapons. They stood to one side of the narrow gap. In his imagination, Kelemvor was already listening to the drivers proclaim their gratitude.

But Adon was not thinking about the drivers at all. The saddlebags containing the tablet were slung over his shoulder. He wished he had given the artifact to Midnight for safekeeping. In addition to being exposed to theft, it would only get in the way during battle. Unfortunately, it was too late to do anything about that now.

Midnight returned to the front window. The ten caravan drivers were lurking at the outer gate, peering into the ward as if they feared the inside of Dragonspear Castle more than what pursued them. They were a strange crew, wearing striped, hooded cloaks that kept their faces hidden in dark hollows.

Midnight was surprised at their lack of urgency. The undead could not be so far behind that they had time to waste.

Finally, she yelled, "You in the caravan! Run for the keep!"

Without any hurry, the drivers started forward. The caravan was halfway to the inner gate when the first corpse clambered through a gap in the outer wall. The zombie wore the same striped cloak as the drivers, though its hood was thrown back to reveal a coarse braid of black hair, eyes lacking any spark of life, and doughy gray skin.

Midnight assumed a terrible creature must have befallen the caravan, slaying half or more of its number and setting the dead against their fellows. Four more zombies climbed into the outer ward and continued after the caravan. The drivers didn't look back. Instead, they concentrated upon leading their horses toward the inner gate.

Down in the ward, Adon and Kelemvor laboriously opened the gate a little more to admit the horses as well as their masters. The zombies were pursuing so slowly that Kelemvor had no doubt that there would be plenty of time to close the gate after the drivers reached safety.

From the tower window, Midnight watched as the last zombie climbed through the outer wall. The chase seemed wrong to her, however. The whole thing had been too slow and too relaxed. Nor did she like how the drivers had responded to her offer of help—without a word of acknowledgment or thanks.

As the first driver reached the gate, an overpowering stench of decay and death filled Kelemvor's nostrils. At first, the odor puzzled him, for the zombies were not close enough for him to smell them. Then, thinking about how slowly the caravan moved, the warrior began to suspect the drivers were not what they appeared to be.

"Close the gate!" he yelled to Adon, grabbing the beam they had used to lever the door into its current position.

"What do you mean?" the cleric demanded, confused. Like Kelemvor, he smelled something foul. But he assumed it was merely the horses—or something in their packs.

The green-eyed fighter cursed and pushed one end of the beam toward the cleric. "They're zombies! All of them! Now, close the gate."

Comprehension dawning in his eyes, Adon took his side of the beam and turned to position it beneath the heavy gate.

But he was too late. The first zombie pushed through the gap. Beneath the driver's striped hood, Adon saw a bloated face and lifeless eyes. The thing's thin lips were pulled back in a grotesque grin, revealing a set of broken yellow teeth.

It raised an arm and clawed at the cleric.

Adon ducked and grabbed his mace, but dropped the beam. For a second the cleric wished that he was still in Sune's grace, still able to turn undead. That wish passed as two more drivers pushed through the gap.

Kelemvor grabbed his sword and hacked at the first zombie's neck. The thing's head rolled off its shoulders neatly, but the body remained standing. It began swinging its fists blindly. Then the next two zombies attacked, both focusing on Adon. One landed a savage blow in the cleric's ribs, and the other backhanded him so violently that his ears rang.

"Run!" Kelemvor yelled. He slashed a zombie's arm off, then backed away a step.

Adon started to obey, but stumbled over the beam and nearly fell. He swung his mace, hitting the closest zombie. Bone cracked and the creature's temple caved in, but it did not fall. Two more drivers stepped forward, one to either side of the cleric.

Midnight heard several dull thuds as her friends' weapons struck the zombies, then ran to the window overlooking the inner ward. She saw Kelemvor hacking at three of the undead that surrounded Adon. Two more drivers were pushing through the gate, and the mage knew plenty more were approaching outside.

Kelemvor slashed, tearing the cloak from the head of a driver. Its eyes were dull and lifeless, and its skin doughy and gray. The fighter slashed again and the driver lost an arm—then pressed forward to counterattack.

Midnight knew her misgivings had been justified: Adon and Kelemvor were as good as dead and the tablet lost, unless she could pluck them from the midst of battle. Remembering the heavy chandelier in the middle of the room, the mage went to the wall and released the rope. The chandelier crashed to the floor. She drew her dagger and cut the rope free, then hastily coiled it.

Down in the courtyard, Adon thought he was doomed. The cleric was surrounded by three zombies that seemed impervious to his mace—or at least immune to the damage he was dealing with the weapon. More undead were entering the courtyard every few seconds. He smashed a driver's ribs and felt them break, then cringed as the zombie raked at his face with four filthy fingers.

To Adon's left, Kelemvor's sword found a target, beheading a zombie and temporarily clearing a small path between the warrior and the cleric. Adon seized the chance to fling the tablet to Kelemvor.

The saddlebags struck the fighter in the shoulder, then tangled around his left arm. Intent upon recovering the artifact, the zombies turned toward the tablet and left Adon alone. Although Adon and Kelemvor did not know this, before his destruction, Bhaal had told Myrkul where Midnight kept the tablet. Accordingly, the Lord of the Dead had instructed the zombies to recover any saddlebags the heroes carried with them.

Although Adon did not know the source of the zombies' information, it took him only an instant to realize they wanted the tablet and knew where it was. "Run!" he called to Kelemvor, stepping forward and cracking a corpse's skull. "Get out of here!"

Kelemvor thought his friend was merely being noble.

"No!" the fighter cried, slicing into a zombie.

The thing did not fall, then two more stepped to its side. All three undead lashed out at the warrior, and he had no choice except to back away. Nevertheless, still having failed to notice that Adon was no longer under attack, Kelemvor yelled, "I got you into this, and I'll get you out of it!"

"I doubt that," Midnight yelled. She stood atop the wall behind Kelemvor, the hastily coiled rope in her hands. The magic-user dropped one end of the rope toward the courtyard. She ran the other end through an arrow loop in the closest merlon and began tying it off.

Kelemvor slashed at a leg, slicing deep into an attacker's knee. The zombie pressed forward, completely unaffected by a wound that would have crippled a living man. The fighter's other two attackers landed powerful blows in his ribs, then two more zombies crowded around and began flailing at him. The warrior retreated another few steps, and a moment later his back was pressed against the wall.

Seeing what Midnight intended and realizing that he could do little to help Kelemvor, Adon screamed, "Up the rope, Kel! I'm safe!" With that, he turned and ran for the nearest stairway.

Midnight finished her knot, then returned to the wall's edge. The rope ended eight feet off the ground, easily within Kelemvor's reach. However, the warrior was so busy fighting zombies that he could not start climbing.

The magic-user climbed onto the rope and slid down, stopping a foot before its end. Midnight knew she lacked the strength to pull the warrior out of battle, but she hoped that with her aid, Kelemvor could grab the rope and quickly climb out of the zombies' reach. "Kel, give me your hand!" she cried.

The warrior glanced up and saw Midnight's outstretched hand, then the zombies landed several blows. He swung his sword viciously, buying himself a foot of breathing space. Immediately, he lifted the saddlebags and placed them in Midnight's hand.

"Take it!" Kelemvor yelled.

At first, Midnight didn't want to obey. But then the zombies turned their attention to her, simply trying to walk over the warrior. She accepted the saddlebags, slung them over her shoulder, then started up the rope. The warrior stayed on the ground and continued slashing at zombies.

A few seconds later, Adon arrived at the top of the wall and helped Midnight climb up the last few feet. After she was safely on the wall, she turned and yelled, "I'm safe, Kel. Come on!"

The warrior immediately sheathed his sword and, ignoring the zombies, turned and grabbed the rope. He pulled himself to the top of the wall as quickly as he could. Midnight cut the rope behind him, then said, "Follow me!"

She led the way back to the tower, entering the first doorway she came to. Though this room lacked an iron chandelier and an age-worn desk, it was similar to the one from which she had taken the rope.

As soon as they were inside, Adon asked, "What now?"

"We've got to think of a plan," Midnight replied, sheathing her dagger. "And we'd better do it before the zombies find a way to get up here."

Kelemvor went to the window and watched the zombies stumble around the ward. "I'm sorry I got you into this," he said. "I just thought—oh, damn it, I just didn't think."

"Don't blame yourself," Adon responded, gripping the fighter's shoulder. "Those zombies would have attacked no matter what you did. Somebody sent them after the tablet."

"It was Myrkul," Midnight sighed. "I told you that he and Bhaal were working together. Well, he must have tried to contact Bhaal and discovered that I had escaped with the tablet."

"Whether Myrkul sent them or not," Kelemvor grumbled, "I should be skinned and roasted alive." He took the saddlebags from Adon and started to remove the tablet. "Maybe I can trick them into following me."

The scarred cleric pushed the tablet back into a saddlebag. "No, Kel. We stand a better chance of surviving if we stick together." Adon had purposely left the tablet in the warrior's hands. In the coming battle, he thought it best to have it protected by their most capable fighter.

Kelemvor frowned and, when Adon did not take the saddlebags back, threw them over his shoulder.

Sensing the fighter's mood, Adon added, "It's better things worked out this way. Otherwise, the zombies would have attacked us by surprise."

"Adon's right," Midnight added, touching Kelemvor's arm. There was nothing to be gained by making the warrior feel bad, and she did not enjoy watching him vilify himself. "Let's just see if we can find the entrance to the Realm of the Dead. After all, we were headed here anyway."

"Where do we start?" Kelemvor asked, peering out the window. To his alarm, the warrior saw that many of the zombies had stumbled onto the stairs and had reached the top of the wall. Worse still, they were coming toward the tower.

The fighter stepped away from the window, saying, "We'd better get out—"

A loud clatter rang through the room, startling all three of the companions. Midnight grabbed Kelemvor's arm and jerked him out the window, then pointed at an arrow lying on the floor. On the stone wall was a fresh scratch where the arrow had struck the stone. Kelemvor nonchalantly picked it up. "Zombies don't use bows," he said. "Where'd this come from?"

"We'll figure that out later," Adon said, fearing the zombies were only one part of Myrkul's trap. "Let's get out of here!" He led the way down the stairs.

They descended the spiral staircase past three rooms, not pausing until they reached ground level. Here, the heroes took a moment to peer into the room on the ground floor. Its only door was the one they were now standing in.

"We'd better go down to the basement," Adon noted frantically, continuing down the dark staircase.

"Wait! We'll be trapped!" Kelemvor objected.

"We're already trapped," Midnight replied, following the cleric.

"And the zombies will probably go up first since they saw you and Midnight go up the wall," Adon added. "Maybe we can sneak out when they climb the stairs."

Kelemvor nodded and Adon led the way down into a dim, dank basement. The muffled whisper of running water echoed from the walls, though no one could identify the source of the sound. High in the middle of the inner wall, a small window opened into the inner ward at ground level. The little light the room received entered through this opening.

Adon briefly considered trying to escape out the window, but quickly rejected the idea. It was large enough to provide ventilation and light, but far too small to accommodate Kelemvor's broad shoulders—or even Midnight's, for that matter.

The room contained only moldering debris. There were sacks of spoiled grain and casks of rancid wine—obviously left by wanderers who had used the tower as temporary lodging—empty, rotting barrels and a coil of moldy rope attached to a worm-eaten bucket. The room's wooden floor was decayed and spongy.

While Adon and Kelemvor listened to the zombies ascend the stairs, Midnight explored the room, occasionally picking away pieces of plank with the tip of her dagger.

After five minutes, Adon shook his head and cursed. "The zombies aren't doing what we'd hoped, Midnight. The ones from the courtyard are still on the ground floor." The cleric paused and looked at Kelemvor. "We're trapped."

"I'll lead the way up," the fighter growled. "Maybe we can fight our way out."

"Not yet," Midnight said, puzzling over the floor. The other rooms in the tower had not had any rot, and she didn't understand why this one should be any different. Then she thought of the bucket and the rope, which were similar to the ones used in wells. She went to the center of the room. "Kel, use your sword to pry up one of these planks! Quickly!"

Although puzzled, the warrior did as asked. A section of floor three feet square came up. The thin, muffled whisper echoing from the walls changed to a quiet roar.

"What is it?" Kelemvor asked.

"An underground stream!" Adon answered, kneeling next to the warrior.

Pointing at the bucket and rope, Midnight added, "It's an emergency water supply, used in case of siege."

Adon smiled and pointed into the hole. "The zombies won't follow us down there!"

"If we have the courage to go ourselves." Kelemvor stuck his head into the blackness.

"What do you see?" Midnight asked.

"A cavern," he muttered. "But it's dark. I can't see the bottom." He pulled his head out.

Midnight kneeled next to her friends and looked into the hole. She could see nothing but darkness, but it sounded as though the stream running under the tower was fairly large.

Kelemvor grabbed the rope and bucket. "I guess we'll have to trust this thing." He tied one end of the rope around a beam on the ceiling, then grabbed it and pulled himself off the floor to test the strength of his knot.

Adon scowled. "Perhaps we'd be wiser to look for something—"

The room grew a shade darker, as though something was blocking the light. Without finishing his sentence, Adon turned toward the cellar window and saw a man's form kneeling on the ground outside. The man had a familiar hawkish nose.

"Look out!" Adon screamed, realizing he was the only one who saw Cyric. The scarred cleric lunged at Kelemvor and shoved him to the ground.

Midnight turned. Something buzzed past her ear and struck Adon with a wet thump. The scarred cleric groaned loudly and dropped to his knees beside her.

"What is it? What's wrong?" Midnight asked.

Adon didn't answer. His eyes rolled back into his head, then he pitched forward into the hole. Midnight lunged and caught him by the shoulder and the bloody shaft that protruded from his ribs. The stick snapped and the cleric's body slipped from the mage's grasp. A moment later, she heard a distant splash.

"Adon!" she gasped, unable to comprehend how she had come to be holding a broken arrow shaft in her blood-smeared hand.

Kelemvor understood perfectly. He was looking at Cyric, who was nocking another arrow. "I'll kill you!" the fighter roared, rushing to thrust his sword out the window.

"You missed your chance," the thief replied, easily retreating out of Kelemvor's reach. "But you should know that I was aiming for you just then. That foppish cleric got in the way."

"I haven't missed *my* chance," Midnight hissed, turning to face the window. At the sound of Cyric's voice, her heart had turned as cold as ice, and she had thought of the perfect way to kill him. The incantation for a cone of cold appeared in the mage's mind. She pointed her finger at the window and called upon her magic.

Cyric hit the ground and rolled, expecting to meet some hideous magical death. Instead, a wave of black frost rolled out of the window. As the thief cringed on the ground, the frost coalesced into a black ball and zipped past him, ricocheting from one of the keep's walls to another. Wherever it touched, the stones sprouted hoarfrost and icicles, then crumbled to dust. The ball finally bounced over the wall and, leaving a trail of icy destruction in its wake, went bounding off into the High Moor.

Breathing a sigh of relief, the hawk-nosed thief scrambled away from the window. Now that Kelemvor and Midnight knew he was on their trail, it would be much more difficult to kill them.

After watching Midnight's spell misfire, Kelemvor peered out the window. Cyric was nowhere in sight. "You missed," he reported, still too numbed by Adon's death to react.

Midnight did not respond. She lay curled up on the floor, gasping for breath and sweating uncontrollably. Her body ached from head to toe, and the magic-user felt as though willpower alone held her spirit inside her body. She recalled Bhaal's warning that she would burn herself up if she did not learn how to wield Mystra's magic.

That was exactly what it felt like she had done. Any spell wore a magic-user down, and part of a mage's training involved increasing her body's tolerance to magical energies. But Midnight, newly gifted with the ability to call upon a limitless supply of magic, did not yet have the endurance to withstand such energies. In theory, she could call upon her magic to do almost anything, but she now understood that the effort might leave her a lifeless husk of flesh and energy.

When he turned around, that was exactly what Kelemvor feared he was seeing. "Midnight!" he gasped.

For the first time since Adon had entrusted it to him, Kelemvor set the Tablet of Fate aside. He dropped the saddlebags, knelt beside Midnight, and took her into his arms. "How can I help?" the fighter asked softly. "What can I do?"

Midnight wanted to tell him to hold her, to keep her warm, but she was afraid to speak. Right now, she needed her strength just to stay conscious.

Kelemvor heard the shuffling of heavy steps on the stairway, and he knew the zombies had discovered their hiding place. His first thought was to charge the stairs, but he knew the undead would tear him to pieces. That would leave Midnight alone and at their mercy.

Instead, he cut the bucket away from the rope and threw it aside. The fighter tied the free end of the rope around Midnight's waist. He intended to lower her into the cavern, then climb down after her.

He quickly realized he did not have time. The first zombie appeared in the door just as he slipped the mage into the hole. Kelemvor ignored the thing and began lowering Midnight. Two more of the walking corpses entered the room.

Midnight only knew that Kelemvor was lowering her into the darkness and that her strength was slowly returning. With the cavern walls echoing its bubbles and gurgles back toward her, the stream sounded incredibly large, more like a small river.

A few moments later, her descent stopped and she found herself hanging in darkness. Though it sounded as if she were only a few feet above the stream, there was no way for the mage to confirm or deny that suspicion. Midnight looked up and saw a dim square of light. There were forms dancing around it, but she could not make out any details.

Back in the tower's basement, the first zombie ignored Kelemvor and picked up the saddlebags containing the Tablet of Fate. The fighter finished lowering Midnight, then grabbed his sword and hacked at the zombie. The thing's arm fell off and it dropped the tablet. But before Kelemvor could retrieve the artifact, the zombie's fellows joined it and all three attacked.

The fighter slashed at them to no avail. He connected solidly with the one whose arm he had already lopped off, opening a gash in its abdomen and temporarily stunning it. Heedless of their own safety, the other two corpses closed in, flailing wildly.

Forced to retreat away from the tablet, Kelemvor stumbled into the pit in the middle of the room. He grabbed the rope to keep from falling, then leveled a vicious slash at one of his attackers. The zombie's head flopped off its neck and dropped to the floor. Another of the undead threw itself at the hand Kelemvor was using to hold onto the rope. The fighter instinctively slashed and connected. Then the stroke continued past the zombie's body and the warrior could not draw back quickly enough to avoid cutting the rope.

Midnight heard Kelemvor scream, then the rope popped and went slack. She dropped into the stream, felt the current grab her, then began fighting to keep her head above water. Though she was still exhausted from the misfired spell, she knew that she had to find a reservoir of strength or drown.

Two splashes sounded to Midnight's left as Kelemvor and the sword he had dropped hit the water in quick succession. The mage tried to swim toward the disturbance, but she was too weak and the current was too strong.

A moment later, Kelemvor called to her. "Midnight?

Where are you?"

"Here," she croaked. In the rushing water, she barely heard her own voice and knew it would not be audible to her lover. Midnight tried to swim toward the fighter, but the stream simply swept her away.

Kelemvor had more strength than Midnight, but he didn't try to swim out of the current. He knew that the mage had to be downstream and was determined not to lose her. Allowing the tablet to fall into Myrkul's hands was bad enough, but Kelemvor was unwilling to face life without Midnight.

The warrior swam downstream with all his might. He paused every now and then to cross the current, hoping to find Midnight. It was a good plan, but the fighter had underestimated the power of his strokes. He was quickly so far ahead of the mage that he stood no chance of meeting her.

Kelemvor continued his search for fifteen minutes before growing so exhausted that he could only concentrate on survival. For another quarter-hour, the stream swept the fighter and the magic-user farther into darkness. Sometimes it rushed into long passages completely filled with water, and both Midnight and Kelemvor believed they would drown before they bobbed back to the surface, exhausted and gasping for breath. At other times, they bounced against rocks or the cave's walls. Despite the pain of such encounters, though, they always clutched and grasped at the slick surfaces, hoping to latch onto something and pull free of the current.

Neither one drowned nor pulled free. Both Kelemvor and Midnight continued into the darkness, cold and blind, aware of nothing but the rush of the stream, the weight of their soggy clothes, and the fetid water they swallowed with every other breath.

After a time—Kelemvor could not say how long he'd been in the water or how many miles he had floated—the stream straightened its course and grew more quiet. The fighter started to remove his clothes, for their weight was only contributing to his fatigue. But a strange slurping sound echoed off the cavern walls, and Kelemvor paused to hold his head above the water and listen. The noise was coming from the middle of the channel.

He swam across the stream, then the current grew faster and the slurping grew louder. Kelemvor turned his body away from the noise, then stroked harder and harder as the current spun him around. Finally, he felt himself being pulled back up the stream. The exhausted fighter lowered his head and swam with all his strength. At last, he broke free and continued downstream.

The twisting current had been the edge of a whirlpool, the warrior realized. It had been a small one, or he would never have broken free, but the effort still left him exhausted.

Then Kelemvor remember Midnight.

"Midnight!" he called. "There's a whirlpool. Swim to the right!" He called this warning over and over again, until at last he could no longer hear the sucking sound of the whirlpool.

Even if she had been close enough to hear the warning, Midnight could have done nothing to avoid the danger. She was too drained to swim or even to pull off her heavy clothes. Her limbs were numb and clumsy with cold and exhaustion, her lungs burned every time she took a breath, and her mind was incoherent with fatigue.

When the stream straightened its course ahead of her, Midnight let herself drift into the center of the channel, relieved for a respite from the turbulent currents. While the slurping sound grew louder, she held her head out of the water and drew ten delicious, uninterrupted breaths. Then, as the water became faster, the fatigued mage pushed her feet downstream—and felt herself spiraling downward.

She had slipped into the whirlpool without realizing what it was, and now she barely cared. Midnight simply held her breath and relaxed as the water carried her away.

❧ 12 ❧

Black Ice

While Kelemvor and Midnight struggled to keep from drowning, Midnight's misfired magic skipped along the High Moor. Wherever the ebony globe touched, the earth turned to black ice. It glanced off a maple tree and the sap congealed in the trunk. It bounced into a stag and froze the blood in the animal's veins.

Nearly an hour later, the black ball tumbled into a creekbed and could not escape. It rolled downhill, dashing from one side of the gully to the other, leaving a ribbon of black ice in its wake. The gully emptied into a small, rocky canyon. The globe ricocheted from one wall to another, changing dripping springs into sable icicles.

As the ball bounced down the canyon, the underground stream carried Kelemvor farther away from the whirlpool. Finally, the current grew swifter and water filled the cave completely. At first, the fighter was not concerned, for his lungs were full of air and the stream had dragged him through a dozen similar passages. But two minutes passed and the warrior's lungs ached to draw another breath. He swam to the top of the stream, scraping at the ceiling in a vain search for air pockets. His head grew light and, to keep from inhaling, he clamped a hand over his nose and mouth. For a minute or so more, the cavern did not open up and Kelemvor remained submerged.

Then, as unconsciousness threatened to take him, the current died away. The warrior floated upward and a dim, greenish radiance lit the water. Kelemvor realized he had escaped the cavern. But his lungs still screamed for air and an unreasoning voice told him to breathe.

Kelemvor kept his hand pressed over his face. With what remained of his strength, he swam. Ten seconds later, he broke the surface and gulped down a dozen breaths.

He was in a small mountain lake—no more than a large pond, really. There was a small beach a hundred feet ahead. To the fighter's right, a waterfall plunged into the lake from a ninety-foot cliff. The small creek feeding the waterfall ran down the center of a narrow, rocky canyon.

Something black and spherical was bouncing down that canyon, rebounding from wall to wall. Though he had not seen the destruction the ball left in its wake, a terrible feeling of apprehension washed over Kelemvor. He began swimming for the shore, fighting his own weariness and the cumbersome weight of his wet clothes. He thought about stopping to shed his pants and boots, but that would have taken too much time.

Kelemvor was halfway to shore when the sphere reached the cliff. The waterfall turned into a cascade of black ice. The ball skipped into the air, then fell toward the lake.

Seeing what had become of the waterfall, Kelemvor swam harder, kicking and stroking madly despite the agony in his limbs. The ball fell steadily, inexorably, toward the lake. Kelemvor was only twenty-five feet from the shoreline when the globe touched the water.

Beneath the sphere, a black circle of ice appeared. The ball skipped away, touching down twice and leaving two more icy patches in its wake. As the globe bounced out of the lake, the black circles began to expand.

Kelemvor continued to swim. Ten feet from shore, an icy vise grabbed at his ankle. The warrior kicked free and swam two more strokes, then his hands touched bottom. The water suddenly grew frigid, especially around his legs. He tried to stand, but found his thighs and waist locked in merciless jaws of ice. Trying to break free, he threw himself forward— only to come crashing down in shallow water, his chin barely past the shoreline.

The ice continued to form, advancing toward the fighter's

shoulders and threatening to trap his arms and chest. Kelemvor could not let that happen. He pushed his torso out of the lake and waited while the water froze beneath him. When the ice reached his hands, he moved them to the shore and continued to hold his body out of the water.

The ice stopped forming when it reached his chin. After a moment of silence, the lake began popping and creaking, adjusting itself to the increased volume of frozen water. The ice sheet rose a few inches, then surged three feet forward, leaving Kelemvor and his icy prison well ashore.

As the fighter waited for further adjustments, he examined his situation. He was trapped from his waist to his knees in a sheet of black ice. Below his knees, he could kick freely, whirling cold water around his calves and feet. Judging by what he could feel, the ice was about six inches thick.

In front of him, two inches of snow blanketed tufts of beach grass and capped several dozen pieces of driftwood littering the shore. Beyond that, a steep bank of sand rose ten feet. Six inches of soil topped the embankment, providing meager purchase for a few twisted dwarf pines that perfumed the air with a sweet citruslike odor.

The lake itself was nestled in a hollow at the base of the High Moor. To Kelemvor's left, a single brook—now frozen and black—drained the tiny lake. The only visible inlet was the frozen waterfall, though Kelemvor knew that at least one underground stream also fed the lake.

After his brief examination of his surroundings yielded no easy method of escape, Kelemvor jerked and tried to pull free of the ice. When he failed, he screamed in rage.

His bellow came echoing back to him, as clear and as crisp as when he voiced it. The echo only made the fighter feel more desperate. Kelemvor shrieked again and dug his hands into the sand, then pulled with all his might. A keen ache shot through his shoulders and down his spine. His arms, still fatigued from the long swim, felt as heavy as clubs. Still, he did not stop pulling.

Finally, Kelemvor's muscles began to quiver, then he started shivering and realized how cold he was. The air stung his fingers and his face, while his torso prickled with icy needles. Below his waist, the cold gnawed at his bones, burning his buttocks and thighs with frosty agony.

He worried most about his feet. Despite his tightly laced leggings and well-oiled boots, his feet were soaked. Kelemvor suspected that the stinging in his toes was the first stage of frostbite. If he did not escape soon, the warrior knew he would lose his toes, perhaps even freeze to death.

A crow landed in the low branches of the closest pine, then stared at the trapped fighter with a hungry gleam in its eye. Kelemvor hissed at it. The bird remained perched in the tree, politely waiting for the green-eyed man to die. It could afford to be patient. Judging from its lustrous feathers and plump body, the crow fed itself quite well.

Kelemvor did not enjoy being sized up as if he were a leg of mutton. "C-Come back tomorrow!" he called, the cold causing him to stutter. "I'm not going anywhere."

The crow blinked, but did not leave. Although it was in no hurry to start its feast, the bird did not intend to let some other scavenger claim its prize.

Kelemvor grabbed a piece of driftwood and hurtled it at the black bird. The stick missed and hit the tree next to the crow's. The bird turned its black eyes on the trembling boughs, then looked back at the warrior.

"Just leave me alone," Kelemvor growled, waving his hand at the bird. "Let me die with some dignity."

The hopelessness he felt surprised the fighter. Kelemvor had never been one to give up before the battle ended. But he had never felt this frightened before.

Kelemvor avoided examining that fear too closely. He had faced death many times before, and had never felt as despondent as now. The fighter was afraid of something more than dying. He told himself that leaving the tablet to the zombies was what had upset him.

But he knew that was a lie. Though Kelemvor understood the importance of returning the tablet to Helm, losing it would not produce such anguish. The true reason for his distress was Adon's death, and the uncertainty of Midnight's fate. Though he had no way of knowing what had happened to her, the warrior felt certain she could not have avoided the whirlpool.

Stop thinking, he told himself. Stop thinking before it's too late. Kelemvor suddenly wanted to go to sleep so he could wake up and discover that the zombies and underground stream had been bad dreams.

But the fighter did not dare to close his eyes. Even through his growing disorientation, Kelemvor knew that sleep could be deadly in freezing conditions.

The shivering went away and his muscles began to stiffen. Kelemvor knew he was slipping closer to death. He kicked his legs, then beat the black sheet beneath his chest.

The ice did not crack, did not pop, did not give at all. He was as good as dead, yet was still alive. That makes me undead, Kelemvor thought, like the caravan zombies. He chuckled grimly at this half-formed thought.

But undeath was better than what had happened to Adon and Midnight.

Forget it, he told himself. Thinking about the past will bring nothing but more sorrow. Survive first, then think.

Not thinking was easier said than done. If Kelemvor had not insisted upon rescuing the caravan, had not been so stubborn, his friends would be alive. But the fighter had been stubborn, as he always was. He thought that perhaps he deserved to die.

"Stop it!" He spoke the words aloud, hoping to snap himself into a more alert state of mind.

The crow squawked once, as if suggesting Kelemvor get on with his death.

"Fetch a dagger, then, or a sharp rock," Kelemvor muttered to the bird. "I can't kill myself with my bare hands."

The bird cocked its head, then ruffled its feathers and stared at Kelemvor with a disapproving glare.

Kelemvor stretched forward and grabbed a thick piece of driftwood. The crow prepared to take flight, but Kelemvor had no interest in attacking the bird again. Hefting the branch like a club, the fighter turned to his right as far as he could, then smashed the branch down on the ice.

A loud crack pealed across the lake, echoing off the cliff on the far side. Kelemvor tried to move his leg and found it would not budge. He raised the log and struck again. Another loud crack rolled across the ice-covered lake. The wooden club snapped in two, and one end went skittering across the ice, leaving the fighter holding a two-foot long wooden stake.

The crow squawked several times, then hopped out of the tree. It landed on the shore, just out of Kelemvor's reach, and squawked once more.

Kelemvor considered throwing his stick at the bird, then thought better of the idea. The broken branch was not much of a tool, but it was all he had. Instead of attacking the crow, he grasped the stick as he might a dagger, then hit the ice with its sharp end.

Something gave, so he struck again and again, his movements growing increasingly jerky and erratic. Finally, Kelemvor stopped to see what he had accomplished. The fighter had smashed the end of the branch into a rounded pulp. His hand throbbed with the force of his blows, but the exertion had warmed his body a little.

The black ice showed only the tiniest depression. It was much harder than the driftwood, and the fighter's efforts had done nothing to break it. If he wanted to smash his way free, Kelemvor knew he would have to find something harder than the driftwood, harder than the ice.

Kelemvor thought of the flint and steel in the purse he kept around his neck, but quickly discarded the idea; they were just chips he used to start campfires. They might serve well enough as hard points if fastened onto the end of the stick, but he had no way to do that. Besides, they would certainly be lost if they flew off the end of the stick, and that was a risk the fighter could not take. When he freed himself, he would need the flint and steel to start a fire. If it came down to death, he would use the flint to scratch at the ice, but it would be futile effort and he knew it.

Kelemvor turned his attention back to the shoreline. With

the dulled stick he still held, the warrior could reach other objects. Unfortunately, the only things on the shore were more sticks and the bird. A wave of despair passed over Kelemvor as he decided that he could do nothing to save himself, for the ice was too thick and too hard. He was going to die, like the others . . .

Don't think about them, he told himself. Thinking about them will demoralize you, make you want to die.

And Kelemvor wanted to live. It surprised him, somehow, but he definitely wanted to live.

The crow hopped to within the fighter's reach. The bird pretended to take no notice of Kelemvor, though it was difficult to tell exactly what its black eyes were focused upon. Perhaps the crow was testing the warrior, trying to decide how much longer it would take for him to die.

"I won't hurry on your account," Kelemvor grumbled.

The crow cocked its head, then opened its beak and hissed. Kelemvor thought of the beak pecking at his eyes, of the spiked claws digging at his ears and nose. He winced.

Then an idea occurred to him, though it was born not of wisdom, but of the irrationality that comes with freezing to death. He scratched at the ice with his fingernails and noticed that he had scraped away the slightest bit. Of course, even muddled as he was, Kelemvor knew he would be long dead before working free of the ice with his own nails.

But the crow's claws were sharper than fingernails. And the fighter could see many possibilities for the beak.

As if sensing his thoughts, the crow watched Kelemvor warily.

"I think I'll go to sleep," Kelemvor said, concerned by how thick his speech had become. In his confusion, he feared the crow might not understand him if he slurred his words.

The bird, of course, showed no sign of understanding him at all.

Kelemvor laid his head in his arms, keeping one eye open just enough to watch the bird. It felt good to rest his head, and he noticed that he was finally warm. The warrior was extremely drowsy, and thought the effort of his long swim had finally caught up to him. He closed both his eyes.

Ten minutes later, the crow decided to investigate the im-mobile man. Taking to its wings, the bird approached twice and fluttered overhead without landing. Finally, it settled a foot from Kelemvor's head and stared directly into the war-rior's face. The man's eyes remained firmly closed, and his breath was so shallow it could not be detected.

The crow hopped forward, then pecked at the fighter's nose. When Kelemvor did not stir, the crow pecked again, this time taking a pinch of flesh away in its beak.

Kelemvor woke with a start and saw the black form in front of his eyes. Even as addled as he was, the fighter real-ized the crow was causing his pain. He lunged and his right hand closed on oily feathers. His left hand caught the bird by the leg, and the warrior felt a bone snap.

The crow squawked and slashed with its free foot. Kelem-vor closed his eyes. Sharp claws ripped into his brow. The fighter screamed and the bird pressed harder, trying to rip through the man's eyelids and jerk an eyeball loose.

Kelemvor released the bird and covered his face. An in-stant later, the crow's wings beat the air and the bird was airborne. The fighter wiped the blood from his brow and looked after the bird. The fight had charged Kelemvor's body with adrenaline, and the warrior was thinking clearly enough to wonder why he had ever believed it possible to scratch through six inches of ice with a crow's claw.

"Filthy squab!" Kelemvor called, touching his fingers to the cuts in his forehead.

The crow circled several times, then flew away toward the west. With some alarm, the warrior noted that the sun was sinking and there were only about two hours of day-light remaining.

He began to feel lonely and frightened, and wished he had not chased the bird away. Though it had been waiting to pick his bones, at least the crow had been company.

Kelemvor noted that his legs had gone numb from the thighs down, and that his hands had taken on a blue tint. He was in danger of becoming a lump of ice. The fighter began waving his hands and trying to kick his feet, hoping to get the blood circulating and warm them.

This was only a temporary solution. If he was going to survive, he needed to warm himself. Fortunately, it looked as though the tools to do that were within arm's reach.

Hoping that this was not another confused idea brought about by the cold, Kelemvor started gathering materials to start a fire. Stretching as far as he could, the fighter swept the snow off tufts of beach grass and pulled them out by their roots. He stored the grass inside his shirt, and did not stop gathering it until his shirt was bulging. The warrior was working more by instinct than by thought, for he had started a thousand fires and trusted his intuition more than his muddled intelligence.

Next, he gathered all the driftwood within reach, separating the smaller pieces from the larger. Within minutes, he had three small piles of wood. Finally, he selected his six largest sticks and laid them to his left, side by side so they made a small platform. From experience, he knew that once the fire was burning well, the flames would convert the ice directly to steam. But in the initial stages, the fire had to be kept off the ice.

Kelemvor removed a handful of grass and rubbed it vigorously between his hands to dry it. He laid it atop the platform of sticks and repeated the process until he had a small pile of fairly dry tinder. Then he took the flint and steel from his purse and started striking them together. Five anxious and painful minutes later, a spark caught. One blade of grass began to burn, then two, then several. The fighter put on more grass and, after it started burning, held several twigs over the fire to dry.

Thirty seconds later, Kelemvor began to shiver and could no longer hold the twigs. He laid them on the fire. The wood began to smoke, then one caught. The fighter blew gently on the flame. The other two twigs began to burn.

Kelemvor put his flint and steel away. Minutes later, a small circle of orange flames danced in front of him. The breeze eddied around his body, blowing ash and smoke into

RICHARD AWLINSON

his face. His eyes teared and he coughed, but the warrior
didn't care. To him, the smoke was perfume and the coughing a small price to pay for heat. Soon, he stopped shivering
and his whole torso was warm.

Ten minutes later, Kelemvor no longer felt confused. He
was fatigued and numb below the waist, but he was no
longer drowsy. His motor coordination had returned to normal. The fire had made a small bowl in the black ice, and the
fighter took comfort in seeing that it melted like normal ice.
Now, all he had to do was find a way to break it.

Kelemvor considered starting a fire where his hips disappeared into the frozen lake, but rejected the idea. He could
not reach enough driftwood to melt away that much ice.
What he needed was a way to chip the ice, and that meant
he needed something hard.

The lake was surrounded by all sorts of cliffs, boulders,
and rocks, but there wasn't even a pebble within reach.
They were all buried beneath the sandy beach.

Had Kelemvor still been half-frozen and muddled, he
would have missed the significance of his last thought. However, now that he was warm, his thoughts were focused and
he was mentally alert. With renewed determination, he
grabbed the strongest piece of driftwood within reach and
began digging in the sand in front of him.

Not six inches below the surface, he found the first rock.
It was a round, hand-sized stone useful for throwing, but
not for smashing through ice. He kept digging.

The second stone was a little better, being about the same
size, but with jagged features more suited to chipping. He
set aside this rock, too, and kept digging.

A foot beneath the surface, Kelemvor found the ideal
stone. It was a dark gray thing, featureless and drab. But to
the fighter, the stone was more beautiful than any diamond.
It was as large as he could handle with a single hand. On one
end it had a small, sharp point, and the other end was large
and ideal for gripping.

Kelemvor took the stone, then smashed it into the ice near
his hip. A small spray of black chips shot up. He brought the

rock down a dozen more times, trying to create a crack in the ice. The result was simply a dozen more small chips.

At the top of the slope, wings fluttered. The crow settled beneath its tree, holding its left claw off the ground.

Looking at the injured leg, Kelemvor said, "I'm sorry about the foot."

The crow tilted its head and, unable to stand for long on one foot, settled on the ground as though sitting in a nest.

The fighter smiled and held up the rock. "It looks like dinner will be late," Kelemvor added.

The crow's head bobbed twice. Had Kelemvor's mind been more addled, he might have interpreted the awkward gesture for agreement, as if the crow were saying, "Delayed, but not cancelled."

The fighter decided to ignore the crow and began chipping beneath his chest, where the ice was thinner. To his delight, a large, jagged section broke away. Working toward his waist from this break, Kelemvor managed to start a crack that pointed more or less toward his right hip.

He worked for twenty minutes, pausing every now and then to throw some more driftwood on the fire. In that time, he managed to extend the crack clear to the middle of his hip. Then, as the sun sank toward the moor hills and the sky turned pink, his fire melted through the ice. It dropped into the water, leaving a sizzling and smoking hole two feet to his left.

"No!" Kelemvor screamed.

His only answer was the chill moan of the wind.

The fighter began to grow cold immediately. He tried to pull out of the ice, hoping the crack he had opened was enough to free him. His hips did not budge.

Kelemvor reached for more grass to start another fire, then found he had already used most of it. Worse, only a few sticks of driftwood remained within reach. Even if he did start a second fire, it would never last through the night.

He beat his forehead against the ice and cursed. Already, numbness was creeping back into his hands and fingers, and he knew that there was not much warmth left in his body. At last, Kelemvor allowed himself to think the unthinkable: he had been wrong to insist upon rescuing the caravan. His stubbornness had gotten Adon, and probably Midnight, killed.

"Friends!" he screamed. "Forgive me! Please, Midnight! Oh, Midnight!" He screamed her name again and again and again, until he could no longer bear hearing the hills throw the name back at him.

When he stopped yelling, the crow flapped down to the shore, taking care to land out of arm's reach. It squawked three times, as if suggesting Kelemvor give up and die.

The bird's eagerness enraged the fighter. "Not yet, squab!" he snarled. He grabbed the first stone he had uncovered, the small round one, and flung it at the crow. Though his aim was wide, the crow took the hint and flapped away into twilight. After the bird had gone, Kelemvor picked up his large stone and angrily pounded at the ice on his left. If he was going to die, he was determined to fight until the end.

Kelemvor was so angry that he did not notice the tiny fractures his blows were causing. Five minutes later, a long crack opened in the black ice from his shoulders to the hole the fire had caused. It took only ten minutes more to open a seam all the way to his left hip.

Then, as the warm hues of dusk gave way to the violet tones of night, the section of ice under Kelemvor's chest broke free. The fighter pulled his body forward, no longer clamped into place by the ice at his hips. Without pausing to celebrate, he hauled himself onto the shore and began gathering grass and wood.

After starting his fire, Kelemvor removed his frozen pants and boots to examine his feet and legs. The legs were blotchy and pale, but he thought they would recover given time and warmth. His feet were in worse condition. They were white, numb, and cold to the touch.

Kelemvor had served in enough cold weather campaigns to know severe frostbite when he saw it.

❧ 13 ❧

Dark Awakening

Midnight woke from a deep slumber, her body sore and stiff. She had been dreaming of a dry bed in a warm inn, so the mage was confused and disoriented when she opened her eyes and found something else. The gloom was so thick she couldn't see her own nose, and she was lying face down on cool sand, half in, half out of lapping water. Behind her, a waterfall pounded the surface of a small pool.

The waterfall reminded Midnight of her journey down the subterranean stream and the unpleasant drop through the whirlpool. The magic-user had landed in the dark pond behind her. After that, she had floated aimlessly until she'd reached the shore upon which she now lay.

Midnight had no way of knowing it, but that had been ten hours ago. Fatigued from the misfired cone of cold and the struggle in the stream, her body had collapsed into a restorative sleep as soon as immediate danger passed. The mage now felt physically and mentally rejuvenated, but was still emotionally exhausted. Adon was dead, and that knowledge blackened the joy and wonder of her own survival.

Midnight wanted to blame somebody for Adon's death, and Kelemvor was the easiest one to condemn. If the warrior had not insisted upon aiding the caravan, the zombies would never have trapped the party and Cyric would not have caught them unprepared.

But such reasoning was weak, and Midnight knew it. There were too many coincidences and contingencies. That Cyric would recover so quickly had been unthinkable, and the magic-user still could not imagine how he had. But given the fact that he had, it was inevitable that the thief would catch up and attack. Midnight had been just as blind to that possibility as Kelemvor, and it was not fair to blame the warrior for not foreseeing what she had also failed to predict.

If the blame for Adon's death lay with anybody, Midnight thought it lay with her. She should never have let her friends convince her not to kill Cyric when she had the chance. The magic-user alone had seen how brutal the thief had grown, and she should have known that his willpower and ruthlessness would give him the strength to pursue them.

She would not make the same mistake again. There was nothing she could do to bring Adon back. But if she ever escaped from this cavern and saw Cyric again, she would avenge the cleric's death.

The thought of escaping the cavern turned Midnight's thoughts to Kelemvor, whom she assumed was also in the cave. The warrior had splashed into the stream after her, and that had been the last she'd heard of him. It did not seem unreasonable to assume he had dropped through the whirlpool behind her. He could be sitting thirty feet away, thinking himself alone in dark.

"Kelemvor!" Midnight called, rising to her feet.

Her voice echoed off the cavern's unseen walls, barely audible above the roar of the waterfall.

"Kelemvor, where are you?"

Again, the only answer was her echo.

A depressing thought occurred to her. She had avoided drowning, but that was no guarantee the fighter had. After all, Kelemvor had been carrying the tablet. It would have been difficult to keep from drowning while holding onto the saddlebags.

"Kelemvor," she called, more desperately. "Answer me!"

He did not answer.

Picturing Kelemvor's drowned body floating beneath the waterfall, Midnight drew her dagger. She summoned the incantation to create magical light and performed it. The dagger began glowing with a brilliant white light. It suddenly grew extremely hot and she dropped it, her fingers searing with pain. The magic-user kneeled and thrust her hand into the pool's cool water, irritated that her magic had misfired.

Still, the dagger glowed brightly enough for Midnight to see that she was on the shore of a dark pond. Twenty feet away, the waterfall poured into the cave from a hole in the ceiling, churning the surface of the pond into a dark froth. The ceiling was fifteen feet high and vaulted like the interior of a cathedral. Hundreds of stalactites hung from it, their tips glistening with moisture. Drooping spheres of minerals, with skins as rough and pebbly as dragonhide, sprouted from the walls. In every corner, murky tunnels and alcoves ran back into the depths of the cave.

"Kel!" Midnight called again.

Her voice echoed off the walls, then faded into the sound of the waterfall. She was alone, lost underground. Adon was dead and Kelemvor was gone—maybe dead as well.

As if to emphasize the mage's morbid point, her dagger's light suddenly dimmed and changed to a red hue. She looked down and saw that it had become a puddle of molten iron. It was slowly trickling away, taking the last vestiges of light with it and leaving Midnight in the dark once more.

The magic-user considered her situation. First of all, even if it was impossible to find a way out of the cavern on foot, she realized she was not trapped. If the circumstances became desperate, she could try using her art to escape. Considering the unpredictability of magic, doing that would be risky. But if there was no other option, Midnight would not hesitate to trust her luck.

Once the mage realized she had a way out of the cave, it became easier to think calmly. The second thing Midnight considered was that she was alone. Adon was certainly dead. If Cyric's arrow had not killed him, the fall or the stream had. But the only proof she had that Kelemvor drowned was her own conjecture, and it was born out of solitude and fear rather than sound thinking. After all, Kelemvor was stronger than Midnight, and she had not died. Even burdened with the tablet, his chances of surviving were much greater than hers. It seemed likely that he had washed out of the water in a different part of the cavern.

Finally, Midnight realized that though she did not know where she was, it was somewhere more or less beneath Dragonspear Castle. According to Bhaal, the entrance to the Realm of the Dead was also beneath the castle's ruins.

Midnight concluded that the smartest thing to do was explore the cavern. With luck, she would find either Kelemvor or the Realm of the Dead. Unfortunately, she would need a light. The magic-user thought of using her dagger's molten metal to ignite something as a torch, but did not have anything with her that would burn long enough to do her any good.

She had no choice except to try using her magic again. Midnight removed her dagger's sheath from its belt, then summoned the incantation for creating light. This time, a bright flash appeared. The unexpected burst of light hurt the mage's eyes, leaving her stunned and dazed with white spots swimming in her vision.

A few moments later, her sight returned to normal and the mage saw that she remained in total darkness. Her magic had again failed. Midnight decided to do without light for now, then started walking along the shore of the pond. She moved slowly and carefully, testing her footing with each step and waving her hands in front of her head to locate unseen obstacles.

Every few moments, she paused to call Kelemvor. Soon, Midnight discovered that the echo of her voice provided hints about the size and shape of the cavern. The longer it took the echo to return to her, the farther away from the cavern wall she was. By turning in a circle and calling Kelemvor's name, she could get an idea of the cavern's shape.

Armed with this discovery, she soon circled the pond. It seemed to be about a hundred yards in diameter, though it was difficult to be sure with all of the twists and turns in its shoreline. The only audible inlet was the waterfall, and the only outlet a small brook that trickled out one end.

Since she had found no other exits, Midnight slowly

walked along the brook's edge. The magic-user constantly called Kelemvor's name, always moving in the direction from which it took the echo the longest to return. In the complete darkness, it was difficult to guess time and distance. Still, Midnight soon realized the cave was immense.

Midnight continued to follow the water along its snaking course for what she guessed to be two hours. Occasionally, the corridor broadened into large rooms. From the echoes, it sounded as though dozens of alcoves and side passages opened off of these rooms. Although the magic-user took the time to call down these passages, she was careful not to wander away from the brook. It was the only reliable means of navigation she had. Besides, if Kelemvor had fallen through the whirlpool, she suspected the best chance of finding him lay in following the water.

Eventually, the brook entered a large room and formed another pond. Midnight carefully explored the shores of the pond, but could find no outlet. On one end of the pool, there was a gentle gurgling that suggested the water drained out through a submerged passage. The magic-user sat down in frustration.

For a long time, Midnight tried to puzzle out what might have happened to Kelemvor and what he might be doing as a result. The more she pondered the possibilities, the more it seemed that in the end, Kelemvor would go to Waterdeep. Assuming he had survived, which was the only thing the mage allowed herself to believe, the fighter knew two things that she thought would eventually force him to make that choice. First, the tablet had to be delivered to Waterdeep. Second, Midnight's eventual destination was also the City of Splendors, and if they had a chance of meeting again, it would be there.

As the magic-user contemplated Kelemvor's situation, a white silhouette floated into the cavern from a side passage. It was roughly the shape of a man, but appeared to be made entirely of light. It illuminated everything within twenty feet of it.

"Who are you?" Midnight called, both frightened by the

form and curious about it.

The figure turned and approached to within ten feet of her, then stopped and looked her over without speaking. It had the features of a robust man: heavy beard, square jaw, and steady eyes, all formed with light. The body, also nothing more than white light, had the musculature of someone well acquainted with hard work—perhaps a blacksmith.

After studying her for a moment, the white silhouette turned away without speaking and started toward a corridor opposite the one from which it had entered.

"Wait!" Midnight called, rising. "I'm lost—help me."

The white form paid her no more attention. The magic-user scrambled after it, struggling to stay within the small circle it illuminated. Within a few steps, the sandy shore gave way to pebbles, then the pebbles gave way to large rocks. Despite the treacherous footing, Midnight scurried along behind the white spectre, determined not to lose her light source or the mysterious silhouette.

It did not take Midnight long to notice that the apparition seemed to be following a passage running more or less in one direction. Several times, the tunnel opened into large rooms. In such chambers, Midnight feared she would lose the silhouette, for the caverns were littered with jagged boulders, sudden drops, and sloping floors. Once, she nearly stepped into a deep hole, and another time she had to leap across a crevice. Still, despite having to rush blindly through short expanses of cavern, Midnight managed to stay with the spectre.

After what must have been five hours of exhausting travel, the silhouette drifted into a vast area of darkness. The ceiling was about fifteen feet high, but Midnight could not see the far side of the chamber. As she scrambled after the spectre, the echoes of the rocks she dislodged seemed distant and subdued. The mage called out Kelemvor's name, and the sound of her voice drifted away into darkness, giving her the impression that this chamber was immense.

Midnight continued into the room, following the glowing apparition. Five minutes later, they reached a smooth wall of quarried granite. An expert stone-mason had fitted the blocks so tightly that Midnight could not have slipped a dagger's blade into the seams. The granite itself had been cut and polished so expertly that even the finest thief would slip trying to gain a handhold on it.

The wall ran in both directions as far as the silhouette illuminated, and rose fifteen feet to butt against the ceiling. Her pulse quickening with excitement, Midnight followed the spectre along the wall, running her hand down the slick cold stones.

Finally, they intersected a stone-paved street that entered the wall. Unlike the wall itself, the road showed signs of its incredible age. Some of its cobblestones had cracked or sunk into the ground, while others had become dislodged and lay scattered about.

The street ran beneath the wall in an arched tunnel. A heavy bronze-plated portcullis sealed each end of the vault. To either side of the main arch, there were smaller vaults, just large enough for a man to stand up in. These tunnels were sealed by heavy, bronze-plated doors.

The door on the closest tunnel hung cockeyed and open, and the silhouette entered the vault without hesitation. Midnight slipped past the door and followed. Again, the workmanship in the room was flawless. Each stone was squarely cut and set into place without the tiniest gap, and the keystones had not slipped a fraction of an inch in what Midnight assumed must have been thousands of years.

At the other end of the tunnel, they reached another partially opened door, again plated in bronze. The spectre slipped past it and disappeared. Midnight quickly followed, pushing the door open. Its hinges creaked loudly from a lack of oil.

The street continued straight ahead, save that now curbstones and sidewalks lined it. On either side of the road, gray, square buildings rose to a height of two stories. Made of quarried stone, the buildings had a simple and clean architectural style. On the first floor, a rectangular door led into each dwelling, and on the second story, one or two square windows overlooked the street. Without exception, they were constructed with the finest workmanship, though Midnight did see a few signs of deterioration—loose stones and gaps in the seams between blocks.

But it was not the buildings that caught Midnight's interest. The white spectres of a thousand men and women flitted here and there, their glowing forms illuminating the city in pale, twinkling light. The streets buzzed with the eerie cackle of their conversations.

Upon seeing so many apparitions in one place, it occurred to Midnight that this was a gathering place for shades like the one she had followed into the city. An instant later, she concluded that the glowing white forms were the souls of the dead. Noting that the soul spectres were not paying her any attention, Midnight started down the street. Though frightened, she was determined not to let that fear get in her way. If this city was the Realm of the Dead, then the other Tablet of Fate was hidden somewhere nearby. She intended to get it and leave as quickly as possible. Then she would find Kelemvor.

Halfway down the first block, a soul spectre approached Midnight. He had the form of an elderly man, with wrinkles on his brow and confused, vacant spheres of light where his eyes should have been.

"Jessica?" the man asked, reaching out for Midnight's hand. "Is that you? I didn't want to leave until we were together."

Midnight recoiled, anxiously avoiding his touch. "No. You're looking for somebody else."

"Are you sure?" the spectre asked, disappointed. "I can't wait much longer."

"I'm not Jessica," Midnight answered firmly. Then, more gently, she added, "Don't worry. I'm sure she'll be along when her time comes. You can wait for her."

"No, I can't!" the spectre snapped. "I don't have time— you'll see!" With that, he turned and drifted away.

After the soul spectre left, Midnight continued down the street. Several times, shades approached her, demanding to know if she was a loved one or friend, though they seldom seemed as confused as the old man. Midnight was able to excuse herself with nothing more than polite denials, then continue on her way.

For the first two blocks, the road was lined with empty shops, often with living quarters located directly overhead. Midnight poked her head into the doors of four of the buildings as she went. Each time, a small party of spectres greeted her—twice with polite invitations to join them, once with disinterested rudeness, and once with a rather hostile demand to be left alone.

As Midnight progressed farther into the city, she grew increasingly impressed by the thoughtfulness and planning that had gone into building it. The streets all intersected at right angles, and the blocks were more or less uniform in size. But the dwellings themselves were not drab or uninteresting. The buildings had been designed with a stoic artistry. They had clean, square forms and symmetrical plans that lent themselves to function as well as beauty. Exterior walls were adorned with simple etched lines that echoed the rectangular designs of the structures. Doors were always placed in the center of the building, with an equal number of windows located in similar positions on either side of them. The simple architecture left Midnight with a relaxed, peaceful feeling.

The city's third block was entirely taken by a single structure that rose all the way to the cavern's roof. This building lacked both doors and windows, its only opening being a great arch located exactly in the middle of the block. Midnight went to this arch and entered the massive structure.

She emerged in a great open courtyard. On three sides, it was lined by three-story promenades. Behind the promenades, arched doorways led into spacious rooms. A massive building, supported by white columns of the finest marble, dominated the end of the courtyard to Midnight's left. The altar in its entrance suggested it was a temple.

At the other end of the courtyard, dozens of spectres lounged on the edge of a marble fountain. In the center of the fountain, a magnificent spout of water shot high into the air and turned to mist. A strange harmony, at once unsettling and calming, radiated from the fountain, and Midnight found herself drawn toward its waters.

The spectres near the font seemed oblivious to her presence, so she approached and peered into its pool. The water was as still as ice and as black as Bhaal's heart, but also as clear as glass. The magic-user felt as though she were looking into another world, where peace and tranquility reigned supreme.

Beneath the water lay a great plain of shimmering light. It sprawled in all directions as far as Midnight could see, and she felt as though she could see to the edge of the Realms. The plain was entirely featureless, save that millions of tiny figures milled about on it.

Gazing at the magnificent plain, a mood of serenity and destiny supplanted the mage's sorrow concerning Adon's loss and her anxiety about Kelemvor's absence. She felt it would not be long before she and her old friends were reunited. Midnight did not know why she felt this way, but suspected it had something to do with the vast plain below.

A deep, rough voice interrupted the magic-user's reverie. "I'm sorry to see you here."

Midnight looked up and saw a spectre addressing her. The shade was familiar, and she could not help flinching. The voice belonged to Kae Deverell, but to her, the form would forever be Bhaal's.

"Don't be sorry," Midnight said.

Deverell took a seat on the fountain next to her. "And your friends—I forget their names—how do they fare?"

"I don't know about Kelemvor," Midnight replied, "but Adon's down here somewhere."

"And the halfling?" Deverell asked. "What about Sneakabout?"

"He died in Yellow Snake Pass," Midnight said. She did not elaborate. The memory of Cyric's treachery pained her too much.

Deverell sighed. "I had hoped to hear better news."

A spectre leaped through Deverell and dove into the fountain, then sank toward the plain in long, graceful spirals. The lord commander draped a hand into the water and watched the spectre descend with a mixture of envy and fear.

"Oblivion—how it draws us," Deverell mused. He closed his eyes as though he were pulling a long draft from his mug back at High Horn. Though his hand did not disturb the water's glassy surface, the dark liquid was draining away the pain and anguish that came with being dead. It was also draining away the Cormyrian's memories of life.

At length, he withdrew his hand. The time for him to leap into the pool would come soon enough.

As soon as they died, the souls of the dead were drawn by Myrkul's magic to one of the thousands of places like this, the Fountain of Nepenthe—a pool or well filled with the black Waters of Forgetfulness. In normal times, Myrkul's attraction was so strong that a soul spectre would immediately leap into dark waters, then emerge on the plain on the other side.

With Myrkul barred from his home, however, his magic had been considerably weakened. Many soul spectres were finding the strength to resist his attraction—although only temporarily. All through the Realms, soul spectres were gathered outside long forgotten wells and pools and fountains, vainly attempting to resist the final call of death.

Deverell tore his thoughts away from the fountain and turned to Midnight. "Tell me, who has the tablets now? What will happen to Cormyr and the Realms?"

"Kelemvor has one of the tablets," Midnight said, unaware that she was lying. "And the other is here somewhere."

"Here?" Deverell asked, perplexed. "What would it be doing here?"

"It's in Bone Castle," Midnight explained. "Myrkul took it."

"Then the Realms are doomed," Deverell replied flatly.

"Unless I can get to the castle and recover the tablet," Midnight said, dipping her fingers into the fountain's glistening waters. Unlike Deverell, she caused expanding rings of ripples. The water both chilled and comforted her.

"Stop!" Deverell yelled, reaching for her arm. His fingers closed right through her bones, leaving the flesh cold and numb. "You're alive!"

"Yes," Midnight said reluctantly, unsure what to make of Deverell's reaction.

"Pull your hand out of the water!"

Midnight obeyed, wondering if she had offended the soul spectre by touching the fountain.

This calmed Deverell. "You're alive—and that means there is hope," he said, "but not if you let those waters drain your memory. Now what is this about Bone Castle?"

"That's where the other tablet is," Midnight explained. "I've got to get inside and recover it. Can you take me there?"

Deverell's form grew even whiter, if that was possible. "No," he muttered and turned away. "I'm not ready for the Fountain of Nepenthe. And even if I was, I've never been to the Realm of the Dead."

"This isn't it?" Midnight demanded.

"Not by an arrow's long flight," Deverell said, shaking his head. "We're in Kanaglym, according to the others."

"Kanaglym?"

"Built by the dwarves when the High Moor was fertile and warm."

Midnight could not imagine a time when the High Moor was fertile, much less warm. "But there are no dwarves here now," she observed, looking around the fountain.

"No," Deverell agreed. "They never inhabited it, at least not for long. The town well ran dry within a year of Kanaglym's completion. The dwarves sank a deeper well on the site of the old one. Eventually, they struck a limitless supply of water: the Waters of Forgetfulness.

"Within a month, they realized their mistake and re-named their beautiful well the Fountain of Nepenthe. A month after that, most of them abandoned Kanaglym completely. Those who were too stubborn to evacuate simply forgot where they lived and wandered off into the dark."

"Then this isn't Myrkul's realm," Midnight sighed. "Bhaal said there was an entrance to the Realm of the Dead below Dragonspear. I thought I had found it."

"That you have," Deverell responded, nodding toward the fountain.

"Under the water?"

"Aye. The dwarves dug this well so deep they struck Myrkul's domain," Deverell explained.

"It should be easy to reach, then," Midnight said, peering into the dark pool. "A simple water-breathing—"

"No," Deverell interrupted. "Not through the water. It drains your emotions and your memories."

Midnight was not worried. "I have other ways to pass." She was thinking specifically of teleporting, but a better idea presented itself to her. It was something called a worldwalk, which created an ultra-dimensional connection between planes.

Midnight had never heard of that spell before, but she had a good idea why she would be able to use it. Then, without giving the matter any conscious thought, she realized she knew not only how to perform the incantation, but how it was constructed, the theory that made it work, and that Elminster had developed the original spell.

The magic-user was astonished. There was no reason she should know all that. The information had simply come to her. She decided to see what else she could do. Midnight searched her memory for a complete listing of Elminster's spells. Her mind was immediately flooded with the incantations for, construction of, and theory behind every spell Elminster knew, which seemed an endless list of magic. Reeling from the plethora of information, she turned her thoughts away from the ancient mage's magic. Remembering an interesting spell she had once witnessed, in which a mage interposed a disembodied magical hand between himself and an attacker, Midnight explored her mind for information about that spell. Again, she immediately discovered that she knew everything about it, from how to perform the incantation to the fact that a wizard named Bigby had invented it several centuries ago.

Somehow, Midnight realized, she had acquired an encyclopedic knowledge of magic, almost as though she had access to a mystical book containing every spell ever invented. There was no doubt that this new ability was related to Mystra's power, but the magic-user did not understand why it had come to her at this particular moment. Perhaps it was because she was so close to an exit from the Realms. Or perhaps it was simply another development in her expanding relationship to the planet's magical weave. Whatever the reason, Midnight could not help but feel encouraged. She would certainly need every advantage available if she was to recover the Tablet of Fate from Bone Castle.

Contemplating the task of recovering the tablet brought Midnight's thoughts back to Deverell and his interest in helping her. Turning to the lord commander, she asked, "You're already dead, so what do you care what happens to the Realms?"

"A man's honor does not die with his body," Deverell replied. "As a Harper, I swore to uphold the good and combat evil wherever I found it. That vow will bind me until . . ." He nodded toward the fountain.

"I hope that's a long time," Midnight responded.

Deverell did not reply, for he knew that he didn't have the willpower to resist the fountain much longer. "You look tired. Perhaps you should rest before you go," he said. "I'll watch over you."

"I think I will," Midnight replied. She did not know how long it had been since she had slept, but the mage suspected that there would be little opportunity for rest in the Realm of the Dead.

They went to one corner of the courtyard and Midnight lay down. It took her a long time to fall asleep, and then her rest was filled with dreams and bad omens. Still, she slept as long as possible and when she woke, her body—if not her mind—felt ready to continue her journey.

As she stood and stretched, Midnight noticed that a crowd of several thousand soul spectres had gathered in the courtyard.

"I'm sorry," Deverell said. "When you fell asleep, word of a live woman's presence spread quickly. They've come to look at you, but mean no harm."

Looking at the spectres' envious faces, Midnight felt sad for them. "It's all right," she said. "How long did I sleep?"

Deverell shrugged. "I'm sorry, but I no longer have a sense of time."

Midnight started forward, then a thought occurred to her and she turned to Deverell. "If somebody died at Dragon-spear Castle, would his soul come to Kanaglym?"

Deverell nodded. "Of course. The Fountain of Nepenthe is the closest access to the Realm of the Dead from the ruins."

Midnight turned and addressed the crowd. "Kelemvor, are you here?" she cried. The crowd of soul spectres shifted uneasily and looked from one to another, but nobody came forward. Midnight breathed a sigh of relief.

The magic-user addressed the crowd again, this time expecting a response. "Adon, how about you? Come here so we can talk." Midnight was not sure how she would feel about speaking to a dead friend, but she had to try. "Adon, it's Midnight!"

Adon still did not show himself.

Five minutes later, Deverell said, "Perhaps he is scared, or could not resist the fountain for long."

Midnight shook her head. "That's not like Adon. He isn't one to give up."

Deverell searched the crowd. "Well, he's not coming forward. I don't think you'll gain anything by waiting for him."

Midnight reluctantly nodded. "Perhaps it's for the best. It would only cause us both pain."

"Then, if you're ready," Deverell said, extending a glowing hand toward the Fountain of Nepenthe.

Midnight gathered her courage and nodded. "As ready as I'll ever be."

Deverell led the way through the crowd of soul spectres. When he reached the Fountain of Nepenthe, he stopped and turned toward Midnight. "Until swords part, then."

Deverell's farewell heartened Midnight, for she recognized his words as a warrior's sign of respect. "May your noble heart save your soul," she replied.

The magic-user looked back to the throng of soul spectres, searching for Adon's face or some sign that he had come to see her off. The crowd remained a swarm of impassive and unfamiliar faces.

Midnight turned to the pool, trying to imagine what she would find on the white plain below. Finally, hoping that if her magic was ever going to be reliable, it would be reliable now, she summoned the incantation for Elminster's worldwalk and performed it. A shimmering disc of force appeared over the fountain. Midnight took a deep breath and stepped inside.

*   *   *   *   *

Cyric stood before a small inn, his horse's reins in his hand. The inn was located in the barren prairie between Dragonspear Castle and Daggersford. The tavern and lodge were in a stone building standing in the shade of six maples. The stable sat fifty yards to the west, its corral built over a small stream that provided a constant supply of fresh water.

But the stream was now clogged by dead livestock, and the stable had burned to the ground. At the tavern, the sign of the Roosting Gryphon lay on the snow, half-burned and illegible. The shutters were smashed and splintered, and wisps of greasy smoke drifted out the open windows.

Is there anything for me? the thief's sword asked, the words forming inside his mind as if they were his own thoughts.

"I doubt it," Cyric answered. "But I'll look around." He and the sword—he thought of it as a "she"—had fallen into the habit of addressing each other as companions—even friends, if such a thing were possible.

Please—anything will do. I'm withering.

"I'll try," Cyric replied sincerely. "I'm hungry, too."

Neither of them had eaten since stealing the horse from the six hapless warriors who had "rescued" Cyric. The thief suspected the sword was in far worse shape than he was. For the first part of their fast, the sword had used its dark powers to keep him from feeling the effects of hunger. After Dragonspear Castle, however, she had grown too weak to continue sustaining the thief.

That had been two days ago. Now, Cyric's belly ached with hunger and he was lightheaded and weak with exhaustion. Both he and the sword needed sustenance.

But there had been no chance to feed. After Midnight's attempt to kill him, Cyric had entered the tower, intending to chase Midnight and Kelemvor wherever they went. But as he started down the stairs, the zombies had emerged with the tablet. The thief had assumed that Kelemvor and Midnight had died at the undead creatures' rotting hands.

He had turned to follow the zombies, determined to steal the tablet from them at the first opportunity. So far, the undead caravan drivers had not given him a chance. They had marched far into the snowy plain west of the road, where they would not be observed by passing caravans. Then they had turned north and started walking at a plodding, relentless pace, and had not stopped since.

Finally, because the caravan road ran northwest and the zombies had continued marching straight north, they had intersected the road near the inn. From a hiding place in the snow, Cyric had watched the undead raze the inn before resuming their relentless march. Although the thief was not sure why they had destroyed the tavern, he suspected it had been a mistake. By traveling so far off the road, the zombies were clearly taking pains to avoid detection. They had probably been instructed to kill anyone who saw them. So, when they ran across the inn, they had sacked it. Of course, destroying an establishment on a well-used road would hardly keep their presence secret, but zombies were not smart enough to think of that detail.

Anyway, now that the undead had disappeared over the horizon, Cyric thought it was safe to see if they had left anything behind. He tied his horse to a maple tree, then entered the tavern. A dozen bodies littered the floor, scattered between tables and in the corners. It appeared the men had tried to fight the zombies off with fire, for expired torches lay strewn about the dirt floor. In several places, the torches had touched something flammable, causing fires that still smoldered here and there. It looked as though the flames had fallen just short of engulfing the inn.

"How do you feel about drinking blood from the dead?" Cyric asked his sword.

How do you feel about it? she replied. *Does anybody look good to you?*

"I'm not that hungry," Cyric answered, disgusted.

I am, the sword said flatly.

Cyric unsheathed his sword, then went over to the corpse of a burly woman wearing an apron. In her hand was the handle of a butcher knife, but the blade had been snapped off. Her throat was bruised where a zombie had choked her. Cyric knelt at her side, preparing to slip his sword between the corpse's ribs.

"She's dead," said a man's strained voice. "They all are!"

Cyric quickly rose and turned around. A balding, portly man stood in the doorway, a loaded crossbow in his hands.

"Don't shoot," Cyric said, slowly raising his hands. He assumed the man had seen enough to guess that his intentions were not honorable. The thief was merely looking for a way to stall until he could turn the advantage his way. "This isn't what you think."

The portly man frowned. "What's wrong with you? Why are you so afraid?" The man did not suspect Cyric of anything nefarious. He was in shock and had forgotten the effect that holding a lethal weapon would have on other people.

Gathering his wits, Cyric nodded at the crossbow. "I thought you might have mistaken me for—"

"For a zombie?" the man scoffed, looking at his crossbow and blushing. "I'm not that rattled."

The fat man stepped behind the bar and laid the weapon down. "Will you join me in a draft—compliments of the house? As you see, I'm out of business."

Cyric sheathed his sword and went to the bar. "I'd be happy to."

The portly man poured Cyric a mug of ale, then set it on the counter and poured himself one. "I'm called Farl," he said, offering his hand.

Cyric took the hand. "Well met. I'm Cyric," he replied, forcing as much warmth as he could into his voice. "How did you survive this . . ."

The fat man frowned. "Zombie attack," he muttered flatly. "I was in the basement when it happened. Just lucky, I guess."

The thief narrowed his eyes and stared at the innkeeper for a moment. "Yes," he said. "I guess you were lucky."

"Yes, well, here's to luck, Cyric!" Farl called, draining his mug.

After watching Farl empty his mug in a single gulp, Cyric tipped his own. Unfortunately, his empty stomach rebelled at the strong brew and he could not finish it. He sat the mug down and braced himself against the bar.

"Are you ill?" Farl asked absently. At the moment, he was still too stunned and shocked to feel any real concern for a stranger, but he was too observant a host not to take notice of his guest's condition.

"Nay," Cyric replied. "I haven't eaten in a week."

"That's too bad," Farl muttered automatically, pouring himself another mug. He downed it in one long gulp, then belched quietly into his sleeve. Finally, it occurred to the fat man that Cyric might like something to eat.

"Wait here," the innkeeper said, shaking his head at his negligence. "I'll fetch you something from what remains of the kitchen." He poured another ale and left the room.

Farl is a juicy morsel, the sword urged.

"Aye, he is. But you'll have to wait your turn," Cyric said.

I can't wait any longer!

"I'll decide how long you can wait," the thief snapped.

I'm fading.

Cyric did not answer. He felt foolish for arguing with a sword. More importantly, he found her demanding tone offensive. But he also knew that the sword was being truthful. The color of her blade had faded to white.

Without me, you wouldn't have recovered from Bhaal's wounds, the sword insisted. *Do you want me to starve?*

"I won't let you starve," Cyric said patiently. "But I'll decide what I feed you."

Farl came shuffling back to the door, a large tray in his hand. "Who are you talking to?" he asked.

You owe me Farl! the sword hissed. The words were hot and urgent in Cyric's thoughts.

"I was talking to myself," the thief said. "It's one of the hazards of riding alone."

Farl sat the tray on the counter. He had assembled the best his kitchen had to offer: roast goose, stewed tomatoes, pickled beets, dried apples. "Have a feast," he said. "It'll just go to waste if you don't eat it."

"Then I'll eat until my horse can't carry me," Cyric replied, noting that Farl had brought all the food he would need for some time to come. "Could I have another mug of ale to wash it down?"

"Of course," Farl muttered, taking the mug and filling it. "Have all you like." He smiled weakly.

"Rest assured," Cyric replied. He accepted the mug with one hand and drew his sword with the other. "I will."

The thief reached across the food and struck quickly. He plunged the blade into the fat man's chest while the innkeeper's lips were still twisted in a feeble smile.

Farl made one feeble grab for his crossbow. Then, his brow raised in puzzlement and he collapsed behind the counter. So the blade would stay imbedded in the man's breast, Cyric released his sword's hilt.

The thief grabbed a piece of goose and took a large bite out of it. Then he leaned over the counter and looked at his sword. Speaking around a mouthful of cold meat, he said, "Enjoy your meal."

❦ 14 ❦

The White Plain

As she stepped through the disc, Midnight felt herself disappear from Kanaglym, then reappear on the white plain. Her mind felt as if it had not moved at all, as if it were an anchor and her body had pivoted around it.

As soon as Midnight inhaled, caustic vapors burned her throat and nose. When she tried to focus her eyes, she saw nothing but white and might as well have been looking into the sun. The ground quivered beneath her feet like something alive and restless, and a million droning voices set the air buzzing with a murmur that made her skin tingle.

Gradually, Midnight's vision returned. The worldwalk's shimmering disc hung in the air next to her. It did not seem wise to leave a portal between the planes open, so the mage concentrated on closing it and the gateway disappeared.

A moment later, she began to make sense of the weird information her senses were gathering. She stood on an endless, chalky plain, in the midst of more people than she could count. Unlike the soul spectres of Kanaglym, these creatures possessed material, tangible bodies. Had she not known otherwise, the magic-user would have thought the people on the plain were alive.

To the mage's right was a huge crowd of several thousand. Everyone in the throng faced one direction, their attention fixed on the sky as though watching something Midnight could not see. As she studied the mass of spirits, a murmur rose from its far side, racing toward her like a wave on a stormy ocean. Finally, it broke over her with such volume that she grimaced.

"Tyr!" the crowd called.

Thousands of worshipers had simultaneously called the name of their lord. Midnight could easily imagine the cry crossing the interplanar void and reaching Tyr's ears back in the Realms.

"O Tyr, God of Justice, Balancer of the Scales, answer this, the call of your faithful," the worshipers cried, their prayer clear and understandable despite the number of mouths speaking the words. "When will you deliver us, we who dedicated our lives to your glory, to spreading truth and justice into every corner of our planet, Toril? Hear the appeal of your worshipers, Tyr. Look! Here is Mishkul the Mighty, who brought King Lagost to justice; and here is Ornik the Wise, who judged between the cities of Yhaunn and Tulbegh; and here is Qurat of Proskur, who . . ."

The prayer droned on, proclaiming the loyalty of Tyr's worshipers and listing the accomplishments of each one. Judging from the size of the mob, the litany would continue for days. The mage moved away from the crowd, searching for a hint as to Bone Castle's location.

Often, she encountered huddled groups of people ranging from five or six to ten thousand. In one instance, Midnight encountered a dozen women flailing themselves and screaming devotion to Loviatar, Lady of Pain. Another time, she met a thousand worshipers of Ilmater standing shoulder to shoulder in resolute silence. Occasionally, she saw groups singing praises to gods so ancient their names had been forgotten in the Realms.

Several hours of wandering later, Midnight realized that she would never find her way around the Realm of the Dead without directions. Stopping a rotund man, she asked, "Can you tell me how to find Bone Castle?"

His eyes opened wide in fear. "No—no, I can't!" he snapped. "Why would I know where it is—and why would you want to?" He abruptly turned and fled into the crowd.

Midnight stopped three more people and asked them the same question. The reactions of all three were strikingly similar: each claimed ignorance of the castle's location, and each told her in no uncertain terms that she was a fool for asking. The mage decided to stop inquiring about the castle. For some reason, her question disturbed the dead.

To Midnight's left, someone screamed in terror. The magic-user spun toward the sound. Thirty feet away, a mound of flesh was attacking a woman. The crowd had cleared away from the struggle, so Midnight had a clear view of the conflict.

The woman appeared to have been about forty years of age, with hair as black as Midnight's, save that it was streaked with gray. More interesting to the magic-user was the woman's pendant: a blue-white star within a circle.

Mystra's symbol.

The woman's attacker was a hideous thing. Its head resembled that of a man, with a normal nose, mouth, and ears. But it also had dull fangs that drooled yellow bile and eyes that glowed as red as hot embers. The head sat atop a grotesque body thicker around than a hogshead cask, and long, gangling arms hung from its shoulders. Spongy masses of leathery hide bulged where muscles should have been, and old wounds oozed a foul green pus in a dozen places. The creature's legs were so pudgy they barely held its body off the ground. Still, the mound of flesh tottered after the woman with remarkable speed and grace.

"Come here, hag!" it growled. The beast's voice was so low and guttural that Midnight barely understood the words. In one hand the fat blob carried a rusty scimitar, and in the other a pair of manacles that it waved after the woman.

Because she knew so little about the Realm of the Dead, the mage hesitated to involve herself, but that indecision didn't last for long. She could not allow an attack on one of Mystra's followers. "Leave her alone!" Midnight yelled.

Upon hearing the mage's words, the woman fled toward her. The thing stopped in its tracks, then frowned and shook its head as if it were unable to believe what it had heard. Finally, it grumbled, "She belongs to Lord Myrkul."

As if the explanation were adequate, the beast ran after the woman and smashed the manacles into her head.

Mystra's follower fell in a limp heap.

"Stop!" Midnight ordered, advancing toward the fight. "Touch her and you die!"

The thing paused to stare at the raven-haired woman. Finally, it roared, "Die? Touch her and I die?" It broke into a cackle that sent waves rolling through its fat body. Then it kneeled and placed a shackle on the woman's wrist.

A powerful imprisonment incantation appeared in Midnight's mind. The magic-user hesitated for an instant, then felt the magical weave around her. It was strong and stable, not wavering and unpredictable as it had been in the Realms. Midnight smiled and repeated the spell.

The thing placed a shackle on the woman's other wrist.

After completing the incantation, Midnight started toward the mound of flesh, saying, "I warned you."

The woman's attacker looked up and snarled, then stood to meet Midnight. "You'll rot in—"

The magic-user reached out to the foul creature and touched it, triggering the imprisonment magic. The mound of flesh stopped speaking in midsentence, then froze in place. An instant later, a dark sphere engulfed the fat monstrosity and carried it into the white ground. It would remain there in suspended animation until someone freed it.

Midnight started to tremble, then sat down and closed her eyes. While confronting the ugly mound of flesh, the magic-user had been angry and determined. Now that the fight was over, however, she felt surprisingly queasy and frightened. Although the magical weave had felt stable when she called upon it, Midnight could not help but shiver at what might have happened had her magic misfired.

She tried to put thoughts of failure aside. The incantation had worked flawlessly, and the mage realized that she had no reason to believe that magic was unstable outside the Realms. For several moments, Midnight remained sitting with her eyes closed.

"Do I know you?" asked a man's voice.

The voice seemed vaguely familiar, though Midnight could not place it. She opened her eyes and, to her surprise, saw a hundred people staring at her. The woman Midnight had saved was nowhere in sight. She had vanished without thanking her savior.

The man who had spoken stood directly ahead of Midnight, wearing a scarlet robe trimmed with gold. He was Rhaymon of Lathander.

"What are you doing here, Rhaymon?" Midnight asked, standing. The last time she had seen him was at the trial in Shadowdale. He had been very much alive.

"Then I do know you!" Rhaymon cried, delighted. "I was right!"

However, the cleric didn't answer Midnight's question. In fact, he had died in the forest outside of Shadowdale, when an oak tree's limb became mobile and strangled him. He rarely cared to talk about the experience.

"Yes, you know me," Midnight confirmed. "You testified against Adon and me at the trial for Elminster's murder."

Rhaymon frowned. "Elminster? But he's not dead . . . is he?"

"No," Midnight said quickly. "The trial was a mistake."

Rhaymon frowned, wishing he could remember more about Midnight's trial, for his memories had begun to slowly slip away since he'd come to the plain in the Realm of the Dead. But the cleric did remember that Midnight had not been executed. "I don't remember much about the trial," he admitted. "But you escaped, so, as the faithful of Lathander say, 'a bright dawn made the dark night worthwhile.' "

"I'm not sure I'd say that," Midnight replied, thinking of the people Cyric had murdered to gain her freedom.

Rhaymon did not take note of Midnight's uneasiness. "You were brave to rescue that woman," he said, wagging a finger at her. "But you were also foolish. You won't save her by stopping just one of them."

"What was that thing?" Midnight asked, pointing at the spot where she had imprisoned the mobile mound of flesh.

"One of Myrkul's denizens," Rhaymon explained.

Midnight's heart jumped and she suddenly felt very vulnerable. She noticed that the spectators were still staring at her. "I wish they'd stop watching me like that," Midnight noted uneasily, glaring back at the crowd.

Rhaymon turned and addressed the gapers. "Go on—there's nothing to see here."

When the crowd continued to stare, Rhaymon took Midnight by the elbow and guided her away. "Don't mind them. They're curious about your eyes."

"My eyes?" Midnight asked.

"Yes. A moment ago, your eyes were closed. The dead don't close their eyes, you know." Rhaymon stopped and studied Midnight for a moment. "I suppose that means you're alive?"

"And what if it does?" Midnight asked, looking away and avoiding a direct answer to Rhaymon's question.

"Nothing. It's just unusual." The cleric guided her forward again. "Most dead don't use magic—not unless they're liches. By the way, which are you: undead or alive?"

Midnight sighed. "I'm alive, Rhaymon. And I need your help."

"What do you want?" he asked, leading the way around a group of old ladies—worshipers of Lliira, the Goddess of Joy—rolling on the ground, laughing.

"I need to find Bone Castle," Midnight replied. "The fate of the whole world depends on my success." She did not say more. Until Rhaymon agreed to help, it seemed wise to reveal as little as possible.

"Bone Castle!" Rhaymon exclaimed. "That's in Myrkul's city!"

"Isn't this Myrkul's realm?" Midnight asked.

Rhaymon shook his head. "Not quite. But you can get there easily enough."

"Will you help me?"

"What you say must be true," Rhaymon replied, "or you'd never risk the kind of eternal suffering you'll find in Myrkul's city. I'm sure that Lord Lathander would want me to do what I can."

"Thank you," Midnight said. "Where do we go?"

Rhaymon pointed to his right. "West."

"West?" Midnight asked, searching the barren sky for something by which to tell her direction. "How do know that's west?"

Rhaymon smiled. "I don't. But when you're dead, you acquire a certain sense for this place that I can't explain. You'll just have to trust me on this—and a hundred things like it."

Considering the difficulties she had encountered so far, Midnight thought that seemed wise.

Rhaymon led the way through the milling crowd, pausing or turning aside every now and then to make sure they did not cross paths with a denizen. After what must have been hours of walking, Midnight began to stumble.

"How much farther is it?" she asked.

"A lot farther," Rhaymon answered, continuing forward steadily.

"We've got to find some way to get there faster," Midnight gasped between panted breaths. "I've got to meet Kelemvor in Waterdeep."

"There is no faster way to travel," Rhaymon noted calmly. "Unless you care to attract denizens. But don't worry. Time and distance are different here. Whether it takes you a day or a month to reach Bone Castle, the time that passes on Toril will be only a fraction of the time that passes here."

They continued walking for several more hours, then the mage could go no farther. She collapsed and slept while Rhaymon watched over her. After a long time, Midnight woke refreshed and they continued their journey. The mage took the opportunity to have Rhaymon explain what he knew about Myrkul's realm.

Adjusting his pace so that Midnight walked at his side, Rhaymon said, "Myrkul has two domains: his city in Hades, which is where you are going and which he rules absolutely, and the Fugue Plain, which is a demiplane outside his city that he oversees as part of his duties. When somebody dies in the Realms, his spirit is drawn to one of the thousands of gates between the Realms and the Lord of the Dead's two domains. The spirits of Myrkul's faithful go directly to his city in Hades."

Here, Rhaymon stopped walking and interrupted his lecture. "You might actually beat your friend Kelemvor to Waterdeep, you know."

"How?" Midnight asked, also stopping. The idea of using the Realm of the Dead as a short cut delighted her.

"The chances are good that there's a gate between Waterdeep and Myrkul's city," Rhaymon answered. "If you can escape from the city at all, you can return to the Realms via the gate to Waterdeep."

"Thanks for the suggestion," Midnight replied grimly, starting to walk again.

Rhaymon resumed his pace and his lecture. "Although Myrkul's faithful go directly to his city, everybody else comes to the Fugue Plain, which is really a waiting area for the spirits of the dead. Here, Myrkul's denizens—who were once his worshipers, I suppose—harvest the spirits of the Faithless and the False—"

"The Faithless and the False?" Midnight interrupted.

"The False are those who betray their gods," Rhaymon explained. "The Faithless don't worship any gods."

"What do the denizens do with the spirits?" Midnight asked, thinking of Adon and his break with Sune.

"Take them to Myrkul's city for an eternity of suffering, I'd imagine," Rhaymon noted calmly. "I don't know—but I'm sure you'll find out soon enough."

"No doubt," Midnight replied darkly.

"After the denizens cull out the spirits of the Faithless and the False, the Faithful wait here for their gods to take them to a final resting place in the Planes."

"Then why is the Fugue Plain so crowded?" Midnight asked, eyeing the milling masses.

Rhaymon frowned. "Because this is our final test," he said. "With only one or two exceptions, the gods have chosen to leave us here to prove our worthiness."

"It seems callous to abandon loyal worshipers like that," Midnight observed.

"They haven't abandoned us," Rhaymon answered quickly. "They'll come for us someday."

Midnight accepted this answer, though it was obvious that Rhaymon's statement was founded on hope, not knowledge. For if the gods *were* concerned about their worshipers, the Fugue Plain would have been far less crowded.

They continued their conversations and their trek for another two days. The mage learned little more of significant interest. Eventually, the crowds began to thin, and a dark line appeared on the horizon. Midnight had no doubt that they were getting close to Myrkul's city.

Finally, the dead cleric and the mage reached a point beyond which there were no more milling souls. The dark line on the horizon had changed to a dark ribbon stretching from one side of the endless plain to another.

Rhaymon stopped walking. "I've brought you as far as I can," he said. "Beyond here, I'm no use to you."

Midnight sighed and tried to smile, though she felt lonely and abandoned. "You've done more than enough already," she replied softly.

Rhaymon pointed toward the left end of the ribbon. "I understand the entrance to the city is down there," he said. "I brought you here so you could approach the wall without meeting the denizens as they go to and from the gate."

Midnight took Rhaymon's hand. "Words cannot express my gratitude," she said. "I'll miss your company."

"And I'll miss yours," he replied. After a small pause, he added some last-minute advice. "Midnight, this is not the world of the living. What seems cruel and evil to you is the normal course here. No matter what you find in Myrkul's city, remember where you are. If you interfere with the denizens, you'll never leave."

"I'll remember your advice," she said. "I promise."

"Good. May the gods favor your path," Rhaymon said.

"And may you keep your faith," Midnight responded.

"I will," he answered. "I promise." With that, he turned and walked back toward the souls upon the Fugue Plain.

Midnight turned toward Myrkul's city and started walking. Two hours later, an eerie moan reached her ears and musty whiffs of rot plagued her nose. The magic-user continued at her best pace. The moan gradually became a suppressed wail, and the stench of decay grew stronger and hung more steadily in the air. The wall constantly grew higher and larger, and as Midnight got close to it, she saw that its surface swayed and writhed—as if it were alive.

The mage wondered if the wall was made of serpents. That would explain the absence of sentries. If the wall itself was menacing enough, Myrkul would not need guards.

Midnight continued forward, approaching within fifty feet of the wall. The suppressed wail changed into a cacophony of muffled sobs, the foul smell of decay grew so strong it nauseated her, and the magic-user saw that she had been mistaken about the writhing forms in the wall. What she had taken to be serpents were thousands of squirming legs.

The wall was constructed entirely of human bodies. Men and women were stacked fifty feet high, their bodies turned inward to face the interior of the city. The largest people gave the wall bulk and height, while the smaller ones chinked gaps and filled holes. They had all been sealed into place with a greenish mortar that reminded Midnight of solidified mold.

The hideous barrier was nearly enough to end Midnight's journey. For a long time, she could only stand and stare in sickened shock. The magic-user had intended to climb over the wall, but could not bring herself to grapple the legs. Instead, deciding to the make use of her magic, she summoned and performed the incantation for levitation.

Immediately, her feet left the ground and she rose into the air. Every now and then, Midnight grasped a squirming leg and used it as a guide. A moment later, she pulled herself into a prone position just inches over the top of the wall, hoping to look like just one more body.

A squall of howls and screeches greeted her. The magic-user recoiled and covered her ears. On the other side of the wall, the cries of the dead had been muffled by the space between the Fugue Plain and Myrkul's city. But when Midnight had pulled herself onto the wall, she had crossed from the demiplane into Hades.

The air inside the wall smelled rank and profane, with a caustic bite that scorched her nose and throat when she breathed. The dark gray sky cast only a dim light over the city. Here and there, pinholes of illumination penetrated the murky heavens. From what Rhaymon had told her, Midnight suspected that the tiny lights were gateways between Myrkul's domain and various spots in the Realms.

The city itself sat in a great bowl that sloped down from the wall toward the opposite horizon. The metropolis was so immense that, even from atop the wall, Midnight could only see that the far side disappeared into a haze of indistinguishable detail.

Closer to Midnight, a broad avenue circled inside the wall's perimeter. Twenty feet down the road, thirty whip-carrying denizens were driving several hundred slaves in Midnight's direction. As the group passed beneath her, the magic-user saw that the slaves had remarkably similar, drab features: gray hair, yellow-gray skin, and expressionless gray eyes. But the people they carried had distinctive features. Here was a woman with buckteeth, there was a man with a large nose, and behind him was an obese woman with a triple chin.

Although the mage wanted nothing more than to free the slaves, Rhaymon's warning against interfering with the denizens remained fresh in her mind. Midnight simply turned her head away. After the slave train passed, she turned to watch the city again.

Inside the perimeter avenue stood a countless number of ten-story brownstone structures. These buildings had once been identical, but ages of decay and corrosion had twisted them into a plethora of different shapes. While some remained in pristine condition, many had deteriorated so badly they were little more than stacks of rocks that might collapse at any moment. Others had sprouted twisted minarets and crooked towers, and were now warped into shapes only vaguely reminiscent of their original form.

As Midnight studied the buildings, she observed that structures of similar condition were grouped together.

Then she noticed the city was divided into boroughs of more or less equivalent size. The areas with pristine buildings were divided into orderly blocks with straight, clean streets. Where the buildings were crumbling, the streets were so clogged with rubble that it appeared impossible to traverse them. In areas with twisted and grotesque buildings, the streets were crooked and narrow, curling and winding back on themselves with mazelike confusion. There was no sign of anything that might be Bone Castle, and Midnight did not know where to begin her search.

But she knew she had to get off this wall. After waiting for another caravan of slaves to pass, Midnight pushed herself over the city and floated down to the road that ran along the wall. She paused a moment to reconnoiter the area. One group of three denizens was tottering down the avenue after her, and two more were approaching from the borough directly ahead. Fortunately, both groups were over five hundred feet away, so she sprinted down the avenue away from them. After ten seconds of running, she ducked into a borough of deteriorated buildings that had looked abandoned from the wall.

The thoroughfares were cluttered with rubble and deserted. From the building's windowsills, sputtering yellow lamps cast putrid circles of light into the street. As Midnight passed one of the lamps, she inhaled a breath of the sulfurous vapor. She briefly choked and her skin stung where a wisp of black smoke had touched it.

The magic-user ducked down an alley and clawed over a pile of rubble half as high as one of the buildings. Then she tumbled down the other side and ran into the alley that connected with another street. She turned left and ran halfway down it. Finally, confident the denizens would never find her, Midnight climbed over another pile of rubble and stopped in a blind cul-de-sac.

She needed a guide. In a city of this size, it would be impossible to find Bone Castle without help. Even had she known the castle's location, the city was so alien it would be a simple matter to make a mistake and get killed. Midnight realized she would have to summon help.

Immediately, the incantation for summoning monsters came to mind, along with all of the extraneous information about its creator and the theory behind its construction. It was not a monster she wanted, but after contemplating the original spell for a moment, Midnight saw how she could modify the incantation to suit her needs.

The spell was designed to call an unspecified monster to aid the caster. Instead of a monster, however, Midnight needed to call a person, but had no idea who. By adjusting a few finger manipulations and altering the intonation of the spell's verbal components, the mage thought that she could call someone who both knew his way around Myrkul's city and would be willing to aid her.

Midnight was a little frightened by what she was about to try. Normally, only the most advanced mages altered or created spells. But, considering the knowledge available to her and the stability of the magical weave in the plane, Midnight was confident of success.

After reviewing her adjustments, the magic-user performed the incantation. A moment later, someone began climbing over the rubble in the entrance to her cul-de-sac. Midnight waited anxiously, prepared to dash into a building if the visitor was not what she expected.

A halfling climbed into view atop the rubble, then stopped and frowned at her. He had the same drab features, gray hair, yellow-gray skin, and expressionless gray eyes as the slaves Midnight had seen from atop the wall. In fact, the halfling was distinguishable from those slaves only in size.

Atherton Cooper had no idea how he had come to be in this alley. Just a moment ago, he had been laboring to mortar a struggling woman into the wall.

"Sneakabout?" Midnight asked, peering uncertainly at the short figure.

The halfling's frown deepened. He recognized something in the woman's voice and in the name she had called him. Then he remembered: Sneakabout was his name. "Yes—that's right," he observed. "Who are—"

The answer came to him before he finished asking it. He

had once been friends with the woman who now stood before him. "Midnight!" he exclaimed, sliding down the rubble. "What are you doing here?"

The mage held her arms out to the halfling. "Not what you think," she replied. "I'm alive."

Midnight's comment about being alive kindled a painful realization for Sneakabout and he stopped short of her arms. "I'm dead," he said, unpleasant memories flooding his mind. "Why did you let Cyric kill me?" he demanded.

Midnight didn't know what to say. She had not expected to meet Sneakabout, and was not prepared to justify saving Cyric to someone the thief had murdered. "I wouldn't make the same decision again," she said, dropping her arms.

"That's little consolation," Sneakabout hissed. "Look at what you've done to me!" He ran his hand down his body.

"*I* didn't let Cyric kill you!" Midnight snapped. "You threw yourself at his mercy!"

"I had to!" Sneakabout said, more memories washing over him. He looked away from Midnight's eyes. "He had my sword. I had to get it back or go insane."

"Why?" Midnight asked. So she would be at the halfling's eye level, she sat down.

"It's an evil, cursed thing," he explained, still not looking at the mage. "If you lose it, you must recover it. The man I stole it from died trying to steal it from me, just like I died trying to take it from Cyric."

Midnight suddenly understood why Sneakabout was in the City of the Dead. By pursuing the sword, by living only for it, he had betrayed his god.

"So you're one of the False," she gasped.

Sneakabout finally turned to look her in the eye. "Yes, I suppose I am."

"What does that mean?" Midnight asked. "What is your fate?"

The halfling shrugged, then casually looked away as if his fate was of little concern. "I'm one of Myrkul's slaves. I'll spend eternity mortaring the Faithless into the wall."

Midnight drew a sharp breath.

"What are you worried about?" Sneakabout asked. He turned back with an irritated frown on his face. "I thought you worshiped Mystra? Not that being faithful is much better than being faithless when you're down here. The Fugue Plain is overflowing with the abandoned souls of most of the gods' faithful."

"I'm not worried about myself," the mage said. "A few weeks after he killed you, Cyric killed Adon . . . and Adon died with no faith in the gods."

"Then its the wall for him," Sneakabout said, shaking his head glumly. "I'll probably be the one that mortars him in."

"Is there anything that you can—"

"No!" the halfling snapped, waving his hand to cut off Midnight's plea. "He chose his fate when he was alive. It can't be changed now. If that's why you summoned me—"

"It's not," Midnight said sadly, upset by the halfling's curt response. She wondered if he would be as unwilling to help her recover the tablet as he was to help Adon. Hoping to look more commanding, she stood. "You must take me to Bone Castle."

Sneakabout's eyes widened. "You don't know what you're asking! When they catch us, they'll . . ." He paused and considered his situation. The denizens could do nothing that was worse than what they were doing to him now.

"If you don't help me," Midnight said, taking the halfling by both shoulders, "the Realms will perish."

"What's that to me?" Sneakabout replied, backing away. "With luck, so will Myrkul's city."

"Help me get the Tablet of Fate and return it to Waterdeep," Midnight said, following Sneakabout. "I'll end your misery."

He stopped backing away. "How?"

"I don't know yet. But I'll find a way."

The halfling raised a skeptical eyebrow.

"Trust me," Midnight pleaded. "What do you have to lose?"

Of course, Sneakabout had nothing to lose. If the denizens caught him helping Midnight, they would torture him for eternity—but they were already doing that.

"All right. I'll help," the halfling said. "But realize that you've made a very important promise. If you don't keep it, you might be considered one of the False when you return."

"I know that," Midnight said. "Let's go."

Sneakabout turned and started over the rubble at the end of the cul-de-sac. For several hours, he led Midnight through a maze of twisting alleys and cluttered streets. Occasionally, they entered a region of straight clean avenues. The halfling always crossed these places quickly, then led them back into a deteriorating or twisted borough.

Midnight was glad to have Sneakabout as a guide. Although vaguely aware that they were walking toward the low end of the city, she was completely lost. Even the halfling stopped now and then to ask directions of one of the False. He always confirmed his directions with two or three others.

"The False," he explained, "are not to be trusted. They'll send you straight into a pack of denizens just out of habit."

Finally, noticing that Midnight was stumbling with weariness, Sneakabout led her onto the roof of a decaying building. "You need to rest," he said. "We'll be safe up here."

"Thanks," Midnight replied, resting her head on her arms. As she looked up at the sky, the mage noticed pinholes of light that resembled stars.

Noticing where Midnight was looking, Sneakabout said, "Those are the gates to the Realms."

"Are you sure?" the raven-haired mage asked. From what Rhaymon had told her, she had concluded the same thing. But, since one of the dots would be her escape route, she saw no harm in being certain.

"What else would they be?" the halfling asked. "There are no stars in Myrkul's city."

"If that's an exit," Midnight queried, rolling onto her side, "what keeps the dead and the denizens from using it?"

Sneakabout shrugged. "What prevents men from going to the real stars? They're too far, I suppose, and there are certain barriers. You'd better rest—and eat something, if you have it."

"I'll rest," Midnight replied, realizing she hadn't eaten in what must be days. It did not matter. Even if she had possessed food, she could not have kept it down. The smell and the cries of the damned were simply too unsettling.

A few hours later, she and the halfling resumed their march toward the low side of the city. Sneakabout led the way through mile after mile of cluttered avenues and twisting alleys. Finally, he stopped on a lopsided bridge spanning a river of black ooze.

"We're almost there," he said. "Are you ready?"

"Yes," Midnight replied. Despite her anxiety, she was telling the truth. Thanks to Sneakabout, she felt as fresh as could be expected after wandering Myrkul's realm for the equivalent of almost a week.

The pair continued down the street, then turned into an alley that snaked through one of the chaotic boroughs. A few minutes later, an eerie moan began to drift up the narrow lanes. Sneakabout slowed his pace and moved cautiously forward. Midnight followed half a step behind.

The alley turned sharply to the left. The stench of rot and decay grew so strong Midnight began gagging. She tapped Sneakabout's arm and they stopped so she could get used to the odor. Several minutes later, they moved forward again. The alley joined a broad boulevard, and on the other side of the boulevard was another wall built from human bodies.

Having seen one of the hideous barriers did not minimize the effect of this one. It still turned Midnight's stomach. Now, it also enraged and depressed her because Adon would share the fate of its hapless building blocks.

"This is Bone Castle," Sneakabout said. He pointed to a tall, ivory-colored spire that poked its crown above the barricade. "And that's the keep tower."

Midnight could not believe what she saw. Behind the wall, just a hundred feet away, rose a spiraling tower built from human bones. The tower ended in a steeple. Atop the steeple, lit by six magical torches and in plain view of anybody who could see Bone Castle, was a stone tablet. The mage immediately recognized it as the twin to the one she had left with Kelemvor.

Like a hunter displaying a prized trophy, Myrkul had put

his tablet where all his subjects could admire it.

"There it is!" Midnight whispered.

Sneakabout sighed. "So I see. How are you going to get it?"

"I'm not sure yet," the mage replied, studying the situation. "This is too easy—it doesn't make sense to leave the tablet unguarded."

"Don't make the mistake of thinking it's not guarded," Sneakabout said. "There are thousands of guards."

"How so?" Midnight asked.

"If we can see the tablet, so can all the denizens—and dukes and princes—within sight of Bone Castle."

"Dukes and princes?" Midnight asked.

"Who do you think commands the denizens?" Sneakabout replied. "The dukes rule the boroughs. The princes rule the dukes. Each is more vicious than its vassals."

Midnight nodded. If Myrkul's court was like most others, there would be no shortage of dukes and princes near Bone Castle. "What else?"

"The best way to guard a treasure is to lull the thief into thinking it's unguarded—then trap him when he tries to steal it. I'd expect a magical ward or two near the tablet."

Midnight did not bother asking Sneakabout how he knew so much about theft. Though he had claimed to be a scout, and had proven that he was when he was alive, it was no secret that many halflings learned the basics of thievery to survive. Right now, Midnight was grateful that he had. She would never have been foolish enough to go after the tablet without looking for possible defenses, but it was good to have the halfling confirm her suspicions. "Anything else?"

"That's enough," Sneakabout said. "A thousand guards and a trap or two will safeguard almost anything—unless you happen to have pretty potent magic at your disposal."

Though she knew the halfling had added this last comment to bolster her confidence, Midnight was hardly encouraged. "Let's hope it will be enough." She studied the tower for a moment, considering her plan of attack. "We'll turn invisible—"

"No good," Sneakabout interrupted. "The denizens—

especially the dukes—will see through that without a second glance."

Midnight frowned, then thought of another plan. "All right, then. We'll fly up there, I'll dispel the magical wards. Then we'll take the tablet and be gone."

Sneakabout considered this plan for a moment. "How long will that take you?" His use of the second person was deliberate. He knew he could not go with Midnight.

"Not long," Midnight said confidently.

"Probably too long," Sneakabout answered. "They'll be after you in the time it takes you to fly up there, maybe less."

"Then what can I do?" Midnight gasped.

"You'd better think of another plan," the halfling said. "You can't keep your promise if they capture you."

Midnight fell into a long silence and tried to think of another approach. Finally, she said, "This will work. I'll prepare our escape route before touching the tablet. Then, instead of going to the tablet, I'll bring it to us. We'll be gone in an instant."

"That should work," Sneakabout replied. "But I'll take my leave before you try it."

"Leave?" Midnight asked. "You aren't coming with me?"

Sneakabout shook his head. "No. I'm dead. In the Realms, I'd be undead and more miserable than I am here."

Midnight took the halfling's hand. "You'll never know what your help has meant to—"

"And I don't care," Sneakabout interrupted tersely. He could not help resenting the fact that Midnight would be leaving and he would not. "Just remember your promise."

He pulled his hand away and walked up the alley.

Midnight watched him go, confused and hurt by his sudden coldness. "I'll remember," she said.

Sneakabout turned a corner and was gone.

Midnight looked after him for a moment, once again lonely and more than a little afraid. The mage silently vowed that, after returning the Tablets of Fate to Helm, she would find a way to help Sneakabout, and not only because of her promise.

But the first thing she had to do was recover the tablet and get out of Myrkul's city before she was killed. The magic-user summoned Elminster's worldwalk to mind. Then, remembering what Rhaymon had said about finding her way back to Waterdeep, she began to pick the spell apart, to look at how Elminster had put it together.

It required fifteen minutes of hard concentration for Midnight to understand the intricacies of Elminster's construction. It took another fifteen minutes to alter the incantation so the other end of the portal would seek out the access well to Waterdeep. After finally finishing, Midnight was still unsure she would emerge near the City of Splendors. If she had known which one of the pinholes of light was the gate to Waterdeep, the alteration would have been much simpler. As it was, she would have to trust her fate to the fact that she had done her best.

Satisfied with her preparations, Midnight performed the worldwalk incantation. A tremendous surge of magical energy rushed through her body, tiring her. Still, it was nothing alarming—or even surprising, considering the power of the magic she was summoning.

A shimmering disk of force appeared. Midnight found herself wishing that she could see what lay on the other side, but there was no time for idle contemplation. Next, she summoned the incantation for telekinesis, then performed it with the tablet as the target. An instant later, in response to her probe, the tablet slipped out of its supports and rose an inch into the air.

Without wasting any more time, Midnight willed the tablet to come to her. It moved slowly at first, then began picking up speed, and was soon streaking in her direction. Though the mage could hear nothing above the cries of the Faithless in the wall, Midnight imagined a wild chorus of surprised yells and outraged bellows spreading through the boroughs around the castle. If anybody was looking toward the tablet, they could not fail to notice that Myrkul's trophy was being stolen.

As if to confirm Midnight's suspicions, something rose

into view from the other side of the wall. Huge, batlike wings sprouted from its fat feathered body. With its multifaceted eyes and protruding fangs, the creature's head looked like a cross between a vampire's and a fly's.

The tablet arrived and Midnight caught it. Immediately, she felt magic so powerful she could detect it without a spell. Something was wrong, for the other tablet had no magical aura at all. The magic-user suspected Myrkul had placed a ward or sigil directly on the artifact.

But it hardly mattered at the moment. A dozen more denizens had risen behind the first, and a hundred more forms were approaching from the other side of the keep's bone-white tower. Midnight did not have time to pause for a close examination of the Tablet of Fate.

She stepped into the disk and found herself running up a short corridor of light. The last time she had cast the worldwalk spell, the mage had simply stepped through the disk and appeared on the Fugue Plain. There had been no tunnel. The mage began to fear she had spoiled Elminster's spell by tinkering with it.

Then, thirty feet ahead, Midnight saw a wall of water covering the end of the corridor, as though she was running up the inside of a well. Remembering how she had altered the incantation so the portal would seek the access well to Waterdeep, the mage realized the worldwalk had worked exactly as specified. On the other side of the water lay Toril.

Midnight ran the rest of the way up the tunnel and stopped next to the wall of water. She turned around and tried to close the portal.

The shimmering disk remained in place, and the bat-winged denizen from Bone Castle entered the other end of the corridor. Midnight tried again to close the portal, and again she failed.

The creature smiled, baring its wicked fangs. "It won't work," the creature hissed, its voice like the sound of metal scraping stone. "Wherever the tablet goes, we go."

Two more of the monster's fellows flew into the portal.

"How?" Midnight gasped.

"It doesn't matter," the bat-winged creature said. "Give the tablet back."

Then Midnight understood. The magic she detected on the tablet was one of Myrkul's fiendish traps. He had made it impossible for anyone stealing it to escape his guards. The Lord of the Dead could have used variations on hold portal, dispel magic, gate, passwall, and a number of other spells to make the tablet a homing beacon for his minions.

Exactly how he had done it was unimportant, though. What did matter was that when Midnight took the tablet to Waterdeep, she would unleash Myrkul's hordes—the tablet would hold the gate open for the denizens and draw them through. She couldn't let that happen any more than she could return the tablet to the Lord of the Dead's vassals.

Midnight realized she had to block the corridor, and the perfect incantation for doing so came to her. It was a prismatic sphere, a globe of scintillating colors that the denizens would never penetrate. While they clawed and scratched at its exterior, she would be tucked safely inside.

"Last chance, woman," the bat-winged denizen said, starting up the corridor. "There's no escape."

"That's what you think," Midnight replied.

She performed the incantation. An instant later, a shimmering sphere encased her, at the same time blocking access to Waterdeep.

Midnight's body felt like it was on fire, and her head hurt so badly she could barely think. Within the space of a few minutes, the mage had cast two of the most powerful spells known to mages anywhere. The effort had taken its toll on her body. It didn't really matter, however. The mage was safe as long as the prismatic sphere held out. And in Midnight's case, that could be a long time.

❧ 15 ❧

City of Splendors

After breaking free of the ice and spending a long night next to a small fire, Kelemvor had left the High Moor and walked to the caravan road on his frozen feet. At the roadside, he had stopped and built a roaring fire, then sat down to wait for the blaze to attract help.

While his feet thawed, Kelemvor had puzzled over what to do. Midnight had fallen into the underground stream, and he had no idea what had become of her after that. But it had seemed that the mage's chances of survival were as great as his own, especially if she had called on her magic. Therefore, the fighter had decided to assume she was alive.

Still, Kelemvor had had no idea what Midnight might do. She might have tried to recover the tablet from the zombies, if she even knew that it had been lost. If not, the mage would have tried to go to the Realm of the Dead to recover the other tablet. There had also been the possibility that Midnight thought he was dead, in which case Kelemvor had not had the faintest idea what she would do.

The warrior had quickly realized he could not predict Midnight's actions. The only thing he knew for sure was that she would eventually go to Waterdeep.

After reaching that conclusion, the fighter had considered trying to recover the tablet from the zombies. But, alone, without a weapon and disabled by frostbite, there would have been no chance of success. Besides, given the way the undead had pursued the tablet, Kelemvor had suspected the zombies were no longer at Dragonspear Castle. They had probably already fled toward their master, and

RICHARD AWLINSON

the warrior had not had the vaguest idea where he might be hiding.

In the end, he had decided to go to Waterdeep. There, he would wait for Midnight. If she did not show up, he would recruit help and start out in search of the tablet and his lover.

Fortunately, the fighter had finished his plans before his feet thawed. When sensation had returned, it had been impossible for the fighter to think of anything but pain. He had felt as though he'd stepped into a vat of boiling water, and the torment had continued unabated for twenty-four hours.

A company of ten fast-moving riders had come by in the middle of the warrior's agony. They had loaned Kelemvor a spare horse and invited him to accompany them to Waterdeep.

A day and a half later, they had come across the remains of the Roosting Gryphon Inn. For no apparent reason, the inhabitants had been slaughtered. The company had puzzled over this until a rider found the proprietor's bloodless body. Immediately, the merchants had attributed the carnage to a vampire. But Kelemvor had voiced a suspicion that the attackers were the same zombies that had fallen upon his company at Dragonspear Castle.

Seven days later, camped half a mile off the road, the merchants had discovered the fighter was correct. In the middle of the night, a dozen zombies had wandered into camp, slaying the sentry and half the company before they realized what was happening. Kelemvor, recognizing the zombies' striped robes, had grabbed a sword and tried to organize a defense. But the merchants had panicked, and those who did not perish had fled into the night. The warrior, still limping from frostbite, had made his way to a horse and escaped.

That had been three days ago. Since then, he had been playing an exhausting game of cat and mouse with the zombies. The undead were traveling toward Waterdeep, but were avoiding the road in a clumsy attempt at secrecy. Every now and then, Kelemvor rode close to them to make sure they were still moving to the northwest. The zombies kept tabs on him with scouts, and had tried to ambush him several times. The extent of their success was that the fighter had not slept since the attack on the merchants.

Kelemvor's lack of sleep had taken its toll. As his horse cantered along the road, he had to concentrate on the countryside to stay awake. To the right, a vast, snow-covered plain extended as far as the eye could see. Somewhere out there, Kelemvor knew, were the zombies. To his left lay a brown ribbon of sand that could only be the Sword Coast. Beyond the coast, a glistening, azure plain of water stretched to the far horizon: the Sea of Swords.

The road topped a small hill and the horse stopped of its own accord, then snorted and stomped its foreleg. Kelemvor leaned down to pat its neck, then noticed his mount had smashed some scaled thing. The fighter's first thought was that the scales belonged to a snake, but then he saw fins and gills.

It was a fish.

Kelemvor looked down the road. On the other side of the hill, thousands of wriggling, flopping forms, all crawling inland, covered the plain. It was as if the sea had suddenly become undesirable and the fish were moving inland in pursuit of better water. Though he found the sight disconcerting, the warrior was not frightened. Like almost everyone in the Realms, Kelemvor had become accustomed to such strange sights.

Besides, from the top of the hill, he could see Waterdeep. The road ran for only one more mile, ending at a fortified gate that sat, almost, on the beach of the Sword Coast. To the gate's south lay the Sea of Swords, dotted here and there with the sails of great cargo ships. To the north, a small escarpment, no more than a few feet high, rose from the white prairie. As the slope continued east, it grew both steeper and higher, until it could properly be considered a cliff over much of its length.

Atop this cliff ran a high city wall, dotted at regular intervals by sturdy towers. It was broken only in the center of the escarpment, where the cliff was so tall and steep that no man could possibly scale it. Behind the wall, a hundred stalwart towers proudly held their turrets just high enough to be visible from outside the city. The fighter had no doubt that, at long last, he was looking upon the City of Splendors.

Beyond Waterdeep, a small mountain lifted its crown seven hundred feet above the plains, watching over the city bearing its name. At the top of Mount Waterdeep stood a lone tower, around which flocked birds of enormous size. Even from this distance, Kelemvor could see their bodies and the shape of their wings.

The fighter urged his horse forward. It moved reluctantly, picking its way through the fish migration as though walking down a muddy street and not wanting to soil its hooves.

As he neared the gate, Kelemvor saw that the huge birds over Waterdeep were not birds at all. While they had the wings and heads of great eagles, their bodies and feet were those of lions. They were griffons, and upon their backs they carried men. The fighter could not help but imagine how much easier his journey would have been if his company had possessed such mounts.

In his weariness, Kelemvor was so absorbed by the griffons that, when his horse suddenly stopped, he almost did not realize he had reached the gate. Two men-at-arms stood in front of him, both wearing black scale mail embossed with an upturned, gold crescent moon surrounded by nine silver stars. Behind them stood another man, this one wearing a mixture of green leather and black chain mail, with only the gold crescent moon for a device. Over a dozen similarly dressed men stood in the gate, attending to other travelers.

"Halt and state your name and your business," said the first guard. He avoided stepping too close to the grimy warrior. Though accustomed to unbathed travelers, this one appeared more sullied than normal.

"Kelemvor Lyonsbane," the fighter sighed. He knew he smelled bad. Being cold, hungry, dirty, and exhausted, he suspected he looked even worse.

"And what's your business?"

Kelemvor began to chuckle. The only response that came to mind was that he had come to save the world. He wondered if the guards would believe him.

The other guard stepped forward, irritated by what he perceived as disrespect. "What's so funny?"

Kelemvor bit his lip, trying not to laugh. The euphoria of exhaustion had settled over him and he found it difficult to control his mirth. "Nothing. I'm sorry. There are these zombies that I was following—"

The two guards snickered, but the man wearing green armor stepped forward. "Zombies?" he asked. His employer had told him there might be trouble with zombies in the weeks to come.

"They attacked us and killed one of my friends," Kelemvor responded.

"Your name again?" the guard asked.

"Kelemvor Lyonsbane." The fighter realized he sounded incoherent, if not completely insane.

The guard's eyes widened. This was one of the people for whom he was waiting. "Where are the other two—Midnight and Adon of Sune?"

"I told you," Kelemvor yelled, suddenly angry at having to repeat himself. Though he knew his moods were a result of his fatigue, he could not control them. "Zombies attacked us! Adon's dead and Midnight's gone! She'll be here somewhere—I've got to find her!"

"Relax—you're safe now," the guard said, realizing his employer would be more adept at handling the traveler's incoherence. "I'm Ylarell. We've been expecting you."

"You have?" Kelemvor asked. His mind abruptly shifted gears. "There are zombies out there—you've got to find them!"

"We will," Ylarell murmured. "The zombies won't hurt you in here. Now come with me—there's somebody who wants to see you." The guard took the reins to Kelemvor's horse and led the way through the gate.

After passing through a vacant plaza of snow-covered grass, Ylarell led the fighter to another wall. He said a few words to the guards here, and then took Kelemvor into the city proper. Though the warrior had seen many cities in his time, Waterdeep's size and magnificence stunned him. The streets bustled with carts and pedestrians, all intent on some task that must have seemed important to them. The briny odor of the harbor drifted over the rooftops on the left, where sturdy warehouses were interspersed with shabby tenements. To the right, a thicket of inns and stables stood shoulder to shoulder, packed so close Kelemvor did not see how caravans reached the ones deeper in the ward.

As they passed farther into the city, merchant shops and fine inns lined the streets. Then they entered a residential neighborhood, where grand houses and even a villa or two stood along winding avenues. Finally, Ylarell stopped before a large tower.

"Whom may I say is calling?" The voice came from the base of the tower, though Kelemvor saw no window or door there.

"Ylarell of the Watch, with Kelemvor Lyonsbane."

A door suddenly appeared where none had been before, and a tall, black-haired man stepped out of the tower. "Well met, Kelemvor! I am Blackstaff Arunsun, friend and ally of Elminster. Where are your companions?"

Ylarell interceded on Kelemvor's behalf. "He's in bad shape, milord."

Blackstaff nodded in understanding and retreated into the tower. "Bring him in."

Ylarell helped Kelemvor dismount and took him into a small sitting room. A moment later, Blackstaff led another man into the room. Though ancient, the second man looked every bit as robust as Blackstaff. A full head of hair and a beard as heavy as a lion's mane framed his sharp-featured face.

"Elminster!" Kelemvor growled. In his exhausted state, the fighter had no trouble blaming the ancient sage for the hardships he and his friends had endured. It was apparent to the warrior that Elminster had reached Waterdeep well ahead of him and with a lot less trouble.

"I ought to slit you gizzard to gullet!" Kelemvor snarled.

"I lack the gizzard," Elminster replied, not intimidated. "Now tell me what has become of thy friends."

Kelemvor related the events that had occurred at Dragonspear Castle, making the necessary digressions to explain about Bhaal and Cyric. When he finished, both Blackstaff and Elminster sat in dumfounded silence, pondering the effect of the fighter's report upon their plans.

Finally, Elminster groaned in frustration. He had not counted on Midnight finding her own entrance into Myrkul's realm. "If she went after the second tablet alone, the Realms may be in serious trouble."

Kelemvor was heartened by Elminster's unspoken assumption that Midnight had survived the underground stream. But he was far from encouraged by the sage's concern about Midnight going after the second tablet alone.

Blackstaff stood, already formulating a plan to control the damage. "Ylarell, fetch Gower and meet us at the Yawning Portal Inn. Then gather a patrol to look for the zombies who attacked Kelemvor—we'll need to recover that tablet right away."

Elminster also stood. "The Pool of Loss, my friend?"

Blackstaff nodded. "Gower will show us the way."

The two mages did not say any more. They both knew what had to be done. Located deep under Mount Waterdeep, the Pool of Loss was the closest access well to Myrkul's realm. They were going into Hades to retrieve Midnight and the tablet—if that were still possible. Elminster and Blackstaff quickly turned to leave without any further explanation.

Kelemvor wondered if they had forgotten he was in the room. "Wait for me!" he demanded.

Blackstaff regarded the fighter with equal parts of aggravation and forbearance. "This is beyond you, friend. You've done well to get this far."

"I'm coming," Kelemvor replied, irritated at being patronized.

"You're barely coherent!" Blackstaff objected.

"I'll follow you anyway," the warrior threatened.

Blackstaff looked to Elminster, who studied Kelemvor with cool scrutiny. "He might prove useful," the sage said at last. "Give him a restorative."

Blackstaff lifted his hand and a vial of murky green fluid appeared. He gave the potion to Kelemvor, then noted, "This will numb your fatigue . . . for a while."

Though curious about the vial's contents, Kelemvor did not ask. The wizards were obviously not in a cooperative mood, and he thought it wiser to save his questions for more important things. The fighter drank the potion down. As Blackstaff had promised, he immediately felt refreshed.

Without paying Kelemvor any more attention, the two mages walked south through a maze of twisting alleys and streets, stopping only when they reached a sizable inn. The sign over the door read "The Yawning Portal."

Blackstaff and Elminster entered and, oblivious to the attention of the patrons, went directly into the office. Kelemvor followed, taking a seat at the office's single table. Without being asked, a serving wench brought them each a mug of ale, then left and closed the door.

The owner of the Yawning Portal was a retired, prudent warrior named Durnan the Wanderer. Unknown to his patrons, Kelemvor, and anybody in the room except Blackstaff and Elminster, Durnan was one of the mysterious Lords of Waterdeep, the secret democratic council that governed the city.

As with Durnan himself, there was more to the name of his inn than met the eye. "Yawning Portal" was a tongue-in-cheek reference to the tendency of those who indulged in the tavern's fare to tell tall tales. But the name also referred to a deep shaft, resembling an indoor well, which led into the caverns beneath Mount Waterdeep. That shaft was why Blackstaff had brought his guests here, despite Kelemvor's assumption that this was just where they would meet Gower—whoever Gower was.

Blackstaff and Elminster sat without speaking, so Kelemvor

did not break their silence. Their bearing awed him, but he also thought they were being impolite to a man who had crossed the Realms at their behest. It did not matter, though. They represented his only chance of rejoining Midnight, and he would gladly endure their rudeness to see her again.

Ten minutes later, a stocky, broad-shouldered man entered the office. Ylarell and a ruby-nosed dwarf followed him. Not bothering with introductions, Blackstaff addressed the dwarf. "Gower, you're going to guide us to the Pool of Loss."

The dwarf sighed. "It'll cost you."

"Thy price?" inquired Elminster suspiciously, well accustomed to the dwarven tendency to overvalue service.

"Fifteen—no, make it twenty—mugs of ale," Gower responded, deciding he might as well try for a large fee.

"Done," Blackstaff answered, knowing Durnan would cover the fee without mention of repayment. "But only after we return. We need you sober."

"Seven now—"

"One before we leave, and that's final," Blackstaff grumbled. He turned to the broad-shouldered man. "Durnan, may we use your well?"

Durnan nodded. "Would you like some company into the pool?"

Elminster, who knew of Durnan's prowess, turned to Blackstaff. "If he's as good with the sword as he claims—"

Durnan snorted at Elminster's coyness. "I'll fetch my blade and Gower's mug."

Blackstaff led the way into the next room, which contained an indoor well. Durnan met them there with Gower's ale, a glittering sword, a coil of rope, and a half-dozen torches. After giving torches to everyone and lighting his own from the lamp on the wall, Durnan stuck a foot into the well's bucket. "Let me down slowly, Ylarell. I haven't been in here for some time."

Ylarell lowered Durnan into the well. Blackstaff followed, then Elminster and Gower. Finally, Kelemvor put a foot into the bucket and grabbed the rope.

"Lower away," the fighter said.

Ylarell began cranking, and Kelemvor descended into the dark shaft for several minutes. Ten feet above the bottom of the well, Blackstaff reached out of a side tunnel and pulled the fighter toward him. Kelemvor stepped out, then Blackstaff turned to the dwarf and said, "Lead on, Gower."

Not even bothering with a torch, Gower started down the tunnel. Durnan followed next, then the two mages, and Kelemvor brought up the rear. They descended into a labyrinth of half-collapsed dwarven tunnels and natural passages. On occasion, the company was forced to wade through steaming water, sometimes so deep Durnan had to carry Gower to keep the dwarf's head dry. Finally, they reached a slick passage that dropped into the darkness at an uncomfortable angle. Kelemvor was sure that if someone fell onto it, he would slide all the way to the bottom.

Thinking the same thing, Durnan said, "I'll tie off the rope and we can use it to descend."

"Nonsense," Gower said, sitting down at the edge of the steep passage. "We don't need a rope for this."

With that, he pushed himself forward and slid into the darkness.

Durnan, Elminster, and Blackstaff gave each other challenging glances, but hesitated to follow. Finally, Elminster put his hand on a boulder and said, "Ye could secure the rope to this."

Durnan tied the rope off, then the company followed Gower into the steep passage. The dwarf waited at the bottom, a condescending smirk on his face. The corridor had emerged in cathedral-like room so large the torches did not light the ceiling or the far side. The glowing, white spectres of hundreds, perhaps even thousands, of people were drifting aimlessly about the cavern.

"The Pool of Loss is over there," Gower said, pointing toward the middle of the room. "But there's something strange going on."

"What are those?" Kelemvor asked, nodding at the strange silhouettes.

Elminster did not bother to answer. His attention was fixed on the shimmering dome of scintillating lights that Gower had pointed to.

Blackstaff looked at Elminster. "Are you thinking what I'm thinking?"

"Yes," Elminster said, returning Blackstaff's gaze.

They both looked back to the dome.

"What? What are you thinking?" Kelemvor demanded, poking his head between the two wizards.

As usual, the mages did not answer, but they both suspected that the shimmering globe was a prismatic sphere, one of the most powerful defensive spells a magic-user could cast. They were trying to figure out what it was doing down here.

An instant later, again without saying anything, they started toward the dome. Durnan, Gower, and Kelemvor followed, though Durnan and Gower were much less apprehensive than Kelemvor. They had worked with Blackstaff before and were confident that if it was important for them to know something, he would tell them.

When the company reached the dome, they saw that it sat within a small stone-walled pool. It appeared to be a sphere with the bottom half hidden from view. The fit was so precise that there was not the slightest gap between the stone wall and the shimmering globe. The sphere continually flashed in a pattern of red, orange, yellow, green, blue, indigo, and violet, as though it were a striped ball spinning on its axis.

The mages circled the well for several more minutes, inspecting the dome first closely, then from farther away. Finally, Blackstaff asked, "What do you make of it?"

Elminster frowned and turned to Kelemvor. "Could this be Midnight's work?"

The fighter shrugged. He had no idea what the globe was or whether Midnight could have created it or not. "All I can tell you is that she was growing more powerful all the time. She once—" He searched for the word the mage had used to describe plucking them from one place and depositing them

RICHARD AWLINSON

in another. "She once 'teleported' four of us halfway from Boareskyr Bridge to Dragonspear Castle."

Elminster's eyes widened. "She did?"

"Then she could have cast this," Blackstaff concluded.

Inside the sphere, Midnight had been resting for hours. The magic-user was recovering from performing the worldwalk and prismatic sphere incantations in quick succession. She was completely unaware that help had arrived. The deafening screams and howls of a thousand enraged denizens were drowning out the voices of Elminster and company.

Fortunately, noise was the only thing that had entered the globe. Several denizens had flung themselves against the sphere or tried to assail it with spells. Each time, Midnight had heard a cry of pain or anger as the sphere directed an attack back at its originator.

As long as the sphere remained up, both Midnight and the Realms were safe from the denizens. But the spell would expire soon, and the mage feared it would take most of the strength she had recovered to recast it. While this would keep her safe and the denizens out of the Realms for a little while longer, it was only a short-term solution.

And Midnight did not dare leave the sphere until she countered Myrkul's trap. Until then, the tablet had to stay inside the sphere. Otherwise, she could be creating a passageway for the denizens between Myrkul's realm and wherever she went.

Then, with a start, the mage realized she could use a permanency incantation to indefinitely prolong the prismatic sphere. The gestures and words came to mind easily. It would be as wearing as renewing the sphere, but at least it only had to be done once.

With a sigh, Midnight performed the incantation. The effort drained her, but not completely. Within eight hours or so, she would have the strength to overcome the magic Myrkul had placed on the tablet.

Back outside the sphere, Kelemvor and the other four rescuers were still puzzled.

"These things don't last forever," Blackstaff was saying. "And if Midnight cast it, she's probably around here somewhere."

"Yes—undoubtedly inside," Elminster said. "That's what prismatic spheres are designed for."

"She's inside that thing?" Kelemvor exclaimed. He started toward it, but Durnan quickly restrained him.

"No, my friend," Durnan said. "If you touch it, you won't be fit to feed to the dogs."

"Then how do we get her out?" Kelemvor cried.

"Perhaps we don't want to," Elminster sighed, running a hand through his beard. "The mage who casts a prismatic sphere can enter or leave at will. If Midnight is inside, there's a reason."

"Then what do we do?" Kelemvor demanded.

"We let her know we're here," Blackstaff said. "When I count to three, let's all shout her name."

Their shout might have worked, if not for the cacophony of denizens' screams on the side of the sphere facing Myrkul's city. As it was, however, their voices were lost in the maelstrom of noise, and Midnight never knew her name had been called.

Next, the company tried throwing things into the sphere: bits of clothes, stones, rings. Nothing got through. More often than not, the sphere hurled the items back at whoever had thrown them. Blackstaff even tried to penetrate the globe with a telepathy spell, but it either misfired or the sphere repelled it. The bearded mage was stunned into dumfounded shock for twenty minutes. Kelemvor found Blackstaff's silence a welcome respite from the wizard's condescending manner.

"Well, Elminster, what do we do now?" Kelemvor asked, crossing his arms over his chest.

"We wait," Elminster replied. "The thing will fall after an hour or two."

So they sat down to wait. Eventually, a few soul spectres drifted over and idly gossiped with Elminster and Blackstaff, but Kelemvor, Durnan, and Gower superstitiously

RICHARD AWLINSON

avoided speaking with the dead. Several times, one of the
silhouettes found itself unable to resist the call of the Pool
and tried to enter despite the sphere. In each instance, it
was repelled or disappeared in a white flash.

Four hours later, Blackstaff stood. "This is ridiculous! Nobody can keep a prismatic sphere up this long!"

"Apparently Midnight can," Elminster observed.

"I'm going to dismantle it!" Blackstaff declared.

"That might not be wise," the elder mage replied. "Even if
ye cast all the spells without a misfire, we dare not risk eliminating the sphere without knowledge of why she cast it."

"You can dismantle the sphere?" Kelemvor asked. He
stood and rushed to Blackstaff's side.

"Yes," Elminster explained. "It's a most complicated and
tedious procedure."

"Tell me about it," Kelemvor demanded. Like Blackstaff, he
was tired of waiting.

"Very well," Elminster sighed. "It appears we have nothing
better to do at the moment. A prismatic sphere is in reality
seven magical spheres, each providing a defense against different attacks."

"To dismantle one," Blackstaff interrupted, "you must cast
a cone of cold to destroy the red sphere, which defends
against mundane missiles like arrows, spears—"

"And rocks with messages on them!" Kelemvor finished.

"Precisely," Blackstaff said. "Next, you must use a gust of
wind to—"

"We don't need to dismantle the whole sphere," Kelemvor
exclaimed.

Blackstaff frowned, irritated by the interruption.

Kelemvor ignored the mage, then continued, "All you
have to do is negate the first sphere. Then we can throw
something inside to get Midnight's attention."

Elminster looked doubtful. "I don't like—"

"What other choice do we have?" Durnan said, expressing
an opinion for the first time. "We can't stay down here forever. I have a business to run!"

"Very well," Elminster sighed, reaching into his robe and

pulling out one of his distinctive meerschaum pipes. He gave it to Kelemvor. "She should recognize this—try not to break it. If ye will do the honors, Blackstaff?"

"With pleasure," the mage replied.

Inside the sphere, Midnight had just identified the nature of Myrkul's trap. He had combined powerful variations of locate object and hold portal spells to ensure that his denizens could always follow wherever the tablet was taken. In effect, the locate object spell served as a beacon marking the tablet's location, and the hold portal spell prevented the thief from closing his escape route.

Fortunately, Midnight's prismatic sphere had not closed her escape route, it had merely blocked it. She could leave and the denizens could not follow. Because she had used an incantation to make the sphere permanent, it would never fall. In effect, the door between Myrkul's city and the Realms remained permanently open, but the hallway had been filled with an impassable obstruction.

As Midnight contemplated her discovery, something flew into the globe and landed in her lap. She jumped to her feet and nearly stepped out into the waiting hands of Myrkul's denizens.

Then the raven-haired mage picked up the object and discovered that it was a clay pipe—a distinctive, familiar clay pipe.

Outside the sphere, everyone was breathing a little easier because Blackstaff's spell had not misfired. Also, Kelemvor had tossed Elminster's pipe into the sphere without it rebounding.

"What if she doesn't recognize your pipe?" Kelemvor asked.

At that moment, Midnight stepped out of the sphere, the tablet in one hand and Elminster's pipe in the other. "Does this belong to one of you?" she asked.

"Midnight!" Kelemvor whooped.

They rushed into each other's arms and embraced—but not before Elminster snatched his pipe back.

For a long, uncomfortable minute, Blackstaff, Elminster,

Durnan, and Gower waited while the reunited lovers kissed and hugged each other. Finally, when it became apparent the pair was oblivious to the presence of others, Elminster cleared his throat.

"Perhaps we should attend to the business at hand?" he suggested.

Midnight and Kelemvor reluctantly separated.

Addressing Midnight and pointing at the sphere, Elminster said, "Perhaps ye would care to explain why ye've been hiding inside that thing for the better part of a day?"

"Not here," Gower insisted. "I'm thirsty—and you owe me nineteen mugs of ale!"

"One moment, Gower," Blackstaff said impatiently. "Is it safe to leave?"

Midnight nodded. "Oh, yes," she replied. "We can leave now. The sphere is permanent."

Both Elminster and Blackstaff raised an eyebrow.

"There—you see?" the dwarf said. "Let's go."

With that, Gower started toward the exit. Realizing they could not find their own way back to Durnan's tavern, the others reluctantly followed, barraging Midnight with questions as they walked.

☙ 16 ❧

Myrkul

"No!" Kelemvor hissed. He took the tablet off the floor and put it on the table. "Here's your tablet. Take it and get the other one yourself!"

"This discussion does not concern you, Kelemvor," Blackstaff retorted. He was not accustomed to being addressed so sharply, especially by mercenary warriors.

"That's right, not anymore. And it doesn't concern Midnight, either."

Blackstaff scowled and started to suggest Kelemvor was a coward, but Elminster stepped between the two men. Frowning at Blackstaff, the sage said, "Calm down. We can discuss this like gentlemen, can we not?"

Blackstaff's scowl changed to an embarrassed grimace. Elminster's comment was directed primarily at him, and he knew his friend was right. The young wizard should have enough self-control so that a stubborn warrior did not irritate him. "Forgive me," he muttered. "The stress is telling, I'm afraid."

Kelemvor also relaxed, but did not apologize.

They were in Durnan's office in the Yawning Portal. Midnight lay on the couch, where she had collapsed into a deep sleep. Her black hair was as coarse and as stiff as a horse's tail. Her complexion had faded to the color of ash, and her red-rimmed eyes were sunk deep into their sockets.

The Realm of the Dead had taken its toll on her. Kelemvor could not bear to see her join another battle, which was what Elminster and Blackstaff proposed. "She braved Myrkul's city," the fighter said. "Hasn't she done her part?"

"Others have also sacrificed," Blackstaff retorted. "Ylarell was a fine man."

Kelemvor did not know how to respond. When he and his five companions had returned to Durnan's tavern, a member of the city watch had been waiting with bad news. After lowering Midnight's rescue party into the well, Ylarell had taken a group of men to find the undead Kelemvor had described. The patrol had tracked the walking corpses into the foul-smelling tunnels that carried away Waterdeep's offal and refuse.

The undead had ambushed the patrol two hours later. Ylarell and his company had been winning the battle until an evil-looking human appeared and used magical poison to aid the zombies. Only one guard had survived, and only because he had remained unobserved. The watch commander knew of Blackstaff's interest in the zombies, and had elected to send no more men into the tunnels until he spoke with the wizard.

Connecting what Midnight had learned from Bhaal with some of his own research, Elminster had suggested that the man who had aided the zombies was Myrkul. Now, the ancient sage and Blackstaff wanted to use Midnight and the tablet to bait a trap for the Lord of the Dead.

Kelemvor thought his lover had done enough. More importantly, he doubted she had the strength to face Myrkul. "She's too weak," he said, kneeling at her side.

"Weak as she is," Elminster replied patiently, pointing a gnarled finger at the female mage, "she wields more power than Blackstaff and I together."

"No!" Kelemvor said, standing.

"The decision is hers," Durnan said. He sat slumped in a chair behind his desk, a mug of ale in his hand. "In Waterdeep, no man speaks for a woman unless she asks him to."

"You'll take her over my dead body," Kelemvor snapped, putting himself between Midnight and the others. "Or not at all."

Midnight opened her eyes and reached for the fighter's hand. "Kel, they're right. I must go on."

"But look at you!" the warrior protested, kneeling at her side. "You're exhausted!"

"I'll be fine after I rest."

"You can hardly stand," Kelemvor said, running his hand over her dry hair. "How can you fight Myrkul?"

Elminster laid a wrinkled hand on Kelemvor's shoulder. "Because she must—or the whole world might perish."

Kelemvor dropped his head and stared at the floor. Finally, he looked at Elminster and said, "Can you explain this to me? Why must Midnight draw Myrkul out? Why do we need the other tablet?"

Blackstaff snapped, "Elminster doesn't need to explain himself to the likes of—"

The ancient sage raised a hand to silence the bearded wizard. "He has a right to know," Elminster said.

"While ye and thy friends have labored to retrieve the tablets, this is what I have learned." The sage motioned at the air above the table. "Out of the mists at the beginning of time there came a will who called itself Ao. Ao wished to create an order." Elminster flicked his fingers and a golden scale hung in the air. "He balanced the forces of chaos and order, spending the first eons of his life cataloguing and setting them into opposition."

Dozens of lumps of coal appeared and settled onto the scale's dishes. "By the time he completed his task, the universe had grown too vast and intricate for even Ao to watch over." The scale wobbled and spilled the coal.

"So Ao created the gods." The chunks of coal compressed into glittering diamonds, each with the symbol of a god etched upon it. "To preserve the order, he assigned each god certain duties and powers." The diamonds returned to the dishes and the scales again hung balanced.

"Unfortunately, so he would not need to watch over them constantly, Ao created the gods with free wills. But with free will came ambition and greed, and the gods were soon struggling to increase their power at each other's expense." The diamonds started moving from one dish to another, again unbalancing the scales. "Ao could not stop the struggle without eliminating the gods' free will, so he began to oversee the transfer of powers and duties." In an even stream, the diamonds began moving from one dish to another. The scales steadied.

"And he created the Tablets of Fate to reflect the powers and duties of each god. Now the gods could exercise their ambition, yet the tablets would allow Ao to be sure the Balance was always maintained. But Myrkul and Bane were more concerned with their own aspirations than the Balance."

Two dark-colored diamonds left the dishes and circled the scales in crazy, erratic patterns. "So they took the tablets and hid them away, intending to steal as much power as possible during the confusion that followed."

All the diamonds bounced out of the dishes and whirled about the room. The scales spun and jerked wildly, until at last they overturned and crashed to the table. "In anger, Ao cast all the gods from the Planes, sparing only Helm. To the God of Guardians, Ao assigned the task of keeping the other gods out of the Planes.

"Without the gods to exercise their powers and perform their duties, the Realms began slipping into chaos." The diamonds rained down on the table. "Unless we recover the tablets and return them," Elminster concluded, "the Realms will perish." A bright flash filled the room, then the scales and the diamonds disappeared in wisps of smoke.

Kelemvor could not argue with Elminster's conclusion. Somebody had to return the tablets. But he still did not see why it had to be Midnight.

Before the fighter could voice his thoughts, though, Durnan set his mug aside and spoke. "It seems everybody— gods and mortals alike—should want the same thing: to return the tablets to Ao. I shudder to say this, and I only bring it up to be sure you've considered the possibility, but would it matter if Myrkul returned the tablets?"

"Very much!" Midnight snapped, rising to her feet. Durnan's suggestion appalled her. She had not endured Bhaal's touch, watched Adon die, and braved the Realm of the Dead in order to let the Lord of Decay prevail. "Ao will look favorably upon whoever returns the tablets. Allowing Myrkul that privilege would be worse for the Realms than not returning the tablets at all. Can you imagine a world where the Lord of Decay is favored?"

"Besides," Kelemvor added, "if Myrkul stole the tablets in the first place, I doubt he would return them now."

"True," Blackstaff concurred, surprised to find himself in agreement with the warrior. "He'd be afraid Ao would punish him for his theft."

"We have no choice," Elminster said, laying both hands on the tablet. "We must recover the other tablet from Myrkul."

"But why does Midnight have to do it?" Kelemvor asked. He looked from Elminster to Blackstaff. "Why can't you two do it? After all, you're supposed to be great mages."

"We are," Blackstaff said defensively. "But not great enough to kill Myrkul."

"Kill Myrkul! You're mad!" Kelemvor yelled.

"No," Blackstaff replied, meeting the warrior's heated gaze with a calm demeanor. "Midnight can do it. Shortly before the Arrival, I lost much of my control over magic, as did all mages. But, unlike clerics, our powers did not fade at the moment of the fall or perish entirely. We could see no reason for this. So, while Elminster was investigating what had happened to the gods, I was trying to find out what had happened to magic."

"What did you find out?" Durnan asked, for the first time sitting up straight.

"He discovered that I was in contact with Mystra just before Ao banished the gods," Midnight said. "She gave part of her power to me."

"Correct," Blackstaff replied. "Somehow, Mystra learned of Ao's anger before he exiled the gods. Perhaps Helm warned her, for it's rumored that they were lovers. Be that as it may, Mystra entrusted part of her powers to Midnight, intending to recover that part when she entered our world."

Midnight sighed, "Unfortunately, Bane captured the Lady of Mysteries when she arrived. Kelemvor, Adon, and I had to rescue her." Midnight left out Cyric's name, for she did not care to remember she had called the thief a friend. "While captive, Mystra learned that Bane and Myrkul had stolen the tablets. She tried to return to the Planes to tell Ao, but Helm destroyed her when she tried to fight past him. Her last act was to invest her powers in me so that I could recover the tablets."

"And that's why Midnight must be the one who confronts Myrkul," Blackstaff said, laying a hand on the warrior's shoulder. "She's the only one who can defeat him."

Kelemvor did not bother to object. No matter how much he wanted to deny it, the warrior saw that Midnight was the one who had to confront the Lord of the Dead.

But he still disliked the idea of using her as bait. She would have a better chance of surviving if they attacked Myrkul, instead of allowing the Lord of the Dead to surprise them. "If we must fight Old Lord Skull," he said, "then let us do it on our terms, not his. Maybe we can catch him unprepared."

"Carry the battle to his ground?" Blackstaff asked.

Kelemvor nodded.

"I approve," Elminster said, smiling. "Myrkul will not expect it. The survivor from Ylarell's patrol shall lead us to his lair."

"If that's what Kelemvor thinks is wise, then that's what I'll do," Midnight told them, smiling at the warrior. "But first, I must rest."

"Then I suggest we go to my tower and see if we can't dispel the magic on this," Blackstaff said, picking up the tablet. "If we intend to surprise Myrkul, we can't have his wards detailing our moves for him." He led the way out of the Yawning Portal.

As they stepped into the street, Midnight paused to look at the sky. It was a sickly green instead of blue, and the sun was purple instead of yellow, but she did not care. After enduring the white sky of the Fugue Plain and the drab gray of Myrkul's city, she was just glad to have a sun and sky over her head.

Then she noticed a ribbon of scintillating colors descending from the heavens to the summit of Mount Waterdeep. It was too distant for her to see details, but she suspected it was a Celestial Stairway.

"Don't stare," Elminster whispered. "Most people cannot see it. They will think ye've gone daft."

"I don't care," Midnight said. Still, she tore her gaze from the stairway and followed him down the street.

They had not taken more than a dozen steps before flapping wings startled Kelemvor. The fighter spun around and came nose to beak with a crow on Blackstaff's shoulder. The bird's left leg had been neatly splinted.

The crow screeched in alarm and pecked at Kelemvor, who barely managed to raise an arm and save his eye.

"Leave me alone, dung-eater!" Kelemvor flailed and came away with a handful of feathers.

The crow squawked, then fluttered to Blackstaff's other shoulder. Peering nervously around the wizard's head, the crow croaked what sounded like a sentence.

"Do you know this avian messenger?" Blackstaff asked Kelemvor.

"As well as any man can know the worm that would eat his corpse," Kelemvor responded, glaring at the bird.

"Crow apologizes," Blackstaff said.

When Kelemvor made no move to accept the apology, the bird squawked twice more.

"He says you'd have done the same thing if you were hungry."

"I don't eat crows," Kelemvor replied. "And I don't talk to them, either." He turned away and started for Blackstaff's tower.

* * * * *

Fifteen feet below Kelemvor, in the dark sewer under Rainrun Street, Myrkul suddenly stopped moving. Behind him, twelve zombies also halted, though fetid water continued to slosh around their legs.

"The tablet's in the street, my friends," the Lord of the Dead whispered, as if the zombies actually cared what he was saying. None of his worshipers were with him. Over the past few weeks, the Lord of the Dead had sacrificed his entire Waterdeep sect to provide energy for his magic.

Myrkul stared at the ceiling of the dark passage and absentmindedly touched the saddlebags slung over his shoulder. The saddlebags contained one of the Tablets of Fate—the one his zombies had stolen at Dragonspear Castle.

An hour and a half ago, via the locate object spell he had placed on it, Myrkul had sensed that Midnight had brought the other one to Waterdeep. Immediately, he had set out after the mage, intending to recover the tablet before assuming leadership of the host of denizens he expected to besiege the city at any moment.

But things had not proceeded according to plan. It had taken him far longer than expected to lead his zombies through the labyrinth of Waterdeep's sewers. Now that he had finally arrived, the tablet was being moved. His original intention had been to attack while the tablet was inside a building, where the battle would not be observed by the city watch.

He did not think it would be wise to alter his plan and attack in the streets. Already, he had destroyed one patrol, and the watch commanders would soon grow curious about what had happened to it. Tangling with another did not seem smart, at least not until his denizens gave the commanders something else to worry about.

Unfortunately, something was wrong. The denizens should have arrived right on the heels of the woman. But it was evident that she had spoiled his plan and prevented his subjects—and all the spirits of the dead—from following her to Waterdeep.

Just then, Myrkul sensed that the tablet was moving again. "Let's see where they are taking this tablet," he said to nobody in particular. "Then we will decide what to do." The Lord of the Dead turned and started sloshing back the way he had come.

A hundred feet down the tunnel, Cyric heard the zombies reverse direction and cursed under his breath. He had been in the absolute darkness and stinking water of the tunnels for half a day, following the zombies and their master. His nerves were beginning to feel the effect of close call after close call.

Once, right after he'd entered the sewers, he had come close to stealing the tablet. The zombies had attacked a watch patrol. By the light of the patrol's torches, the thief had seen the tablet slip into the rank water when a watchman had hacked an arm off the zombie carrying the saddlebags. Cyric had ducked beneath the surface and swam through a jungle of legs after it. Two hands had snatched the saddlebags away just as he reached it.

The thief had drawn his sword and surfaced with the idea of attacking whoever had the tablet, but had seen Myrkul casting a spell, then smelled a caustic odor. He had ducked back beneath the water and swam away while a cloud of poison killed the patrol. Since then, Cyric had been following the Lord of the Dead through the sewers, waiting for another opportunity to take the tablet.

As he heard the zombies come closer, Cyric moved up the tunnel ahead of them until his hand touched one of the intermittent ladders that led up to an access hole. The thief climbed up the ladder and remained perfectly motionless as the zombies passed beneath him. He did not come down until the sound of sloshing was a hundred feet away.

Unaware that he was being followed, Myrkul concentrated solely on maintaining contact with the tablet. He followed it through a twisting maze of sewer tunnels. Sometimes he had to pause while Midnight and her company passed through a tangle of streets and followed no direction in particular. Sometimes he had to backtrack when the tunnels took an unexpected turn.

Eventually, however, the tablet stopped moving, and Myrkul was satisfied it had reached its destination. He went down the tunnel to an access ladder, then climbed up and raised the iron cover just enough to see the building into which his enemies had gone.

It was a large tower with no windows or doors—one that

had come to his attention in the past. The tower belonged to Khelben "Blackstaff" Arunsun, one of Waterdeep's most powerful mages.

Myrkul descended back into the cloaca. "We will leave the tablet with Blackstaff for now," he said to his uncaring zombies. "Recovering it would draw attention to us, wouldn't it?" He paused and smiled a rictus grin. "We'll go to the Pool of Loss now, and see what is keeping my denizens. Then, perhaps, we'll worry about the other tablet." The Lord of the Dead turned and led his zombies into the darkness.

A few moments later, when he was confident Myrkul would not see him, Cyric climbed the ladder and looked at Blackstaff's tower. At least one being in the tunnel had been paying attention to Myrkul's words.

* * * * *

The thunder of five hundred hobnailed boots on cobblestone ended a slumber as deep and as restful as any Midnight could recall. She rolled over and buried her face in the feather bed, cursing the city for its noise. An officer barked an order and the soldiers rumbled to a stop outside her window.

Her dim room suddenly seemed as quiet as a graveyard. The silence woke her more fully and quickly than any clamor. At once both curious and frightened, Midnight leaped from her bed and threw her cloak over her shoulders.

At the base of Blackstaff's tower, a voice asked, "Whom may I say is calling?"

"Mordoc Torsilley, Captain of the Company of the White Wyvern, of the City Guard of Waterdeep, for Khelben 'Blackstaff' Arunsun. And be quick about it!"

Midnight threw open her window shutter, which was magically hidden to people on the street. In the courtyard below, over two hundred troops stood at strict attention. Their commander was facing the blank wall at the base of Blackstaff's tower. Each man wore black scale mail embossed with an upturned crescent moon of gold encircled in nine silver stars.

The entire company was fully armed, with halberds in hand and daggers and bastard swords on their belts.

Though all of them kept their attention fixed directly ahead, their faces were far from expressionless. The older men had the grim look of veterans returning to battle, while the younger men could barely keep themselves from trembling.

Midnight's door opened and Kelemvor rushed into the room.

"What's happening?" the raven-haired mage asked.

"I don't know," Kelemvor replied, leaning out her window to study the troops. Though he was no longer a soldier and had no desire to become one again, his heart stirred at the spectacle of a company fully dressed and ready for battle.

"How long have I been asleep?" she asked, hoping the answer would give her some clue as to the excitement's cause.

"Six hours," Kelemvor said, without turning away from the troops. He had seen the look in their eyes many times before, and he knew what it meant. "They're off to battle," the fighter noted. "And they don't think they're coming back."

He turned and limped toward the stairs. Blackstaff's restorative had worn off, and the warrior's feet still suffered the effects of having been frostbitten. "We'd better see what's happening."

Midnight followed him down three flights of stairs to the anteroom on the ground floor. Blackstaff and Elminster were already there, Elminster holding the tablet beneath his arm. Both men looked as though they had not rested in more than a day. While Midnight had slept, the two wizards had been laboring to remove Myrkul's magic from the tablet. She wondered if they had succeeded.

Mordoc Torsilley, commander of the White Wyvern, was just unrolling a long scroll. He addressed Blackstaff. "Are you Khelben 'Blackstaff' Arunsun?" he asked.

"You know who I am," Blackstaff answered. "We've met many times."

Mordoc looked up from the scroll apologetically. "This is

official business, Your Splendidness." He began to read from the scroll, "For the good of all citizens of Waterdeep, and in order to defend the city from its enemies, Khelben 'Blackstaff' Arunsun is hereby commanded—"

"Commanded!" Blackstaff snorted, insulted that anyone would dare use such a term to him. He ripped the scroll out of Mordoc's hands and read the rest silently. Finally, he asked, "I am to take command of the Wyvern Company?"

"Aye, that would be the long and short of it," Mordoc replied, hastily adding, "sir!"

"Incredible," Blackstaff muttered. "I'm no general."

"And our enemy is no army," Mordoc replied.

"What is it then?" Elminster said, irritated at the intrusion. "And be quick about it. We have important business to attend to."

"As near as we can tell, sir, they—"

"Who?" Blackstaff demanded. "What is it you want?"

"Fiends, sir. Hundreds of 'em, and their number is increasing all the time. They came from the caverns beneath Mount Waterdeep, then started pillaging the city. They've got everything from Harborwatch Tower to Snail Street—that's most of the Dock Ward. We've slowed them down, but that's about all. And the griffons are taking a beating from the ones that can fly. Before long, they'll have all of Waterdeep—unless you can stop them."

"The denizens," Midnight gasped. "They escaped the Pool of Loss."

"So it would appear," Elminster replied, scratching his beard. He immediately realized that Myrkul was the only one who could have countered Midnight's spell. But he did not understand why the Lord of the Dead would have bothered. Even for the God of Decay, destroying Midnight's sphere would have been far from easy. Elminster did not see why Myrkul would waste the energy, when he undoubtedly knew what he wanted was in Blackstaff's tower. The old sage and Blackstaff had been unable to dispel the magic the Lord of the Dead had placed on the artifact.

"We'd better act quickly," Blackstaff said to Elminster. At

the same time, he thrust the scroll back at the captain.

"The men are outside, sir," Mordoc said, assuming the black-bearded wizard had been talking to him.

"Men?" Blackstaff retorted. "Take them and begone. I have important matters to attend to."

Mordoc frowned and reached into his cloak. He looked as though he were a dog that had just been kicked, and with good reason. It was not safe to be the one who told Blackstaff Arunsun he had to do something against his will.

Mordoc withdrew a ring, then handed it to Blackstaff. "Sir, the warden of the guard ordered me to give you this."

Blackstaff reluctantly accepted the ring. It belonged to Piergeiron the Paladinson, the only acknowledged Lord of Waterdeep, Warden of the Guard, Commander of the Watch, Overmaster of the Guilds—and a dozen other titles. Blackstaff sighed and slipped the ring onto his finger. He had been summoned to serve his city. If he did not answer Piergeiron's call, he would lose his citizenship. Turning to Elminster, he said, "I have no choice."

Elminster nodded. "Go. It will be better if somebody keeps the denizens at bay. Undoubtedly, they're coming for the tablet."

"You know where to hide it?" Blackstaff asked.

Elminster nodded. "Aye, the vault. Now go."

Before leaving, the dark-haired mage turned to Midnight and Kelemvor. "If you need anything—"

"A dagger," Midnight requested immediately, recalling that hers had melted in the caverns below Dragonspear Castle.

Blackstaff nodded. "Elminster can get it for you." He turned and walked through the wall, saying, "Perhaps this will take only a little while."

"Perhaps," Elminster repeated absently. After Blackstaff left, he remained silent for a long time, puzzling over why Myrkul had released the denizens.

Finally, Midnight ventured to ask, "What now?"

Her question snapped Elminster out of his musings. "Yes— what now? We hide the tablet, I suppose."

"Why?" Kelemvor exclaimed. "I thought we were going to attack Myrkul!"

"The situation has changed," the old sage said. "It appears he is coming to us."

"Which is why we should attack," the fighter maintained. "It's the last thing he'll expect."

"True," Elminster noted thoughtfully. He liked Kelemvor's aggressive strategy, but suspected the warrior had not thought through the details of his plan. "How are we going to sneak up on our enemy when he can track us by our tablet?"

Kelemvor remained confident. "We leave it here, so he thinks we're still in the tower."

"Leave the tablet unguarded?" Elminster objected.

"Why not?" Kelemvor said. "If we defeat Myrkul, we'll be the only ones who know where it is. If Myrkul kills us, at least he'll have to steal it from Blackstaff's tower."

"And how are we going to find Myrkul?" Elminster asked, drumming his bony fingers on a tabletop.

"The same way he's finding us," Midnight replied. "I can locate his tablet as easily as he can locate ours."

Elminster shook his head doubtfully. "Ye know how unpredictable magic—"

"We're fighting for the fate of the Realms," the warrior said forcefully. "We'll have to run a few risks."

"I think we should carry the fight to Myrkul, too," Midnight said. "I, for one, am tired of running. Will you come with us or not, Elminster?"

Elminster raised his eyebrows at Midnight's gentle rebuff. She had just taken leadership of this small company, but that was to be expected. "Of course I'll come," the sage replied. "Ye are going to need all the help ye can get."

Elminster went to the library and took the tablet into Blackstaff's sub-dimensional vault, where he also retrieved a dagger for Midnight. To the sage's consternation, he could not seal the room when he left. After a couple of quick experiments, the ancient wizard determined the door simply could not be closed while the tablet was inside. Myrkul's magic kept it open, in effect raising the sub-dimensional vault back into the normal dimension. The only thing guarding the tablet would be an illusion of a wall.

Still, as nervous as that made Elminster, he realized Kelemvor was right about one thing. If they stopped Myrkul, the tablet would be safe anywhere inside Blackstaff's tower. On the other hand, if Myrkul killed them, it would be better if the tablet was not along. The wizard pushed a bookshelf in front of the vault, then went back downstairs.

While Elminster hid the tablet, Midnight performed her locate object incantation. She nearly went mad as it misfired, flooding her mind with the present location of every item she had ever owned. However, after collapsing in a confused heap for a few minutes, the mage sorted through the jumble of contradictory directions and focused on Myrkul's tablet.

By the time Elminster returned, she and Kelemvor were ready to go. After accepting Blackstaff's dagger from the sage, Midnight led the way into the courtyard, a queasy feeling of dread settling in her stomach. Her magic was pulling her south and a little east, the same way a lodestone pulled toward north. She started down Swords Street, brushing past hundreds of people rushing in the opposite direction.

"We're going toward the battle," Kelemvor observed, elbowing a path through the mass of refugees. In the distance, columns of smoke rose over the city.

They had not walked more than two hundred feet before Midnight sensed the tablet was now more to the east than the south. She turned onto Keltarn Street and walked down a short block, to where it joined the Street of Silks.

"That's strange," she said, pausing at the intersection. "It's to our north now."

The mage led her friends up the Street of Silks into another throng of refugees. She feared her magic had become unreliable. Still, the sensation of being pulled toward the tablet was clear and strong, so she continued forward.

Two hundred feet later, Midnight turned west. "The tablet's

over there." She pointed across a solid block of buildings.

"This way, then," Kelemvor said, running up the Street of Silks to where Tharleon Street joined it. He turned west down the narrow alley, then waited for Midnight and Elminster to catch up.

"It's straight ahead," Midnight said.

They walked down the street until it reached Swords Street again. Blackstaff's tower stood across the avenue and to the right.

"We've made a circle!" Kelemvor observed.

"Perhaps I located the wrong tablet," Midnight said meekly, trying to sort through the confusion in her mind.

"I don't think so," Elminster grumbled. He pointed across the road and to the north, at a figure in a black robe. The man carried saddlebags over his shoulder. He was walking straight toward Blackstaff's tower, violently pushing aside anyone unfortunate enough to get in his way.

"Myrkul!" Midnight cried.

"Yes," Elminster replied. "He's come for the other tablet."

Kelemvor drew his sword. "And he doesn't know we're behind him." The warrior started across the road.

So she could summon another incantation if needed, Midnight stopped concentrating on the tablet. The three allies crossed the street and moved up behind Myrkul, finally getting a clear shot at his back just as he reached the tower.

Midnight summoned a lightning bolt. "Cover your eyes," she warned.

The instant Kelemvor and Elminster obeyed, the mage pointed at Myrkul's back and uttered the words to the incantation. A loud crackle filled the air. A dozen blue streaks leaped off Midnight's finger and shot into Swords Street, striking buildings and people. Tiny blasts flared wherever the bolts touched, gouging small craters in walls and burning fist-sized holes into bodies.

Myrkul stopped at the tower's entrance and turned around. He saw Midnight, flanked by Elminster and Kelemvor, staring in horror at the results of her botched incantation. The Lord of the Dead had not expected to find the trio outside the tower, but it did not concern him. He had ways of occupying them while he retrieved the tablet.

Myrkul gestured at the sewer entrance behind Midnight, then entered the tower. A cry of alarm spread up the street. Kelemvor turned in time to see several soggy corpses climb out of the sewer. They wore the same striped robes of the undead that had stolen the tablet at Dragonspear Castle. The skin on their faces was wrinkled and decaying, and their expressions were dull and lethargic.

"Zombies!" the warrior gasped.

"Ignore them!" the ancient wizard yelled. "Into the tower."

Kelemvor and Elminster ran for the tower. Behind them, they dragged Midnight, who was still dazed and anguished by the destruction her spell had caused. When they reached the tower, Myrkul was nowhere in sight, though the rank odor of sewage still hung in the air.

"Upstairs!" Elminster said. "In the library!"

Kelemvor led the way up the spiraling staircase, advancing slowly and cautiously. Midnight followed, while Elminster came last. The first zombie entered the tower just as the ancient sage stepped onto the stairs.

On the second floor, Elminster told the mage and the warrior to stop outside a closed door. "The tablet's in there—which means Myrkul is, too," he explained.

"We can't use magic," Midnight whispered. "I've already hurt too many people."

"Nonsense," Elminster growled. "If we don't stop Myrkul, the citizens of Waterdeep will be dead anyway."

"Elminster's right. Waterdeep's a battlefield now," Kelemvor said. "Innocent people are going to die no matter what. The only thing we can do—must do—is win the battle."

The first zombie appeared around the bend in the staircase. Elminster calmly turned and touched one of the stone stairs, then whispered a complicated chant. Kelemvor moved to meet the advancing zombie, but a stone wall sprang up where the sage had touched the stairs.

"It worked," Elminster sighed. He turned toward the door. "Be ye ready, Midnight?"

She nodded, but did not speak.

Elminster looked at Kelemvor, and the warrior kicked the door open. Midnight stepped into the room, searching for the dark-robed figure they had seen in the streets.

"There's nobody in here!" she reported.

Kelemvor and Elminster peered over her shoulder. The library was, indeed, deserted. One bookshelf had been tipped over, revealing a section of blank stone wall.

Elminster cursed, then said, "He's already got our tablet!"

"There's only one place he could have gone," Kelemvor yelled.

"Up!" Elminster confirmed. "Quickly, before he escapes."

They started up the stairs, pausing to look into the rooms on each floor.

Meanwhile, Myrkul slipped the second tablet into the other side of the saddlebags. Then he slung the bags over his shoulder and stepped out of Blackstaff's vault into the library.

"Remarkable," he said, walking over to the stairway and examining Elminster's wall. "*They* are hunting *me!*" He thought for a moment, then added, "We can't have mortals trying to destroy me, can we?"

Myrkul cast a passwall spell at the stone barrier blocking the stairway. A rectangular section of stone separated itself and began hopping down the stairs as though it were alive.

Myrkul watched the stone crush one of his zombies, then disappear around the bend in the staircase. His spell's misfire did not concern the Lord of the Dead. He would soon have plenty of undead to call in Waterdeep.

"Up the stairs!" Myrkul said. "Kill the woman and her friends. They've caused me too much trouble already."

As the zombies shuffled past, Myrkul contemplated his next move. He would return to the Pool of Loss to call the spirits of the dead. After harvesting the energy of their souls, he would go to the Celestial Stairway. With luck, Helm would let him pass, for he now possessed both tablets. Then the Lord of the Dead would destroy Ao. Everything was again proceeding according to plan.

On the flat roof atop Blackstaff's tower, Kelemvor could not believe Myrkul had escaped so easily. "Where is he?" he roared.

Elminster turned to Midnight. "You can't trace the tablet anymore?"

Midnight tried to reactivate her locate object magic, but it was gone. "I can redo the incantation, but it'll take a minute," she replied.

"We don't have time. Let's go," Kelemvor said, rushing back down the stairs. Midnight and Elminster followed.

Ten steps later, the warrior came face to face with Myrkul's undead. The lead zombie opened a long gash in the warrior's shoulder. Kelemvor reacted instantly, backing away and countering with a backhanded slash that removed the corpse's arm. In the same breath, the fighter kicked the thing, knocking it down the stairs and into the zombie behind it. Both corpses fell.

"Run!" Kelemvor screamed.

Elminster took Midnight's arm and fled back up the stairs. As they retreated, a third zombie climbed over the pile in the stairway. Kelemvor waited for it, then hacked at its neck with two savage slashes. The thing's head came free with a pop, then dropped to the stairs and rolled away. The body remained standing, flailing its arms.

The two zombies Kelemvor had knocked over regained their feet and pushed past their headless comrade, intent on tearing the warrior to pieces. He backed up the stairs slowly, slashing periodically to stall his attackers.

Outside the trap door leading into the stairwell, Midnight turned to Elminster. "We've got to help him," she cried.

"Kelemvor can take care of himself," Elminster said. "Let's use the time he's buying us. How can we retrieve the tablets?"

Midnight tried to summon some magic that would help, but all she could think of was her lover. Occasionally, the clang of steel on stone or a loud grunt rolled out of the stairway to announce that he still lived. Each time, the sound grew closer, so Midnight knew the sage was right. Kelemvor was buying time and not simply throwing his life away. Still, she could think of nothing but helping him.

Midnight returned to the stairwell.

"Where are you going?" Elminster demanded. "The tablets—think of the Realms!"

"In a minute!" Midnight retorted.

She found Kelemvor staggering up the stairs, covered from head to foot with scratches and small wounds, scarcely beyond the reach of two pursuing zombies. Midnight paused, trying to think of something to halt the corpses.

Kelemvor slipped on a small stone and nearly fell. The rock bounced toward the zombies, and then an incantation came to Midnight. She performed it as quickly as she thought of it, and the stone instantly became a boulder.

It smashed into the first zombie, crushing him. Then it slowed its descent and bounced into the second corpse, knocking it off its feet. The boulder tottered on a stair for a moment, then reversed direction and sluggishly started rolling uphill. It gained momentum steadily, and a moment later the rock was bouncing up the stairs as rapidly as it had started down them.

Midnight pointed at the boulder and screamed, "Look out!"

Kelemvor took two steps, glanced over his shoulder and saw the boulder. He dropped to his belly and it bounced over him. Midnight barely jumped out of the way as the huge rock shot out of the stairwell and arced away into Waterdeep.

The warrior scrambled out of the stairs behind it. He slammed the trap door shut, then hopped on top to prevent the zombies from opening it.

"Perhaps now we can attend to the tablets?" Elminster suggested, tapping his foot impatiently.

Midnight glanced at the stairwell. Kelemvor looked secure enough for the moment. "I have something in mind," she said. "But I don't know how much good it will do. I can only grab one of the tablets with the spell, and it won't stop

Myrkul from coming after us."

"We'll handle Myrkul when he gets here," Elminster said. "Right now, our only concern is getting the tablets back."

Midnight nodded, then closed her eyes, envisioned a tablet, and performed an instant summons incantation.

At the bottom of the tower, Myrkul was about to step into the courtyard when the saddlebags suddenly became unbalanced and slid off his shoulder. He picked them up and looked into the side that had grown lighter. It was empty.

He cursed an oath so profane that even one of his clerics would have winced, then turned and ran back up the stairs.

On top of the tower, Midnight stood staring at the tablet in her hands. Until now, her magic had not fatigued her. But the instant summons was complicated and demanding, and she felt slightly weakened.

"Marvelous," Elminster said. "Call the other one, and we'll be on our way."

"How are we going to get off the roof?" Kelemvor demanded, still standing on the door. The zombies were pressing on the other side, but did not have the leverage to push the fighter off.

"We'll think of something," Elminster replied.

Midnight shook her head. "I'm tiring. Even if the incantation doesn't misfire, I won't have anything left to fight Myrkul." She did not doubt the Lord of the Dead was coming at this very moment. "You summon the other Tablet of Fate, Elminster."

"I can't," the sage replied. "I haven't studied that spell in years. But I *can* get us off this roof if you get the other tablet."

The comment reminded Midnight that, as powerful as he was, Elminster still had to study his spells and impress their runes on his mind.

"I'll try," Midnight sighed, setting the first tablet down.

She called the instant summons incantation to mind again, then pictured the other tablet and performed it. An instant later, a storm of fist-sized rocks appeared over the tower and pelted the trio mercilessly.

"It failed!" Midnight said, feeling a little dizzy. Her body ached where a dozen stones had hit her, and her muscles burned with fatigue.

The trap door bucked beneath Kelemvor, then it flew open, launching him into the air. He landed six feet away and rolled to his feet, still holding his sword.

A zombie climbed out of the stairwell. Kelemvor charged, cleaving the corpse in two with a slash so vicious he nearly threw himself off his feet.

"Myrkul!" he screamed, staring at a dark-robed man behind his zombies.

Kelemvor's sword suddenly changed into a huge snake and slithered around his body. The serpent's scales were covered with a filthy green ooze, and a forked, black tongue flickered from its mouth. Myrkul shrugged. He had intended to heat the sword and burn the warrior's hands, but he would be just as happy if a snake strangled the man to death.

The serpent wrestled Kelemvor to the floor, then Myrkul sent his remaining zombies out onto the roof. Midnight grabbed her tablet and backed away. Elminster, however, calmly waited for Myrkul's corpses to leave the stairway. Then he cast a spell he hoped would take them by surprise.

To the sage's immense relief, a swarm of fiery globes leaped from his hand, each one striking a corpse in the chest. Most of the spheres carried the zombies off the tower roof. Some exploded into miniature fireballs that reduced the corpses to piles of ash and charred bone. In an instant, the meteor swarm had destroyed Myrkul's protectors.

After hearing Elminster's voice and seeing the fiery trails streak over the stairwell, Myrkul knew he would have to confront the woman and her friends alone. They had dared to hunt him, and when that failed, they had stolen a tablet off his person. The trio would continue to harass him until he destroyed them. Sighing in exasperation, the Lord of the Dead prepared a defensive spell and climbed out of the stairwell.

Elminster was the first to see Myrkul step onto the roof.

Kelemvor was being strangled by the snake, and Midnight, tablet beneath her arm, was rushing to her lover's aid. The Lord of the Dead wore a black hood pulled over his head. Beneath the hood, he had scaly, wrinkled skin covered with knobby lesions, black, cracked lips, and eyes so sunken that his face looked like a skull. Fiery blue embers burned where his pupils should have been. The saddlebags containing the other tablet were slung over his shoulder.

Elminster began to throw an ice storm at the avatar, but Myrkul lifted a hand and cast the silence spell he had prepared. Everything within five feet of the ancient sage suddenly fell quiet, as did the mage himself. Without the ability to speak aloud, Elminster could not complete the verbal component of his spell and it did not go off.

Noticing what had happened to Elminster, Midnight shifted her attention from Kelemvor to Myrkul.

"Come, my dear," the Lord of the Dead said, his voice guttural and rasping. "Give me the tablet. I will spare your friends."

Midnight had no time to bandy promises with the god. She called a simple magic missile to mind, dropped the tablet, and performed the incantation. A dozen golden bolts leaped from her fingers and struck Myrkul—then dissipated harmlessly, leaving a golden aura clinging to the Lord of the Dead's putrid form.

Myrkul lifted a hand and examined his new radiance, then laughed at her botched spell. "How you taunt me, mortal!"

Midnight found herself trembling and feverish. Although the incantation was normally a rudimentary one, its potency had increased with her power. It had taken more out of her than she'd expected.

Myrkul held out his hand. "Once more, give me the tablet." He turned toward Kelemvor and gestured at the snake. The serpent drew tighter around the warrior's throat and his face immediately turned purple. "You have only a little time before your friend dies."

Even for an instant, the mage did not believe Myrkul

would keep his word and spare her lover. She had no intention of doing as asked, but neither could she bear watching Kelemvor die. Hoping the appearance of indecision would buy her time to think, Midnight tore her gaze away from Myrkul and looked out over the city.

To the south, great pillars of black smoke rose from the city's North Ward. Midnight could even hear distant screams and faint clashes of steel. Dozens of griffon riders were battling tiny forms in the air. A few griffons rode over other quarters of the city, acting as messengers or scouts trailing enemy groups that had broken through the line. One griffon, carrying two riders, was flying toward Blackstaff's tower.

The riders were too distant for Midnight to identify and she had no idea why they were coming toward the tower. Whatever their reason, she did not think they would arrive in time to save her and her friends, or to prevent Myrkul from getting both the Tablets of Fate.

"What is your decision?" Myrkul demanded.

"You win," Midnight said, kneeling to retrieve the tablet at her feet. At the same time, she summoned the most powerful spell that came to mind: temporal stasis. The incantation was so difficult it would probably drain her, perhaps even burn her up completely, but she had no choice. If it worked, Myrkul would be trapped in suspended animation. Then she and her friends could deal with him at leisure. If it did not work, Myrkul would win.

Midnight cleared her mind, then performed the incantation. A wave of fire rushed through her body and she collapsed to the roof. Her muscles ached and her nerves tingled as though she had fallen onto a bed of needles. The mage tried to breathe, but lacked the strength to open her mouth. A curtain of darkness descended over her eyes.

Midnight forced herself to stay alert, the curtain to draw back, and her lungs to expand. Gradually, her vision returned and, weak as she was, the mage could see again. Myrkul stood motionless, the saddlebags containing the other tablet still slung over his shoulder.

Without its creator's will to guide it, the snake wrapped around Kelemvor seemed confused and uncertain. It was squeezing less fiercely now, its attention turned toward the Lord of the Dead's motionless form. The warrior also seemed dazed, but managed to slip an arm inside the coil squeezing his throat, preventing the serpent from choking him.

Midnight stood and, carrying her own tablet, stepped toward the motionless god. The embers that served as Myrkul's eyes flared.

"I—I'm not finished quite yet," the Lord of the Dead croaked through quivering lips. The avatar's whole frame was shaking. He was breaking free of the spell.

As she looked into the Lord of the Dead's eyes, Midnight's heart sank. It seemed nothing could stop him. Then the mage noticed a gray streak plummeting out of the sky. The griffon she had noticed earlier was diving to attack Myrkul's back. Midnight dropped her eyes to the roof, not wanting to alert the evil god to the bravery of the griffon riders. Although the attack would stun Myrkul, it would not kill him. The magic-user knew she had to find a way to take advantage of the surprise.

While Midnight and Elminster, who was still under the influence of the silence spell, prepared to take advantage of the griffon attack, Kelemvor took several deep breaths and recovered some of his strength. He thrust his other arm through the coil around his neck, then grabbed the snake's head. Locking one hand onto the upper jaw and the other onto the lower, he pulled in opposite directions with all his might. An instant later, bone popped and the warrior ripped the jaws apart. The serpent's body slackened and it began writhing in pain. Kelemvor slipped out of its grasp. He pitched the slimy, squirming thing over the side of Blackstaff's tower, then turned toward Myrkul.

Myrkul saw Elminster coming toward him and turned stiffly to meet the attack. But the old sage stopped five feet away, confusing the Lord of the Dead. Then Myrkul realized he could no longer hear.

Midnight, still trembling from the effort of the temporal stasis spell, summoned the incantation for disintegration and another for a dimensional door. If she could destroy the avatar's body, the god's essence would disperse. Then, through the dimensional door, the mage could shift the explosion high over the Sea of Swords, where it would do far less harm.

An instant later, the griffon struck. Because of the silence surrounding Elminster, Myrkul did not hear the whisper of its wings and was taken by surprise. The god fell onto his left side, and the saddlebags with the tablet slipped off his shoulder. The beast followed the god to the roof and sank all four claws into the avatar's body. One of the griffon riders jumped off the creature's back. Even as the man's feet touched the roof, the great beast flapped its wings to rise again.

Myrkul squirmed and grabbed at the saddlebags, barely clutching them into his grasp.

Seeing what was happening, Kelemvor charged across the roof. As the griffon lifted the god into the air, the warrior threw himself after the tablet. His hands clutched the bottom of the saddlebags, then Kelemvor pulled the tablet from Myrkul's grasp. He landed on the roof and rolled away.

Pain shooting through his avatar's body, Myrkul felt himself being lifted off the roof. He made one last grab for the saddlebags as Kelemvor rolled away, but the griffon had already carried him too far into the air.

Myrkul twisted around so he could look up toward the rider. "You will all pay for this!" he cried, shaking his bony fist.

As she watched the griffon carry Myrkul into the air, Midnight prepared her incantations, but stopped short of performing them. If she destroyed the avatar, the rider was certain to die in the mayhem that followed. The magic-user went to the edge of the tower and watched the griffon fly over Blackstaff's courtyard, Myrkul still struggling in its claws. The great beast continued flapping, all but ignoring the writhing body in its grip.

Then the Lord of the Dead stopped struggling and pointed at the griffon rider. An instant later, the soldier slumped over. He slipped out of the saddle and plunged toward the cobblestoned street below.

Midnight performed the disintegration incantation. A green ray shot from her hand and touched Myrkul. The avatar's body gleamed briefly, then a brilliant golden flare erupted over the city. Midnight quickly cast the spell for a long range dimension door and transferred the dying avatar to a spot high over the Sea of Swords, far from Waterdeep.

There was a loud crack as the avatar fell into the door, and another burst of light washed over the city from the west. The explosion caused by Myrkul's death was like a second sun rising over the sea west of Waterdeep. When it died away, there was no sign of the griffon, its rider, or Myrkul. A brown murk hung in the air east of the tower, where the avatar had been seconds earlier.

The murk settled over a two block area. Wherever it touched, plants withered and people fell to the ground choking. Whether they were built of stone or wood, the buildings turned to dust and collapsed, and even the streets themselves crumbled. Within moments, two square blocks of Waterdeep had been turned into a desolate, brown waste.

Midnight sank to her knees, shivering with exhaustion and remorse. Hundreds of people had died when Myrkul's essence settled on them. She could not help feeling responsible for their deaths.

Somebody walked up behind her.

"I *had* to destroy Myrkul," she whispered, still staring at the poisoned area. "What else could I have done?"

"Nothing else," answered a familiar voice. "You cannot be blamed for saving the Realms."

Midnight stood and, ignoring the wave of dizziness that rushed over her, turned around. "Adon!" she cried.

❦ 17 ❦

CYRIC

Cyric stopped just inside the stairwell and concealed himself in the shadows. The overhead trap door opened onto a circular roof, where several people were talking. Though the voices were muffled, he suspected that two of them belonged to Kelemvor and Midnight. The thief had watched them follow Myrkul into the tower.

Cautiously, Cyric went up the stairs and looked out onto the roof. Elminster was picking up one of the Tablets if Fate and putting it into the saddlebags Kelemvor and company had been using as a carrying case since Tantras. The thief could not believe who was standing next to Midnight. "Adon!" he hissed, his voice barely audible.

I thought you killed him? his sword said, the words forming within his mind.

"So did I," Cyric whispered.

The thief frowned and shook his head. He had seen the arrow sink into Adon's ribs with his own eyes, then watched the cleric tumble into a dark cavern. It hardly seemed possible that the scarred cleric was alive.

Your old friends have an uncanny knack for survival, the red-hued sword observed.

"I know," Cyric replied. "It's beginning to irritate me."

Midnight was more surprised than Cyric to see Adon. "You're alive!" she exclaimed, throwing her arms around the cleric. The magic-user was still too fatigued to be standing on her own, however, and her knees buckled.

Adon dropped his mace, caught the mage, and gently lowered her to a seated position. "Are you well?"

Midnight nodded wearily. "Yes—just fatigued."

Kelemvor joined them and cradled Midnight's head in his lap. "This business has taken its toll on her," he said.

"I'll be fine," Midnight replied. "I need rest, that's all. Now what happened to you, Adon?"

"I don't really know. After Cyric's arrow hit me, I fell into an underground stream and was carried away. The next thing I remember is waking up in the care of a gnome named Shalto Haslett—he claimed I'd been clogging up his well."

"How did you get to Waterdeep?" Kelemvor asked, remembering his own harrowing journey. "You couldn't have healed quickly enough to walk."

"Shalto had a crow carry a message to Waterdeep. Then somebody named Blackstaff sent a griffon for me."

"Blackstaff!" Kelemvor and Midnight said simultaneously.

"I wonder how long Elminster has known you're alive?" Midnight asked, glancing toward the ancient sage.

"And why he didn't tell us?" Kelemvor added.

Adon shrugged. "You'll have to ask him. All I know is that I'm glad I arrived when I did."

Elminster approached, the saddlebags in his hands. Both Midnight and Kelemvor turned to the wizard and angrily began asking their questions, but no words came out of their mouths. Myrkul's silence spell still clung to the sage, deadening the sound of the pair's voices. But from their irritated expressions and the gestures directed at Adon, Elminster could guess what they wanted to know.

He and Blackstaff had decided not to tell Kelemvor and Midnight of their companion's survival for good reason. The wizards had not wanted to distract the pair from the task at hand. Shalto's message had only said that Adon was alive and needed transport to Waterdeep. Without knowing what condition the cleric was in, the wizards had not wanted to raise Midnight's and Kelemvor's hopes.

Elminster tried to explain these things via gestures, but only succeeded in confusing and angering the fighter and the mage further. Finally, he simply shrugged his shoulders and looked away.

To his alarm, he saw that his work was not yet over. Myrkul's denizens did not seem to have noticed the destruction of their lord, and were still savaging the troops in the Dock Ward. Elminster gave the saddlebags to Adon, then turned to Midnight and went through the somatic motions for a dispel magic spell.

Midnight quickly understood what Elminster wanted. But, despite wanting to hear why he had not told them about Adon's survival, she was hesitant to call on her powers again. The fatigued mage was loath to risk the danger of a another misfired spell. Besides, she was still weak and feared that casting the incantation would drain what little remained of her strength. Midnight shook her head.

Elminster urgently pointed toward the south.

Midnight and the others turned. The battle had drawn closer. The city was burning as far north as Piergeiron's Palace. Between Blackstaff's tower and the palace, a hundred separate battles raged in the sky. The combats were graceful, looping things that seemed to move in slow motion. The dark specks circled each other, trying to climb higher than their opponents one moment, then swooped down to attack in the next. Midnight could tell Waterdeep's guardsmen from Myrkul's denizens only by the size of the griffons.

Every now and then, a speck plummeted out of the sky and disappeared into the maelstrom in the streets below. On the ground, the battle had progressed much farther north. Midnight could clearly see companies of black-armored guardsmen and green-armored watchmen lined up to make a stand along Selduth Street, which ran east and west. In front of their lines, approaching along the north-south running avenues, were thousands of the grotesque denizens common to the Fugue Plain in Hades. As the denizen horde moved northward, it drove before it the battered and bloodied remnants of dozens of guard companies that had already thrown themselves against the swarm.

Every now and then, some mage within the defending ranks would loose a fireball or hail storm at the advancing denizens. As often as not, the spell misfired, coating the streets with snow or showering the magic-user's own ranks with sparks and flame. Even when a spell did work, it seldom affected the denizens. Magic missiles bounced off their chests harmlessly, and lightning bolts simply dissipated into the advancing throng with no effect.

Realizing Waterdeep had little hope of repelling the denizens unless something changed, Midnight motioned for Elminster to stand away so she could speak. Then she performed the incantation to dispel the magic on the old sage. Immediately, a wave of fatigue shot through her body and her vision darkened. Midnight collapsed, trembling, into Kelemvor's arms, then slipped into unconsciousness.

Kelemvor clutched her close to his body. "Wake up," he whispered. "Please, wake up."

Adon knelt and touched his fingers to Midnight's throat. "Her heartbeat is still strong," he noted softly.

Kelemvor slipped Midnight into Adon's arms, then stood and went over to Elminster. "What did you make her do?" he demanded.

"Calm thyself," Elminster said, relieved to see that Myrkul's spell no longer plagued him. "Midnight will recover. She did nothing more than exhaust herself."

The wizard went to the edge of the tower and looked down at the battle. The denizens had driven the remnants of twenty shattered companies into the line along Selduth Street. Waterdeep's defenders had opened holes in their ranks to allow the routed troops to pass.

"And she did so in a good cause," Elminster said, pointing at the denizens. "They're coming for the tablets."

"Why?" Kelemvor asked. "Myrkul's gone!"

"Apparently they don't know that," Elminster replied, "or they don't care. In either case, I must stop them."

"How can one man stop a host of those things?" Kelemvor demanded.

"Ye were a soldier. What's the best way to demoralize an army?"

Kelemvor shrugged. "Starve it or cut it off from its home. But who—"

"Precisely!" Elminster said. "Cut it off from home."

He addressed both Kelemvor and Adon. "When Myrkul's horde begins to retreat, take the tablets to the Celestial Stairway. But don't move before that or the denizens will come after ye. Do ye understand?"

Adon nodded. "But where is the Celestial Stairway?"

Elminster frowned as though the answer were obvious. "Up there," he said, pointing toward the summit of Mount Waterdeep.

"Two more questions before you go," Kelemvor said.

"All right, but be quick about it."

"First, what are you going to do?"

"I'm not sure," Elminster replied. "Go to the Pool of Loss and close it off, I suppose. Since the denizens aren't from our plane of existence, that should draw their attention away from the battle."

"But you'll need hours to get there," Kelemvor objected. "Even if you can make it back to the Yawning Portal through the battle—"

A condescending smile creased Elminster's lips. "My boy, have ye forgotten who I am? What's thy second question?"

Kelemvor frowned, not entirely satisfied with Elminster's first answer. Still, he knew the sage wouldn't explain himself further. The fighter asked his second question. "Why didn't you tell us Adon was alive?"

Elminster actually looked embarrassed. "Yes—well, Blackstaff and I discussed that matter. There's no time to explain at the moment. Perhaps when I return."

With that, the sage went to the stairwell, already plotting his strategy. First, he would cross into another plane, where there would be no need to worry about the unpredictability of magic. Then Elminster intended to travel to the other side of the Pool of Loss and reseal it from there. It might be tiring, but the ancient wizard did not think it would be beyond him.

As the sage stepped into the stairwell, Cyric slipped into a room on the tower's top floor. The thief had been watching and listening to everything that occurred on the roof.

It's good you didn't steal the tablets immediately, his sword commented. *Even I could not have defended you from an army of denizens.*

Cyric did not reply. Instead, he waited for Elminster's steps to descend well past his door. Then the thief returned to his position at the top of the stairwell, waiting for an opportunity to attack.

A few minutes after the wizard left, Midnight regained consciousness. She immediately noticed Elminster's absence, and feared she had dispelled the sage with Myrkul's spell. "Elminster," she asked weakly. "Where is he?"

"The Pool of Loss," Kelemvor replied. "He went to seal it."

"As soon as the denizens start retreating, we're to take the tablets to the top of Mount Waterdeep," Adon said.

Kelemvor turned to the cleric. "What makes you think the denizens will retreat?" the fighter asked doubtfully. "Elminster's one man against an army."

"We'll have to wait and see," Midnight replied. "I need to rest anyway."

They turned to watch the battle. In the air, the superior number of griffon riders appeared to be holding their own against the flying denizens. The battling specks had moved no closer. On the ground, the story was different. The denizens had just reached the line at Selduth Street and were ripping through it with the force of a tidal wave.

Waterdeep's second rank of defenders charged Myrkul's denizens while the foul creatures were busy destroying the first rank. Each soldier stayed long enough to slash two or three times, then quickly retreated to form a new line. At the same time, a third rank of pikesmen formed behind the second, prepared to utilize the same hit-and-run tactics.

The strategy took its toll on the denizen army, leaving two hundred of their bloated, leathery bodies in the street. But it took a heavier toll on Waterdeep's defenders, who lost two men for every denizen. Still, it was the only strategy that worked, so the defenders repeated it over and over, retreating farther north and closer to Blackstaff's tower.

Finally, the battle reached Keltarn Street, which ran west

from the Street of Silver. It crossed the Street of Silks and ended, scarcely five hundred feet from Blackstaff's tower, at Swords Street. The denizens were advancing up all three north-running avenues: the Street of Silver, the Street of Silks, and Swords Street.

In accordance with the normal strategy, the Company of the Manticore fell back along the Street of Silver, leaving the denizens a clear path down Keltarn Street. To the Manticore commander's surprise, the denizens turned down Keltarn Street and fell on the flank of 3rd Watch Regiment, who were defending the Street of Silks.

Within seconds, the 3rd Watch Regiment perished. The denizens from both the Streets of Silver and Silks started down Keltarn Street toward the Company of the Chimera, the last group of defenders on Swords Street.

"That's it," Kelemvor said. "We'd better run before they break through."

"But Elminster—," Adon objected, waving his mace like an accusing finger.

"Did not succeed," Midnight interrupted. "And I doubt I've the strength for even one more spell."

Kelemvor reached down to help the raven-haired mage stand, and Adon cast a last glance over the battle. "Wait— they just might hold," he said.

All three companions turned just as the denizens reached Swords Street. The Company of the Manticore was charging down Keltarn Street behind the denizens. At the same time, the 5th Watch Regiment, which had been held in reserve, was rushing to reinforce Swords Street.

Kelemvor did not think even these developments would stop the denizens. "We can't take that chance," he said.

Cyric decided to make his move while the three companions were still trapped on Blackstaff's tower. He drew his short sword and slipped onto the roof as quietly as he could, moving toward Kelemvor's back.

Midnight saw Cyric first. "Kel!" she screamed.

"What?" the warrior asked, bewildered.

Cyric rushed forward, taking advantage of the fighter's

confusion. He wanted to finish the warrior quickly. The others he would take his time with. But as long as Kelemvor remained alive, he was dangerous.

"It's Cyric!" Midnight yelled.

Kelemvor spun to face his attacker. Cyric's blade flashed past the warrior's chest, missing its target by a hair's breadth. The fighter yelled in astonishment. Realizing he still had the advantage, the thief stepped forward and slipped an ankle behind the stocky warrior's knee. Kelemvor tried to retreat and Cyric tripped him.

As the warrior fell, Adon slipped to Cyric's right, the saddlebags over his shoulder and his mace in his hand. Midnight stepped to Cyric's left.

The thief raised his sword to finish Kelemvor.

"Stop!" Adon screamed, stepping within striking range of Cyric's head.

To the thief's right, Midnight also stepped forward. She did not feel very threatening. Her arms quivered with fear for her lover's life, and the mage was so exhausted it might prove impossible to lift her hands for an incantation.

"Don't be foolish," Cyric snarled. "Drop your weapons or I'll slit Kel's throat."

"You'll do it anyway," Adon replied. "At least you'll die, too."

The cleric raised the mace over his head, but Midnight shook her head. "What do you want?" she demanded.

"The same thing I've always wanted," Cyric replied. "The Tablets of Fate."

"So you can become a god," Midnight mocked. "Ao will never make a god of a thief and a murderer."

Cyric burst out laughing. "Why not?" he asked. "This is the same overlord who created Bhaal, Bane, and Myrkul!"

Midnight frowned. It had never occurred to her that Ao might be an evil god or one who did not care about good or evil. However, that didn't matter at the moment. She stepped back, summoning a magic missile incantation.

"He dies!" Cyric screamed, recognizing the look of concentration in Midnight's eyes. "The tablets, now!"

Midnight looked at Adon. "Let him have them," she said,

dropping her hands to her sides.

"No!" Kelemvor exclaimed. "He'll kill me anyway."

The fighter started to rise, and Midnight knew Cyric would strike. Midnight's only hope of saving her lover lay with her magic. She quickly performed an incantation, pointing her fingers at the thief.

Twenty golden bolts flashed from her fingers—then missed their target and arced away into Waterdeep. An instant later, the ground rumbled. Twenty different buildings shot into the heavens, leaving long plumes of golden flame in their wakes.

Midnight's knees buckled and her head began to swim. She stumbled backward two steps, but did not allow herself to fall. Her magic had failed her.

The misfired incantation astonished the men, but only for an instant. "Bad luck," Cyric sneered. He turned his attention back to Kelemvor, who was rising to his knees.

Adon stepped forward, swinging his mace. Cyric's anger changed to fear. Kelemvor had forced him into a mistake. The thief swung his right leg up and thrust his heel into Adon's ribs, using the bloodstained hole in the cleric's shirt as a target. His foot connected with a satisfying thump.

The cleric bellowed in agony and dropped his mace and the tablets, then doubled over and collapsed. His lungs burned with each breath, and he felt as though another arrow had pierced his ribs.

Kelemvor lunged, hoping to topple Cyric before the thief regained his balance from kicking Adon. But Cyric anticipated the attack and sidestepped the lunge easily. As the fighter flew past, the thief stepped around behind him.

Cyric could not help smiling. From his position, and with both Adon and Midnight all but helpless, he could easily wound the warrior, yet spare his life. Instead, the thief thrust his sword into Kelemvor's back, putting all his weight behind it, burying the blade as deep as possible.

As Cyric plunged his weapon into the fighter's back, Midnight saw that the wound did not bleed, and that the sword was drinking her lover's blood. A sick, guilty anger came over her. Screaming in rage and anguish, the mage pulled her dagger and found the strength to charge.

The fighter felt his life draining away. "Ariel," he whispered through the pain. As his vision blurred, Kelemvor Lyonsbane wondered if, perhaps, he'd done enough good in the short time he was without his curse to be remembered as a hero. Then he died.

At the same time, Adon tried to stand. However, his body wouldn't do what he wanted it to. When he pressed against the roof, his arms simply quivered and jets of agony shot through his torso.

Cyric calmly pulled his sword out of Kelemvor's back and turned to meet Midnight's attack. He blocked the magic-user's wild stab, knocking the dagger from her hand and sending it off the tower. Turning his parry into an attack, the thief dropped his blade beneath the mage's arm and lunged.

But Midnight was quicker than Cyric expected. She sidestepped his attack, then raked her fingernails across his face. The mage had forgotten about the denizens, the tablets, and even her own life. At the moment, all she wanted was to make Cyric pay for killing Kelemvor.

The hawk-nosed man screamed, then knocked Midnight down with a powerful kick. She landed flat on her back six feet away. The thief's face stung, and he could feel blood dripping down his cheek. "You hurt me!" he snarled, more astonished than angry.

"I'll kill you," she said, standing up. Her words were calm and even.

"I don't think so." Moving so quickly and so smoothly that Midnight did not see the blow coming, the thief rushed forward and drove his sword into her abdomen.

Midnight felt a sharp pain, as if Cyric had kicked her again, and her breath left her lungs. She looked down and saw the sword hilt protruding from a gash in her robe, the thief's hand still wrapped around it. Her intestines began to burn, then the sword began sucking her life away. Too shocked to resist, the magic-user clutched at the hilt and tried to pull it out.

Cyric pushed, keeping the blade imbedded in the wound. "Just a few seconds longer," he said, "and you'll be with Kelemvor."

Midnight began to feel detached from her body, as though she and it were separated by miles.

"I won't die," she hissed.

"Won't you?" Cyric asked, twisting the blade.

"No!" Midnight cried.

She released the sword, then straightened three fingers and jammed them into the thief's throat as hard as she could. The strike nearly smashed his larynx. Choking and gasping, he stumbled away, pulling the sword out of the mage's body.

Midnight collapsed into a sitting position. She held her hands over her wound, which had begun to bleed.

Cyric swallowed and cleared his throat several times, attempting to restore the normal passage of air. Finally, he lifted his sword and started toward Midnight again. "For that, you die in pain," he gasped.

Barely capable of focusing on the thief, Midnight raised a hand and pointed it at him. She tried to summon an incantation that would kill him, but the pain in her stomach clouded her head and she could not think clearly. Her mind simply filled with a jumble of nonsensical words and meaningless gestures.

Just then, a fierce round of battle cries came up from Swords Street. Watching Midnight over his shoulder, Cyric went to the edge of the tower to see what had happened. Just a hundred yards from the base of Blackstaff's home, the Company of the Manticore and the 5th Watch Regiment were engaged in a confused, whirling melee with Myrkul's horde. Human and denizen bodies alike lay stacked two and three deep, and blood ran down the gutters in streams. The buildings lining the street were scorched and half-destroyed from the desperate magic that wizards had flung into battle without regard to misfires or precision.

As Cyric watched, a group of denizens broke through the

line. Five mages directed spells at them, resulting in a spray of colors, an unexpected rain shower, and two miniature tornadoes. But one of the spells went off correctly, and a fireball engulfed Myrkul's warriors. To Cyric's surprise, the magic reduced the denizens to charred lumps. A dozen of Waterdeep's soldiers gave a rousing cheer, then rushed over to seal the gap the attackers had been trying to exploit.

And from what Cyric could see from the tower, the battle was going badly for the denizens all across the city.

The battle was turning, though Cyric could not see the reason. In fact, Elminster had finally reached the other side of the Pool of Loss and closed the portal. The loss of contact with Hades was demoralizing the denizens. It was also weakening much of their invulnerability to spells, fire, and weapons, which was due to magic emanating from Myrkul's realm.

Cyric decided that it was time to take the tablets and find the Celestial Stairway. He turned back to the middle of the roof, where Midnight barely sat upright. The mage continued to point her hand in his general direction. Her face was too masked in pain for the thief to tell whether or not she was concentrating on magic.

Cyric considered stabbing Midnight again. But then he looked at her wound and the pool of blood in which she sat. Recalling some of the incredible things he had seen her magic do, the thief decided it would be wiser to let her bleed to death on her own. Besides, with the tide of battle turning, he did not think there was much time to waste.

The thief went over to Adon and pulled the saddlebags out of the cleric's grasp. Adon feebly tried to rise and stop him, making it as far as his knees.

"Thanks," Cyric said cheerfully. Taking aim at the bloody spot on the cleric's shirt, the thief kicked him as hard as he could—twice. "I'd kill you, but I don't have any time to waste."

Then Cyric threw the saddlebags containing the Tablets of Fate over his shoulder and left the tower.

❧ 18 ❧

Ao Speaks

After Cyric left Blackstaff's tower, Midnight collapsed and fell unconscious. Adon dragged himself to her side. He tore a ragged piece of cloth off the mage's sleeve and used it to stanch the bleeding from her wound. The bandage did not work completely, but at least the flow slowed to a trickle.

As they lay on the roof, Adon watched Waterdeep's soldiers defend the city. At first, the guard companies and watch regiments simply kept the denizens from breaking through their lines again. Then, as the attackers' charge lost momentum, the defenders started beating the horde back. Within minutes, Waterdeep's troops were advancing, and a short time later they were pursuing the denizens back toward the Dock Ward.

But the defeat of Myrkul's host did little to encourage Adon. Each time he took a breath, his lungs filled with fire, and each time he exhaled, bolts of pain shot through his torso. Periodically, he fell into fits of uncontrollable coughing and wheezing. Cyric's contemptuous kicks had broken two ribs, in addition to mangling Adon's already injured lungs. Several times, the cleric tried to find the strength to stand and go after Cyric and the tablets. A wave of unbearable agony always forced him back to his knees.

Forty minutes later, a griffon carrying two riders approached Blackstaff's tower and landed. A tall, black-haired man leaped off the beast, examined Kelemvor's bloodless body, then inspected the rest of the scene. Finally, he walked over to where Adon and Midnight lay.

"What happened?" Blackstaff demanded, not bothering

with introductions. The wizard had never met Adon, but he had no doubt about the cleric's identity.

"Cyric took the—" Adon fell into a violent attack of coughing and could not finish the sentence.

After waiting a few moments for the fit to pass, Blackstaff said, "Wait right here—I'll get something to help."

He disappeared into his tower, then returned an instant later with two vials of murky green fluid. "This is a restorative. It will ease your pain." He gave one to Adon, then kneeled and poured the other into Midnight's mouth.

Adon accepted the vial and drank it down. Although he had never met Blackstaff Arunsun, the black-bearded man's bearing left little doubt of his identity. As the mage had promised, the potion dulled the cleric's pain and put an end to his coughing. Though Adon felt far from hardy, he found the strength to stand.

"Cyric has the Tablets of Fate!" Adon said. "You've got to—"

Midnight opened her eyes. "Khelben?" she said. "Do you have the tablets?" She still felt dizzy and weak, but her strength, like the cleric's, was slowly returning.

Instead of answering Midnight's question, the bearded mage began asking his own. "What happened to Kelemvor? Where's Elminster?"

Midnight and Adon each tried to answer a different question simultaneously. The result was a garbled mumble.

Blackstaff held up his hand. "Let's start from the beginning. Midnight?"

Midnight told Blackstaff about tracking Myrkul back to the wizard's tower. She quickly explained how the Lord of the Dead had stolen the tablet from the vault, then described how they had lured the god back to the roof and destroyed him. "By the time we recovered both tablets, his denizens were closing in on your tower," she finished. "Elminster went to the Pool of Loss to cut them off from Myrkul's city."

"Then Cyric attacked," Adon said. He briefly recounted how Cyric had injured him again, killed Kelemvor, stabbed Midnight, and finally taken the tablets and left.

When the cleric was softly relating the specifics of the green-eyed fighter's death, Midnight turned away and tried in vain to hold back her tears.

Blackstaff considered the story for a minute, then said, "I'll go and retrieve Elminster from the Pool of Loss—"

"What about Cyric and the tablets?" Adon interrupted. "You've got to catch him before he reaches the Celestial Stairway!"

"Patience, Adon," Blackstaff said calmly. "Unless he knows where the Stairway is, Cyric will not find it easily. Only people of extraordinary power can see it. We have plenty of time to locate him and recover the tablets."

The wizard had no way of knowing that Cyric was at that moment hiking up the side of Mount Waterdeep that faced the sea. On top of the mountain, he saw a wide, ever-changing ribbon of colors he did not doubt was his destination.

Perhaps it was the fact that he possessed both of the Tablets of Fate. Perhaps, in recovering the tablets, he had established that he was as extraordinary as Blackstaff and Midnight. But whatever the reason, the Celestial Stairway had appeared to Cyric the instant he set foot on the mountain.

Back on Blackstaff's tower, however, the bearded mage remained oblivious to Cyric's progress. "When Elminster and I get back, we'll recover the tablets and return them to Helm." Although he did not say it, the wizard was concerned for his old friend's safety. If Elminster was as tired as Blackstaff, the ancient sage could be in trouble. "For now, I'll send someone to look after you two."

"You can go get Elminster," Midnight said. "But I'm going after Cyric now. You don't know that murderer like I do." She looked toward the Celestial Stairway, fearing in her heart that the thief was already standing at its base.

"I'm going, too," Adon added.

"But you're wounded!" Blackstaff objected. He pointed at the bloodstains on their clothes. "Both of you!"

"I feel well enough to fight," Adon said. With his broken ribs, the cleric knew he would be risking further injury to his lungs. But at the moment, his own safety did not matter as much as preventing Cyric from returning the tablets.

"The potion only numbs your pain," Blackstaff cautioned. "It does not heal your injuries. You'll collapse the instant you exert yourselves."

"I'll take that chance," Midnight growled, in no mood to wait for Elminster—or anybody else—to avenge Kelemvor's death. She was aware of her wound, but it caused her only a little discomfort. Blackstaff's potion was an effective one. "Do you have another dagger I can borrow?" she asked.

"And where's my mace?" Adon muttered, struggling to keep the weakness out of his voice. Though his pain had subsided, he still felt far from strong. But he was not going to let Midnight go after Cyric alone.

Blackstaff shook his head, frustrated by their insistence. He said, "As you wish. But allow me to persuade a pair of griffon riders to lend you their wings."

The wizard went to his rider and held a brief conversation. The griffon took to its wings and flew toward the south, then Blackstaff disappeared into his tower. A minute later, he returned with the weapon the mage had requested. Soon, two griffons landed atop his tower.

"The griffon riders will take you wherever you wish to go," he said flatly. "But I've instructed them to bring you back the instant you show signs of pain. Elminster and I will return within the hour. Will you at least be here to meet us?"

Midnight glanced at the corpse on the roof, then said, "Assuming we haven't found Cyric, yes." She had no intention of returning if they found the thief, for all that would matter then was revenge. Looking back at Blackstaff, she added, "Thanks for your help."

Blackstaff smiled weakly. "No . . . thank you. What you've done has benefitted us all. Good hunting!" The wizard turned back to his tower.

Midnight and Adon went to the griffons. The riders, eyeing the pair's wounds doubtfully, helped them into the passenger saddles.

"Where to?" asked Adon.

Midnight looked at the ribbon of scintillating colors rising off Mount Waterdeep. "Whether Cyric knows it or not, he must go to the top of the mountain. It's wisest to look up there first."

"That's easy enough," said one of the riders. "We keep our griffons there."

Five minutes later, the griffons landed just north of the mountain's summit. A stone tower stood atop the peak, and a covered stable sat fifty feet to the east. Inside the stable were over two dozen griffons, all of which had suffered serious injury—torn wings, gashed heads, broken legs. An even greater number of men tended the beasts' injuries. The griffons were not the only ones who had suffered. Human groans rolled out of the tower's door, as well.

Midnight and Adon dismounted, then looked around the peaktop eyrie. Directly ahead, the northern ridge of Mount Waterdeep descended at a gentle grade, gradually disappearing into the magnificent temple complexes and grand villas of the city's wealthy Sea Ward. To the east, the mountain dropped away steeply, ending in the sheer cliff that marked the western boundaries of the Castle Ward. The eight spires of Piergeiron's Palace poked over the head of the cliff. Beyond the spires, the city of Waterdeep stretched across the benchland like a magnificent diorama, complete with smoking chimneys and fluttering flags. Behind Midnight and Adon, to the south, a series of wooden piers and granite battlements girded the murky waters of the harbor.

To the west, the peak fell away in a hundred-foot cliff. The terrain then sloped down five hundred feet to a defensive wall guarding the base of the mountain. Below the wall, a precipice plunged into the azure waters of the Sea of Swords.

But it was not what lay below the mountain that caught Midnight's interest. A shimmering path of amber and pearl rose off the top of the peak and disappeared into the heavens. The translucent path simultaneously looked solid and immaterial.

As Midnight watched, the stairway changed from amber and pearl into a set of white steps. A moment later, it shifted again, this time becoming a ramp of pure silver. The stairway continued changing forms every few seconds.

"What are you looking at?" asked Adon. The only thing he saw to the west of the peak was a cliff.

Midnight pointed at the air above the cliff. "The Celestial Stairway," she said.

Adon peered at the sky. He still saw nothing. "I'll have to take your word for it."

The griffon riders showed the pair through the tower and stable, but there was no sign of Cyric. As she left the tower, Midnight concluded, "Cyric's not here." The mage noticed that all the walking and climbing stairs had caused her wound to bleed more heavily, and she felt a little dizzy.

"Then it will be difficult to find him," Adon said, sitting down on the steps to the tower. Unlike Midnight, his injuries were causing him a great deal of distress. Though Blackstaff's potion had taken the edge off the cleric's pain, he was having trouble breathing and he felt extremely weak.

"We'll find him," Midnight growled. "When we do, I'll kill him."

The mage's stomach stirred uneasily. She had never plotted in advance to use her magic to kill someone. To her, magic had always been a defensive shield, a means of earning respect and power, a joyful art—never a weapon to be used in anger or for vengeance.

"I won't make the mistake of stopping you again," Adon said, remembering bitterly that he had talked his friends into sparing Cyric's life. He could not help being angry with himself. If he had kept quiet, Kelemvor would be alive right now. "But I'll kill him first if I can."

The griffon riders frowned and exchanged uneasy glances. They were accustomed to death and combat, but their charges sounded as though they were contemplating murder. Blackstaff had said nothing about the strangers being exempt from the normal laws of the city.

"I'm not sure you should be talking like that," one of the riders said. "Blackstaff said—"

"Quiet!" Midnight hissed, looking toward the south. "Into the building, quickly!"

Cyric was standing on the south side of the summit, studying the backside of the griffon eyrie. The saddlebags containing the tablets were slung over his left shoulder, and he held his sword in his right hand.

In order to make it more difficult to see him from the streets of Waterdeep, the thief had hiked up the back side of the mountain. Then he had circled around the far side of the cliff before climbing to the summit. Though he did not expect anyone to prevent him from taking the tablets to the Celestial Stairway, it always paid to be cautious.

Cyric was glad he had been careful. From Waterdeep, he had seen that there was a tower and stable on the summit of the mountain. But he had not expected the tower to be close to the Celestial Stairway, or to find so many guardsmen milling about.

After studying the area for a few more minutes, the thief continued toward the staircase. There really was no reason for the griffon riders to stop him. Besides, even if they tried, he suspected he could rush the last hundred feet to the stairway before they could detain him.

From the tower's door, Midnight watched Cyric advance toward the Celestial Stairway. Finally, when he was fifty feet from both the staircase and the tower, when Midnight believed Cyric could not escape, she prepared to attack.

"Now!" the mage cried, stepping out of the tower.

Adon rushed out behind her, followed by the two griffon riders. As they charged, Midnight tried to summon a death incantation, but found she was too weak. The gestures and words necessary for the spell were only blurs in her consciousness.

When Cyric heard Midnight's cry, he did not waste time wondering why she was not dead. The thief immediately understood that despite her wound, the magic-user had found the strength to beat him to the mountaintop and set up an ambush. Reacting instantly, he sprinted toward the Celestial Stairway.

As Cyric ran, a deep voice boomed from the stairway. "No! Stop!" The words were so loud they echoed over Waterdeep like thunder.

A figure in glistening armor appeared and started down the stairs. The armored man stood nearly ten feet tall, and his body seemed stocky and powerful. His eyes were sad and compassionate, though they had a cold edge that hinted at his merciless devotion to duty. The Unsleeping Eye of Helm adorned the god's shield.

The two guardsmen immediately stopped and kneeled. The entire complement of soldiers atop the peak came out of the tower and stable. Upon seeing Helm's magnificent figure, they also fell on their knees and did not move. Several frightened griffons took flight.

The battle between the soldiers of Waterdeep and Myrkul's denizens raged on, but the sight of Lord Helm further undermined the creatures' lines. On the other hand, the brave guardsmen and watchmen were heartened by the god's appearance over the city. Many prayed for divine intervention as they hacked their way through the routed denizen horde.

Down in Waterdeep, tens of thousands of refugees from the battle stopped what they were doing and looked toward the mountaintop. Several thousand correctly guessed that only a god could have spoken so loudly. They began drifting toward the slopes of Mount Waterdeep in the vague hope of glimpsing the speaker. Helm's voice frightened many others, and they began seeking shelter in basements and cellars. Most citizens simply stood dumfounded and stared at the mountaintop in fear and awe.

Unlike the citizens of Waterdeep, the booming voice did not stun Cyric. He continued running toward the Celestial Stairway. The thief did not think Helm's command was directed at him. Even if it had been, he was not about to stop until he had delivered the tablets.

The god's command caused Adon to hesitate, but Midnight did not even pause. Cyric had killed Kelemvor and Sneakabout, had tried to kill her and Adon, and had betrayed them all. The mage did not care who commanded her to spare his life. She continued after the thief, her dagger in hand.

Helm met Cyric at the bottom of the stairway, then stepped in front of him protectively.

"This life is not yours to take," the God of Guardians said, glaring at Midnight.

"You have no right to command me," Midnight screamed. She slowed her pace to a walk, but continued toward Cyric.

"He must pay for his crimes," Adon gasped, coming up behind Midnight.

"It is not my duty to judge him," Helm said flatly.

Watching Midnight carefully, Cyric stepped to Helm's side and gave him the saddlebags. "I have recovered the Tablets of Fate," the thief said.

Helm accepted the artifacts. "I know who recovered them," he replied, coldly staring into Cyric's eyes. "As does Lord Ao."

Adon, who could not see the reproach in Helm's gaze, cried, "He's lying! Cyric stole those from us, and he killed a good man to do it!"

Helm turned his craggy, emotionless face toward the cleric. "As I said, I know who recovered the tablets."

Midnight continued toward the stairway. Her legs felt weak and unsteady. "If you are aware of Cyric's evil, why do you accept the tablets from him?" she demanded.

"Because it is not his duty to pass judgment," said another voice. It was hardy and resonant, without hint of anger or compassion. "Nor is it his prerogative."

A figure two feet taller than Helm stood fifty yards up the staircase. Though his face showed no particular age—he could have been twenty or he could have been a hundred and twenty—his hair and beard were as white as alabaster. The being's face, neither handsome nor ugly, had even, symmetrical features that would not draw notice on any street in the Realms.

However, he wore a remarkable robe that would have distinguished him in the most elaborate court in Faerun. It fell as any cloth might, with wrinkles here and pleats there. When she looked at it, though, Midnight felt she was staring into the heavens. The robe was as black as oblivion, dotted by millions of stars and thousands of moons, all arranged in a pattern that was not quite perceivable, but which gave the whole robe a beautiful, harmonious feel. In some places, bright swirls of light lit small areas. The swirls were balanced in other areas by regions of inky darkness.

"Lord Ao!" Helm acknowledged, bowing his head in supplication.

"Bring me the Tablets of Fate," Ao commanded.

Helm opened the saddlebags and removed the tablets. In the god's mighty hands, the two stones looked small, almost insignificant. Helm took the tablets to Ao, then kneeled on the stairway to await further commands.

Ao studied the tablets for several minutes. In a hundred places throughout the Realms, the avatars of the surviving gods fell into a deep trance as Ao summoned their attention.

"On these artifacts," the overlord said, sending his voice and image to all of his gods. "I have recorded the forces that balance Law and Chaos."

"And I have returned them to you," Cyric said, daring to meet Ao's gaze.

Ao looked at the thief without approval or disapproval. "Yes," he said, stacking the tablets together. "And here is what it amounts to!" The overlord of the gods crushed both tablets in his hands and ground them into dust.

Midnight cringed, expecting the heavens to come crashing down. Adon cried out in grief and astonishment. Cyric watched the dust fall from between Ao's fingers, an angry frown creeping down his face.

Helm jumped to his feet. "Master, what have you done?" the god asked, his voice betraying his fear.

"The tablets mean nothing," Ao said, addressing all of his gods, no matter where they were. "I kept them to remind you that I created gods to serve the Balance, not to twist it to your own ends. But this point was lost on you. You saw the tablets as a set of rules by which to play juvenile games of prestige and pomp! Then, when the rules became inconvenient, you stole them . . ."

"But that was—," Helm began.

"I know who took the Tablets of Fate," Ao replied, silencing Helm with a curt wave of his hand. "Bane and Myrkul have paid for their offenses with their lives. But all of you were guilty, causing worshipers to build wasteful temples, to devote themselves so slavishly to your name they could not feed their children, even to spill their own blood upon your corrupt altars—all so you could impress each other with your hold over these so-called inferior creatures. Your behavior is enough to make me wish I had never created you."

Ao paused and let his listeners consider his words. Finally, he resumed speaking. "But I did create you and not without purpose. Now, I am going to demand that you fulfill that purpose. From this day forward, your true power will depend upon the number and devotion of your followers."

From one end of the Realms to another, the gods gasped in astonishment. In far off Tsurlagoi, Talos the Raging One growled, "Depend on mortals?" The one good eye of his youthful, broad-shouldered avatar was opened wide in outrage and shock.

"Depend on them and more," Ao returned. "Without worshipers, you will wither, even perish entirely. And after what has passed in the Realms, it will not be easy to win the faith of mortals. You will have to earn it by serving them."

In sunny Tesiir, a beautiful woman with silky scarlet hair and fiery red-brown eyes looked as though she were going to retch. "Serve *them*?" Sune asked.

"I have spoken!" Ao replied.

"No!" Cyric yelled. "After all I went through—"

"Quiet!" Ao thundered, pointing a finger at the thief. "I do not care to be challenged. It makes me fear I have made a poor choice for my new god."

Cyric's eyes went blank and he stared at Ao in shock.

"It is the reward you sought, is it not?" Ao asked, not taking his eyes off the thief.

Cyric stumbled up the stairway. "It is indeed!" he exclaimed. "I will serve you well, I swear it. You have my gratitude!"

A deep, cruel chuckle rolled out of Ao's throat. "Do not thank me, evil Cyric. Being God of Strife, Hatred, and Death is no gift."

"It isn't?" Cyric asked, furrowing his brow in puzzlement.

"You desired godhood, control over your destiny, and great power," Ao said. "You will have only two of these—godhood and power—to exercise as you will in the Realm of the Dead. And all of the suffering in Toril will be yours as well, to cause and inflict as you wish. But you will never know contentment or happiness again."

Ao paused then and looked at Midnight. "But the thing you have desired most, Lord Cyric, will never come to pass. *I* am your master now. You serve me . . . and your worshipers. I believe you will find that you now have less freedom than you had as a child in the alleys of Zhentil Keep."

"Wait," the new God of Strife cried. "I don't—"

"Enough!" Ao boomed, turning his palm toward Cyric. "I know you will perform your duties well, for they are the only thing you are suited to."

Midnight's heart sank. With Cyric ruling the Realm of the Dead, she could never keep her promise to rescue Sneakabout.

"Forgive me," the mage whispered, turning away from the stairway. "Some promises cannot be kept." She feared Cyric had been right about the nature of life. It was a cruel, brutal experience that ended only in torment and anguish.

"Midnight!" Ao called, turning his attention to the magic-user.

At the sound of her name, Midnight slowly turned to face the master of the gods. "What is it?" she demanded defiantly. "I'm injured and fatigued.. I have lost the one man I loved. What more do you want from me?"

"You have something that has no place in the Realms," Ao said, pointing a long finger at her.

She immediately knew he meant Mystra's power. "Take it. I have no further use for it."

"Perhaps you do," Ao responded.

"I am too weary for riddles," she snapped.

"I have lost many gods during this crisis," Ao said. "As punishment for their theft, I will leave Bane and Myrkul dispersed. But Mystra, Lady of Mysteries and grantor of magic, is also gone. Even I cannot restore her. Will you take her place?"

Midnight looked at Cyric and shook her head. "No. That was not the reason I recovered the tablets. I have no interest in corrupting myself as Cyric did."

"What a pity you view my offer that way," Ao replied, gesturing at Cyric. "I have taken one mortal for his malevolence and cruelty. I had hoped to take another for her wisdom and true heart."

Cyric snickered. "Waste no more breath on her. She lacks the courage to meet her destiny."

"Accept!" urged Adon. "You must not let Cyric win! It is your responsibility to oppose him—" The cleric stopped, realizing that Midnight had more than fulfilled any responsibilities she had. "Forgive me," he said. "You are as brave and as true a woman as I have ever known, and I believe you would be a worthy goddess. But I have no right to tell you what your obligations are."

At the mention of obligations, Midnight thought of her promise to Sneakabout, then of the faithful souls waiting for deliverance in the Fugue Plain. Finally, she imagined her lover's spirit wandering the vast white waste with millions of other dead souls. Ao's offer might give her the means to spare Kelemvor that eternal misery, to rescue the Faithful from their undeserved torture, even to keep her promise to Sneakabout. If so, Midnight knew Adon was correct—she did have a duty to answer the overlord's call.

"No, you're right," the mage said, turning to Adon. "I must go. If I don't, the deaths of Sneakabout and Kelemvor will have meant nothing." She took the cleric's hands and smiled. "Thank you for reminding me of that."

Adon smiled in return. "Without you, the future of the Realms would be very dark."

Ao interrupted their conversation. "What is your decision, Midnight?"

The mage quickly kissed Adon on the cheek. "Good-bye," she said.

"I'll miss you," the cleric replied.

"No you won't," Midnight said, a smile crossing her lips. "I'll be with you always." She quickly turned and stepped onto the stairway, which had become a path of diamonds, and went to stand opposite Cyric.

Addressing Ao, she said, "I accept." Then she turned to Cyric and added, "And I'm going to make you regret your betrayals for the rest of eternity."

For an instant, Cyric was afraid of Midnight's threat. Then, the thief remembered that he knew the mage's true name, Ariel Manx. He smiled weakly and wondered if that would have any power over Midnight now that she was a goddess.

Ao lifted his hands. The Celestial Stairway and everything on it disappeared in a column of light. The brilliant pillar blinded Adon and the thousands of citizens who had been looking at the top of Mount Waterdeep in that instant.

In sunny Tesiir, Tsurlagoi, Arabel, and in a hundred other cities where the gods had taken shelter, similar pillars of light flared and rose into the heavens. Finally, in Tantras, where the God of Duty had fallen against Bane, the scattered shards of Torm's lion-headed avatar rose off the ground and drifted back together. A golden pillar of light shot out over the sea, then rose into the heavens, and Torm also returned home.

Epilogue

"So, this is where you've been hiding!"

Blackstaff's voice brought an abrupt end to Adon's uneasy slumber. Though still unable to see, the cleric knew he was lying in the eyrie's mess hall, alongside a dozen more suffering men. Shortly after Ao's ascension, Blackstaff's restorative potion had worn off and Adon had collapsed. Some of the riders had brought him into the tower and laid him out with their wounded.

"We've been looking for you for—well, for a few minutes anyway," Blackstaff said sheepishly. It had been over six hours since he had parted company with Adon and Midnight. At the Pool of Loss, the young wizard had found Elminster inside a prismatic sphere, besieged by denizens on both sides of the gate to the Realm of the Dead. Since Blackstaff had exhausted himself fighting in the streets, it had taken a while to free his friend.

"We might have known a malapert lad like ye wouldn't wait for us before returning the tablets," Elminster added, feigning irritation.

Blackstaff laid a hand on Adon's shoulder. "Well done, Adon!" he said. "Come, let's go to my tower, where I'll see that you're cared for properly."

Blackstaff and Elminster transferred Adon to a litter, then started across the mess hall.

"Make way!" Blackstaff boomed.

Eventually, the cleric's bearers reached the other side of the crowded room and stepped into a brisk night wind. It carried the promise of snow, as it should at that time of year.

Blackstaff started to turn to the right, but Adon stopped him. "I'd like to pause in the fresh air before we go back to the city." Although he was happy the Realms had been saved, Adon's heart was heavy with Kelemvor's death and Midnight's absence. The cleric wanted to take a peaceful minute to pay tribute to his friends.

Adon lifted his head toward the heavens and a tear rolled down his scarred cheek. The night wind stole the drop from his face and blew it toward the sea, where it would join a million other tears and be forgotten.

Perhaps that was for the best, Adon thought. It was time to forget the pain of the past, to forgive the neglect of the old gods. Now was the time to look to tomorrow, to forge stronger unions with the gods and shape the Realms in a better, more noble image.

As Adon contemplated the future, a circle of eight points of light appeared before his eyes. At first, he thought the lights were a blind man's fancy and tried to make them go away. But they didn't fade. In fact, they grew stronger and brighter, until at last he recognized them as stars. In the center of the ring, a stream of red mist continually bled toward the bottom of the circle.

"Midnight!" Adon said, realizing that he was seeing the new goddess's symbol. A wave of tranquility rolled through his body, filling his heart with a deep sense of harmony. A moment later, he felt strong enough to sit up in his litter.

"What's wrong?" Blackstaff asked, turning to Adon.

The cleric could see Blackstaff's tall form clearly. Behind the mage, one drunken griffon rider was leading another from the stable toward the tower.

"Nothing's wrong," Adon said. "I can see again."

"Ye also seem much stronger," Elminster commented.

"Yes," Adon sighed, pointing at the circle of stars overhead. "Midnight cured me."

Blackstaff looked at the stars. "That's one of the new constellations," he said. "It appeared this very evening. Do you know what it means?"

"It's Midnight's symbol," Adon replied. "And I swear by its

light and the name of Lady Midnight that I'll gather a host of worshipers to honor it!"

Blackstaff studied the stars. "Then let me be your first."

One of the drunken riders stumbled into the wizard, nearly causing him to drop Adon's litter.

Blackstaff whirled on them. "Watch where you're going, dolt! Can't you see we have an injured man here?"

"Sorry, sir," said the first rider. "He's blind."

"Bring him closer," Adon murmured, motioning at the blind man. He laid a hand on the man's eyes. The cleric silently called upon Midnight to restore the soldier's vision.

The blind rider shook his head several times, then blinked his eyes twice. Finally, he looked Adon over from head to foot, as if he could not believe what he saw. "You cured me!" he cried, falling to his knees beside Adon's litter.

Elminster frowned at the rider. "We'll have none of that, now," the sage said. "Adon's just doing what he does best."

Blackstaff smiled. "It appears life is returning to normal."

The dark-haired sage was correct. With the gods back in the Planes to resume their duties, life was returning to normal all over the Realms. On the river Ashaba, which had been running with a current so swift no man would brave it, a fisherman pushed his boat out onto the gentle, slow currents he remembered. With luck, he would return at dawn with enough trout to feed his family for a week.

In Cormyr, an army of sycamore trees that had been besieging the capital city suddenly retreated. They marched back into the forest from which they had come, each tree searching for the particular hole from which it had ripped its roots.

But not everything in the Realms went back to the way it was before the night of Arrival. North of Arabel, where Mystra had fallen against Helm, great craters of boiling tar dotted the countryside, making travel through that region a twisting, worrisome experience. Where Midnight had rung the Bell of Aylan Attricus and Torm had destroyed Bane, the northern quarter of Tantras and all the fields around it remained inert to magic, much to the delight of those who had offended vengeful mages. Below Boareskyr Bridge, where Bhaal's avatar had fallen to Cyric's blade, the Winding Water ran black and foul. No living thing could drink from the river's polluted waters between the ruined bridge and Troll-claw Ford, over a hundred miles to the south. These scars and a dozen others would remain for generations, grim reminders of when the gods walked the world.

But Toril was not the only place to change as a result of Ao's wrath. In the Fugue Plain, god after god appeared in the air, ready to search out and call home the spirits of the Faithful. First came Sune Firehair in a blazing chariot of glory. The Goddess of Beauty had a rosy complexion and scarlet eyes, with long crimson hair that waved in the breeze like a banner. She wore a short, emerald-green frock that complemented her generous figure and provided a colorful contrast to her ruby visage. Sune's chariot swooped low over the endless plain, dragging great tails of flame behind her. As she passed, her faithful grabbed hold of the flaming tails and were carried along with the goddess, basking in the fiery radiance of her beauty.

Then Torm arrived, garbed head to foot in gleaming plate armor, his visor raised to reveal his sturdy countenance and steady gaze. The God of Duty charged across the plain on a magnificent red stallion, calling for his faithful followers to fall in behind him. Soon he was riding at the head of an army greater and truer than any that ever walked the Realms.

Next came snowy-haired Loviatar, dressed in a gown of white silk, with a pinched mouth and cruel fiendish eyes. Her chariot was drawn by nine bloody horses, which she drove with a barbed whip of nine strands. Beguiling Auril, Goddess of Cold, followed in a coach of ice, irresistibly alluring despite her blue skin and aloof bearing. Then, with her green, seaweed hair and the face of a manatee, came Umberlee, followed by all of the other gods who had abandoned their duty for so long.

As the deities collected their faithful from the Fugue Plain, a small, matronly halfling walked through the confusion toward the city where the Faithless and False languished. She had gray hair, sprightly eyes, and moved with a determined gait. The woman was Yondalla, provider and protector of all halflings. At the request of a fellow god, she was going to the city of suffering to investigate the case of a halfling named Atherton Cooper who had lost his way and been trapped there.

Finally, after all the other gods had collected their faithful, came the Wounded Lady, the new Goddess of Magic. Although her long sable hair and the sublime features of her face remained unchanged, Midnight seemed even more alluring and enchanting than she had been as a mortal. Her dark eyes were more secretive and enigmatic, flashing now and then with hints of both great sorrow and implacable determination. The Wounded Lady rode upon an alabaster unicorn that left a translucent, glittering trail in his wake. When Mystra's faithful stepped onto the sparkling path, they were whisked along behind the Goddess of Magic.

At last, when all the Faithful had been gathered from the Fugue Plain, the gods returned to their homes with their charges. Midnight and her mount went to the Plane of Nirvana, that place of ultimate law and regimented order, where there were always equal parts of light and dark, heat and cold, fire and water, and air and earth.

As they approached Nirvana, Midnight's faithful saw an infinite space filled with circular subplanes hanging in the air. The subplanes were arranged in every direction, locked to each other at the edges like the gears of a clock. Each planar level rotated slowly, and its revolution was transferred to adjacent levels through its gears, so that the entire plane spun in unison. Midnight's mount turned in the direction of the largest subplane, carrying his mistress and her faithful toward their new home: a perfectly symmetrical castle of tangible magic.

In another castle, very different from Midnight's new home in Nirvana, Lord Cyric sat in silence, brooding. His defeated denizen army swarmed about him, and the cries of the damned in the wall around his city drifted to his ears.

The new God of Strife and Death liked his new home, though he found his master, Lord Ao, troublesome. Perhaps given time, Cyric mused, I will find a way to revolt against the overlord of the gods.

As Ao watched Midnight and the other gods return home with their faithful, he felt a deep sense of relief. At last, his gods might start fulfilling the tasks for which they had been created.

The overlord was sitting cross-legged and alone, surrounded by a void so vast that not even his gods could comprehend it. Of all the states of being he could assume, this one was his favorite, for he was at once in time and disconnected from it, at once the center of the universe and separate from it.

Ao turned his thoughts to Toril, the young world that had consumed so much of his attention lately. Surrounded by a hundred planes of existence and populated by a variety of fabulous beings both sinister and benevolent, it was one of his favorite creations—and one that he had come close to losing, thanks to the inattentiveness of its gods.

But in two of its inhabitants—Midnight and Cyric—Ao had found the fabric of the Balance, and he had called upon them to right the world. Fortunately, they had answered his call and bound the fulcrum back together, but it had been a dangerous time for Toril. Never again would he allow his gods to threaten the Balance so severely.

Ao closed his eyes and blanked his mind. Soon, he fell within himself and entered the place before time, the time at the edge of the universe, where millions and millions of assignments like his began and ended.

A luminous presence greeted him, enveloping his energies within its own. It was both a warm and a cold entity, forgiving and harsh. "And how does your cosmos fare, Ao?" The voice was at once both gentle and admonishing.

"They have restored the Balance, Master. The Realms are once again secure."

ABOUT THE AUTHOR

The Avatar Project, which consists of both game and book releases, is the combined effort of a number of TSR staff members and talented free-lance authors. Richard Awlinson is TSR's pseudonym for *Waterdeep*'s author, Troy Denning.

FORGOTTEN REALMS

FANTASY ADVENTURE

EMPIRES TRILOGY

HORSELORDS
David Cook

Between the western Realms and Kara-Tur lies a vast, unexplored domain. The "civilized" people of the Realms have given little notice to these nomadic barbarians. Now, a mighty leader has united these wild horsemen into an army powerful enough to challenge the world. First, they turn to Kara-Tur.

DRAGONWALL
Troy Denning

The barbarian horsemen have breached the Dragonwall and now threaten the oriental lands of Kara-Tur. Shou Lung's only hope lies with a general descended from the barbarians, and whose wife must fight the imperial court if her husband is to retain his command.

CRUSADE
James Lowder

The barbarian army has turned its sights on the western Realms. Only King Azoun has the strength to forge an army to challenge the horsemen. But Azoun had not reckoned that the price of winning might be the life of his beloved daughter.

FANTASY ADVENTURE

▪ THE HARPERS ▪

A Force for Good in the Realms!

This open-ended series of stand-alone novels chronicles the Harpers' heroic battles against forces of evil, all for the peace of the Realms.

The Parched Sea
Troy Denning

The Zhentarim have sent an army to enslave the fierce no-mads of the Great Desert. Only one woman, the outcast witch Ruha, sees the true danger—and only the Harpers can counter the evil plot.

Elfshadow
Elaine Cunningham

Harpers are being murdered, and the trail leads to Arilyn Moonblade. Is she guilty or is she the next target? Arilyn must uncover the ancient secret of her sword's power in order to find and face the assassin.

Red Magic
Jean Rabe

One of the powerful and evil Red Wizards wants to control more than his share of Thay. While the mage builds a net of treachery, the Harpers put their own agents into action to foil his plans for conquest.

DARK SUN WORLD

PRISM PENTAD

Troy Denning

The Verdant Passage

The immortal sorcerer-king, Kalak, has reduced the city of Tyr to a place of utter desolation, forcing Agis, a maverick statesman, Sadira, a half-elf slave girl, and Rikus, a man-dwarf gladiator to become reluctant leaders of rebellion. *On sale now.*

The Crimson Legion

Tithian, the new king of Tyr, liberates the slaves . . . and plunges the city into chaos. Only Rikus, the gladiator slave who sparked the rebellion, can save the city from the mighty army sent from Urik to destroy it. *On sale April 1992.*

The Amber Enchantress

Sadira, the beautiful sorceress loved by both Rikus and Agis, is torn between the dark power of sorcery and the use of the Good Magic needed to protect the planet's fragile ecology. *On sale October 1992.*